HE HAD STALKED HER LIKE THE PREDATOR HE WAS....

And now he was above her, his face harsh yet sensual, his eyes black, burning coals.

It was happening too fast. Trapped beneath his powerful body, Tempest couldn't move, couldn't breathe. Yet when his teeth scraped the swell of her breast, the erotic enticement sent her arching toward his mouth.

But fear beat at her as his body pinned hers, taking possession as if he had every right to her, as if he were invading her soul so deeply that she would never get him out.

She felt his teeth pierce her breast, sink possessively into her skin, and instantly she stiffened.

But his mind pushed into hers, breaking through every barrier until they were completely one. She felt the heat of her own skin sliding over his, her blood, hot with life and light, flowing into him, his insatiable hunger and terrible need. She saw the erotic images in his head, the things he would do to her. She saw his iron will, his ruthlessness, his merciless, predatory nature.

Darius was everywhere she was. In her body, in her mind, in her heart and soul.

And, God help her, she could deny him nothing....

Books by
Christine Feehan

DARK GOLD
DARK MAGIC
DARK CHALLENGE
DARK FIRE
DARK LEGEND
DARK GUARDIAN
DARK MELODY
DARK DESTINY
THE SCARLETTI CURSE

Christine Feehan

DARK FIRE

AVON

An Imprint of HarperCollinsPublishers

This is a work of fiction. Names, characters, places, and incidents are products of the author's imagination or are used fictitiously and are not to be construed as real. Any resemblance to actual events, locales, organizations, or persons, living or dead, is entirely coincidental.

AVON BOOKS
An Imprint of HarperCollins*Publishers*
10 East 53rd Street
New York, New York 10022-5299

Copyright © 2001 by Christine Feehan
Cover art by John Ennis, www.ennisart.com
ISBN 978-0-06-201945-5
www.avonbooks.com

First Avon Books paperback printing: November 2010

Avon Trademark Reg. U.S. Pat. Off. and in Other Countries,
Marca Registrada, Hecho en U.S.A.
HarperCollins® is a registered trademark of HarperCollins Publishers.

Printed in the U.S.A.

10 9 8 7 6 5 4

For my daughter, Manda.
Many thanks for giving me such joy, for bringing
Skyler into our lives and hearts, for just being you.

Special thanks to the staff at Konocti Harbor Resort and
Spa, who are always helpful, manage to come up with
terrific concerts and are genuinely great people.

DARK FIRE

Chapter One

Flashlight and wrench in hand, she was crawling out from under the troupe's huge touring bus when he first caught sight of her. She was small, almost childlike. At first he was certain she was, at most, a teenager, dressed in baggy overalls, her wealth of red-gold hair pulled back into a ponytail. Her face was grimy, smudged with oil and dirt. Then she turned slightly, and he could see high, firm breasts thrusting against the thin cotton top beneath the bib of her overalls.

Darius stared at her, entranced. Even in the night her red hair gleamed like flames. That he could tell her hair was red stunned him. Dark, predatory, immortal Carpathian male that he was, he had not seen colors, only black and white, in more centuries than he could count. He had not disclosed that information, his accompanying loss of emotion, to his younger sister, Desari, who remained, as she had for eons, sweet and compassionate and everything good that female Carpathians were. Everything that he was not. Desari depended on him, as did the others in their troupe, and he did not wish to distress her with the knowledge of how close he was to either facing the dawn—and his own destruction—or turning vampire, undead instead of immortal.

That this little unfamiliar woman in baggy overalls had captured his attention was shocking to him. But she had a sway to her hips that sent a deep need jolting hard within him. He caught his breath and followed her from a distance as she moved around the touring bus to disappear from his sight.

"You must be tired, Rusti. You've been working all day!" Desari called out.

Darius couldn't see Desari, but, as always, he was able to hear his sister's voice, a blend of musical notes that could turn heads and influence all living things.

"Grab some juice out of the fridge in the trailer, and relax for a few minutes. You can't fix everything in one day," she continued.

"Just another couple of hours and I'll have this up and running," the little redhead answered. Her soft, husky voice touched Darius in the very core of his being and sent blood surging hotly through his veins. He stood still, transfixed by the unexpected sensation.

"I insist, Rusti," Desari said gently.

Darius knew that tone, the one that ensured she got her way. "Please. You have the job as our mechanic. It's obvious that you're exactly what we need. So knock off for the night, will you? Watching you work so hard makes me feel like a slave-driver."

Darius sauntered slowly around the motor home toward the small, red-haired woman and his sister. Beside tall, slender, elegant Desari, the petite female mechanic he had not yet met looked like a scruffy child, yet he couldn't take his eyes from her. She laughed throatily, tightening his body to an aching heaviness. Even from a distance he could see that her eyes were a brilliant green, large and heavily lashed, her face a perfect oval, with high cheekbones and a wide, lush mouth just begging to be kissed.

Before he could hear her, she disappeared again, walking beside his sister around the back of the broken-down touring bus to the rear door. Darius simply stood there, frozen to the spot in the darkness. Night creatures were stirring to life, and Darius allowed his gaze to wander the campsite, noting the various colors around him. Vivid greens, yellows, and blues. He could see the silver of the bus, the blue lettering on the side. The little sports car nearby was fire-engine red. The trail bikes secured to the bus were yellow. The leaves on the trees were bright green, veined with darker hues.

Darius inhaled sharply, pointedly drinking in the stranger's scent so that he could always find her, even in a crowd, always know where she was. Strangely, she made him feel as if he wasn't so alone anymore. He hadn't even met her yet, but simply knowing she was in the world made it seem a completely different place. No, Darius had not told his sister how bleak and empty his life had been or how dangerous he had become, but his gaze, when it rested on the redhead, had been hot and possessive, and something fierce and primitive within him had raised its head and roared for release.

Desari came striding back around the bus alone. "Darius, I did not know you had risen. You are so secretive these days." Her large black eyes scanned him speculatively. "What is it? You look . . ." She hesitated. *Dan-*

gerous. The unsaid word shimmered in the air between them.

He nodded toward their mobile home. "Who is she?"

Desari shivered at his tone, then rubbed her palms up and down her arms as if she were cold. "We discussed the need to hire a mechanic to go on the road with us, to keep the vehicles in shape so we could protect our privacy. I spoke to you of placing an ad, with a special compulsion embedded in it, and you gave your approval, Darius. You said that if we found someone the cats could tolerate, you would permit it. Early this morning Rusti appeared. The cats were out with me, and neither of them objected to her."

"How is it that she made it to the camp through our safeguards, the barriers that protect us during the daylight?" he inquired softly, a hint of menace in his even voice.

"I honestly don't know, Darius. I scanned her mind for any hidden agendas and found none. Her brain patterns are different from those of most humans, but I could detect only her need for work, honest work."

"She is a mortal," he said.

"I know," Desari replied defensively, aware of the heavy, oppressive weight in the air signaling her brother's censure. "But she has no family, and she has indicated a need for a great deal of privacy herself. I don't think it will bother her if we're not around during the day. I told her that, because we work and travel mostly at night, we often sleep during the day. She said that suited her fine. And we do really need her to keep our vehicles running properly. You know it's true. Without them we'd lose our facade of 'normalcy.' And we can handle a human without any problem."

"You sent her into the trailer, Desari. If she is there,

why are the cats not with you?" Darius asked, his heart suddenly in his throat.

"Oh, my God." Desari paled. "How could I make such a mistake?" Stricken, she ran toward the door of the motor home.

Darius was there before her, jerking open the door and leaping in, crouching low, ready to fight the troupe's two leopards for the small female body. He froze, motionless, his long black hair falling across his face. The red-haired woman was curled up on the couch with one large panther on either side of her, dwarfing her in size yet pushing against her hands, seeking attention.

Tempest "Rusti" Trine stood up quickly as the man burst into the touring bus. He looked wild and dangerous. Everything about him screamed peril and power. He was tall, sinewy like the cats, and his long dark hair was shaggy and untamed. His eyes, as black as night, were large and mesmerizing and as penetrating as those of the two panthers. She felt her heart jump, and her mouth went dry.

"I'm sorry. Desari told me I could come in here," she offered appeasingly, trying to move away from the cats as they continued to nuzzle her for attention, nearly knocking over her small frame with each nudge. They attempted to lick her hands, which she avoided, since their rough tongues could take the skin off her.

Desari shoved into the bus past the large man and stopped, wide-eyed and shocked. "Thank God you're all right, Rusti. I never would have told you to come in here alone if I had remembered the cats."

That is not something you should ever forget. Darius delivered the reprimand in a soft whip of velvet straight into his sister's mind, using their familiar mental pathway. Desari winced but made no protest, aware her brother was right.

"They seem quite tame," Rusti ventured hesitantly, touching first one spotted feline head and then the other. The slight trembling of her hands betrayed her nervousness—of the man, not the leopards.

Darius straightened slowly to his full height. He looked so intimidating, his broad shoulders seeming to fill the bus, that Rusti actually stepped backward. His eyes bored straight into hers, his gaze holding her prisoner, searching her very soul. "No, they are not tame. They are wild animals and do not tolerate close contact with humans."

"Really?" Mischief danced for a moment in the woman's green eyes, and she shoved the bigger cat away. "I didn't realize. Sorry." She didn't sound sorry; she sounded as if she was making fun of him.

Somehow Darius knew, without a shadow of a doubt, that this woman's life would be tied to his for all eternity. He had found what Desari's new partner, Julian Savage, called his lifemate. He allowed burning desire for her to flare briefly in his eyes and was satisfied when she stepped back again. "They are not tame," he repeated. "They could tear apart anyone entering this bus. How is it you are able to be with them safely?" he demanded, his voice deep and compelling, that of a man obviously accustomed to instant obedience.

Rusti's teeth scraped across her lower lip, betraying her nervousness, but her chin went up defiantly. "Look, if you don't want me here, it's no big deal. We haven't signed a contract or anything. I'll get my tools and leave." She took a step toward the door, but the man was a solid wall, blocking her way. She glanced behind her, judging the distance to the rear door, wondering if

16

she could make it before he pounced. Somehow she was afraid that running would trigger his own predatory instincts.

"Darius," Desari objected gently, laying a placating hand on his arm.

He didn't so much as turn his head, his black eyes remaining on Rusti's face. "Leave us," he ordered his sister, his voice soft and menacing. Even the cats grew uneasy, pushing close to the red-haired woman whose green eyes flashed like jewels.

This man called Darius frightened Rusti in a way no one else ever had. There was stark possessiveness in his eyes, a sensual cruelty around his beautiful mouth, an intensity burning in him that she had never witnessed before. She watched her only ally desert her as Desari reluctantly obeyed her brother, leaving the luxurious touring bus.

"I asked you a question," he said softly.

His voice sent butterfly wings brushing at her stomach. It was a black-velvet weapon, a sorcerer's tool, and it sent heat curling unexpectedly through her body. She felt the color creeping up her neck and into her face. "Does everyone do everything you say?"

He waited, as still as a leopard poised to pounce, his unblinking eyes fixed on her face. She felt a strange compulsion to answer him, to reveal the truth. The urge beat at her head until she rubbed her temples in protest. Then she sighed, shook her head, and even attempted a smile. "Look, I'm not certain who you are, other than Desari's brother, but I think we've both made a mistake. I saw the ad for a mechanic and thought this job would be something I'd like, traveling with your band around the country." She shrugged carelessly. "It doesn't matter. I can just as easily move on."

17

Darius studied her face. She was lying to him. She needed the job. She was hungry but too proud to say anything. She covered her desperation well, but she needed work. Yet not once did her green eyes waver from his black stare, and her entire body bespoke defiance.

He moved then, gliding close to her so fast that she didn't have a chance to run. He could hear her heart pound, hear the rush of blood, of life, through her veins. His gaze rested on the pulse beating so frantically in her neck. "I think this job will suit you perfectly. What is your real name?"

He was too close, too big, too intimidating and powerful. Up close she could feel the heat radiating from his body, the magnetism he exuded. He wasn't touching her, but she felt the warmth of his skin against hers all the same. She had an urge to run as fast and as far as she could.

"Everyone calls me Rusti." She sounded defiant even to her own ears.

He smiled in an infuriatingly male way that told her he knew she was afraid of him. The smile did nothing to warm the black ice of his eyes. He bent his head slowly toward her until she could feel his breath against her neck. Her skin tingled in anticipation. Every cell in her body went on alert, screaming a warning.

"I asked you what your name is," he whispered into her pulse.

Rusti took a deep breath and made herself remain perfectly still, unflinching. If they were playing a game, she was not going to make a wrong move. "My name is Tempest Trine. But everyone calls me Rusti."

His white teeth flashed again. He looked like a hungry predator eyeing its prey. "Tempest. It suits you. I am

18

Darius. I am the guardian of this troupe. What I say goes. Obviously you've made the acquaintance of my younger sister, Desari. Have you met the others?" He felt an unfamiliar rage rip through him at the mere thought of any of the other men around her. And in that moment he knew that until he made Tempest his, he was extremely dangerous, not only to mortals but to his own kind as well. In all his centuries of existence, even in the early years, when joy and pain still existed for him, he had never experienced such jealousy, possessiveness, or any other emotion remotely like it. He had not known what rage felt like until that moment. It was sobering to realize just how much power this small human woman wielded.

Rusti shook her head. She edged away from his intensity, from the way he made her heart pound in alarm, glancing frantically at the rear door. But Darius was too close for her to make good her escape. So she looked to the big cats, then focused and aimed her thoughts at them, a talent she had had since birth, though one she would never admit aloud.

The smaller of the two leopards, the one with the lighter coat, moved between her and Darius and showed her teeth in a warning snarl. Darius reached down and laid a calming hand on the cat's head. *Be still, little friend. I would not harm this one. She seeks to leave us. I feel it in her mind. I cannot allow such a thing. You would not wish it either.*

At once the cat moved to position itself in front of the rear door, leaving Rusti no chance of escape. "Traitor," she hissed at the leopard under her breath, forgetting herself.

Darius rubbed the bridge of his nose thoughtfully.

19

"You are an unusual woman. You communicated silently with the animals?"

She looked guilty, ducking her head, her eyes shifting away from him as she pressed the back of her hand to her soft, trembling mouth. "I don't have a clue what you're talking about. If anyone's communicating with the animals, it's you. The cat's in front of the door. Not only everyone but every*thing* obeys you, huh?"

He nodded slowly. "Everyone in my domain, and that now includes you. You are not to leave. We need you as much as you need us. Did Desari assign you a place to sleep?" He felt not only her hunger but also her fatigue. It beat at him, inside him, so that his every protective male instinct roared to life.

Rusti stared up at him, measuring her options. Somewhere deep inside herself, she knew that Darius had taken away her choices. He would not allow her to leave. She saw that in the merciless line of his mouth, the implacable resolve stamped on his features, and his soulless black eyes. She could pretend if she wanted to, leave it unspoken between them, not challenge him. Power clung to him like a second skin. She had been in dangerous situations before, but this felt entirely different. She wanted to run . . . and she wanted to stay.

Darius reached out and tipped up her chin with two fingers so that he could stare directly into her green eyes. Two fingers. That was all. But it felt as if he had put chains on her, bound them together in some inexplicable manner. She felt the impact of his gaze burning into her, branding her as his.

The tip of her tongue nervously moistened her full lower lip. Darius's body clenched in hot, hard, urgent demand. "You are not going to run, Tempest. Do not think you can get away. You need the job. We need you with us. Just follow the rules."

"Desari said I can sleep in here," she found herself answering. She didn't know what she was going to do. Down to her last twenty dollars, she had been certain this was the perfect job for her. She was an excellent auto mechanic, she enjoyed traveling, she liked being alone, and she loved animals. And something about this particular help-wanted ad had jumped out at her, drawn her to this place, these people, as if it was meant to be. It had been strange, almost a compulsion she couldn't resist to find these people, so sure was she that the job was meant for her. She should have known it was too perfect. Without thinking, she sighed softly.

Darius's thumb feathered lightly over her chin. He felt her tremble, but she stood her ground. "There is always a price to pay," he observed, as if reading her mind. His hand moved to her hair, and he fingered the red-gold strands as if he couldn't help himself.

Rusti stood very still, like a small animal caught out in the open by a stalking panther. She knew he was extremely dangerous to her, yet she could only stare up at him helplessly. He was doing something to her, mesmerizing her, hypnotizing her with his burning black eyes. She couldn't look away from him. She couldn't move. "How high is the price?" Her words came out strangled-sounding and husky. She couldn't tear her gaze away from his no matter how much her mind screamed at her to do so.

His body moved close, closer still, until his hard frame seemed to imprint itself on the softness of hers. He was everywhere, surrounding her, enveloping her until she was a part of him. She knew she should try to move, to break the spell he was weaving around her, but she couldn't find the strength. Then his arms closed around her, drew her into him, and her heart turned over at the gentleness in a man of such power and enormous strength. He whispered something soft and soothing. Something compelling. A sorcerer's seduction.

She closed her eyes, the world suddenly hazy and dreamlike. She felt as if she couldn't move, as if she didn't want to move. She waited almost breathlessly. His mouth brushed her right temple, moved across her ear, feathered across her cheek to the corner of her lips, breathing warmth, leaving little dancing flames wherever he touched. She felt torn in two. One part of her knew it was so perfect, so right; the other urged her to run as fast and as far as she could. His tongue stroked across her neck, a velvet, rasping caress that curled her toes and sent heat pooling deep within her. His fingers curved around her nape, drawing her even closer. His tongue stroked a second time. A white-hot sensation pierced her skin exactly over her frantically beating pulse. Pain sliced through her, then gave way instantly to erotic pleasure.

Rusti gasped, found some deep reservoir of self-preservation, and squirmed, pushing at the muscles of his chest. Darius shifted subtly, but his arms remained tight and unyielding. Drowsiness slipped over her, a willingness to give him whatever he wanted.

She felt divided into two selves, one locked helplessly in the dark embrace, the other looking on in shock and horror. Her body was hot. Burning. Needing. Her mind accepted him and what he was doing. Taking her blood, staking his claim on her. Somehow she knew that he was not trying to kill her but possess her. Knew also that he was not anything human. Her eyelashes swept down, and her legs buckled.

Darius slipped one arm under Tempest's knees and lifted her, cradling her against his chest as he fed. She was hot and sweet and unlike anything he had ever tasted. His body was on fire for her. Still feeding, he carried her to the couch, savoring the essence of her, unable to stop himself from taking what was rightfully his. And she *was* his. He felt it, knew it, would accept nothing less.

Only when her head lolled back on her slender neck did he realize what was happening. Swearing eloquently to himself, he closed the wound in her neck with a sweep of his tongue and bent to check her pulse. He had taken far more blood than she could afford to give. And his body still throbbed with a relentless, savage demand. But Tempest Trine was a small woman and not of their race; she could not afford such a blood loss.

Worse, what he was doing was strictly forbidden, breaking every code, every law he knew. Every law he himself had taught to the others and demanded they follow. Yet he couldn't stop himself. He had to have this woman. True, a mortal female could be used for sex, a simple pleasure of the body, if one could still feel such things. And as long as one did not drain the life from her entirely, a mortal female could also be used for sustenance, to feed upon. But not both, and never at the same time. It was taboo. Darius knew that if she hadn't fainted from the blood loss, he would have taken her body with his. Not once but again and again. And he would have killed anyone who tried to stop him, who tried to take her from him.

Had it happened, then? Was he turning vampire? The one thing every Carpathian male feared—was it happening to him? He didn't care. He only knew that Tempest Trine was of the utmost importance to him, the only woman he had ever wanted in centuries of a lonely, barren existence. She made him feel. She made him see. She brought life and color into his bleak world, and now that he had seen it, felt it, he would never go back to total emptiness.

Cradling her on his lap, he started to tear open his wrist with his teeth. But something stopped him. It didn't seem right to feed her that way. Instead, he slowly opened his immaculate silk shirt, his body unexpectedly tightening even more in anticipation. One fingernail lengthened into a razor-sharp talon and sliced a thin line across his chest. Then he pressed her mouth to the wound. His blood was ancient and powerful and would replenish her quickly.

At the same time he reached for her mind. In her unconscious state, it was relatively easy to take control, to command her to do his bidding. Still, he was astonished at what he discovered. Desari was right. Tempest's mind did not follow the usual human pattern. It was more like that of the cunningly intelligent leopards he often ran with. Not exactly the same, but definitely different from the normal human brain. For the moment it didn't matter; he easily controlled her, demanding that she drink to replenish what he had taken from her.

Out of nowhere an ancient chant came into his mind. He found himself saying the words of a ritual, uncertain where they came from, knowing only that they must be said. He murmured them in the ancient tongue of his people, then repeated them in English. Bending over Tempest protectively, stroking her hair, he breathed the words softly into her ear. "I claim you as my lifemate. I belong to you. I offer my life for you. I give you my protection, my allegiance, my heart, my soul, and my body. I take into my keeping the same that is yours. Your life, happiness, and welfare will be cherished and placed above my own for all time. You are my lifemate, bound to me for all eternity and always in my care." As he uttered the words, he felt a curious shifting in his body, a release of a terrible tension. He also felt the words weaving tiny threads between her soul and his, his heart and hers. She belonged to him. He belonged to her.

But it wasn't right. She was a mortal. He was Carpathian. She would grow old; he never would. Still, it didn't matter. Nothing mattered to him except that she was in his world, that she was beside him. That it felt right to him. She fit with him as if she had been fashioned only for him.

Darius closed his eyes and held her to him, savoring the feel of her in his arms. He closed his wound himself and laid her among the pillows lining the couch. Very gently, almost reverently, he cleaned the dirt and grime from her face. *You will not remember this when you awaken. You will know only that you took this job and are now part of our crew. You know nothing of what I am or that we exchanged blood.* He reinforced the command with a hard mental push more than sufficient to convince a human.

She looked so young in her sleep, her red-gold hair framing her face. He touched her, his fingers possessive, his black eyes burning fiercely. Then he turned to regard the large cats. *You like her. She can speak to you, can she not?* he asked them.

He could feel their answer, not in words but in images of affection and trust. He nodded. *She is mine, and I will not give her up. Guard her well while we sleep until the next rising,* he silently commanded them.

The two cats rubbed against the couch, trying to get as close as possible to the woman. Darius touched her face once more, then turned and left the mobile home. He knew Desari would be waiting for him, and her gentle doe-eyes would be accusing.

She stood leaning against the front of the trailer, confusion on her beautiful face. The moment she saw him, she looked anxiously at the bus. "What have you done?"

"Stay out of this, Desari. You are my own blood, the one I most love and treasure, but—" Darius stopped, amazed that he could express that emotion honestly for the first time in centuries. He did feel love for his sister again. It beat in him, real and strong, and his relief was tremendous at not having to reach for and feign remembered emotions. He recovered his composure and continued. "But I will not tolerate your interference in this matter. Tempest will stay with us. She is mine. The others will not touch her."

Desari's hand went to her throat, and her face paled. "Darius, what have you done?"

"Do not think to defy me, or I will take her far from here and leave you all to go your own way."

Desari's mouth trembled. "We are under your protection, Darius. You have always led, and we have always followed you. We trust you completely; trust your judgment." She hesitated. "I know you would never hurt this girl."

Darius studied his sister's face for a long moment. "No, you do not, Desari, and neither do I. I know only that, without her, I will bring danger and death to many before I am destroyed."

He heard her swift intake of breath. "Is it that bad, Darius? Are you so close, then?" She did not need to use the words *vampire* or *undead*. They both knew intimately of what she spoke.

"She is all that is standing between the destruction of

26

mortals and immortals alike. The line is fragile. Do not interfere, Desari. It is all the warning I am capable of giving you," he said with a merciless, implacable resolve.

Darius had always been the acknowledged leader of their small group, ever since they were all children and he had saved them from certain death. Even as a mere youth he had reared and protected them, given them his all. He was the strongest, the most cunning, and the most powerful. He had the gift of healing. They relied on him for his wisdom and expertise. He had steered them safely through the long centuries without thought for himself. Desari could do no other than support him in this one thing he asked. No, not asked. Demanded. She knew Darius was not exaggerating, not lying, not bluffing; he never did. Everything he said, he meant.

Slowly, reluctantly, Desari nodded. "You are my brother, Darius. I am with you always, whatever you choose to do."

She turned as her lifemate abruptly shimmered into a solid state beside her. Julian Savage still took her breath away, the sight of his tall, muscled frame, the striking, molten-gold eyes that always reflected love back to her.

Julian bent to brush Desari's temple with the warmth and comfort of his mouth. He had caught her distress through their psychic link and instantly returned from hunting prey. When he turned his gaze on Darius, his eyes were cold. Darius met that gaze with one equally chilling.

Desari sighed softly at the two territorial males measuring each other. "You two promised."

Instantly Julian leaned into her, his voice extraordinarily tender. "Is there a problem here?"

Darius made a sound of disgust, a rumbling growl deep

in his throat. "Desari is my sister. I have always seen to her welfare."

For just a moment the golden eyes flickered over him, cold with menace. Then Julian's white teeth gleamed in a semblance of a smile. "It is true, and I can do no other than be grateful to you."

Darius shook his head slightly. He was still unused to tolerating the presence of any male not of his own small group. Accepting his sister's new lifemate traveling with them was one thing; liking it was quite another. Julian had been raised in the Carpathian Mountains, their native land, and though he had been forced into a solitary existence, he had had the benefit of years of training in their ways, of adult Carpathian guidance during his fledgling years. Darius knew Julian was strong and one of their people's most skilled hunters of vampires. He knew Desari was safe with him, but he couldn't quite relinquish his own role as her protector. He had had far too many centuries of leadership, of learning the hard way, through experience.

Some centuries ago in their almost-forgotten homeland, Darius and five other Carpathian children had seen their parents murdered by invaders who thought them vampires and carried out their ritual slayings: a stake through the heart, beheading, with garlic stuffed in the mouth. It had been a frightening, traumatic time as Ottoman Turks overran their village while the sun was high in the sky, just as their parents were at their most vulnerable. The Carpathians had tried to save the mortal villagers, standing with them to fight the invasion despite the fact that the attack had come when the Carpathian people were at their weakest. But there were far too many assailants, and the sun was too high. Nearly everyone had been massacred.

The marauding armies had then herded the children, mortal and immortal alike, into a straw shack and set it on fire, burning the youngsters alive. Darius had managed to fabricate an illusion to cloak the presence of a few of the children from the soldiers, a feat unheard of at his age. And when he noticed a peasant woman who had escaped the bloodthirsty assailants, he had cloaked her presence as well and forced a compulsion upon her. He embedded within the woman a deep need to flee and take with her the Carpathian children he had saved.

The woman took them down the mountain to her lover, a man who owned a boat. Though sailing the open seas was rarely attempted in that century, since tales of sea serpents and falling off the earth abounded, the marauders' cruelty was a worse fate, so the small crew took their vessel far from their shores in an attempt to flee the steadily advancing army.

The children had huddled together in the precarious craft, all terrified, all shocked at the hideous deaths of their parents. Even Desari, a mere infant, was aware of what had happened. Darius had kept them going, insisting they could make it if they stuck together. A terrible storm had come up, washing the crew overboard, the sea rising up to claim the sailors and the woman as efficiently as the Turks had massacred the villagers. Darius had refused to yield his charges up to such a fate. Although still very young, he already had an iron will. Holding the image of a bird in their minds, he forced the children, as young as they were, to shape-shift with him before the ship went down. Then he had flown, clutching tiny Desari in his talons, leading them to the nearest body of land, the shores of Africa.

Darius had been six years old, his sister barely six months. The other female child, Syndil, was one. With them were three boys, the oldest four years of age. Compared to the familiar comforts of their homeland, Africa seemed wild, untamed, a primitive, frightening place. Yet Darius felt responsible for the safety of the other children. He learned to fight, to hunt, to kill. He learned how to exert authority, to take care of his group. Carpathian children did not yet have the extraordinary talents of their elders—to know the unknowable, to see the unseeable, to command the creatures and natural forces of the Earth, to heal. They had to learn these techniques from their parents, study under those who would teach them. But Darius didn't allow those limitations to stop him. Though he was just a little boy himself, he would not lose the children. It was that simple to him.

It had not been easy to keep the two girls alive. Female Carpathian children seldom survived the first year of life. At first Darius had hoped other Carpathians would come and rescue them, but in the meantime he had to provide for them as best he could. And as time passed, the memory of their native race and ways faded. He took the few rules imprinted on him from birth, what he could remember of his talks with his parents, and he devised his own ways and his own code of honor by which to live.

He harvested herbs, hunted animals, tried every nutritional source on himself first, often sickening himself in the process. But eventually he learned the ways of the wilds, became a stronger protector, and ultimately the group of children became much closer than most families, the only ones like themselves in their remote world. The few of their kind they had encountered had already turned, become the undead, vampires feeding on the lives of those around them. Always it was Darius who took the responsibility of hunting down and destroying the dreaded demons. His group was fiercely loyal to, fiercely protective of, one another. And all of them followed Darius without question.

His strength and will had carried them through centuries of learning, of adapting, of creating a new kind of life. It had been a shock to discover, a few short months ago, that others of their kind, Carpathian and not vampire, still existed. Darius had been secretly afraid that all males of his kind eventually turned, and he feared what would become of his wards if he did. He had lost all emotion centuries earlier, a sure sign a male was in danger of turning. He never spoke of it, always afraid the day would come when he would turn on his own loved ones, relying on his iron will and private code of honor to prevent such an outcome. Already, one of the males among them had turned, become the unthinkable. Darius glided away from his sister and her lifemate, thinking of Savon. Savon had been the second oldest boy, the closest of friends, and Darius had relied on him often to hunt or to watch over the others. Savon had always been his second in command, the one he trusted to watch his back.

He stopped for a moment beside a huge oak tree and leaned against the trunk, remembering that horrible day a few months earlier when he had found Savon crouched over Syndil, her body a mass of bite marks and bruises. She was naked, blood and seed seeping from between her legs, her beautiful eyes glazed with shock. Savon had then attacked Darius, going for his throat, ripping and tearing nearly fatal wounds before Darius had time to realize that his best friend had become what all the males feared becoming most. The vampire. The undead. Savon had brutally raped and beaten Syndil and was now trying to destroy Darius.

Darius had had no choice but to kill his friend and incinerate his body and heart, having had to learn the hard way how to destroy a vampire properly. For the undead could rise again and again from the most mortal of wounds unless certain techniques were used. Darius had had no one to instruct him in those techniques, only an eternity of instincts and mistakes to correct. After that terrible battle with Savon, Darius had lain for some time deep within the soil, healing himself.

Syndil had been largely silent in the months since, often taking the shape of a panther and staying with the other cats, Sasha and Forest. Darius sighed. It was only now that he could feel the deep sorrow sweeping over him for Savon, the guilt and despair that he had been unable to see it coming and find a way to help his friend. After all, he was their leader; he was responsible. And Syndil was like a lost child, with such sadness, such wariness in her beautiful dark eyes. He had failed her most of all, failed to protect her from one of their own, thinking in his arrogance that his leadership, the unity among them, would prevent the ultimate depravity one of their species could experience. He still could not look Syndil fully in the eyes.

And now he was breaking his own laws. But, he wondered, had he made up those laws so the "family" would have a code to live by? Or had his father told him of these matters? Or had they been imprinted on him before birth, as certain other knowledge had been? Had he been better friends with Julian, they might have shared more information, but for centuries Darius had always learned for himself, remaining self-contained, private, answering to no one, accepting the consequences of his own actions and mistakes.

Hunger bit at him, and he knew he had no choice but to hunt. The campground they had chosen to stay in for a few days was deep within a California state park, little used and, at the moment, empty. A highway ran close by, but he had spread an invisible warning net between it and the camp, creating a sense of oppression and dread in humans who might think of stopping there. It wouldn't harm the humans, just make them wary. Yet it hadn't deterred Tempest.

Darius thought about that as he shape-shifted on the run, his body contorting, stretching. Muscles and sinew soon encompassed a loose, supple leopard's powerful frame, and Darius loped silently through the forest toward a more popular campsite situated near a deep, clear lake.

The leopard covered the distance quickly, scenting prey, circling to stay downwind and low in the bushes. It observed two men fishing from the reed-covered shore, talking to each other in short bursts of speech.

Darius paid no attention to their words. In the body of the cat he slunk close to the ground. Carefully positioning each large paw, he crept stealthily forward. One of the men turned his head toward the sound of laughter coming from the campsite. Darius stopped, then resumed his slow-motion progress. His prey turned his attention back toward the lake, and in absolute silence the leopard edged ever closer, then crouched low, powerful muscles bunched and waiting.

Darius sent forth a silent call, enveloping the shorter of the two men, drawing his prey to him. The man's head went up, and he turned toward the leopard waiting in the brush. He dropped his fishing pole into the lake and began to lurch forward, one foot in front of the other, eyes glazed.

"Jack!" The other man grabbed the sinking pole, twisting around to stare at his friend.

Darius froze both men with a mind block and shape-shifted back to his own form as "Jack" approached the big cat. It was the only safe thing to do. He had found that the cat's hunting instincts made it dangerous to use its body to feed. The leopard's sharp canines pierced and killed its prey. It had taken several trial-and-error episodes on his part as a child, not powerful or skilled enough for hunting, to learn what was acceptable and what was not. Until he was grown he had had no choice but to use the leopards and their abilities, and he accepted the responsibility for the Africans who had died, for it was the only way he could keep the other children alive.

Now he kept the other man calm and accepting with the ease of long practice, a method perfected long ago. He bent his head and drank his fill, careful not to take too much. He didn't want his prey sick and dizzy. Helping the first man to a sitting position in the brush, he summoned the other one to him.

Finally sated, he slowly allowed his body to reshape. The cat snarled silently, its instinct to pull what appeared to be carcasses deeper into the trees and finish consuming them, blood and meat. Darius fought the urge and padded on cushioned paws back toward the touring bus.

His group now traveled together as musicians, modern-day troubadours, going from city to city singing, as often as possible, in the small local venues Desari preferred. The constant travel also preserved their personal anonymity even as their outward fame grew. Desari had a beautiful voice, haunting and mesmerizing. Dayan was a superb songwriter, and his voice, too, captured audiences and held them spellbound. In the old days the troubadour life had allowed them to travel from place to place without close scrutiny, and no one could notice or compare their differences from others. Now, with the world growing smaller, maintaining privacy from fans was a much more difficult feat. Thus, they made every effort to act and appear "normal," including using inefficient, imperfect, automotive travel. And thus their need for a mechanic to maintain their caravan of vehicles.

Darius made his way back to the campsite and shape-shifted as he entered the motor home equipped with every luxury. Tempest was in a deep sleep, due, he was certain, to the fact that he had been greedy in the taking of her blood. He should have tried to control himself, to deprive himself of the unexpected ecstasy of it.

Just looking at her made his body ache with a relentless, urgent demand he knew was not going to go away. He and this fiery little woman, would have to learn to strike some sort of balance. Darius was unaccustomed to opposition. Everyone always did as he bade without question. He could not expect a tempestuous human woman to do the same. He tucked the blanket more closely around her and bent to brush his mouth against her forehead. His thumb skimmed the softness of her skin, and he felt a jolt throughout his body.

Darius collected himself and directed a firm command to the leopards before stalking out of the bus. He wanted Tempest safe at all times. Though the cats slept the day away, as did Darius and his family, the leopards gave the troupe semblance of security, guarding the bus while the troupe members were resting and restoring themselves deep within the ground. He directed the cats' protective instincts to include Tempest above all.

Chapter Two

Vampire. Tempest sat up slowly, wiping at her mouth with the back of one trembling hand. She was in the Dark Troubadours' touring bus, on the sofa bed, lost in a sea of pillows, a blanket covering her. The two leopards pressed close to her were sleeping. The sunlight was trying in vain to filter through the dark curtains covering the windows. It must be late afternoon, with the sun so low. She was weak, shaking. Her mouth was dry, her lips parched. She needed liquid of some kind, any kind.

When she tried to stand, she swayed slightly before finding her balance. She remembered every horrifying detail of the night before, even though Darius had commanded her to forget all of it. She had no doubt he was capable of commanding most human beings to do his bidding, but somehow he hadn't managed to do so with her. Tempest had always been a bit different, able to communicate with animals, to read their thoughts as they could read hers. That trait must have provided her partial immunity to Darius's mental push, though he likely thought he had successfully destroyed her memories of what he was and what he was capable of doing.

She put a hand to her throat, searching for a wound, realizing that she *wasn't* immune to his blatant sex appeal. She had never felt such chemistry in her life. Electricity had arced between them, sizzling and crackling. And it was humiliating to acknowledge that, however much she'd like to think so, he wasn't completely to blame. She hadn't been able to control herself around him either. Which shocked her. Terrified her.

So okay. The man was an honest-to-God vampire. She would scream and fall apart later. Right now the important thing to do was get out. Run. Hide. Put as much distance between herself and that maniac as she could possibly manage before nightfall, when vampires allegedly arose. Right now, he had to be sleeping somewhere. God help her if he was in a coffin somewhere in the bus. She wasn't about to drive a stake through anyone's heart. It wasn't going to happen.

"Go to the cops," she ordered herself softly. "Someone has to know about this."

She lurched her way to the front of the bus. Glancing in a mirror to assure herself she still had a reflection, she winced at her appearance. The vampire had to be pretty hard up to come after someone who looked the way she did—like Frankenstein's bride.

"Sure, Tempest," she said to her image, "you tell the police. Officer, a man bit my neck and sucked my blood. He's the guardian—uh, bodyguard—for a real popular singer and band. He's a vampire. Please go and arrest him." She wrinkled her nose at herself and deepened her voice. "Sure, miss. I believe you. And who are you, anyway? A homeless, penniless young woman with a record of running away from every foster home we ever put you in. Let's say we take a nice ride to the funny farm. After all, you do spend a lot of time talking to animals." She made a moue with her lips. "Yeah, that'll work."

She found the bathroom, which proved amazingly luxurious, but cleaned up quickly rather than admiring her surroundings, showering, gulping as much water as she could. She changed into faded blue jeans and a fresh cotton top from the small backpack she always had with her.

The moment she headed for the exit, however, both cats lifted their heads alertly and made sounds of protest. She sent them her regrets but slipped out before they could stop her by body-blocking the doors. She could feel their intentions, knew Darius had instructed them to keep her there should she awaken. Both snarled and screamed in anger as she made good her escape, but she didn't hesitate, slamming the door behind her and running away from the bus.

She spent several minutes trying to locate the toolbox she always carried with her, but it was nowhere to be found. Cursing under her breath, she headed for the highway and began to jog. As soon as she put some miles between herself and that creature, she would be happy. Wouldn't you know she would find a vampire? Probably the only one in existence.

She wondered why she wasn't fainting with fright. It wasn't every day a person met a vampire. And she couldn't even tell anyone. Ever. She would go to her grave the only human being alive to know that vampires really existed. She groaned. Why was she always getting herself into trouble? It was so like her to go out on a simple job interview and manage to encounter a vampire.

She jogged for three miles, thankful that she liked to run, because not one single car had driven by in all that time. She slowed her pace and reached up to wrap her sweat-dampened hair into a ponytail again to get it off her neck. What time was it? Why didn't she own a watch? Why hadn't she checked the time before she took off?

After another hour or so of jogging and walking, she finally flagged down a car and managed to get a short ride. She felt abnormally tired and terribly thirsty. The couple who picked her up bubbled over with goodwill, but they wore her out with their energy, and she was almost glad to say good-bye and resume her jogging and walking.

But this time she didn't cover much ground. She was so tired, her body felt like lead, and each step she took felt as if she were wading through quicksand.

She sat down abruptly on the side of the road. Her head was beginning to pound with alarming force. She rubbed her temples and the nape of her neck, hoping to alleviate the pain.

A small blue pickup truck pulled up beside her. It was a measure of her weakness that she could barely find the strength to get to her feet and go to the driver's window.

The man was about forty, compact, and muscular. He smiled at her, his eyes holding a hint of worry. "Something wrong, miss?"

Rusti shook her head. "I need a ride, though, if you're going any distance."

"Sure, hop in." He pushed a pile of clutter from the seat to the floor. "The truck's a mess, but what the heck?"

"Thanks. The weather looks like it's going to turn nasty." And it did. Unexpectedly, dark clouds began to float across the sky.

The man glanced up through the windshield. "Crazy. The weather reports said clear and sunny. Maybe those clouds will just drift on by. I'm Harry." He stuck out his hand.

"Tempest." She slipped her hand into his for a brief shake, but the moment she touched him, her stomach lurched and her skin crawled.

His thumb brushed the back of her hand just once, sending a chill down her spine. But Harry released her immediately and put the truck back into gear, his eyes on the road. Rusti huddled as far from him as possible, fighting her rising nausea and wild imagination. But the moment her head was against the back of the seat, tiredness overtook her, and her lashes kept drifting down.

Harry glanced at her with obvious concern. "Are you sick? I could take you to the nearest doctor. I think there's supposed to be a small town a few miles up this road."

Rusti tried to rally. She shook her pounding head. She knew she was pale, and she could feel small beads of perspiration dotting her forehead. "I jogged for several miles. I think I just overdid it." But she knew that wasn't the problem. For some reason every cell in her body was protesting the distance she was putting between herself and Darius. She knew it. Felt it.

"Go to sleep, then. I'm used to driving alone," Harry advised. "I usually have the radio on, but if it bothers you, I can do without it."

"It's not going to bother me," she replied. Her lashes would not stay up no matter how hard she tried to stay awake. She was exhausted. Had she picked up a bug?

41

Suddenly she sat up straight. Could vampires have rabies? They turned into bats, didn't they? And couldn't bats carry rabies? She was okay with bats, but that didn't mean she liked vampires. What if Darius had infected her with something?

She realized Harry was staring at her. He was probably thinking he had picked up a nutcase. Deliberately she settled back against the seat and closed her eyes. Could a person become a vampire with one bite? One little bite? She squirmed, remembering the dark, sensual heat burning through her body. So okay. Maybe a big bite. The memory, the feel of his mouth on her neck, made her throb and burn, flooding her with flames all over again. She found her hand creeping up to her throat to cover the spot, to hold the erotic memory in the palm of her hand.

She nearly groaned aloud. Darius definitely had infected her with something, but it wasn't rabies. Weariness continued to invade her body, deadening her limbs, so she gave up the fight and allowed her eyes to close.

Harry drove for fifteen minutes, casting quick, covert glances at his hitchhiker. His heart was pounding loudly in his chest. She was small and curvy and had fallen right into his lap. He never looked a gift horse in the mouth. Glancing at his watch, he was satisfied to see that he was ahead of schedule. He was meeting his boss in a couple of hours and had time enough to indulge his fantasies with the little redhead.

The ominous clouds had thickened and darkened, occasionally issuing small veins of lightning and a rumble of thunder. But it was still early evening, around six-thirty, and Harry watched for a grove of trees where he could pull off the road into a private area and remain undetected by any passing cars.

Rusti jerked awake when a hand fumbled clumsily at her breast. Her eyes flew open. Harry was leaning across her, tearing at her clothes. She slugged him as hard as she was able to in the small confines of the truck. But he was a big man, and his fist clipped her behind her ear, then smashed into her left eye. For a brief instant she saw stars, then everything went black, and she slid farther down into the seat.

Harry's mouth covered hers, wet and slimy. Again she struggled wildly, raking at his face with her fingernails. "Stop! Stop it!"

He slapped her over and over, his other hand squeezing her breast hard, hurting her. "You're a whore. Why else would you get in here with me? You wanted this. You know you did. That's okay, honey, I like it rough. Fight me. It's great. It's what I want."

His knee pressed hard against her thigh, holding her down so that he could tear at the waistband of her jeans. Rusti's hand found the door handle, and she wrenched at it and jackknifed out onto the ground. Scrambling on all fours, she tried to get away.

Overhead the skies unexpectedly opened up, and the dark clouds emptied onto them like a waterfall. Harry caught her ankle, dragging her back over the gravel toward him. Grabbing her other ankle, he flipped her over so hard it drove the air from her lungs.

Lightning flashed, sizzled, and arced from cloud to cloud. She saw it clearly as she stared up at the sky. Rain fell in silver sheets, drenching her. She closed her eyes as Harry struck her repeatedly with his clenched fist. "Feels good, feels real good, doesn't it?" he rasped. His eyes were ugly and hard, glaring down at her with hatred and triumph.

Tempest fought him with every ounce of strength she possessed, kicking at him when she could draw her legs up, beating at him until her fists were bruised and aching. Nothing seemed to help. The rain poured down on them both, and thunder growled, shaking the ground.

There was no warning whatsoever. One moment Harry's weight was pressing down on her body, the next he was jerked backward by some unseen hand. She heard the thud as her attacker landed hard against his truck. She tried to roll over, sick to her stomach. Every muscle hurt. She managed to make it to her knees before she vomited violently, again and again. Her eye was swelling shut, and with the rain, wind, and abruptly falling darkness, it was hard to see what was happening.

She heard an ominous crack, the sound of a bone breaking. She crawled almost blindly toward a tree and dragged herself unsteadily up to brace herself on the trunk. Then arms surrounded her, drew her toward a solid chest. Instantly she erupted into a fighting, struggling wild thing, screaming and blindly flailing.

"You are safe, now," Darius crooned softly, battling down the beast raging in his body. "No one is going to hurt you. Be calm, Tempest. You are safe with me."

At that moment she didn't care what Darius was; he had saved her. She clutched his jacket and burrowed close, trying to shrink from the terrible brutality and disappear into the shelter of his body.

Tempest was shaking so hard that Darius was afraid she would collapse. He lifted her into his arms, holding her close. "See to the mortal," he snapped over his shoulder to Dayan, his second in command.

Darius carried Tempest's small, battered body into the

comparative shelter of the trees. She was a mess, her face swollen and bruised, tears streaming down her cheeks. She was hunching into herself, rocking back and forth, far too reminiscent of Syndil after Savon's attack for Darius's comfort. He simply held her, allowing her to cry, his arms strong and comforting.

Before he had risen, the warning of the cats had reached him that Tempest was fleeing. He had slowed her down as much as he could, making her exceedingly tired. Then he sent the clouds to darken the skies so that he might rise early without the sun hurting his sensitive Carpathian eyes, without burning his Carpathian skin. The moment he could, he had launched himself skyward, commanding Dayan to follow him. Together they streamed across the night toward her, Barack racing after them in the sports car at Darius's command.

Now each tear she shed tore at him, ripping into his soul as nothing else had ever done. "You have to stop, baby," he whispered softly into her hair, "you will make yourself sick. It is all right now. He is gone. He will never touch you again." *Or anyone else.* Dayan would destroy any evidence that Tempest had ever been in that blue pickup. Her attacker would drive himself into a tree and break his neck farther down the road.

Darius found his own hand trembling as he stroked her hair, his chin rubbing the silkiness just because he had to. "What made you leave? We offered the perfect job for you. And you will have me to look after you."

"Lucky me," Rusti said wearily. "I need some aspirin."

"You need sleep and time to heal," he corrected gently. "Come home with us, Tempest. You will be safe there."

Tempest clutched her head, but every single place Harry had punched her throbbed and hurt, each worse than the other. She hated that anyone should see her like this, and she certainly had no intention of going anywhere with Darius, especially when his sister and the rest of his group would witness her humiliation.

She pushed ineffectually at the solid wall of his chest, wincing when even her palms hurt. Darius caught her hands and examined them carefully, then brought each to his mouth. His tongue moved over her fingers in a rasping caress that sent a shiver through her body but, oddly enough, soothed the pain. "I can't go back there, not like this."

He could hear the anguish in her voice, the degradation and shame she felt. He realized she had not even looked up at him.

"This was not your fault," he said. "You know that, Tempest. This man tried to rape you because he is depraved, not because you did anything to incite him."

"I was hitchhiking," she confessed in a low voice. "I never should have gotten into his truck."

"Tempest, if he had not found you, he would have found another girl, perhaps one without anyone to look after her. Now let me see your face. Do you think you could take it out of my shirt long enough for me to assess what damage he has done to you?" Darius made an effort to lighten his tone to help put her at ease.

She could not believe how gentle he was. She could feel his enormous strength, his tremendous power, yet even his voice was tender. It brought fresh tears to her eyes. She had run away from him thinking him a monster, yet it was he who had saved her from a real monster.

"I just can't face anyone yet." Tempest's voice was muffled against him, but he could hear her determination. She was getting ready to make her next bid for freedom.

Darius turned then, with her cradled in his arms, and began striding back toward the road. The rain beat down on them relentlessly, but he didn't seem to notice. He took her a distance away so that she wouldn't have to see the horror of what he had done to her attacker.

"I need to sit down," she finally objected, "on solid ground." Suddenly she realized her shirt was in tatters and her bare skin exposed. She gasped out loud, attracting his instant attention, his black gaze moving broodingly over her.

Then he laughed softly to calm her anxiety. "I have a sister, honey. I have seen the female body before." But he was already lowering her feet to the ground and shrugging out of his jacket. Very gently he enveloped her in it, taking the opportunity to look at her more closely. Already dark bruises were marring the perfection of her fair skin, and a faint trickle of blood seeped from the corner of her mouth. Darius had to look away from that temptation. He caught a glimpse of more bruises on the creamy swell of her breast, along her narrow rib cage, and on her smooth stomach.

Rage swept through him, turbulent and unfamiliar. He wanted to kill the man over and over, to feel his neck snap beneath his hands. He wanted to rend and tear like the leopards he had spent so much time studying, so much time learning from. He fought down the killing rage until it simmered and seethed just below the surface but where she could not possibly see it.

His natural instinct was to heal her, using the curative agent in his saliva, but he refrained, not wanting to alarm her further. There would be time enough when he got her home and could put her to sleep.

Tempest was aware that Darius could see her, even in the dark. Curiously, she was no longer afraid of him. She stared at the toes of her dirty running shoes, uncertain what to do. She was sick and dizzy, she hurt everywhere, and she wanted to curl up in a ball and cry. She had no money, nowhere to go.

Darius reached out, ignored the way she flinched from his hand, and wrapped his long fingers possessively around the nape of her neck. "I am going to take you home. You can soak in the tub, I will fix you something to eat, and no one will see you but me. Since I have already seen you, it is all right." His tone seemed to request agreement, but she heard command in his voice.

"We have to call the police," she said softly. "I can't let him get away with this."

"He will not commit such an atrocity again, Tempest," he murmured softly. He could hear the engine of a car speeding toward them, and he identified it as their own. "Has my sister introduced you to any of the other band members yet?" he inquired, deliberately distracting her so that she wouldn't ask any questions.

Tempest sat down right where she was, on the side of the road in the pouring rain. Furious at himself for acceding to her demand to stand when he knew she was too weak, Darius ignored her protest and swung her back into his arms as if she were a child. For once, she didn't protest, didn't say anything. She turned her face into the warmth of his chest, burrowed close to the steady, reassuring beat of his heart, and lay passively in the safety of his arms, shivering from shock and the cold rain.

Barack had made the drive in record time. He liked the speed of modern cars and took every opportunity to hone his racing skills. He stopped exactly in front of Darius, his face, through the windshield, a mask of darkness. The youngest of the men, he had retained remnants of the easygoing boy they had all been so fond of until Syndil was attacked and they began to trust no one, not even themselves.

Darius pulled open the car door and slid in, never relinquishing his hold on Tempest. Her eyes were closed, and she didn't look up, didn't acknowledge the vehicle. It worried him. *She is in shock, Barack. Thank you for getting here so quickly. I knew I could count on you. Get us home with the same speed.* Darius spoke to his friend on their mental pathway rather than aloud.

Shall I wait for Dayan? Barack inquired, using the same mental path that was familiar to all five of his people.

Darius shook his head. Dayan would make better time flying, even in the storm. As would he, if he were willing to frighten Tempest to death by whisking her through the air. He was not. Indeed, he knew that his unfamiliar emotions were feeding the intensity of the storm he had created.

Tempest didn't speak on the long drive back to the campsite, but Darius was aware that she was awake. Not once did she doze off. Still, her hold on her self-control was tenuous at best, so he stayed quiet to avoid saying or doing the wrong thing, anything that might make her want to run away again. He couldn't let her go. The attack had only proved to him how much she needed him, too, and the last thing he wanted to do was create a situation where she feared him or challenged his authority.

Julian Savage was lounging lazily against the motor home as they drove up. He straightened with his casual strength, a ripple of muscles that revealed his power, as Darius slid from the seat of the car, the small, red-haired woman held unbelievably protectively in his arms.

"I know something of the healing arts," Julian offered softly, although he strongly suspected that Darius would refuse his help. The man's hold on the woman was fiercely possessive; Darius would never turn her over to another man.

Darius flicked Julian a smoldering black glance. "No thank you," he answered tersely. "I will see to her needs. Please ask Desari to bring Tempest's knapsack to the bus."

Julian was careful not to allow a glint of humor to show in his eyes. Darius had a soft spot after all. And she had red hair. Who would have guessed? He couldn't wait to tell his lifemate. With a slight salute, Julian sauntered away.

Darius jerked open the door to the motor home, entered it, and gently placed Tempest on the couch. She rolled into a ball, facing away from him. He touched her hair, his hand lingering, trying to convey comfort. Then he turned the tape player on low, so Desari's haunting recorded voice could fill the silence with healing, shimmering beauty. Next he filled the tub with hot, scented water and lit special candles, their aromas also designed to promote healing.

Darius didn't turn on the overhead lights. He could see perfectly without them, and Tempest wouldn't want them. "Come on, baby, into the bath," he said, lifting her tenderly but quickly, giving her no chance to protest. "The herbs in the water will sting at first, but you will feel better afterward." He seated her on the edge of the huge tub. "Do you need help with your clothes?" He kept his voice strictly neutral.

Rusti shook her head quickly, then regretted it when her head pounded and her eye throbbed. "I can take care of myself."

"I do not think we will get into that right now. You are not up to a sparring match." The slight teasing note in his voice surprised him even more than it did her. "Get into the tub, honey. I will be back with your clothes and a robe. You can eat when you get out." He bent to light two more aromatic candles and let their flames flicker and dance on the water and walls.

Rusti undressed slowly, reluctantly. It hurt to move. She was numb inside, too worn out and shell-shocked even to worry about what Darius was or what he wanted from her. She knew he believed he had successfully erased her memory of what he had done to her the night before. Even now, with the horror of *this* night surrounding her, she still felt the burning heat of his mouth on her neck. She slipped into the steamy tub, gasping as the water lapped at her sore body.

Why did strange things always happen to her? She was careful, wasn't she? She slid beneath the water, the stinging from her eye and mouth taking her breath away. When she came up, she lay against the sloped side of the tub and closed her eyes, resting. Her mind stayed mercifully blank. She couldn't think about Harry or what she might have done to bring on his vicious attack. He had wanted to hurt her, and he had.

"Tempest, you are falling asleep." Darius didn't mention that she was moaning softly in distress.

She sat up quickly, arms covering her breasts, water sloshing out of the tub. One eye, a vivid green, stared up at him in alarm, the other swollen and purple. She had quite an interesting array of colors sweeping across her face and body, proof of her vulnerability, yet she still managed to look defiant. "Get out," she demanded.

Darius smiled, a flash of white teeth. It reminded her of a predator's silent challenge. He held up both hands, palms out. "I am only trying to help you not to drown. Dinner is ready. Here is a robe."

"Whose is it?" she asked, suspicious.

"Mine." It was the truth and yet not the truth. He had created it easily, instantly, from natural fibers, a trick learned over the centuries. "I will close my eyes if it makes you happy. Come out of there." He held up a huge towel for her.

"You aren't closing your eyes," she accused him as she stepped into it. He was staring at a particularly nasty bruise on her rib cage. It embarrassed her that he could see the damage her attacker had inflicted; she didn't stop to think why it didn't embarrass her that he was seeing her naked.

Obediently he closed his eyes, but the vision of her—small, forlorn, hurt, and so alone—stayed with him. He felt her slender form enclosed in the towel beneath his hands before he allowed himself to look at her. She appeared more childlike than ever. And for the moment Darius treated her that way, drying her shivering body impersonally, pretending not to notice her soft, satiny skin, her curves, her tiny rib cage and narrow waist. He toweled the red-gold strands of hair, dark now with moisture.

"I can't stop shaking," Tempest said, her voice a mere thread of sound.

"Shock," he said gruffly. He wanted to hold her in his arms, take away what had happened to her. "You are in shock. It will pass." He quickly wrapped her in the warmth of the robe because he couldn't stand seeing her skin so bruised and swollen. He hated the way her eyes avoided his, as if she had something wrong and was ashamed.

"Put your arms around my neck, Tempest," he ordered

softly, his voice a blend of huskiness and hypnotic power.

Rusti reluctantly complied, and he lifted her up, forcing her to look into his black, burning eyes. She almost groaned. She could get lost in his eyes. No one should have those eyes.

"I want you to hear me this time, Tempest. This was not your fault. You did nothing wrong. If you need to place blame on someone other than the man who attacked you, place it where it belongs: squarely on my shoulders. You would never have left if I had not frightened you."

She made a sound of protest, of fear. She told herself it was because the candles suddenly went out, leaving the bathroom in darkness, but she knew it was more than that.

He held her gaze, not allowing her to slip from his mesmerizing possession. "You know it is true. I am used to telling everyone what to do. And I am very attracted to you." He winced inwardly at the understatement of that particular comment. "I should have been more gentle with you."

Darius carried her into the dining area and placed her in a chair at the table. A bowl of steaming soup was waiting for her. "Eat it, honey. I slaved over this for you."

Tempest found herself attempting a smile. It stung her mouth, then she felt it inside her, spreading warmth. No one, as far back as she could remember, had ever treated her with so much caring. No one had ever made her a bowl of soup.

"Thanks for coming after me," she said, stirring the broth, trying, without seeming to, to see what was in it.

He sat opposite her, took the spoon from her with a little sigh, dipped it into the soup, and blew on it. "You eat this stuff, not play with it," he reprimanded, and he held the spoon to her mouth.

Reluctantly she complied. Astonishingly enough, it was good. Who would have suspected a vampire could cook? "It's vegetable soup," she stated, pleased. "And it's very good."

"I do have my talents," he muttered, remembering all the various broths he had concocted for the baby girls, trying to keep them alive. Since Carpathians did not eat meat, he had worked with roots, berries, and leaves, trying everything on himself first, poisoning himself more than once.

"Talk to me," Tempest pleaded. "I don't want to start shaking again, and I can feel it coming on."

Darius held another spoonful of soup to her mouth. "Has Desari told you much about us?"

She shook her head, concentrating on the warmth the soup provided.

"We travel a great deal, giving concerts, you know. Dayan and Desari are our singers. That is Desari's voice you are listening to on the tape. She is very good, is she not?" There was pride in his voice.

Tempest liked his way of speaking, an Old World, old-fashioned manner she found oddly sexy. "She has a beautiful voice."

"Desari is my younger sister. Recently she found her—" He broke off, then tempted her with another spoonful of soup before continuing. "She found a man she loves very much. His name is Julian Savage. I do not know him very well, and we sometimes have trouble getting along. I suspect we are rather alike, and that is the problem."

"Bossy," Tempest supplied knowingly.

The black eyes rested possessively on her face. "What was that?"

This time she did grin. It hurt, but she couldn't stop herself. She suspected no one ever challenged or teased this man. "You heard me."

His eyes burned suddenly with an intensity, with a dark, dangerous hunger that took her breath away, that made her think of the leopards he kept as companions. She pulled her gaze from his. "Keep talking. Tell me about everyone."

Darius slid a hand over her damp hair and found the nape of her neck. His fingers curled around the slender column, liking the way she fit into his palm. Desire slammed into him, hard and unexpected, even as he was deliberately trying to view her as a child in need of his protection. He had touched her only to comfort her, but he didn't let go. He cursed himself for his lack of control. He needed the contact with her, needed to feel her, to know she was real and solid and not some figment of his imagination.

"Barack and Dayan also play in the band. Both are talented musicians, Dayan a guitar player without equal. He writes many of our songs as well. Syndil—" He hesitated, unsure what to reveal about Syndil. "She plays the organ, the piano, just about any instrument. She recently suffered a trauma, however, and has not gone up on stage for a while."

Tempest's gaze jumped to his. She caught his sorrow before he had time to conceal it. "Something happened to her like what happened to me."

His fingers tightened around her neck. "But I did not get there in time to stop it—something I will regret for all eternity."

She blinked and looked away from him quickly. He

had said "for all eternity." Not "until I die" or any of the other expressions a human might use. Oh, Lord. She didn't want him to guess that her memory of what he had done to her hadn't been erased, as he'd wished. But what if he intended doing it again, and this time it worked?

A knock on the door had Tempest jerking around, her heart pounding. Darius rose gracefully, fully aware of Syndil's presence outside the mobile home. He moved with fluid grace toward the door.

Tempest couldn't keep her eyes off him. He was incredibly graceful and supple, sinewy muscles rippling beneath his silk shirt. He walked silently, like one of his great cats.

"Darius." Syndil refused to meet his eyes. She was staring at her shoes. "I heard what happened and thought perhaps I could help in some small way." She handed him Tempest's toolbox and backpack. "Perhaps you would allow me to see her for a moment?"

"Of course, Syndil. Thank you for your concern. I appreciate any aid you can render." Darius stepped back to allow her entry. He didn't allow the hope for her recovery to flare even for an instant in his eyes. He followed the woman he regarded as another younger sister to the table. "Tempest, this is Syndil. She would like to speak with you if you are feeling up to it. I will clean the kitchen. The two of you will be more comfortable in the sleeping quarters."

Tempest managed a small smile. "That's his nice way of ordering us out of here. Everyone calls me Rusti," she told Syndil, oddly without shame before this other wounded woman.

As she slipped past Darius, he reached out to catch her hair and give a small tug. "Not everyone, honey."

She sent him a quelling glance over her shoulder, forgetting for a moment her swollen eye and bruised mouth. "Everyone *else*," she corrected.

Darius allowed her hair to slide through his fingers, savoring the contact with her, however slight it was.

Tempest walked carefully, not wanting to jar her bruised ribs. Syndil gestured to the couch, and Tempest sank into the soft cushions. Syndil examined her face. "Did you allow Darius to heal you?" she inquired.

Her voice was beautiful, satin soft, haunting and mysterious. Tempest knew immediately that she, too, was a creature like Darius. It was in her voice and eyes. But as hard as she tried, she could detect no evil in Syndil, just a quiet sadness.

"Is Darius a doctor?" she asked.

"Not exactly, but he is talented at healing others." She looked down at her hands. "I did not allow him to help me, and that hurt both of us more than I can say. Be stronger than I was. Allow him to do this for you."

"Darius arrived before I was raped," Tempest said bluntly.

Syndil's beautiful eyes filled with tears. "I am so glad. When Desari told me you had been attacked, I thought . . ." She shook her head. "I am so glad." She touched a swollen bruise with a gentle fingertip. "But the man hurt you. He hit you."

"It's far worse to be hurt on the inside," Tempest said, pulling the throw pillows around her as if fashioning them into walls to keep her safe.

Chapter Three

Syndil stared at Tempest for a long moment. Then her breath escaped in a long, slow hiss. She sat down and leaned forward to try to read Tempest's expression. "It happened to you. Not this time, but sometime in your past. You know what it is like. The fear. The revulsion." Her eyes sparkled like black ice, like crushed jewels. "I scrubbed myself for three and half hours, and months later I still do not feel clean." She ran her hands up and down her arms, anguish reflected in her enormous eyes.

Tempest glanced toward the kitchen to assure herself that Darius could not hear them. "You should get counseling. There are places, Syndil, people who can help you put your life back together again."

"Is that what you did?"

Tempest swallowed hard, feeling the familiar nausea that arose every time that particular door started to crack open. She shook her head, pressing a hand to her stomach. "I wasn't in a position to seek help. I was simply trying to survive." Once more she glanced toward the kitchen, then lowered her voice still further. "I never really knew either of my parents. My earliest memories are of a dirty room where I ate off the floor and watched grownups put needles in their arms, legs—every vein they could find. I didn't know which of the adults was my mother or father. Occasionally the authorities would scoop me up and dump me in foster homes, but mainly I lived on the streets. I learned to fight off drug dealers and pimps and every other man that happened by. It was a way of life, all I knew for several years."

"That is when it happened to you?" Syndil asked, her eyes so filled with pain that Tempest wanted to gather her into her arms. At the same time she wanted to run, to never have to relive that particular time in her life again. She couldn't bear it, not on the heels of Harry's attack.

"No, it might have been easier if it had been some sleazy drunk or junkie or even one of the pimps, but it was someone I trusted," Tempest confessed in a low voice, the words forced out of her by some bond between her and Syndil, a bond forged by a terrible trauma they both shared.

"It was someone I loved and trusted, too," Syndil admitted softly. "As a result, I do not know how to trust anyone now. I feel as if he killed that part of me. I cannot perform in the band. I loved playing; the music has always been inside me, and now I cannot hear it. I feel dead without it. I cannot stand to be alone with any of the males I grew up with, men I have always loved as my family. I know they worry for me, but I cannot change what has happened."

Tempest twisted a length of red-gold hair around her

finger. "You have to live, Syndil, not simply exist. You can't let him rob you of your life, your passions."

"But he did. That is exactly what he did. I loved him like a brother. I would have done anything for him. Yet he was so brutal, and his eyes were so vicious as he hurt me, as if he hated me." Syndil turned away. "It changed all of us. The men now look at one another with suspicion and distrust. If such a transformation could happen to Savon, perhaps it could happen to one of them, too. Darius has suffered terribly, because, as our leader, he feels responsible. I have tried to tell him he is not, but he has always cared for and protected us. I know that if I could get over this, it would ease his suffering, but I cannot." She looked at her hands. "The others do not treat me as they once did. Barack especially does not seem to trust me. They watch me all the time now, as if it were my fault."

"Likely they are watching you protectively, not suspiciously. But you are not responsible for what anyone else is feeling, Syndil. You can overcome this, just as the others will in their own time and in their own way. You won't forget it—it might haunt your life and even your relationships—but you can be happy again," Tempest assured her.

"I have never spoken of this to anyone, not even Desari. I am sorry. I came here to help you, but I speak only of myself. I want to scream and weep and crawl into a hole. You are very easy to talk to."

Tempest shook her head. "You have to find a way to go on."

"Please tell me what happened to you, how you were able to cope."

In the kitchen, Darius stirred, reluctant for Tempest to endure any more trauma. But he wanted to know, he had to know, and he realized it was important for both women to be able to discuss the traumatic events they had suffered.

"I met a great lady who was working at one of the homeless shelters I landed in. I was seventeen at the time. She let me live at her house. I used to steal cars and soup up the engines just for the fun of it. Ellen made me realize I could put my mechanical skills to better use and make a good living while I was at it. She helped me get my high school equivalency diploma, and after that she got a me good job at a garage with a friend of hers. It was great for a while."

"But something happened," Syndil guessed.

Tempest shrugged pragmatically. "Ellen died, and I had nowhere to stay again. As soon as I was without protection, my boss showed his true colors. He caught me off guard. I trusted him; he was Ellen's friend. I really didn't expect it of him." She closed her eyes against the vivid memories crowding in, the way he had slammed her into a wall, knocking the breath out of her, leaving her dazed and completely vulnerable to his attack.

"Did he hurt you?"

"He wasn't gentle, if that's what you mean, and I had never . . . been with anyone. I decided it wasn't something I ever wanted to try again." She shrugged, trying not to wince when her ribs protested. "Unlike you, I've never had a family. I'm used to being on my own and working things out for myself. I've always had to learn everything the hard way. It's different for you. You had a life, a family. You know what love is."

"I cannot imagine myself with a man ever again," Syndil said sadly.

"You have to try, Syndil. You can't just withdraw from the world, from your family. Some of it has to be up to you. Ellen always told me to play the cards I'm dealt, not wish for another hand. You can't change what happened to you, but you can see to it that your life isn't destroyed by it."

Listening from the kitchen, Darius vowed to himself that the group would play in the city where that garage owner lived sometime soon, and he would pay him a visit. Still, this was the first time he had heard Syndil talk to anyone about what had happened to her, and he felt a sense of great relief. If she could talk to Tempest, perhaps they both would benefit from the experience.

He could feel weariness beating at his little redhead. Her body was sore, and shock was exhausting her. He knew she had jogged much of the distance she had managed to put between them, and she'd had no money for food or lodgings. He didn't want to interrupt the women, but Tempest was visibly sliding down into the sofa cushions when he glanced at them from the doorway.

Syndil realized it at once. "I will talk to you when you are more rested, Rusti. Thank you for sharing your experiences with me, a virtual stranger. I think you managed to help me more than I did you." She waved at Darius as she exited the trailer.

Darius glided toward Tempest in his silent, intimidating way. "You are going to bed now, honey. I will not listen to any arguments."

Tempest was already lying down. "Does anyone else besides me ever get the urge to throw things at you?" She sounded drowsy, not combative.

Darius hunkered down beside her so he was at eye level with her. "I do not think so. If they do, they do not have the audacity to tell me."

"Well, I think throwing something at you is the only way to go," Tempest told him. Her eyes were already closing, and her voice was weary and sad despite her heavy words.

Darius stroked the wealth of red-gold hair away from her face, his fingers soothing her scalp. "Do you? Maybe tomorrow might be a better time to try it."

"I have a very good aim," she warned him. "It would be easier on you if you just quit giving me orders."

"That would ruin my reputation," he objected.

A smile curved the corners of her mouth, emphasizing the thin red cut at the side of her lip.

Darius resisted the impulse to lean down and find that small cut with his tongue. "Go to sleep, baby. I am going to do my best to take away some of your soreness. Before you fall asleep on me, I made you an herbal concoction that will help you rest better."

"Why do I feel as if you're taking over my life?"

"Do not worry, Tempest. I am very good at managing lives."

She could hear the laughter in his voice, and an answering smile found its way to her mouth. "Go away, Darius. I'm too tired to argue with you." She settled deeper into the pillows.

"You are not supposed to argue with me." He focused on the glass on the counter in the kitchen. It floated from there to his palm easily. "Sit up, honey. You have to drink this whether you want to or not." He slipped his arm behind her back and lifted her so that he could press the glass to her lips.

"What does it taste like?" she asked, suspicious.

"Drink it, baby," he instructed.

She sighed softly. "What's in it?"

"Drink, Tempest, and stop giving me your sass," he ordered, practically tipping the contents down her throat.

She coughed and sputtered but managed to get most of the herbal mixture down. "I hope there were no drugs in that."

"No, it is all natural. It will make you sleep easier. Close your eyes again." He placed her back among the pillows.

"Darius?" She said his name softly, drowsily, and it seeped into his soul and tightened his body to an urgent ache.

He reached above her head to the shelf of candles his family made, searching forests and marshes for the ingredients that would produce the aromas they needed. "What, honey?"

"Thank you for coming after me. I don't know if I could have gone through it again." She was so tired, the words slipped out, revealing far more than she would have willingly disclosed.

"You are very welcome, Tempest," he acknowledged seriously. Darius gathered a few candles, and turned off all lights, plunging the motor home into darkness.

A small cry of alarm escaped Rusti's throat. "Turn on the lights. I don't want them off."

"I am lighting candles for you, and you are not alone, honey. No one can hurt you here. Just relax, and let that drink take effect. You will fall asleep, and I will do what I can to ensure that you wake up without so much pain. If you like, I can bring the cats in to keep you company."

"No. I'm always alone. It's safer that way," she murmured, too far gone to watch her words. "I take care of myself and answer to no one."

"That is what you used to do before you met me," he corrected gently.

"I don't know you."

"You know me. With the lights on or off, you know me." He bent once more to brush his mouth lightly in her hair. Her heart nearly stopped, then began to pound. "Tempest, leave off all this unnecessary fear. I would never harm you. You can trust me. You feel it in your heart, in your soul. Lights do not stop bad things from happening. You know that, too." But he lit the candles anyway so that the soft glow would reassure her and the aromas would soothe her.

The herbal drink he had given her was beginning to take effect, her eyelids growing too heavy to hold up. "Darius? I hate the dark. I really do." Still, she drifted with his tide, not asking herself why she felt so safe and comforted with him when she was so uneasy with the rest of the world, when he was not even human.

He stroked her hair gently, silently giving her a small mental push toward sleep. "The night is a beautiful place, Tempest. When you are feeling a little better, I will show you."

His hands were soothing, and she relaxed beneath his caressing fingers, breathing in the aromas of the candles. Darius began a soft chant. It was not in English; she had never heard the language. The words seemed to seep into her, brushing like butterfly wings in her mind, and she wasn't sure if he was whispering them out loud or not.

Darius continued the chant long after he was certain Tempest was in a deep sleep. Only then did he lean down and inhale the fresh scent of her to take into his keeping. His mouth moved over her temple, the lightest of contacts, then feathered down to her swollen eye. His tongue bathed the bruised tissue with the healing agent of his kind. Finally, after so long a wait, he could find the tempting corner of her mouth and lave the cut with his tongue. He took his time, enjoying his work, holding her mind with his, continuing the chant to keep her asleep.

His palm moved down her throat, then slid across her shoulder, taking the robe with it, leaving soft, satiny skin bared in its wake. His tongue found the edge of a nasty bruise and traced it down over the swell of her breast. Tempest moaned and moved restlessly, fighting the layers of the hypnotic trance. She was strong, her mind oddly different, hard to control when he was indulging temptation and using his energy to heal.

Darius was intrigued and puzzled by her difference from other humans. In all the centuries of his existence, he had never run across a mortal's brain pattern like hers. Because of their earlier blood exchange, it was easier to stay in the shadow of her mind, their bond stronger than before. And he was also beginning to realize the enormity of his own emotions, of the consequences of his actions and of binding her to him with the ritual words.

Tempest was no ordinary woman he was simply sexually attracted to. It went far beyond that, far beyond the boundaries he had previously accepted in relationships. His allegiance had swung completely to this one small woman, even above his own people, those he had protected, hunted for, killed for, led through centuries of turmoil and change.

Darius sighed and lapped gently at a huge, colorful bruise on Tempest's rib cage. He knew he would protect her first above all others. He traced the delicate line of her jaw. What was it about her that made him feel more loyal to her than to his own family, his own kind?

In her mind he found great courage and a tremendous capacity for compassion and understanding. He studied her body, so fragile and delicate, so perfect. With a little sigh he pulled the edges of her robe together and brought the blanket up to her chin. He sent himself seeking outside his own body and into hers, a feat he had rarely attempted on a human. It required far more concentration than with one of his own kind.

He found each bruised internal organ and slowly repaired them from the inside out. He was becoming intimate with her mind, with her body, like a lover, though he had not yet shared her body or mind in the way he wanted.

Darius. His sister's mental call to him brought him back to his own body.

What is it? he responded.

I sense your hunger. Go hunt. We will look after Rusti. Do not worry, brother. She will be safe with me.

Only you. The command came out before he could censor it, more from jealousy than from fear that anyone in their group would choose to harm Tempest. When his sister laughed softly, the hauntingly beautiful notes brushing in his mind, he cursed at himself for revealing his lack of control.

Shut up, Desari. He said it without rancor, his voice a blend of mesmerizing sorcery and affection.

How the mighty have fallen.

I notice that man of yours keeps you on a tight leash, he retaliated.

You need to feed, Darius. Even the cats can feel your hunger. I will, all by myself, watch over Rusti.

Darius sighed softly. Desari was right. He couldn't afford to start the cats fussing; they could wake the dead if they got upset enough. He rose reluctantly. He didn't want to leave Tempest, for he sensed the nightmares lurking not far from her, but he padded to the door, where Desari waited on the other side.

He stepped outside and inhaled the night, allowing the wind to carry him information about creatures hidden in their dens, about human prey in the vicinity. Sasha and Forest pressed close to him, rubbed up against him. He felt their sharp concern. Darius automatically reassured them he would hunt, would feed. He stretched, loosened his muscles, and began to run, shape-shifting as he did so. The two cats flanked him, eager to hunt. The band would move on soon in order to make their next scheduled performance, but while in a town, the leopards had to eat meat provided for them by their Carpathian companions. Despite the ample prey all around them, the cats were forbidden to hunt except in the wilds, which was partly why the troupe tried to camp often in remote forests, parks, and preserves, allowing the leopards to utilize their natural skills, keeping them happy.

Darius's frame contorted, stretched, a muzzle lengthening and rounding as he bent, sinewy bands of muscles sliding to cover his body. Like stiletto blades, claws extended, then retracted until he needed them. His spine lengthened and became extremely flexible, shoulder blades widening themselves, giving him greater lateral balance. Padded paws allowed him to run silently. Black fur rippled, itching for a moment as it spread to cover the rapidly converting framework of muscle.

The leopards were always quick, agile, cunning, and extremely dangerous. Often the hunter of a leopard became the prey. Of all the cat species, they were the most intelligent. Their brain development, Darius knew, was often compared to that of porpoises, and he had first-hand knowledge, centuries of it, of their ability to reason. But as always, when they went on a hunt together, Darius directed them.

Sasha and Forest preferred to hunt from tree limbs, leaping onto unsuspecting prey from above. As a young child Darius had learned patience from their species. Now he, too, could wait and watch, remain completely motionless and silent or creep without detection through forest or jungle, stalking, belly to ground, inch by inch, with incredible muscle control. When he pounced, he did so with incredible swiftness, like those from whom he had learned the art. Early on, however, it had become apparent to him that, predatory as male Carpathians were, he could not afford to stay long in the body of a leopard, an untamed and instinctive killer, without destroying, rather than simply feeding from, his "prey."

Leopards used their long, sharp canines to grab, hold, puncture and tear. Their razor-sharp claws could slice through flesh like a knife. Though clever and bold, incredibly intelligent, they had quick mood swings that made them highly unpredictable. Still, their minds were always working, always meeting a challenge. Male Carpathians were far too close to the species to feed in precisely the same manner, to subdue the predatory beast raging within themselves while in the body of a leopard. It required the man, with his code of honor, his knowledge of right and wrong, rather than the law of the jungle, to feed without killing.

Darius had great respect for leopards, knowing they were every bit as dangerous as he was, and he never lost sight of the wild traits in himself or in the cats. They were both silent, unseen predators, and when they went bad, just as his own species could, they became the devil incarnate.

Right now, with the night enfolding him, with the scent of fresh game abundant, he felt the joy of the hunt, for many years the only pleasure he had known. Leopards were normally solitary hunters, but centuries ago Darius had learned to summon various cats together so that he might study the skills he needed. As a child he had not been strong enough to hunt alone, so he had developed his mental abilities before his brawn. And that had helped him stay sharp, hone his ability to mentally force compliance even as he acquired the skills of the hunter.

Of all the cats, the leopard could be the most dangerous man-eater, often turning the tables on the professional hunters who tracked them. They were stealthy enough, bold enough to go silently into a camp and drag a victim out, most often undetected. Thus it was necessary to keep Sasha and Forest under control. There were many humans camping and tramping through these woods. The cats knew he hunted the humans, taking his sustenance from them, yet they also knew they were forbidden to bring down such easy prey. At times they were disgruntled and sulky over the standing order. He directed them toward the deer and other fauna in the area, wanting no possible mistakes. Sasha and Forest must feed first so they would be preoccupied with devouring their prey when he hunted for fresh blood.

They moved as a unit, exploring the terrain. Darius scented a small herd of deer feeding tranquilly nearby. Like the mobile radar systems they were, the leopards proceeded silently. Their long whiskers, tapered to fine tips, read air currents and objects, so the cats and Darius could feel their way relentlessly forward toward their intended prey.

Darius chose the target, searching for the two weakest animals in the group. The leopard ordinarily chose the easiest kill, the most unwary, the one that wandered inadvertently close to the tree the leopard was utilizing.

Sasha protested with a lift of her lip, but Darius pushed at her mind even as he drove his much heavier shoulder into her as a reprimand.

She reacted with a silent snarl but leapt agilely into the limbs of a large evergreen. Stretching out her long body, she lay motionless, her amber eyes fixed on her prey. The doe moving toward her was older than Sasha would have liked, but Darius was huge, a good two hundred pounds of heavy, ferocious muscle, and neither cat attempted to defy him for long.

Forest circled downwind of the stragglers in the herd toward the deer Darius had selected for him. He sank low into the bushes, his mottled fur blending easily with the vegetation. The doe was wary, lifting her muzzle every now and then, searching the air for a hint of danger. Forest moved an inch, froze, then moved again.

Darius took up a position near the two deer, intending to drive them back if, for some reason, they got spooked, though Sasha and Forest were far too experienced to expose themselves or allow the wind to carry their scent to the prey. Darius further helped by simply stilling the wind, holding it away from the deer until Forest was within a scant foot of his doe and Sasha's prey was directly beneath her tree limb. The big cats exploded into action simultaneously, startling the rest of the small herd. Deer ran in total panic, scattering through the trees, but the two victims remained behind.

Darius left the cats after throwing a warning field around them, creating a dark, oppressive feel to the thickened air that would keep out any human campers or hunters who might wander too close to where the cats were feeding. Sasha and Forest knew the rules, but instincts as old as time had ruled them before their Carpathian companions did.

Darius moved unerringly through the woods toward the human campsite. In his present form he could leap easily over fallen tree trunks or any other obstacle in his path. He reveled in the feel of his ropy muscles sliding under fur. Before losing his emotions he had always loved the night, and now, at long last, he could truly enjoy it, not through dim memories or by touching his sister's mind, but through his own senses. The damp ground beneath his feet, the stirring of nocturnal creatures, the power surging through him, the wind blowing through the trees, making them sway and dance in rhythm. He even reveled in the relentless, aching hunger in his body.

Tempest. She had brought colors into his world. Emotions. She had brought life back to the nearly dead. She allowed him to feel his love for and devotion to his family; it no longer need be feigned, a faint memory of emotion. Now, when he looked upon Desari, his heart warmed. When he saw Syndil, it was through the eyes of compassion, of deep affection.

But what was he going to do about Tempest? She was human. It was forbidden to join with her. Yet he had spoken the ritual words to merge them. He had shared blood with her, and he would again. He knew it. The thought of her taste had his mouth salivating and his body hardening with a savage, relentless ache. She was addicting, her blood sating his terrible hunger as nothing else ever had. He knew, when his body claimed hers, that he would feast on her blood, would crave the exchange between them. The mere idea of her mouth against his skin was unbearably erotic.

He pulled his mind sharply from the vivid picture. Already he had problems controlling his urge to mate with Tempest, to claim her completely. He owed it to her to let her get to know him. Still, she was made for him, his other half. He felt it in his heart, his mind, his very soul. When she grew old, he would choose to grow old with her, and he would choose the dawn. He made up his mind to go quietly from the world when she did.

With that decision came peace. Desari had Julian now, and Barack and Dayan were capable of looking after Syndil. He would have his years with Tempest, long, happy years filled with love and laughter and the beauty of the world around them. He knew that his decision meant that he could no longer seek the restoring solace of the earth. Already he couldn't bear to be separated from Tempest for long. And she needed his protection.

The smell of prey was heavy in his nostrils. A tent rose up in front of him, strung beneath a canopy of trees. Inside a male lay beside a female. The leopard crept stealthily into the canvas shelter, the smell of hot blood rushing through him and the beast within roaring for release. Crouched over the male's strong, healthy body, Darius concentrated on Tempest. That softened the inner predator and allowed him to take his human form, to ensnare the couple with a veil of sleep, of acquiescence. The male turned to him and offered his throat. Darius felt the familiar sharpness of his fangs lengthening against his tongue and bent his head to drink.

The first hint of unease hit him as he closed the pinpricks, ensuring that he left no evidence that he had been there. He shape-shifted, slipping covertly out of the tent before releasing the couple from the thrall of acceptance. The woman moaned softly, turned over, and moved closer to the male for protection. He reacted, even in his sleep, sliding his arm around her waist.

Darius began to move quickly through the preserve,

his body low and streamlined, swiftly and silently maneuvering amid the thick vegetation. He paused several yards from Sasha and Forest. The male leopard was still gorging himself, crouched over his kill. Sasha was already in the trees, the remainder of her carcass in the branches, cached for the following day.

He continued on, his mind unexpectedly rippling with nightmare figures. A tall, burly man with huge arms and an intricate tattoo of a king cobra on his bulging biceps. When the muscle moved, the snake's fangs would open wider. Slowly the man turned his head, his grin obscene and filled with triumph. The garage owner who had assaulted Tempest.

Darius thrust his mind sharply into Tempest's. The images were coming from her even in her sleep. Her distress was now so vivid, the broadcast so loud, that the cats behind him picked it up. He heard their familiar, eerie screams and sent them a quick command to be silent, to follow him straight to the camp.

It required his full attention to hold Tempest's mind with his, but centuries of honing his skills stood him in good stead. He soothed her, directing her thoughts away from the nightmare.

Desari already had the trailer door open and stood aside as the huge leopard leapt easily into the vehicle, shape-shifting as it did so. Darius landed solidly on two feet, striding toward the couch. "She is afraid, a nightmare," he stated softly, crouching beside the slight figure, barely sparing his sister a glance. "Leave us."

He knew Desari watched him for a long moment, felt her concern. He was acting totally out of character with Tempest, and it was obvious he had feelings for her. His very posture screamed of possession, of protection.

"She is human, brother," Desari said quietly.

74

Darius emitted a low, rumbling growl of warning, the sound vibrating in his throat. Desari put a protective hand to her own throat and turned wide eyes on Julian, who had instantly materialized at the door the moment Darius issued the warning. Hastily Desari stepped outside. The tension remained high between her brother and Julian. They could not be considered friends by any means. Both were protective of her, but both were strong, powerful men who went their own way, made their own rules. As a result, their relationship was tenuous at best. Placing a hand squarely on Julian's chest, Desari pushed her lifemate away from the trailer. He responded by wrapping his arms around her waist and lifting her against his strong body, his mouth finding hers, at once hungry and tender.

Darius ignored the entire byplay, his attention centered completely on Tempest. Her hair spilled around the pillow, and his hand, of its own accord, moved to capture the thick mass in his palm. His body tightened, clenched in an unrelenting ache. She looked so young and vulnerable in her sleep. Tempest tried to appear tough, but Darius knew she was in need of someone to protect her and share her life. She was so alone. It was in her mind. Sharing her thoughts and memories as he was doing, he discovered the same aching loneliness in her as dwelt deep within his own soul.

Still, she was different from him in that she was filled with compassion and gentleness, everything he was not. For all the damage that had been done to her, she had no thoughts of revenge, no bitter hatred, only a quiet acceptance. She also had a firm resolve to stay clear of entanglements, to lead an uneventful, solitary existence.

The patterns of her mind were interesting. She preferred the company of animals. She could understand them easily, their body language, their thoughts. She could communicate with them without words.

Darius inhaled her scent, took it into his lungs, his body, and held it there. She was unique among humans, the way she could read the animals around her. It didn't distress her—she loved animals—but the reactions of humans to her gift were always negative. Darius leaned down to lay his head over hers, beating back the rise of the beast within him roaring for freedom. His every instinct was to claim her irrevocably for all time. His body needed hers desperately. The wild craving for the taste of her was riding him hard.

But she needed rest and care. She deserved some kind of courtship. It was her very vulnerability that kept the beast in him leashed. Darius knew himself well, his strengths and weaknesses. He was as merciless and harsh as the land he had grown up in. He was as savage and relentless as the leopards he had run with. He killed without emotion, without malice, but he killed when he deemed it necessary and never looked back.

Tempest belonged to him. Somehow, and he had no idea how it had happened, a human was his other half. Her soul meshed with his, the jagged edges sealing perfectly together. He knew her body was made for his, that he would find in her the same fire that smoldered within him.

Sleep deeply, honey, with no bad dreams. I will watch over you. He murmured the words softly in her mind, filling her head with pleasant dreams, with things he remembered from his childhood. The beauty of the savanna, the mystery of the monsoon, the abundance of colors, of animals. He conjured up the excitement of his first hunt with the leopards. He had tried to drop from the branches of a tree as he had seen the older animals doing but had landed feet in front of his intended victim, inadvertently sending it scurrying out of reach. He found himself smiling at the memory, smiling as she was doing in her sleep.

His hand closed over hers. Waterfalls, the magnificence of frothy, foaming water cascading hundreds of feet. Crocodiles, antelope. A pride of lions. With the details came the smells and feel and lulling heat of Africa. He shared it all with her, replacing the terrible events of her day, of her past, replacing her nightmare with something beautiful.

You're a remarkable man, Darius.

He went still. Not a muscle in his body moved. Even his breathing ceased. He examined her face. She had spoken to him telepathically. It was not on the same path used among his family. It was different, more intimate. But it was her voice; there was no mistaking that. Somehow, in her compulsion-and-herb-induced sleep, she was still aware of his presence in her mind. It was unbelievable that a human could have such powers.

He examined her mind again. It was nothing like the human minds he was accustomed to. It intrigued him, its layers and compartments, as if she had things neatly filed and locked away. Perhaps he had been too complacent about her.

You can hear me? he asked in her mind.

Don't you want me to hear you? Why else are you telling me of all these wonderful places and exciting memories if you didn't want me to hear you?

He again noticed the velvet huskiness of her voice, like a drowsy caress, a lover turning her body mindlessly into his. Did she always sound that way? Did the others hear that sexy, erotic note in her voice?

This way of communicating does not frighten you? he asked.

I'm dreaming. I don't mind dreaming about you. You're sharing my mind; I'm sharing yours. I know your only wish is to help me sleep without nightmares.

Could it be that simple? Did she believe she was dreaming the whole thing? Darius brought her hand to the warmth of his mouth. He was smiling as he kissed her knuckles. Her hand was still bruised from her fight earlier in the day. Without conscious thought, he stroked his tongue over the dark purple-and-blue mark. *Sleep, baby. Sleep deep, and worry about nothing. Allow your body to heal.*

Good night, Darius. Don't you worry so much about me. I'm like a cat: I always land on my feet.

Chapter Four

Tempest woke slowly, as if emerging through a layer of hazy clouds. She was sore, every muscle protesting when she moved, yet not nearly as much as she had expected. She sat up, looking warily around her. Her body was alive with feeling, her skin sensitive beyond belief. She remembered the horror of the attack on her like a vague nightmare. What was vivid and sharp, every detail imprinted forever in her mind, was the memory of Darius's tongue caressing every bruise, taking away her pain and fear, replacing it with erotic, burning pleasure. She wanted to believe that one was a nightmare and the other a romantic dream, but Tempest always looked reality in the face. It was how she lived, how she survived. She might lie to someone else if it was necessary but never to herself. The things Darius had done in her dream world were all too real. She had been in some kind of a trance, half awake, half asleep. And they had talked to one another using only their minds, in much the same way she communicated with animals, only using words, not just images. Telepathy.

She took a deep breath and looked around her. She was alone in the luxurious motor home except for the two leopards, who each opened a sleepy eye at her stirring but did not seem inclined to get up. Tempest pushed a hand through her hair. Should she strike out on her own or take her chances with whatever kind of creature she had stumbled onto?

She hadn't had much luck with humans and had always preferred the company of animals. Last night, when her mind had connected with Darius's, she had recognized his brain patterns as being like an animal's in many respects. He had highly developed instincts and senses like those of the leopard. She knew he was a formidable hunter, but she had detected no evil in him.

Darius could have killed her anytime he wanted. He could have used her for food, if that was what these creatures did. But he hadn't done either. He had come after her when she was in trouble. He had treated her gently and compassionately. And he had tenderly attempted to heal her bruised body and take away the worst of her memories. The cost had not been small to him. Darius wanted her. She had felt the burning heat in him. She had been all but helpless, yet he hadn't acted on the demands of his body. She had felt his enormous energy drain out of him and into her while he was healing her. He had been extremely tired after using his great strength to ease her suffering, and she had even felt a gnawing, biting, insatiable hunger, his mind merging with hers until she was uncertain where her feelings left off and his began.

She sighed and pushed at the hair falling loose from

the thick braid he had woven. No one ever had treated her as Darius had. He was kind and thoughtful, even tender, but for all that he wasn't an easy man to be around. Especially when she was so used to being on her own. His arrogance, his complete confidence in himself and his abilities, had a tendency to set her teeth on edge. Obviously he was accustomed to deference to his every wish. She was accustomed to being utterly independent. She bit at her lip, her teeth scraping back and forth as she thought it out.

Darius wasn't just arrogantly expecting obedience from her. It was far more than that. Hard possession lit the depths of his eyes, gave them a burning intensity, revealing a hunger only for her. "No, way, Rusti," she whispered aloud to herself. "That maniac is used to protecting and controlling everyone around him, so don't let your hormones start running away with you. And vampires are out of the question. You didn't want to get together with the neighborhood pimp; I don't think this is a much better choice. You have to leave. Vamoose. Run. Get out."

Yet she knew she was going to stay. Emitting a little groan, she covered her face with her hands. She had no money, no family, no home. Maybe if Darius slept during the day, and she slept all night, they would get along fine. She peeked out between her fingers. "As if I believe that will happen. That man wants to rule the world. His own private empire." She wrinkled her nose and mimicked his voice, " 'My domain, Tempest.' Remember that he rules everything and everyone in his domain," she told herself.

She glanced at the clock on the wall. It was three in the afternoon. If she was going to get the other vehicles running and earn her keep, she would have to do it soon.

Groaning aloud as her muscles protested, she slid out from under the blanket and made her way to the bathroom. The shower felt good on her aching body and helped to clear away the cobwebs in her mind. As always she swept her hair up out of the way and dressed in a T-shirt and blue jeans, pulling on overalls to keep them semi-clean while she worked.

She was surprised to find the refrigerator fully stocked with fresh vegetables and fruits. She also spotted various breads and pasta. Somehow she knew Darius was responsible for the supplies.

Having learned at an early age to improvise meals, she made an artichoke and mushroom sauce to put over pasta and ate leisurely though sparingly, her stomach still upset from the previous days' events. Finally she cleaned up and went out to take a look at the troupe's car, truck, and motor home.

The afternoon sun was sinking, but it was hot and humid even under the canopy of trees where she was working. Still, she enjoyed the peace of the woods. A slight breeze came up about an hour after she began work, which relieved her discomfort a bit. For the most part, she was so focused on what she was doing, she didn't think of anything else. She finished her adjustments to the motor home by five o'clock and took a short break to drink some cool water and check on the cats.

The red sports car basically needed only a tune-up, and since the group seemed to carry a small-parts department with them, she was able to find what she needed easily. Tempest rather enjoyed working on the little car and was satisfied when it purred at her as she started it up. She took it up the winding ribbon of a road, putting it through several gear changes, driving as if on a race track. A few miles from the camp she pulled over to adjust the timing.

She was standing over the engine, listening to it, when the first wave of uneasiness washed over her. Keeping her head beneath the gaping hood, she lifted her eyes and searched the area around her. Someone was watching her. She knew it. She had no idea where her heightened awareness came from, but she was positive she was right.

Tempest? The voice was, as always, calm and tranquil. But Darius sounded far away. *Tempest, what is it?*

Her fingers clenched around the small instrument in her hand. They weren't going to play pretend with one another anymore. They couldn't pass this off as a dream. *Someone is watching me,* she responded. *It feels . . .* She paused, searching for the correct word to describe her uneasiness. When none came, she did what she did with the animals: She sent an impression of her emotion.

A small silence ensued as Darius evaluated the information. *He troubles me also. You are not within the perimeter I set. Did you not feel the wrenching when you passed through it?*

Rusti frowned. *You set perimeters for me? What does that mean? You have a set distance I'm allowed to travel?* She was outraged, forgetting for a moment her unwanted watcher.

Do not give me trouble, honey. Just do what I say. There was a hint of amused exasperation in his tone. *I knew you were trouble the minute I laid eyes on you. Make a slow visual sweep of the surrounding area. Very slow. Really look. I will see what you see.*

Rusti did as he ordered because she was curious to see what might happen. Her eyesight was good, her senses alert, yet she did not discover what was unsettling her.

It was a strange feeling to share her mind and eyes with another being. She wished she'd brought the cats with her.

It is too late to show good sense now, Tempest. You should have stayed where you were, out of harm's way, as you were supposed to do. There is a man with a pair of binoculars watching from the small wooded area to your left. I can make out the bumper of his car. Tempest felt her heart thud in alarm. *There is no reason to fear him. I am with you now. It would be impossible for him to hurt you.*

But what if he approaches me? I know you are far away. I feel it.

Darius sent her a wave of reassurance, pouring warmth and strength into her. He would never allow another male to treat her as Harry the attacker had. Never again. He meant it. A vow to himself. A vow to her. Rusti swore she could feel him wrap a protective arm around her. She didn't stop to think that it might not be good idea to lean so heavily on his strength when she was bound to resent his dominating ways. She allowed herself to breathe again, allowed her heart to slow back to normal.

Keep working, honey. He is about to make his approach. Just act normal. I will know if you need my intervention.

She took a deep breath, let the air out slowly, and bent once more to fine-tune her adjustment. She forced herself not to look up until she heard the man's car. The Mustang was pale blue and the engine super hot. She could tell by listening to it.

Closing the hood, she greeted the visitor. "Wow. That thing can go, can't it?"

The man unfolding himself from the Mustang's driver's seat grinned at her, showing lots of teeth. A camera hung around his neck. He was dressed in a rumpled suit, and his tie was loose. "She's the fastest thing I've had in years. I'm Matt Brodrick." He held out his hand.

For some reason Rusti was reluctant to touch him. She could feel the dread taking hold, swamping her. She made herself smile and wiped her palm on her jeans. "Sorry, I'm a bit greasy," she explained.

"That looks like one of the cars belonging to the Dark Troubadours. Are you a member of the band?"

There was real curiosity in his voice and a hint of some emotion she couldn't name. Rusti tilted her chin, her green eyes clearly suspicious. "What's your interest?"

"I'm a fan. Desari has a voice straight from heaven," the man answered, showing even more teeth. When she continued to regard him in silence, he heaved a sigh. "I'm a reporter."

She made a face. "Then you know I'm not a member of the band." She held up her toolbox. "I'm their mechanic."

He glanced around them. "Where's their camp? I've been up and down all these roads but haven't spotted it. I know they're somewhere nearby."

"And you think I'll just offer you that information out of the kindness of my heart?" She laughed.

Even in deep earth, miles away, Darius felt his body clench and harden at the sound of her laughter. She was like a carefree child, living each separate moment as it came, heeding nothing before, nothing in the future. The beast in him was growing, fighting for freedom. The fangs in his mouth lengthened to lethal points. He knew he was dangerous, he had always been dangerous, but now, with Tempest close to another male, he had passed the point of self-control. He had no other reason for existence, and he would not give her up. Ever.

Christine Feehan

"For money then?" Now the reporter's teeth looked shiny, his eyes as hard as stone, something cunning in his expression.

"Not a chance," she instantly denied, even though she could certainly use funds. "I don't betray people for money or anything else."

"I've heard some strange things about the group. Will you at least confirm or deny some of the reports?"

Tempest stowed her toolbox on the floor of the little sports car. "Why bother? You people make up whatever you want to. You write it and print it regardless of whom you might hurt."

"Just a couple of questions, okay? Is it true that they sleep during the day and stay up all night? That they all have some strange illness that makes it impossible for them to go out in the sun?"

Tempest burst out laughing. "That is so like a reporter. You must work for one of those disgusting little exploitation rags. Where do you idiots come up with this stuff? You must have a very vivid imagination. I can't say it was great meeting you, Mr. Brodrick, but I've got to go now."

"Wait a minute." Brodrick caught at the door of the car before she could close it. "If I'm wrong, say so. I don't want to print garbage."

"So if I tell you the truth, you'll actually print it, not make up some new sensational tale just to sell your rag?" Her green eyes flashed at him in pure challenge.

"Absolutely I will."

"Right at this moment, the band and their bodyguard are out hiking. They've been hiking up in the hills for the last hour or so. We have to be on the road this evening to make their next gig on time, so they're taking one last break. Then we'll eat dinner and get out of here.

Print that, Mr. Reporter. It's a little mundane, but they also put on their pants one leg at a time, just like everybody else." Rusti had a deep sense of loyalty, and Darius and his family had supported her solidly. If an exploitative journalist like this one suspected anything out of the ordinary with them, she was not above telling a few lies to shield them, even with her own reservations about the group.

"You saw them an hour ago?" Brodrick demanded.

Rusti glanced pointedly at her watch. "Nearly two hours ago. I expect them back any time now. And they'll expect the vehicles to be running smoothly so we can get out of here. I doubt if any of them will be sunburned—they use sunscreen like everyone else I know—but if they are, I'll call you. How's that?" She slammed the door with unnecessary force. "In case you're interested, Desari is prone to mosquito bites. She uses bug repellent along with sunscreen. Would you like to know the brand?"

Good girl, Darius approved, his pride in her growing.

"Come on," Brodrick protested, "give me a break. I'm just doing my job. You know she's news. My God, she has a voice like an angel's. Every major recording company is begging for a deal, and she's still playing little clubs. She could make millions."

Rusti laughed again. "And what makes you so certain she hasn't? Is it so terrible for her to do what she loves? She's an entertainer. She likes the intimacy of small crowds. It isn't the same in a huge stadium; she can't make the same connection with the audience. And there wouldn't be any such connection in a recording studio." She was picking the information straight from Darius's mind. She looked up at Brodrick. "I feel sorry for you. You must hate your job, prying into people's lives with no real understanding of who they are. Money isn't everything, you know."

Brodrick clamped his hand on the door. "Take me back with you to their camp. Introduce me. If I could get an exclusive interview, it would do a lot toward making my boss happy with me."

"Not a chance," she said. "I don't know you, and you ask pretty stupid questions. Any reporter worth his salt would come up with something better than whether or not Desari sleeps during the day. If you gave a performance that ended at two o'clock in the morning, then met with people, including reporters, for another couple of hours, you'd probably want to sleep, too. So what kind of dumb question was that?" Rusti injected as much contempt into her tone as she could muster. "I'll tell you what. When you figure out something worthwhile to ask her, I'll see what I can do for you. But I refuse to put my own job on the line for an idiot."

She then slowly maneuvered the little car away from the reporter's side. In the rearview mirror, she kept an eye on him as she drove off. *He might follow me, Darius. Should I lead him away from the camp?*

You will come straight home, Tempest. And next time do not leave without protection.

She sent him an image of wringing his neck. *I have lived alone all my life, you overbearing, king-sized pain in the butt. I don't need anyone's protection, and I'm sure not asking permission to go anywhere I choose. You have enough people to boss around already, so give it a rest.*

I can see I need to turn my complete attention to getting you in hand, honey. Fortunately, I am up to the task. He sounded far more complacent and sure of himself than she liked.

The way his voice poured over her skin like warm

honey and filled her body like molten lava, pooling wickedly low within her, was stranger than anything she had ever encountered. Her own body was betraying her. Weren't some things in life best left alone, vampires among them?

Tempest. You closed your mind to mine. What is it? Do you think me so formidable that I should not hear your thoughts when you are angry with me? It does not change what is.

Nothing is, Darius. How can you talk to me this way, anyway? She decided the best defense was an offense. Let him try to answer that one. *Is it because you can talk to animals the way I do?* She believed in giving everyone a gracious out.

So you are admitting to that now. We might actually be getting somewhere.

She glanced in the rearview mirror again. She was flying down the narrow, twisting road, skidding through turns and taking one or two off-the-beaten-path trails. She didn't see any distant dust to indicate the reporter was following her, but she had a feeling he was trying to do just that, and she refused to lead him back to the camp.

Darius knew that to be completely safe he still needed one hour before he could rise. Locked in the ground as he was, he feared for Tempest's safety unless she did as he ordered and returned to the area within the perimeter he had set. He considered forcing his will on her. It was tempting, since she was being so ridiculously stubborn, but he would monitor her for now and hope she complied. Only if it became necessary would he compel her to do his bidding.

He liked her mind. He liked her independence, her sense of freedom, her spirit. She would learn she couldn't get away with defying him, but for now he wanted to handle her as delicately as possible.

Darius? Her voice was soft, hesitant, brushing his mind like the touch of fingers on his skin. Flames swept through his body, setting him on fire. He had to have her soon. Time was running out on his control. He needed her desperately.

I am with you, baby. Do not sound so forlorn.

That's not how I sounded, she replied, but he caught the echo of her thoughts. *Did I?*

Come home, honey. Everything will work out. You do not have to singlehandedly defend Desari from this reporter.

He is not just a reporter.

Darius was silent. How had *she* known that? *He* knew it. Several attempts had been made on Desari's life recently. He had read Brodrick's aura, found him to be deceitful, covering his lethal intentions with what he supposed to be charm. Tempest had been unable to read all that, but she had sensed a hidden agenda and done her best to divert the alleged reporter. She had done a good job, too. She'd sounded sincere and open, then contemptuous enough to lend authenticity to everything she said.

You don't have to believe me, Darius. Tempest sounded hurt.

Of course I believe you, honey. Now get back here where I do not have to worry about you. It was clearly an order.

Rusti sighed heavily. He wasn't getting it. She didn't want anyone worrying about her. As she approached within a mile of the campsite, she felt a curious shifting around her; the air seemed heavy and oppressive. At once she realized she had encountered a barrier of some sort. It created a sense of dread in her, as if she needed to turn around. Why was she feeling it now? Was Darius amplifying the perimeters he insisted she observe?

She tossed her mane of red hair, green eyes blazing defiance. He was not going to rule her as he did all the others. They treated him like some kind of Greek god. She groaned aloud. Why had she come up with that particular analogy? Just because he looked like one, acted like one? There went her hormones, running amok again.

Deliberately she began to think of things like taking the little red car for a spin down the highway, far from bossy men. She could hear Darius laughing softly, not in the least worried she would actually steal the car and defy him. *Don't bet on it,* she snapped as she parked directly behind the motor home and got out.

The four-wheel-drive truck was next on her to-do list. It was more important to get it than the dirt bikes into top shape. She lifted the hood and, as always when she worked, focused only on what she was doing, blocking out everything and everyone else.

Darius rose at the precise moment it was safe to do so, bursting from the earth with so much power that soil spewed upward like a geyser. The sky was a soft gray, not yet completely dark, but the canopy of trees cast deep shadows and aided in protecting his eyes. He inhaled, scenting the air around him, taking in each detail, every story the wind had to tell him.

The ever-present hunger gnawed at him, but this time his body, hard and heavy, was making unfamiliar, relentless demands, filled with a terrible need as insatiable as his hunger. He forcibly controlled the inner beast roaring for release and strode around the bus. He spotted Tempest perched precariously on the front grill of the truck, wielding a wrench that looked as if it weighed more than she did. Even as he approached her, her small body swayed, then teetered on the brink of disaster. She attempted to grab the edge of the hood but slipped backward with a small sound somewhere between alarm and annoyance. Clearly it wasn't her first fall.

Darius moved with blurring speed to catch her before she hit the ground. She landed in his arms. "You are more trouble than any woman I have ever encountered. Have you made a study on the best ways to drive a man insane?"

Tempest thumped his heavy muscled chest. "You scared me to death. Where did you come from? And put me down."

His body savored the feel of her, so soft against his hardness. Her face had smudges of grease on it, but she was beautiful all the same. "My heart cannot take any more incidents. What did you think you were doing?" he said gruffly.

Tempest squirmed to remind him to put her down. "My job." He was enormously strong, his body as hard as an oak tree, but his skin was like hot velvet. She could feel the rush of blood through her, hot and needy. It scared her to death. She shoved hard at him. Darius didn't appear to notice. Instead, he started striding away from the campsite. Her heart began to pound. He reminded her of a great warrior claiming his prize. He held her as if he had a right to her, as if she belonged to him.

Darius carried Tempest into the woods, away from open spaces, finding cooler shadows. Her scent beckoned him, and he found himself burying his face against the slender column of her neck. Her pulse beat frantically, drawing his attention. Her silken hair fell against his head, brushing flames over his skin. A sound welled up in his throat as his self-control slipped precariously. There was such danger in this madness. He knew better, but nothing mattered anymore but having her.

Rusti felt the warmth of his breath on her skin. Felt molten heat. And her body clenched in expectation. She circled his head with her arms, drawing him closer without even realizing what she was doing. His need was so great, it beat in him so strongly, that she could feel it swamping her, overwhelming even her sense of survival. His heart matched the rhythm of hers, strong and frantic. She felt the sweeping caress of his tongue along her neck, and her heart skipped a beat, her insides going liquid in anticipation.

"Darius, don't." She whispered the words, meant to make it a command. It came out a husky plea of need.

His mouth moved over her skin, sending waves of fire beating at her. *I have no other choice. What you ask is like trying to stop the wind. It is inevitable between us. Accept me. Accept what I am.* She felt the gentle lapping of his tongue, an erotic, hypnotic rasp of velvet. Her head arched back, exposing the vulnerable hollow of her throat. Heat spiraled through her body as his teeth sank deeply into the offering and he fed hungrily, voraciously on her sweetness. Nothing else would ever sate his hunger again. Nothing. His body burned, needed, demanded. She lay in his arms, drowsy, in a dark, magical dream world, on fire for him.

Somewhere in the woods an owl hooted. From inside the bus one of the cats screamed restlessly, the sound eerie in the twilight. Tempest drew in a deep, shuddering breath, her sense abruptly coming back to her. She was lying in his arms, a willing sacrifice, her body moving against him with an unknown hunger. Her breasts felt full and aching, her nipples hard and pushing against her thin shirt. She felt drowsy and heavy-eyed yet sin-

Christine Feehan

fully wanton. She began to struggle wildly, her fists flailing at Darius.

He pulled himself from a world of pure feeling, stroking his tongue over the pinpricks to seal the tiny points of evidence. "Be calm, honey. I am not hurting you." He rested his forehead against hers. "I will take this incident from your mind and wish that I could do so from my own as well." She was trembling in his arms, her enormous eyes wide with shock, her face pale.

"It's okay, Darius. It was just a surprise," she whispered. "I know you wouldn't hurt me." She made another attempt to get out of his arms.

Darius tightened his hold on her. "I am not going to give you up. I cannot. I do not expect you to understand, and I cannot explain adequately. I have been doing for others all of my existence. I have never had anything for myself; I never wanted or needed anything. But I need you. I realize you cannot accept what I am, but it does not matter to me. I wish I was able to say that it did, but I will not give you up. You are the only one who can save me. Save the others from me. Mortals and immortals alike."

"*What* are you, Darius?" Tempest stopped fighting him. She knew she had no hope of getting away from him unless he allowed it. Her voice was the merest thread of sound. Her heart was slamming against his chest so rapidly, she was afraid it might explode. At once his black eyes caught and held hers, and she felt herself falling forward into their dark, fathomless depths.

"Be calm, honey. There is nothing to fear." He enfolded her in waves of tranquillity, a soothing, peaceful sea of reassurance.

As much as she wanted to, she couldn't look away. There was such an intensity about Darius. He was as still

94

and solid as the mountains, as hard as granite, yet so gentle with her. When he looked at her, a burning hunger lit his eyes, a hard possession. He was ageless. Timeless. With a relentless will. He would never swerve from his chosen path. And he had chosen her.

She reached up to touch her throbbing neck. "Why me?"

"In all the world, in all these centuries since emotions left me, I have been so alone, Tempest. Utterly alone. Until you. Only you bring me color and light." He inhaled, taking her scent deep within his lungs. He needed relief from his body's relentless demands. "Do not worry, you will not remember any of this."

Still held captive by his black gaze, Rusti shook her head slowly. "I remember the last time, Darius. You didn't erase my memory."

His black-ice eyes didn't waver, didn't blink as he accepted the nearly impossible as fact. "You ran away because of what I am." He said it without expression, as if her revelation was not of paramount importance.

"You have to admit, it isn't every day a vampire bites one's neck." She made a feeble attempt at humor, but her fingers curled convulsively in his thick mane of jet-black hair, betraying her nervousness.

"So I am responsible, after all, for the attack on you." Darius was assessing the possibility of what she had said. It had to be true. Humans generally required little effort to control. But likely with the difference in her brain patterns, he should have used a much harder mental push to induce forgetfulness. What courage she must have to face him again. To know what he was, and yet remain as she had this night to face him.

"Of course you weren't responsible for what Harry did," she denied huskily, desperate to tear her gaze from his. She was drowning in those eyes, trapped forever. His arms were iron bands around her, locking her to him. She should have been far more afraid of him than she actually was. Had he succeeded in mesmerizing her?

"Yet you stayed this time, knowing I took your blood," he mused aloud. "You didn't try to leave, even believing me something as evil as a vampire."

"Would it have done me any good?" she asked, for once wanting to meet his eyes, wanting to see his expression.

He didn't so much as flicker an eyelash. His features were as etched granite, sensual yet immovable. "No," he answered her honestly. "I would find you. There is nowhere in this world I cannot find you."

Her heart pounded again. He could hear it, could feel the vibration echoing through his own body.

She drew in a breath. "Are you going to kill me? I'd just as soon know now."

His hand moved over her hair in a slow caress that sent butterfly wings brushing at her stomach. "You are the only one in this world, mortal or immortal, who, I can say with complete conviction, is perfectly safe. I would give my life to protect you, but I will not give you up."

There was a small silence while she studied his implacable features. She believed him. Knew he was as merciless and dangerous as any wild predator. He watched her throat work, a small, agitated attempt to swallow.

"All right," she conceded. "Then there isn't much point in running away, is there?" Her mind was in chaos, making it impossible to think what to do. What could she do? More importantly, what did she want to do? She bit down hard on her lower lip.

A small dot of ruby red welled up on that lush, trembling lower lip. A temptation. An invitation.

Darius groaned aloud, the sound coming from his soul. She couldn't do that, tempt him beyond endurance, and get away unscathed. He bent his head to hers, his mouth hard and possessive. His tongue found that tiny dot of sweetness, swept it into his keeping, savored it. But he couldn't stop there. Her lips were satin soft beneath his. Trembling. Enticing. God, he wanted her. Needed her. Hungered for her.

Open your mouth for me.

I'm afraid of you. The words held tears, held fear, yet she was helpless against her own burning need. Tempest did as he ordered.

Time stopped for Rusti, and the world fell away, until there was only the hard strength of Darius's arms, the heat of his body, the width of his shoulders, and his perfect, perfect mouth. He was a mixture of domination and tenderness. He swept her up with him, caught in a whirling kaleidoscope of colors and feelings. Nothing would ever be the same again. She would never be the same again. How could she be? He was branding her heart. Branding her soul. He was crawling inside her and taking over so that she breathed only him.

His hunger was beating at him, at her. She was the only thing in his world that was solely for him. She was fire, hot, silky fire racing through his veins, and he never wanted it to stop. Only when she gasped, her lungs laboring, did he lift his head, his black eyes burning with possession over her face. Tempest was very pale, her eyes enormous, her lips holding the imprint of his.

She was so weak, she was grateful Darius was still cradling her in his arms. Her legs felt like rubber. "I think I'm going to be like one of those ridiculous heroines in an old-fashioned novel and faint," she murmured against his neck.

"No, you are not." He attempted to feel guilt—he had taken her blood, and she was so small and fragile that any blood loss could make her weak—but Darius was not one to waste time on regrets. How could he regret what was as natural and inevitable as the tide? She was his. Her blood was his. Her heart and soul belonged to him.

Very gently, tenderly, he ran a caressing hand over her silky hair and down her soft cheek to lay his palm against her throat. His fingers curled slowly around her neck, his thumb feathering the delicate line of her jaw. He wanted to touch every inch of her, explore every secret, intriguing shadow and hollow, memorize her luscious curves.

"Darius." Her green eyes found his black ones. "You can't just decide you own me. People don't own one another anymore. I'm not certain what you are, but I gather you weren't born here or even in this century. I was. I value my independence. It matters to me that I make my own decisions. You don't have the right to take that from me." She tried to choose her words carefully, accepting that she was to blame for her own behavior, that this wasn't all Darius's fault.

She had wanted to kiss him. She admitted it. She touched her swollen lips, a little awed. No one should be able to kiss like that. It was like falling off the edge of a cliff, soaring through the skies, touching the sun. It was like burning, going up in flames, until there was no more Tempest Trine, no thinking individual, only mindless, impossible passion.

"Darius, did you understand what I said?"

"Did you understand what *I* said?" he countered softly

98

between his white teeth. "I know it is not an easy thing to accept one such as me, but I have given my eternal allegiance and protection to you, and that is no small thing, Tempest. It is for all time."

"It isn't that I can't accept what you are. I don't even know what that is yet, really." She squirmed suddenly. "Put me down. Please. I feel very—" She broke off, not wanting to admit to feeling defenseless, but the word shimmered between them all the same. "Please, Darius. I want to talk about this and not feel at such a disadvantage."

His hard mouth curved, taking away the almost cruel, implacable edge as if it had never been. Slowly he lowered her feet to the ground. She was half his size and had to tip her chin up to look at him. "Do you feel at more of an advantage now?" he asked softly, amusement in his black-velvet voice.

Chapter Five

Tempest glared at him, her green eyes flashing like emeralds. "Very funny. We have to get a couple of things straight. Maybe I'd rather take my chances here with you than out in the world right now, but not if you're going to keep dictating to me. There have to be a few ground rules. None of this . . . this . . . whatever you call this." She waved her hand to encompass everything. Kissing. Taking her blood. Seducing her. Ordering her around. Setting perimeters. All of it.

His black gaze never left her face. His eyes were as still as those of a leopard scenting prey. Avid. Burning. Intense. He took her breath away with his eyes. Hypnotized her. Cast a spell over her. Tempest pulled her gaze from his, from the seductive, black velvet trap. "And stop that, too," she said decisively, despite the fact that he made her hungry for him.

"Stop what?"

"Stop looking at me that way. It's definitely out. You can't look at me that way. It's cheating."

"How am I looking at you?" His deep voice dropped even lower, the cadence soft and husky. Mesmerizing.

"Okay, that's out, too. No talking in that tone of voice," she declared staunchly. "And you know very well what you're doing. Act normal."

His white teeth gleamed at her, nearly stopping her heart. "I am acting normal, Tempest."

"Well, then, that's out, too. No acting normal." With both hands on her slender hips, she glared challengingly at him.

Darius glanced away to hide the sudden smile pulling at his mouth. He rubbed the bridge of his nose thoughtfully. "That is a great number of rules, all of which seem impossible. Perhaps a more feasible plan might be in order."

"Don't even start with that infuriating, superior-male-amusement thing you do. It sets my teeth on edge." She was frantically attempting to backpedal, to put some emotional space between them so she could breathe. He needed to stop looking so male, too. That would help some. Suddenly dizzy, she sat down rather abruptly on the carpet of pine needles. Surprised, she blinked up at him.

Darius hunkered down beside her, cupping her face in his palm. "Just do as I ask, and everything will be fine, honey."

She caught at his thick wrist for support. "Did you listen to anything I said?"

"Of course I did. I can repeat your nonsense verbatim if you like." He wrapped an arm around her, so that she could lean into the shelter of his body. "Just sit here for a moment. You will feel better soon. I may have gotten a bit carried away, but your blood does not need replacing."

Her green eyes widened. "Don't even think about it, Darius. I mean it. I've read books. I've seen movies. I refuse to become a vampire."

His mouth quirked again. Sexy, intimate, the tiny gesture produced a rush of heat in her bloodstream, and she had to look away from him to save her soul. No one had the right to look the way he did.

"I am not a vampire, honey. The undead has chosen to lose his soul. I have endured, still alive, if lately only barely, these many long centuries."

"What are you then?" Tempest asked, reluctant to hear his answer yet excruciatingly curious.

"I am of the earth, wind, and sky. I can command these things, all things of nature. I am of an ancient race with powers and properties often mistakenly associated with those of vampires. But I am not vampire. I am Carpathian." He watched Tempest, anticipating the many queries she would likely raise in response to his pronouncement.

She tipped her head. "So, have there been many?"

"I do not understand the question." He appeared genuinely puzzled.

"Women like me. Do you collect women so you have a ready food supply?" She asked it flippantly because his proximity was making her blood rush.

His fingers tangled in her hair. "There are no other women. There have been no other women. *You* belong to me. Only you."

She wasn't certain she believed he'd had no other women, but she found she wanted it to be true. "Gee, do I feel lucky," she said. "It's not every day I get bossed around by a vam—Carpathian. I've been on my own and taking care of myself for as long as I can remember, Darius, and I like it that way."

His hand had slipped to the nape of her neck, his attention caught by the softness of her skin. "It seems to me you have not done a particularly good job of it. Face it: You need me."

She batted his hand away, afraid of the fire pooling low in her body. He wasn't safe. Nothing about him was safe, not even casual conversation. "I don't need anyone."

His black eyes burned over her face, hard possession in the set of his mouth. "Then you will learn to do so, will you not?"

Her heart jumped at the soft, warning note in his voice. He could sound so menacing when he chose. Fear flickered in the depths of her eyes, and her green gaze skittered away from his dark one. "Darius, I really am afraid of you." The admission came out under her breath.

For a moment she was certain he hadn't heard her, but then his hand stilled on the nape of her neck, hot and possessive. "I know you are, Tempest, but there is no need for it, and you will get over it."

A flutter of anger gave her courage. "Don't be so certain I'll just let you take over my life."

"If you feel you can do no other than attempt to defy me, by all means, you are welcome to do so, but I warn you, I am not an easy man to cross." His voice was velvet soft, and all the more menacing because of it. There was a hard strength in his fingers as they circled her soft throat.

"Since I'm already afraid of you, that isn't exactly news, Darius," she said, her heart thumping in rhythm to her words. "It isn't as if I haven't been afraid before.

It isn't exactly a new experience for me. But I've always managed." She tilted her chin defiantly.

Darius bent his head close, his eyes like glinting ice. "You are afraid of the loss of freedom, Tempest, not of me. You are afraid of the untamed passion in you that rises up to meet the passion in me. It is that, not me, that you fear."

She pushed at the wall of his chest with both hands. He didn't budge. "Well, thank you very much for that analysis," she snapped, all at once stormy. "What would the others think if I told them you were acting this way?" she challenged. "Are they so far under your thumb that they'd help you?"

He shrugged with casual, fluid grace, reminiscent of a leopard stretching. "It would not matter to me one way or the other. It might break up our family, it might cause bloodshed, but in the end, the outcome would be the same. I will not give you up, Tempest."

"Oh, shut up," she said rudely, exasperated with him. "There isn't much to like about me once you get to know me. I'm always in trouble; it just happens. I'll make you crazy."

His hand closed over her fragile wrist, his thumb finding her pulse unerringly. "You already make me crazy," he replied softly. "You will do as I say soon enough, and then I will not have to worry so much."

"It isn't going to happen in this lifetime," she announced, glaring at him. "And as I have only this one, you're in for a big disappointment."

His laughter was low and amused, rife with that mocking male superiority that said she would be easy enough to handle. "Come on, honey. The others will be rising soon. We have miles to travel this night to stay on schedule. The cats will need to feed before we go." He did not add that all of his family would have to do the same. He sensed her deep fear that he wanted her to use for sustenance, that perhaps he intended the rest of them to use her, also. He wanted to reassure her but knew mere words would not help.

He reached down and pulled her to her feet. She was so unexpectedly light for a woman with such an iron will, and he was so enormously strong, he felt he might fling her into the sky if he wasn't careful.

The moment she was standing, she jerked away, wiping her palms on her jeans, glaring at him. He might rule everyone around him, but she wasn't about to stand for his nonsense. She wasn't going to become a food supply for anyone. And she certainly wasn't going to have some male fantasy figure dominating her life. She might have a penchant for trouble, but she wasn't stupid.

Darius glanced down at her transparent, expressive little face as they walked back toward the camp. She could not hide her thoughts from him anymore, now that he realized the differences in her mind. His earlier troubles served him right for being so complacent and sure of himself in his dealings with her. She was an unusual mortal, yet he hadn't considered that he would have to delve deeper than he normally would. Aside from thinking too much, Tempest had an interesting mind, a way of focusing in on one thing only and blocking out everything else.

She stumbled a little, and he slipped an arm around her shoulders despite her little shrug of retreat. By nature, Tempest was accepting of others. She also understood the way animals reasoned, their survival instincts. So it would require her only a step or two to accept the Carpathian way of life.

Darius knew she could accept it as long as it didn't

encroach on *her* way of life. Tempest lived like a nomad. That was essentially the same way his group lived, but she preferred a solitary existence. She understood an animal's way of life, had strong survival instincts herself, but she had less understanding of people and why they did the things they did. Growing up in a crack house, with mothers selling their children for drugs, selling their own souls for the drugs, she had decided at an early age that she wanted little to do with people, and nothing had happened since to change her mind.

Rusti inched away from the warmth of Darius's body. She didn't like the way he made her feel, that out-of-control rush of hungry need. He was too dangerous, too powerful, far too used to getting his way in all things. She liked her quiet, independent life. Solitude suited her. The last thing she needed was to be caught up in Darius's bizarre troupe of followers.

She sighed, unaware that she did so. She couldn't stay with the Dark Troubadors. The sanctuary they had seemed to offer was rapidly turning into something she wasn't equipped to handle.

Darius glanced down at her bent head, the faraway, pensive look on her face, the sadness reflected in her large eyes. He laced his fingers through hers. "There is no need to worry so much, honey. I have sworn to protect and care for you. I do not take such oaths lightly."

"This isn't exactly something a person can prepare herself for, Darius. Even if you're a . . . a Carpathian rather than a vampire, whatever you are isn't altogether human. I know that when you communicate mentally with me."

"Are you so certain that *you* are completely human? When I merge my mind with yours, I observe brain patterns different from those of ordinary mortals."

She winced, looking as if he'd struck her. "I know I'm different. Believe me, you aren't telling me anything I haven't heard before. You can't call me anything I haven't already been called. Freak. Mutation. Frigid. You name it, I've heard it."

Darius stopped abruptly, forcing Tempest to do the same. He brought her hand to the warmth of his mouth. "I did not mean it that way. I admire what you are. If either of us is a 'mutation' from the norm, Tempest, it is me, not you. I am in no way human. I am an immortal. And I can assure you that you are neither a freak nor frigid. Your heart and soul were simply waiting for mine. Not everyone can hand themselves over to just anyone. A few know that the giving of the treasure of one's body, one's intimacy, is sacred, meant solely for the one they were made for, their other half. Perhaps those who taunted you were jealous of that knowledge in you because they were in far too much of a hurry to wait or because they held themselves too cheap."

Her long lashes hid her emerald eyes. "I'm not a virgin, Darius."

"Because some man forced himself on you?"

"I think you have a false impression of me. I'm no angel, Darius. I've stolen cars, souped them up, gone for joy rides. I've always rebelled against so-called authority figures, probably because the ones I knew left a bad taste in my mouth. It always amazes me how the most self-righteous people, the ones forever preaching and pointing fingers at others, often do the most underhanded and dishonest things. Once I could support myself, I came up with my own code of honor, and that's what I live by. But I'm no saint, and I never have been. The places I come from don't breed saints."

Darius was becoming familiar with every nuance of

her voice. She sounded slightly sad, accepting of her brutalizing childhood but angry with herself for trusting others during those terrible years. Trusting them and having them let her down. That was why she preferred the solitary existence she had chosen, and he could sense her determination not to give it up, despite her need to. The job as mechanic to their traveling band had represented the ability to support herself and be free from the demands of intimate, prolonged contact with other people. He was taking that away from her.

"Perhaps it would be easier on you if I removed your memories of what I am. I could do it properly, Tempest," he offered. He found himself reluctant to do so, however. Somehow he wanted her to accept him as he was.

She shook her head adamantly. "No. If you did something like that, I would never be able to trust anything you said or did."

"You wouldn't remember, and it would take away your unnecessary fears. It does not make sense to me that you should remain afraid of us when we regard you as family," he said reasonably.

"No, don't do that to me," she insisted.

For a moment his dangerously predatory eyes moved over her face, a red flame flickering in their depths, reminding her of a wolf, a relentless hunter. What did she know of him? Only that he was not human but "Carpathian," allegedly immortal. And that he believed he had a right to her. She knew little of the unusual powers and properties he'd mentioned, but she felt them radiate out of his every pore. She could be lulled into a false sense of security because he often treated her gently, even tenderly.

But Darius was first and foremost a predator, yet with all the cunning and intellect of a human. He was dark, mysterious, dangerous, powerful, and very, very sensual. It was a formidable combination. Tempest nearly groaned aloud. How was she going to get out of this mess? His thumb was feathering over her knuckles, sending darts of fire racing through her bloodstream. Why did she have to be attracted to him? Especially if he was more beast than man? Was it because he was the first male who had ever treated her with such care? Was it because he was so utterly lonely and in need?

"Stop thinking so much, Tempest," he repeated softly, a hint of laughter in his velvet voice. "You are making things seem worse than they are." He was becoming tempted to remove her memories despite her reluctance just to ease her fears, yet he was selfish enough to want her to know what he was and have the courage to stay with him anyway.

"Right," she groused, "like that could happen."

Darius enjoyed the way she fit beneath his shoulder. He even enjoyed the way she defied him. He was aware that she had no idea of the power he wielded, the things he was capable of doing, but he felt fully alive with her. The wind rushed over them, blowing her soft hair around her face. He heard the rustle in the trees as the leaves swayed to the music of the breeze. He found himself smiling for no reason, when it had been many centuries since he had smiled at all. He had forgotten the feeling of happiness. Here, in the trees, with the night upon them, the wind calling to him, wild and free, and Tempest tucked beneath his shoulder, he felt both happiness and a sense of belonging.

Rusti glanced up at Darius, a little overwhelmed that she was acting as if all was normal when she should have been running screaming into the sunset. His face was a sensual work of art, carved with harsh yet beautiful lines.

If she had to describe him to someone else, she wasn't certain what she would say. He was power personified. Danger personified. And he was so incredibly sexy. Mesmerizingly so.

She closed her eyes. Well, that settled it, then. She couldn't look at him. She went up in flames every time she did. "Why couldn't you be a nice, ordinary man?"

"What is ordinary?" he asked, amused.

"You didn't have to have those eyes," she accused, flashing a glare at him. "Your eyes should be outlawed."

Warmth flowed into his heart, a curious, melting sensation. "So you like my eyes."

Her long lashes instantly veiled her expression. "I didn't say that. You're conceited, Darius—that's one of your biggest problems. You're arrogant and conceited. Why would I like your eyes?"

He laughed softly. "You like my eyes."

She refused to give him the satisfaction of agreeing. The campsite was just ahead through the trees, and she could hear the laughter of the others. Desari's musical voice was distinctive. It was soft and dreamy, even more mesmerizing than the others'. Tempest had noticed immediately the same hypnotic quality in Darius's voice.

"Everyone should stop following your orders, Darius," she scolded, her green eyes peeping up at him through long lashes. "It's the only possible way to save you. No one ever questions you."

"Perhaps because they trust me to know what is right," he said softly, gently.

She watched him inhale, dragging the night scents into his lungs, and knew instinctively that he was scanning the area, testing the campsite, ensuring to his satisfaction that it was safe. As they emerged through the thick stand of trees into the open, where the others waited, she felt the impact of several pairs of eyes on her. She stopped, her teeth sinking into her lower lip, her heart somersaulting alarmingly. She hated being the center of attention.

Darius stepped in front of her, easily blocking her small body from sight. He bent close to her. "Go shower. The others need to hunt this night before we leave. The cats can feed, then we will split up and meet at the next campsite. You will ride with me."

She wanted to argue with that, but more, she wanted to be away from the others, away from their inquisitive stares. Wordlessly, she turned around and hurried to the motor home. It felt like a sanctuary, as if it was already her home.

She took her time in the shower, enjoying the hot water cascading over her skin. It was difficult to close her mind to thoughts of Darius, but it was the only safe thing to do. She knew she wouldn't be able to stay long with him always around, but if she could hang in long enough to get across the country, maybe things would work out. And it was, after all, Desari who had hired her, putting her on a generous salary. Desari would give her the money the minute she asked for it; she could tell that Darius's sister was like that.

When she had gathered enough courage to quit hiding in the bus and face the group, the campsite appeared empty. A slight noise revised her first impression. Warily she made her way to the small red car. The man peering into the open hood was the one who had been driving the night before.

At the time she had barely glanced at him. Now, studying him, she realized he was, typical of the other band members, incredibly handsome. He had long dark hair, a mischievous look around his dark eyes, and his mouth had a sultry, moody kind of sexiness. She could easily see that this Troubador must be a hit with females of every age on the tour.

He looked up and grinned at her. "So, we meet at last, Tempest Trine. I am Barack. I was beginning to feel left out. Darius, Desari, Julian, and Syndil all speak highly of you. I figured they must have told you I was the group's bad boy and that you were avoiding me as a result."

Tempest found herself smiling. How could she not? Her natural wariness dictated that she keep her distance from him, but his ready grin was contagious. "No one warned me, but I can see they should have."

He patted the car lovingly. "What did you do to make her purr like this?" There was genuine interest in his voice. "I turned on the engine, and she sounded so happy to see me."

"Don't you work on cars? You sure can drive them."

Barack shook his head. "I keep thinking I'll get around to studying it, but there are always so many things to get in the way."

"That's unusual," Tempest said before she could censor her words. "Normally a serious driver and auto enthusiast like you is interested in what's below the hood." She wanted to kick herself for the inane remark. Like Darius, Barack probably slept during the day and used other "powers" at night. She made herself look casually away. "Where are the cats? I haven't seen them in a while."

"Feeding. We have to hit the road tonight, so Darius is allowing them to hunt, as is their right." Barack ran his gaze appreciatively over the small redhead. She was different from other mortal females. He knew she was different, but he couldn't put his finger on exactly how.

But he could hear her heart beating strongly, the ebb and flow of blood in her veins. Hunger was ever present, gnawing at his insides. Like the others, he should have gone to the campground only a few miles away and fed, but checking out the newly tuned car had intrigued him.

"Come over here, Tempest." His voice was low and compelling. He smiled, a flash of white teeth. "Show me what you did to the engine." His hunger was growing as he listened to the rush of blood in her veins.

Rusti didn't like his smile now, didn't like the way he was watching her. She glanced around. "I have to pack my tools and things, get ready to leave. I can show you later."

Shock registered on his handsome face, complete amazement. It occurred to Rusti that no one had ever turned Barack down before. There must have been a hidden compulsion in his voice she had failed to respond to. More and more she realized she was in over her head. If Darius had been the only one she had to deal with, maybe she could have done so successfully—at least long enough to get her across country. But they were all like him. She began backing away.

Barack instantly looked contrite. "Hey, I didn't mean to frighten you. I am not like the one who attacked you. Desari hired you. That means you are under our protection. Seriously, do not fear me. I have never had any woman fear me."

Rusti forced herself to stand her ground and made herself smile. "I'm just a little nervous after yesterday. Once the others get back, I won't be so tense." But at the moment she felt as if she had stumbled into a nest of rattlesnakes.

"We are friends, Tempest. Come here. Show me what you have done to make this machine purr."

She could feel his mind reaching to calm hers, to compel her to do his bidding. Which was worse? Allowing him to use her for a food source or allowing him to realize she knew exactly what he was? Would he then kill her? She decided it might be dangerous to let him know he wasn't controlling her, so she made herself stumble toward him, fear and revulsion choking her. She didn't want this man touching her the way Darius did.

For a moment interest at that thought swirled enough through her mind to push down her fear. Why, if the notion of being used for food sickened her, did she find the way Darius bit into her neck blatantly erotic?

Okay. She had lost her mind totally, she decided. That was the only answer. She had to get out of this jam and find a way to run for it. Produce a suddenly sick aunt in need out of thin air.

She was close to Barack now, his body crowding hers. Her stomach churning, feeling close to tears, she tried to hold herself very still. He was murmuring something to her; she could hear the words buzzing in her mind, but they had no meaning. She wanted to push him away and run. She couldn't stand it; she couldn't. She tried to equate what he was about to do with a simple animal bite, but her stomach revolted, and involuntarily she arched her neck away from his hot breath.

Waves of distress nearly choked her as his fingers curled around her arm. He was enormously strong, quelling her struggles with a viselike grip. A small sound escaped, a note of terror. Inside her mind Tempest could hear herself screaming, though no sound emerged from her closed throat. She was in the middle of real nightmare with no way out.

Then, without warning, not even a rush of wind, a huge black panther hit Barack squarely in the chest, a full two hundred pounds of fury driving the man back and away from Tempest. Barack hit the side of the car hard, the air knocked from him, then landed on the ground on his back, the cat driving straight for his throat.

Vaguely aware of Desari, Julian, another man, and Syndil beginning to emerge from the trees but stopping, frozen in horror, Rusti sought to calm the wild cat. In its mind she found a red haze of killing fury, like nothing she had ever encountered. She ran forward, still trying to soothe it, whispering to it, commanding. Only when she was near Barack, a Barack who was not even struggling for his life, who instead lay submissively beneath those terrible teeth, did she comprehend that the cat was Darius. Shocked, she continued to approach the cat.

"Rusti, stay back!" Desari called out to her. She tried to move forward to help Barack, to stop Tempest, but Julian was restraining her, literally lifting her off her feet, his strong arms around her waist.

The terror on Desari's face, echoing in her voice, registered with Tempest, but even with her own heart pounding in alarm, she reached for Darius, past the fierce fury of the animal to find the man. She knew him. She wasn't exactly certain how, but she knew he was there, somewhere inside that killing rage. *Darius. It is over. Barack did nothing but frighten me. Come back to me.* She kept her tone a soft, trusting plea, much like what she used first with a frightened animal. Soothing, with a belief that it would respond. She somehow knew that Darius would not respond to any of the others and that if she didn't stop him, the cat could very well end Barack's life.

This had happened because of her. That knowledge, like his identity, came to her seemingly out of nowhere, but she was certain of it, and she felt a rush of wonder that anyone could have such a depth of feeling for her. *Please, Darius, for me—release Barack and come to me.*

The panther snarled, exposing long, razor-sharp canines, but at least he wasn't sinking them into Barack's throat. The cat crouched low, vicious, its body frozen into utter stillness, only the tail twitching restlessly, angrily, back and forth. Barack lay under the cat, totally submissive, well aware of who had attacked him. The silence was filled only with his heavy breathing and the cat's snarling rage.

"Darius." Tempest was a heartbeat from the cat's teeth. Cautiously she laid a hand on the heavily muscled back. Her voice was soft, warm honey. "I'm all right. Look at me. He didn't hurt me. He really didn't."

A collective gasp went up, as much for her knowledge as for her courage. It was now obvious to all that she knew the identity of the great cat. Desari clenched Julian's hand in hers, suddenly afraid. No human could know of their existence and live. It placed them all in jeopardy. How did Tempest Trine know? Neither Darius nor Barack would have been so careless as to forget to expunge her memories. Yet how could they do such a thing as destroy the woman who had the courage to save one of their lives, as Tempest was clearly attempting to do?

The black panther moved, ever so slightly shifting its weight, placing its neck beneath Tempest's palm. *Please, Darius, I'm hanging on to my courage by a thread. Help me out. I want to get away from everyone. This is very frightening. All of it. And I don't understand it, so come to me and explain it.* In spite of her determination to be brave, her hand was trembling as it lay on the great cat's back.

Tempest felt Darius's control seeping slowly back into

his mind, felt the man overcoming the beast's rage. The panther moved against her, inserting itself between her and the fallen man. It pushed her away from Barack's supine figure, farther even, toward the trees and away from the prying eyes of his family. Then the leopard padded behind her, directing her into the deeper woods, its walk so silent, she felt she could hear leaves falling.

Back at the campsite the group released a long, collective sigh of relief. Dayan moved first, reaching down and pulling Barack to his feet. "Close call. What the hell did you do?" His voice was accusing. No one ever crossed Darius.

Barack held up his hands. "Nothing. I swear it. I was going to feed, that's all. Nothing else happened. He went berserk on me."

Syndil's slender hand fluttered to her throat. "Could Darius be turning? Darius is never out of control. Could it be happening?"

"No!" Desari cried out, somewhere between fear and outrage at the betraying thought. "No, Darius cannot turn. He is too strong."

Julian slipped an arm around her waist, a slight grin on his face. "None of you know, do you? Darius has not turned. He will never turn. Not now. He has found his lifemate."

"What are you talking about?" Dayan asked.

"These things were never taught to you," Julian mused softly, more to himself than the others. "You were not raised among other Carpathians. What is often second nature to us is not even known to you." His grin widened. "It is not known to Darius. Life is about to become quite interesting around here, boys and girls."

"Stop spouting nonsense, and tell us what you mean,"

Desari commanded, her soft, dark eyes beginning to smolder. "Should we be protecting Rusti?"

"The only one safe is Tempest. Each Carpathian male must find the light to his darkness. It is his only salvation. Without that woman, his lifemate, he will eventually be forced to choose the dawn and eternal rest, or he will succumb to the madness of the undead and lose his soul for all time. Become vampire. There is only one woman for each male, one other half."

"But Tempest Trine is human," Dayan objected. "This cannot be. We have been aware that there exists the other half of our heart, our soul, out there somewhere. A quest to find the proper mate must be made, as you found Desari, Julian. But Tempest is not a Carpathian."

"There are a handful of human women," Julian answered slowly, "all having some form of psychic ability, who can be lifemates to Carpathians. No doubt Tempest Trine is one such female. She wandered into your midst seeking a job but was likely drawn to do so because she was connected to Darius," he explained. "Funny, is it not, how fate has a way of bringing two linked souls together? Do not attempt to intervene between them and, for God's sake, do not touch that woman. Should you do so, Darius will be more beast than man, his every instinct to protect and care for her, to keep her from any others who might threaten her or her connection to him. He is more dangerous at this time than at any other." Julian grinned again. "Leave him to it; he will figure it out eventually."

"I should talk to him, explain," Desari said.

"I did not hear him asking for explanations, did you?" Julian prompted, his arms gathering her close to him. "It is best—and safest—not to interfere in the process of joining lifemates."

"Wait a minute." Barack leaned his long frame against the red car. "You lost me somewhere. I know Darius took her blood; I could smell his scent on her. Are you telling me that he would use her body, too? Isn't that combination strictly forbidden with mortals? Darius himself taught us this."

"Tempest appears to be different," Julian said. "She cannot be classified as a normal mortal; therefore, the rule does not apply."

Syndil's doe-eyes, normally soft and loving, were glinting fire at Barack. "You sought to feed on her? That is beneath you. She was under our protection. You are so insensitive, Barack. Always the playboy. You cannot leave women alone, not even those traveling with us practically as family. Rusti had a terrible experience yesterday. Did you give that a thought when you went to satisfy your own urges?"

"Syndil." Barack looked hurt. Syndil had a sweet, loving nature and was never angry, never upset with any of them.

"Do not 'Syndil' me, Barack. Are you so lazy that you had to feed from a woman protected by our family? I suspect you think so much of your charm that you thought she would be grateful to provide for you."

"It was not like that. I was merely overly hungry, having waited too long to feed. I would not have harmed the woman. And I had no idea she belonged to Darius. Hell, I never would have touched her had I known. He was going to rip my throat out, Syndil. You should be sympathizing with me. Look at my chest. He ripped open my skin. Won't you come heal it for me?" Barack gave her his most imploring, boyish pout.

"Perhaps next time you will think twice before you go chasing after women," Syndil replied and whirled away.

"Hey, wait a minute." Barack trailed after her, desperately trying to get back into her good graces.

"Have we all lost our minds around here?" Dayan demanded. "Soft, sweet Syndil is acting the shrew. Desari is acting like a lovesick calf. I do not know you well, Julian, but you seem to be enjoying Darius's discomfort far more than is seemly, and bad-boy Barack is chasing after Syndil like a lost puppy. What the hell is happening?"

"Your leader has found his lifemate, Dayan," Julian said happily, "and is clueless, totally clueless, about how to deal with her. Finding your lifemate leaves you feeling as if someone punched you in the gut and stole your sanity. Your Darius is used to having his way in all things, simply commanding whatever he deems correct. But now I suspect he is in for the shock he so richly deserves."

"He will simply force his will upon Tempest," Dayan said confidently, "then everything will return to normal."

"Forcing your will on your lifemate is in the same category as cutting your own throat. Not a wise idea. Still, watching will make for much fun," Julian said smugly.

Chapter Six

Once in the thick shelter of the trees, the panther's muscled form contorted and reshaped, shimmering in the blue darkness to become the solid frame of a man. Tempest watched, leaning for support against a tree trunk, wondering if she had somehow found Alice's rabbit hole in the middle of a California state forest.

Darius noted her unnatural pallor, the shock in her enormous eyes. Her soft mouth trembled, and she was twisting her fingers together in agitation, her knuckles white. He knew that if he approached her, she would run. "You know you are not afraid of me, Tempest." His voice was a whisper in the night, a part of the night.

Tempest looked around her. The color of night was deep blue, almost black, but mystical and beautiful. The trees rose as shadows toward the gem-scattered sky. Little tails of mist drifted slowly, lazily, knee-high along the forest floor. "Why do you seem as if you are such a part of all this?" she asked. "As if you belong to the night, but something beautiful, not dark and ugly? Why is that, Darius?" she asked again softly.

"I do belong to the night. I am not of the same race as you. I am not human yet not beast or vampire."

"But you can become a leopard?" The incredible feat was nearly impossible to believe, even though she had witnessed it with her own eyes.

"I can become the mouse scampering across the field, the eagle soaring high in the sky. I can be the mist, the fog, lightning and thunder, a part of the atmosphere itself. But I am always Darius—the one who has vowed to protect you."

Tempest shook her head. "This isn't possible, Darius. Are you sure I didn't fall and hit my head or something? Maybe we both ate a weird mushroom, and we're on some psychedelic trip together. This isn't possible."

"I can assure you, I have done this all my life. And I have existed nearly a thousand years."

She held up a hand to stop him. "One weird thing at a time. I'm hearing this stuff, but my brain is refusing to process it."

"Do you know I would not harm you, Tempest? Do you know that much?" he asked insistently, his black gaze drifting over her face like fog.

In her deepest soul, beyond the human workings of her brain, Tempest knew it was the only certainty she had. Darius would not hurt her. She nodded slowly and saw relief light his eyes for a moment. Then he sobered again.

"I did not mean to expose you to the others' appetites. In truth, it did not occur to me that any would use you for such a thing when you were under our protection. I inadvertently subjected you to a terrible moment, but in truth, you were not in any danger. In Barack's defense, he likely thought he could manipulate your memories, as is generally easy to do with human prey, but he would not have harmed or killed you, simply fed, as, smelling my scent on you, he assumed I had. Please accept my apology."

His voice wrapped itself around her and found its way into her heart.

She sighed softly and tried not to think too much about the word *prey*. "You know what, Darius? None of it matters. I don't have to understand, because I can't do this. You can see that now, can't you? I have no way to deal with this. It's better if I just get out now."

His black eyes never once blinked, never left her face. She found her heart beating faster, threatened in some elemental way she didn't understand. "It isn't as if I would ever say anything to anyone. They'd lock me up if I did. You know you don't have to worry."

His black eyes were merciless, boring into her deeper and deeper until they penetrated her soul. She found it difficult to breathe. "Darius, you know I'm right. You have to know. We aren't two different races trying to find some common ground. We're two different species."

"I need you."

He said the words so quietly that she barely heard them. He made the statement starkly, utterly without embellishment. There was no mental push, no other form of persuasion. Still, the way he said it was like an arrow piercing her heart. She had no defense against those three words. No way to combat the truth of them. The truth she heard in his voice.

She stared at him for a long moment; then, without warning, she picked up and flung a handful of leaves at him. "You don't play fair, Darius. You really don't. You have those eyes and that voice, and now you go and say something like that."

A slow smile softened the hard edge of his mouth. "I knew you liked my eyes." He sounded immensely satisfied. He didn't appear to move, but all at once he was towering over her, his body close enough to share its warmth. His hand found her throat, and his palm lay still so that her pulse beat into its center.

"I didn't say I liked your eyes," she corrected. "I think they should be declared illegal. They're sinful." She lifted her chin belligerently at him, trying to hold her ground against something she didn't even understand.

"I meant my apology, honey. I will never place you in such a position again. I will make certain the others are aware you are under my personal protection at all times." Darius bent his dark head toward hers, drawn to the seduction of her velvet lips.

Tempest's breath caught in her throat, and she shrank back against the tree trunk and held up her palms to push against the hard wall of his chest. "I'm thinking maybe we shouldn't do this. It's safer, Darius, really, for both of us to just not touch."

His smile climbed to his eyes, spreading heat through her body. "Safer? Is that what you think? It is always far safer to do what I wish."

He hadn't moved, not a single inch, despite the pressure she was putting on his chest. Tempest sighed softly. "You would say that. Personally, Darius, I'm at the point where I might run screaming into the forest, or doubt my own sanity and have myself committed. Don't push me any harder right now."

"Do you think you could stand on your own without the tree trunk supporting you?" Amusement tinged his voice.

Tempest patted the tree trunk, reluctant to find out. She was quite proud of the showing she'd made so far. No fainting. No hysterics. None of the things a sane woman would do. But she didn't want to fall on her face. Her long lashes swept down for a moment. Darius easily read the faint self-mocking humor mixed with concern on her transparent face, the sudden determination just before she shifted, ducking beneath his arm to stand on her own. He liked that, her sense of humor, her ability to laugh at herself in the most extreme situations.

She grinned at him. "Well, it worked."

He held out his hand. "Come on, honey. We can just walk and talk."

She regarded him suspiciously. "Just walk and talk. That isn't code for some other weird activity, is it?"

Darius actually laughed. His fingers tangled with hers, captured her hand, and brought it against the heat of his body. "Where do you come up with your nonsense?"

Her emerald eyes sparkled at him. "I can get worse. Much worse."

"You are trying to scare me away."

She laughed in spite of herself. "I think you do a better job at scaring people than I do. You win hands down. No contest."

His arm slid around her waist to lift her smoothly over a fallen log. He didn't miss a stride, and she couldn't stop herself from comparing him to the jungle cat she now knew he could become. He moved in the same silence, with the same grace. "What does it feel like to change like that?"

"Into a leopard?" Darius wondered at her question. He hadn't thought of what it felt like in hundreds of years. The mystery. The beauty. How wondrous it was to shape-shift. Her question brought up the total exhilaration, the awe he'd felt as a child experimenting until he perfected the art, until he could shift in midair, on the run, even when using preternatural speed. "It is an incredible feeling of power and beauty to experience the essence of the animal, its speed and energy and stealth, all miraculously in my own body."

Tempest moved with his rhythm, ambling nowhere in particular. He was so perfectly proportioned, his body its own miracle, strength and power in every muscle, every cell, and he carried it with a casual ease of which he didn't even seem to be aware. "It's fascinating when I communicate with an animal," she admitted. "I would love to be able to actually see things through their eyes, smell and hear things as they do. Can you do that? Or are you still really you?"

"I am both. I can use their senses, their abilities, yet I can also reason, as long as nothing triggers an overwhelming instinct."

"Like a survival instinct."

Darius glanced down at the top of her head. The moonlight was spilling through the trees, touching the red-gold of her hair to turn it to flame. She was so beautiful, he had no choice but to run a caressing hand over the silken strands. "That is what you are to me. A survival instinct. You feel it, too."

Her long lashes lifted enough for him to catch a glimpse of vivid green before she looked away. "I don't know what I feel." She pulled her hand away and sent him a quick look of censure. "We aren't going there, remember? You stay a foot away from me, and you don't do any one of those things I mentioned to you before."

His husky answering laughter sent flames dancing in her blood. She glared at him. "Laughing is out, too."

He caught her small waist and lifted her easily to the

top of an enormous downed log, so that the two of them stood close, his hands resting lightly on her hips as she looked down. Ferns grew abundantly on the forest floor, shades of green carpeting the area in a curious aqua in the blue of the night.

The scenery was so beautiful that she couldn't find her voice, not even to reprimand Darius for forgetting to measure the inches between them. She tried not to be aware of his hands on her, touching her as if she belonged to him. He leaned his dark head so close that her breath caught in her throat. Her neck throbbed in anticipation, and the flames began to crackle and sizzle, threatening to consume her. She felt the heat of his breath exactly over her telltale pulse.

"Listen to the night. It is speaking to us," he said softly.

For a moment she could hear only the beating of her own heart. It pounded in her ears, drowning out every other sound. He carefully turned her around and drew her back against the shelter of his body. "Be still. Be calm. It is there in your mind, Tempest. Find the stillness first. It is there that you begin to learn." His voice whispered over her skin like black velvet. Mesmerizing and perfect. Sheer magic.

Darius was casting a spell, weaving it tightly around her, not simply with the hypnotic power of his voice, or the hard strength of his body but with the night itself. She had never noticed that the darkness had such vivid colors of its own. The moon was shining through the canopy of trees, bathing the world in a soft, iridescent silver. The leaves glistened like gems as the breeze blew gently through them.

The low sigh of the wind was the first sound she could identify clearly after that of her own heart. Darius's arms

127

tightened around her, locking her against his much larger frame. Tempest had an aversion to tight spaces, and she always avoided being too close to men, especially when she was alone and they were strong. However, instead of making her feel threatened, Darius made her feel safe and protected.

"Really listen to it, Tempest, with your heart and mind as well as your ears. The wind is singing softly, whispering tales. There, very close to us—do you hear it? The wind has carried to us the sound of fox kits."

She tilted her chin, straining to catch a single note of what he could hear. Fox kits. Could he really know that? As if reading her mind, Darius placed his lips against her ear. "There are three of them. They must be very young; they're barely moving around."

Tempest felt his lips move in her hair, as if he had accidentally, not by design, brushed against the strands. Self-preservation finally took over, and she attempted to step away from him. But her foot hovered over empty space. She had forgotten she was atop a log. Only Darius's arms kept her from a fall.

He laughed softly, that infuriating, male, mocking amusement. "I was right. You need me. You need a keeper."

"I wouldn't if you weren't driving me insane all the time," she accused him, but she was clutching at him all the same.

"Allow me to merge my mind more fully with yours. I can teach you to listen, to hear the true sounds of the night. My world, Tempest." He glanced down at the slender fingers curled around the thickness of his arm. She was so fragile, so delicate, a small but hugely courageous woman. She was born for him. His heart and mind, his very soul recognized hers. Every cell in his body reached for her, needing, hungry, with an intensity that would never be assuaged.

Darius could feel her slight body trembling against the hardness of his. A fierce, protective instinct rose in him, swamping him with the sheer force of it. He wanted to carry her off to his lair, keep her safe from the everyday dangers of the world around them, keep her close and protected at all times. But he realized that, no matter how strong his feelings, she was mortal, and she had grown up in a different world, one he could never go back and change for her. It had shaped her character as surely as the ages and dangers he had faced had shaped his. He could not move her too fast. The demands of his body and soul had to take second place to her fears, groundless though they might be.

"If you merge your mind fully with mine, will you be able to read my every thought?" she asked anxiously.

He ruffled her hair, affection in the caress. "You mean as I already do?"

Her emerald eyes flashed at him. "You can't read *every* thought I have," she said decisively.

There was a short, telling silence. She tilted her head back to look at him. "Can you?" This time her voice definitely wobbled.

Darius wanted to kiss that worried look right off her face. "Of course I can."

Her teeth tugged at her lower lip. "You couldn't before. I don't think you can, Darius."

"You merge with me every time you communicate mentally with me. It may have taken me a few times to figure out your differences from others, but once I did, it allowed me to slip in and out of your mind at will." His fingers curled lovingly around the nape of her neck. "If you like, I could share some of your memories with you. The little alley you favored behind a Chinese restaurant. You were fond of its unusual cobblestones."

This time Tempest made a lunge to break free, but Darius caught her firmly, imprisoning her within the circle of his arms. "Not so fast, honey. You were the one implying I was telling you falsehoods."

She stood stiffly. "Nobody says *falsehoods* anymore. Your age is showing."

He laughed again, amazed that after centuries of loneliness and utter lack of emotion, he could find himself laughing so readily. There was joy in the night itself, joy in the world, in the very act of living. "That was not nice, Tempest," he scolded her, but his voice was so gentle, it turned her heart over.

"No merging, Darius. I think we should do something semi-normal. Say, just talking. Talking is good. Not anything strange, just the usual. Tell me about your childhood. What were your parents like?"

"My father was a very powerful man. He was often referred to as the Dark One. He was a great healer among our people. I understand that my elder brother has since taken his place among our kind. My mother was gentle and loving. I remember her smile. She had a spectacular smile." The words conjured up the memory for him, the rush of warmth.

"She must have been wonderful."

"Yes. I was only six when she was killed."

Her fingers tightened on his arm in sympathy. "I'm so sorry, Darius. I didn't mean to bring up a sad memory."

"No memory of my mother could be bad, Tempest. When I was six, the Ottoman Turks overran the village near our home and murdered nearly everyone. I was able to get out"—he gestured in the general direction of the campsite—"with a few others. My sister, Desari, along with Syndil, Barack, Dayan, and one other. After that, we were cut off from the rest of our people."

"At six years of age? Darius, what did you do? How did you survive?"

"I learned to hunt from the animals around me. I learned to feed the others. It was a time of great hardship. I made so many mistakes, yet every day was a new, exciting experience."

"How did you get separated from your parents, your people?"

"There was a war. Human villages were being wiped out—people our families considered friends. Our adults decided to stand with the humans. But the soldiers attacked after the sun had risen, when Carpathians are at their most vulnerable, when they need to go to ground. And there were so many soldiers, vicious and cruel, determined to wipe out the entire region, to rid themselves of all of us, as they considered us vermin, vampires. Unfortunately, adults of our species have no power, no strength, when the sun is high, so it was a slaughter, a useless waste of lives. So many died that day, humans and Carpathians alike, women and children. Many of our race were subjected to ritual 'vampire' killings—beheaded and staked through the heart, my parents among them."

Darius's voice was soft, melancholy, distant, as if part of him was centuries away from her. In his arms, Tempest turned to reach up and touch his mouth with her fingertips. "I'm so sorry, Darius. How terrible for you." Tears were glistening on her long lashes, making her eyes luminous. Sorrow for him, for his lost parents, for the boy he had been, throbbed in her heart.

Darius touched a teardrop, catching it on the end of his finger. "Do not weep for me, Tempest. I never want

Christine Feehan

to bring tears to your heart. Your life has been a hard one, too. At least before I lost emotion and color, mine was filled with the love of my old family, and then of my new family for hundreds of years. The boat I and the others escaped our war-torn homeland in took us across the ocean before going down in a violent storm. We were on our own, I the oldest, but we made it to the shores of Africa, and we had great adventures in those years and since—before the darkness gathered in me and spread across my soul."

She watched him bring his finger to his mouth to taste her shimmering teardrop, his black eyes sensual, his perfect lips alarmingly enticing. She swallowed convulsively, afraid she might fling herself into his arms just to taste his mouth again and be forever lost in the burning intensity of his eyes. "What darkness, Darius? What are you talking about?"

"I have felt nothing these last long centuries. After a certain point, evidently a Carpathian male loses his emotions and is in danger of turning vampire. Because I had others depending on me, I fought off the beast within me. But for eons now I have seen no colors, felt no joy, no need for a woman, no laughter, and no love. I have not even felt guilt over necessary killing. Only my hunger was in me. Strong and terrible and always upon me. The beast in me grew until he was always fighting for freedom, raging for release. Then, into that darkness, you came, bringing me color and light and life." Darius said it softly, honestly, meaning every word. His hand came up to capture her mass of red-gold hair, to crush it to his face so that he might inhale the fragrance of her. "I have more need of you than does any other in this world. My body claims yours as its own. My heart recognizes yours. My soul cries out for yours,

132

and my mind seeks the touch of your mind. You are the only woman who can tame the beast and hold me to this earth, to the path of goodness and light. The only one who can keep me from destroying mortals and immortals alike."

Tempest bit at her lower lip again. The things he said to her were almost more than she could comprehend. They made her nervous, even as he made her more aware of herself as a desirable woman than anyone ever had. "Let's not get carried away, Darius. I've agreed to travel with the band for a while, but saving the world is a little beyond my specialties. I wield a mean wrench and all, but relationships totally elude me."

She could be flippant with her answers, but her heart had melted at his every word. His Old-World elegance and charm somehow seemed to provide a balance to the danger clinging to him like a second skin. Sexual magnetism was also second nature to Darius, and Tempest didn't try to delude herself into thinking she was immune.

"It will be in the best interests of all concerned that you remain free from any other relationships," he said softly.

Her emerald eyes flashed a brilliant green before she turned away from him again, too tempted by his perfect mouth to stare at it for long. "Let's walk, Darius. I think it's safer than standing here on a log over looking a cliff. Much safer."

His arm curved around her waist, and he bent forward, his warm breath caressing the nape of her neck. "Run if you must, baby, but there is nowhere to go except back to me."

She firmly removed the thick band of his arm from around her waist, proud of her decisiveness. If his body continued to be in contact with hers, they were both going to go up in flames. The only sane thing to do was to put an ocean or a glacier between them. Maybe the entire polar ice cap.

His infuriating laughter followed her as she jumped off the log and began stalking away. "Reading your mind is becoming very interesting, honey. We could always settle down in an igloo."

"Not a chance. You'd melt the darn thing. Then where would we be? I told you, none of that mesmerizing-eyes thing. And maybe you should try wearing a mask." His sexy laughter had to go, also. Definitely had to go. It was wreaking havoc with her bloodstream. Making it hot, molten, so thick and heavy that she was going to throw herself at him and beg for relief if he didn't stop. Then he'd be sorry. Yeah.

She turned around and glared at him. "Okay. Do the lizard thing."

He studied her face. "The lizard thing?" he echoed. Then an unholy smile touched his sensuous mouth. "Lick your skin? With pleasure. Just tell me where." Deliberately he bent close to the pulse in her throat, his eyes all at once burning, the laughter fading.

Tempest shoved him, hard. If the velvet rasp of his tongue touched her skin, she would be lost. "Get away from me." She took two running steps in growing alarm. "I mean it, Darius. Or we'll have to get a chaperone."

"You said you wanted the lizard thing." His hand shackled her wrist, chaining her to his side.

"I meant scales. You need scales. If you were a little crawly thing, I wouldn't feel I was risking my honor walking in the woods with you." She was laughing in spite of herself.

"If I shape-shifted into a lizard, you would run screaming back to camp." Darius knew that Julian and Desari had already departed in the touring bus with the cats. Dayan, Syndil and Barack were at that very moment cramming themselves into the fast little car Barack loved so much. He could hear Barack pleading with Syndil to talk to him, trying to convince her that he wasn't really a rat.

Darius took advantage of Tempest's momentary pause to gain possession of her hand. His fingers laced firmly through hers and drew her beneath the protection of his shoulder. "If I changed, I would want to show off and do a Komodo dragon for you."

Tempest allowed several heartbeats to go by while her imagination digested that one. "Don't we have to go somewhere tonight? I thought you had a tight schedule to keep. Let's leave Komodo dragons out of the picture. You're scary enough in human form."

They were drifting back toward camp, walking through the layer of fog that was thickening along the forest floor. It was eerie and beautiful, making the woods a magical, mystical place. Tempest liked the feeling of strength in Darius's hand, the heat of his body warming hers, the easy, fluid way he moved with the suggestion of tightly leashed power. Most of all she loved the way his eyes burned possessively over her, the way his chiseled, perfect mouth tempted her.

Darius stopped so abruptly, she ran into him. He had turned to face her, his features dark and sensual in the moonlight spilling through the canopy of trees. He looked what he was, a lord of power, a sorcerer without compare. Tempest could only stare up at his masculine beauty, lost in the hunger in his eyes.

She couldn't breathe when he was so close to her. His eyes darkened until they were merciless with hunger, with raw need. His hands slid down her arms to rest on her hips, to urge her body even closer to his. The midnight blue of the air mixed with the silvery sheen of the moon and came together with the white bank of fog, surrounding them, cutting them off from the rest of the world.

Darius bent his head slowly to hers, drawn by some power other than his own, beyond even his comprehension. All that mattered at that moment was that he feel her satin-soft mouth beneath his. That he taste the wild honey of her. That he take control and end their mutual misery. He had to do this. It was as necessary to both of them as breathing.

His lips were firm yet velvet soft, moving over hers, gently coaxing her response. He felt her shift beneath his hands, glide right inside him, wrap herself tightly around his heart. His teeth tugged gently, insistently, until Tempest had to comply with his unspoken demand and open her mouth to him. The ground beneath his feet whirled alarmingly, but his mouth was fastened to hers, transporting him through time and space to somewhere he had never been.

Without conscious thought, without meaning to do so, Darius found her mind with his and merged them together, sharing his erotic fantasies, his joy in her existence. Sharing the way his body came to life and raged for her, needed her. Hungered for her.

Pure feeling. He was soaring high without wings, freefalling through space, and all the time the flames were leaping higher. He was lost in her, would always be lost in her. Her skin was so soft, her hair like silk. She was the miracle of life itself.

It was all there, sweeping Tempest along in the vortex of his passion, catching her desire and magnifying it until she didn't know where she left off and he began. Until they were one being consumed with fiery hunger. There was no room for self-preservation, no room for modesty; her need was every bit as great as his own.

His arms tightened possessively, sweeping her into the shelter of his hard masculine frame. Deep within his body, his blood thickened to molten lava, a firestorm sweeping through his entire system until he knew he was going up in flames.

We have to stop. The words brushed like butterfly wings in his mind, breathless, erotic, filled with the same hunger and need threatening to consume them both, threatening his very control. Yet there was something else. Something new. Because their minds were merged, he recognized it for what it was; fear as elemental as time itself.

Darius pulled himself back to reality, away from the urgent demands his body was making and back toward a semblance of sanity.

Tempest was on fire, no longer herself but a part of Darius. They were one single and complete entity. She clung to him, the only safe anchor in a wild storm of magic. Darius lifted his head so that his mouth hovered inches from hers. They stared at one another, drowning in each other's eyes, awed that they could produce such a conflagration with only a kiss.

Tempest retreated, a subtle feminine withdrawal from him, trying to find herself and cool the terrible heat searing her body. She touched her mouth with her fingertips, unable to believe that she had helped to generate such flames.

"Do not say it, honey. I know exactly what you are going to say." That infuriating male amusement tinged his husky voice.

Tempest shook her head. "I don't think I can talk. Honestly, Darius, you're lethal. We just can't do this. It's too dangerous. I expected lightning to start arcing between us."

He shoved a hand through his dark mane of hair. "I swear I was hit by a bolt. White-hot and jagged, tore right through me."

Her smile was tentative but there all the same. "So we agree. No more of that."

Darius wrapped an arm around her body and found she was trembling. "I think plenty of that is the answer, Tempest. We have to learn to control it. The more practice we have, the better we will be."

"Better?" Tempest pressed a hand to her mouth, her eyes enormous. "We don't dare get any better at it, Darius, or we could set the world on fire. I don't know about you, but I don't feel so great right now." Her body was heavy and aching for relief, sensitive to the slightest touch. Each time Darius brushed against her, darts of fire raced through her. She needed him, needed his body. "If we had any sense, we'd put half the world between us."

Darius brought her knuckles to the warmth of his mouth and was intrigued by two small scars on them. His tongue examined the faded white marks, a slow, velvet rasp of heat. Tempest closed her eyes against the smoldering desire in his eyes, against his blatant sensuality. This time she knew the instant conflagration wasn't caused only by her. She didn't do things like this, didn't seek instant intimacy. Ever. Who would have thought such a small touch, one look, could reduce her to liquid heat and an ache that would never stop again?

"Darius, you have to stop." She was half laughing but very near tears. "I have no idea what to do. I mean, you're a vampire."

He shook his head. "Not vampire, honey. God help us all, never that. I explained to you that the vampire has chosen eternal darkness, has chosen to lose his soul. You are my soul, my strength, the light to my dark. I am Carpathian, even though I was not raised with our people and my ways are somewhat different. I do not know the Prince of our people, the one who has undertaken to keep our species from extinction. I did not even know he existed or that my elder brother still lived until a few weeks ago."

Tempest began to laugh. "Isn't there *anything* normal we can converse about? Say, the weather? Unusual weather we're having." If he continued to talk to her about things her brain refused to comprehend, she was afraid she would lose her mind. Everything was happening far too fast.

His grin was teasing. "Would you like me to create a storm? We could make love in the rain."

"We can find the others and pretend there's safety in numbers," Tempest suggested firmly, ignoring the way her body went into meltdown at his outrageous suggestion. "I can see which of us is the practical one, and it isn't you." She tugged at his hand, leading him back toward the camp.

He followed her for a few minutes in puzzled silence. Finally, curious, he cleared his throat. "Tempest? Where exactly is it that we are going? Not that I mind—I will follow wherever it is you wish us to go—but to my recollection, this trail winds around a rocky ravine. It is unsafe."

She could feel the color rising beneath her skin and creeping up her neck. When she attempted to untangle her fingers from his, he clung to her like glue. She felt like kicking him in the shins. It was bad enough that he set her body on fire, but now she was completely flustered, while he looked the same as ever—calm, implacable, completely invincible.

"Just where is the camp, then?" she demanded through clenched teeth.

For a moment Darius stared at her. Then he blinked, wiping out the mocking amusement she was certain she had seen swirling in the depths of his eyes. He regarded her with a perfectly sober expression that made her want to *really* kick his shins. It took a goodly measure of self-control to keep from doing it.

"Don't lecture me. I normally have some sense of direction," she protested. "You must have put a spell over me or something. Just lead the way. And wipe that expression off your face while you're doing it."

He walked in silence, his body unconsciously protective toward hers. "What kind of spell did I put over you?" he asked gently, his voice that pure, mesmerizing, hypnotic cadence she couldn't seem to resist.

"How should I know?" she asked petulantly. "For all I know, you studied with Merlin." She regarded him with suspicion. "You didn't, did you?"

"Actually, honey, he was my apprentice," he said.

She put both hands over her ears, her fingers still entwined with his. "I don't want to hear this. Even if you're kidding, I don't want to hear this."

They reached the clearing, and Tempest stopped to stare at the empty grove. Only the truck remained. Not so much as a stray paper wrapper indicated that anyone had ever been there. She was destined to be alone with Darius whether she wanted it or not. "This isn't a conspiracy, is it?"

Darius laughed softly as he opened the door to the truck. "My family probably thinks I have lost my mind, but they would never conspire against you."

"But they would conspire *for* you," Tempest said with sudden insight. She tilted her head at him. "What would they do if this Prince of your people didn't like something you did?"

Darius shrugged casually with his natural arrogance. "I would not want my family to do other than stay out of my business. I have long taken care of myself and my own concerns. I answer to no one. I never have, and I would be unable to do so at this late date." His hands spanned her waist, and he lifted her effortlessly, depositing her on the seat of the truck. "Fasten your seat belt, honey. I would not want you to leap out at the first sign of trouble."

She was muttering under her breath as he slid behind the wheel. In the close confines of the truck, he seemed more powerful than ever. The width of his shoulders, the strong columns of his thighs, the heat of his body. Tempest swallowed the groan caught in her throat. His masculine scent beckoned to something wild and untamed in her. Her fingernails tapped out a nervous rhythm on the dashboard. "You know, Darius, maybe I should just take a bus."

He heard the shadow of desperation in her voice and chose to ignore it. After starting the engine, he reached over to touch her soft skin just once, his fingertip running down her cheek.

The feathery touch sent her heart racing. She knew he heard, knew he was aware of her blood rushing through her veins, was aware of her body ready for and needful of his. With a little sigh she sank down into the seat and laid her head back, closing her eyes.

Chapter Seven

She was lonely. Tempest thought about that as she brushed out her hair and stared thoughtfully into the mirror in the bathroom of the troupe's motor home. The long night had been like a beautiful dream, Darius talking softly to her in the intimacy of the small truck cab, his voice, such a perfect blend of notes, relating interesting bits of history, making it come alive for her. His arm sweeping her next to him, ensuring that her safety belt was snug. The warmth of his body seeping into hers.

They had driven for hours, the night sky unfolding before them, the ribbon of highway their guide. She had become drowsy, her head falling onto his shoulder and settling there. She hadn't intended that to happen, but it felt right. Darius made her feel safe and cherished. It was in his voice, in the heat of his eyes, in the way his body sheltered hers.

Tempest sighed aloud. She didn't want to get used to

the feeling. Nothing lasted forever, and ultimately it was better to rely on herself. She didn't want to fall into a seductive trap, no matter how silken it was. In any case, Darius was far too powerful to even contemplate such a foolhardy act. But she could dream, and it seemed as if she was doing a lot of that lately.

She was lonely without Darius. At many times in her life she had experienced loneliness, but this was different. This felt as if a part of her was missing, a dark void she couldn't fill or escape on her own.

She had awakened late again, another bad habit she was developing. It was well after three in the afternoon. She put it down to traveling all night. No wonder the troupe slept during the day. How else could they keep up such an insane schedule?

She peered closely at her reflection in the mirror. Her bruised eye should still be deeply purple, swollen, and ugly, but only the faintest smudge of blue remained. Darius had healed her. Color crept up her face, and her body leapt to life as she remembered how. It was easier to recall it as an erotic dream. *Darius*. She missed him while he slept, God only knew where.

Disliking the way her eyes were shining, she swung away from the mirror. It was bad enough that she had lingered in the shower like a lovesick calf, dreaming of him. His eyes. His mouth. His voice. The way his body rippled with strength.

"Oh, for heaven's sake." She glared at the lavish interior of the motor home. "You're acting worse than a teenager," she told herself. "He's arrogant and bossy and strange. Keep that in mind when you're going ga-ga over his looks. He's a man. That's bad enough. And he's worse than a man. He's a . . ." She searched for the right explanation. "A *something*. Something you don't want any part of. Now go check the oil. Something mundane, ordinary. Something you can relate to."

Just before dawn he had carried her to the bus they had by then overtaken, after driving all night. She closed her eyes and could still feel the strength in his arms, the way the hard muscles of his chest felt against her soft breasts. In the early streaks of light she could see his face, sensual, beautiful, yet as harsh as time itself. He had carried her gently, carefully into the bus and laid her on the couch among the pillows. His tenderness as he covered her with a quilt was forever etched in her heart. The kiss he brushed over her temple still held traces of fire.

And her neck. Tempest pressed a hand to her neck, then turned back to the mirror to look once more. His mouth had left a burning brand there, marking her as his. She could see the evidence, the odd mark that throbbed and seared and called to him. She covered it with her palm and captured the scorching heat there.

"You are in so much trouble this time, Rusti," she murmured softly. "I don't even have a clue how I'm going to get you out."

She attempted to eat cold cereal but found she was more lonely than hungry. She wanted to see his mouth, the way he quirked it, slow and sexy. She wanted to see the black burning of his eyes. The cereal tasted like cardboard. Why was it erotic when Darius took her blood, when the thought of any other doing such a thing sickened her? What made it repulsive when Barack had bent close yet made her entire body clench in anticipation of Darius? She touched the mark with a fingertip this time.

"You are not going to sit here daydreaming, Tempest," she declared staunchly, vaguely wondering why she was calling herself the name Darius insisted upon. "Go do

144

something, anything, but stop acting stupid."

She took only a few minutes to clean up and, after petting the sleepy leopards, went outside. The heavy drapes at the windows had blocked the light out of the bus so that the day seemed brighter than ever, and she had to squeeze her eyes shut against its brilliance. The breeze was soft and playful, tugging at her hair and clothes, rustling leaves and blowing pine needles here and there about their new campsite.

The air smelled fragrant with both pine and wildflowers. Water bubbled somewhere close by. Tempest fiddled halfheartedly with the bus engine, fine-tuning until she was satisfied. The wind made her feel more lonely than ever. Colors seemed so much more vivid when Darius was around. Everything was more vivid when Darius was around.

Obsession. Was that what this was? Tempest filled a water bottle and slid it into her knapsack. She would go hiking, wade in the stream, and cool off. Wash him away. Whistling, she pushed her hands into her pockets and started off, determined that Darius's presence was no longer going to haunt her. But a feeling of dark oppression began to overtake her as she walked farther from the camp.

She tried singing, but her heart seemed heavy, her legs like lead as she took each step. A terrible sorrow was growing in her. She needed to see Darius, touch him, know that he was alive and well. She found the thin ribbon of a stream and followed it until it widened and poured in a frothy silver blanket over an outcropping of rocks. She took off her shoes and strode in. The icy cold cleared her head enough that she could reason again.

Darius was not dead or hurt. Nothing was wrong. The bond between them was growing because he merged his mind more often with hers. They shared an intense intimacy that was not meant for humans. Without his mind touching hers, she was feeling the loss. That was all. It was simple. She just had to learn to live with it.

Tempest waded farther out into the stream so that the water poured over her knees and the current urged her to follow its course. She became aware of the insects in the air, their constant hum, their buzzing about. They were darts of color, a whirring of gossamer wings. She listened in the way Darius had taught her, in utter stillness, with the water flowing around her and her mind centered on the tiny creatures teeming with life.

Tempest watched a brilliant blue dragonfly hover above the stream. Very slowly she looked around and saw butterflies gathering. So many beautiful colors, wings beating in the air. They came from everywhere, brushing up against her, landing on her shoulders, her arms. Entranced, she stayed attuned to them until she feared she was gathering too many. Abruptly she released them, and they gracefully began to take flight.

Musical notes seeped into her mind as the birds began a concert, a rivalry of sound. Various species vied for air waves and tried to outdo one another. She listened intently, repeating the sounds in her mind until she was certain she had each separate song, each meaning, before she answered them.

One by one she called them to her. Holding out her arms, she sang to them, coaxed them, her throaty warbling luring the birds from their branches and nests. They flew around her, circling low, dipping to inspect her warily before settling on her arm.

Chattering and scolding, the squirrels came next, rushing forward to stop at the edge of the water. Slowly, with great care, Tempest made her way toward them, all the time still talking quietly to the birds. They fluttered around her, cooing and singing, trilling their favorite tunes to her. Two rabbits moved hesitantly into the open, wiggling their noses at her. Tempest stayed very still, reaching out only with her mind to include them in the circle of communication.

It was a bird that first warned her of danger. Riding an air current high above them, its sharp eyes caught a stealthy movement in the brush several yards from the gathering. It keened an alarm, cautioning those below that they weren't alone. Tempest turned around quickly as the birds took flight and the squirrels and rabbits raced to safety. She was left alone in the clearing, her bare feet still in the water. The man partially hidden in the thick brush was busy taking a series of pictures. He looked all too familiar and, worse, all too triumphant. He had obviously taken photos of the animals swarming around her.

Tempest sighed and ran a hand through her hair. At least she hadn't managed to draw out anything major or exotic. No bears or fox or minks. But she could still see the reporter's tatty little rag with her picture on the front, captioned *Birdwoman of the Dark Troubadours*. What a great article that was going to make. How did she manage to get herself into such messes?

"Hello again. You seem to be following us around," she greeted Matt Brodrick, hoping she didn't sound as afraid as she felt. She hated being alone with men, and this meandering stream in a remote wooded area was about as alone as it got. "Did you get some good pictures?"

"Oh, yeah," he answered, allowing the camera to hang loosely around his neck. He began to move toward her, looking cautiously around. "Where's the bodyguard?" he asked with great suspicion.

Tempest's feet moved of their own volition, wading backward into the middle of the stream as Matt Brodrick strode toward her.

"I thought that bodyguard stuck to you like glue."

"Where would you get an idea like that? I'm the mechanic, not a band member. He sticks to Desari, the lead singer, like glue. That's his job. I can give him a message the next time I see him if you'd like." Something about Brodrick made her uneasy. She knew he was more than a nosy reporter trailing after the troupe, but what he wanted, she couldn't guess.

"Someone tried to kill her a couple of months back," Brodrick said, watching her face carefully. "Did they tell you that? Did they mention that when the attempt was made, two other members of the band were shot also? This group can be dangerous to be around."

She went still inside. He was telling the truth; she could feel it. But he had deliberately told her in the quiet solitude of these woods to shock her, to see if he could shake her up. Tempest inhaled, taking in fresh air, pushing out the terrible fear. She began to move in the direction of the current even as she gave a casual shrug. "It has nothing to do with me. I fix cars, that's all. You're probably in as much danger as I am if someone is trying to hurt Desari and you're always hanging around."

She glanced up at the sky. It was a clear, beautiful day, clouds like cotton balls floating serenely high above them. "It's probably some crazed fan. You know the type. Desari is sexy and beautiful. She draws all kinds of attention. Sometimes so much attention isn't a good thing." Some of nature's tranquillity seeped into her mind.

Or was it Darius again? He was far from her; she couldn't touch him even when her mind, of its own accord, reached out to find his. She met only blankness, yet she sensed he was helping her. She could feel something of his characteristic calm entering her and helping her toward the stillness that better attuned her to nature.

Brodrick was stalking her along the edge of the stream, careful to keep his wingtips dry. "More likely someone knows what they are." His eyes bored into her. "You were warning me, weren't you, trying to tell me if I stayed around here I could get hurt?"

"Where did you get an idea like that?" Tempest wished she'd thought of it. She was allowing him to intimidate her, when maybe he was just as scared. "I don't read slimy tabloids, Brodrick, so maybe you should tell me what you're looking for. I take it you plan to use those pictures of me. I'm not a celebrity, and, in any case, what would be the point? So I prefer animals to people. I have an affinity for them. You print that, and all you'll do is maybe lose me my job. How is that going to help you accomplish whatever it is you want?"

Brodrick was studying her. She was standing with the sun behind her, so he didn't spot right away the love bite on her neck. When he did, he made a strangled sound and scrambled backward, hastily reaching inside the neckline of his shirt to drag out a silver cross. He held it out in front of him, facing her.

Tempest stared at it a moment without comprehension. Then, as the significance sank in, she burst out laughing. "What are you doing, you idiot? You're nuts! You really believe the junk you print, don't you?"

"You're one of them. You bear the mark of the beast. You're his servant now," he accused hysterically. The sun shining on the silver glared into her eyes.

Tempest touched her neck with her fingertips. "Who is *he*? What beast? I'm beginning to think you're insane. My boyfriend was playing around and gave me a hickey. What did you think it was?"

"They're vampires, the lot of them," Brodrick said. "Why do you think they sleep during the day?"

Tempest laughed softly. "Is *that* why there's so many coffins in the bus? Wow. I never thought they were vampires."

Brodrick swore angrily, furious that she would make fun of him. "You won't be laughing at me when I prove it to the world. We're on to them. We have been for some time. We're traced them over the last fifty years, and they haven't aged a bit."

"Who are 'we'? And you have proof of this?" Her heart was in her throat, but she forced the taunting grin to remain on her face. "You don't look fifty yourself, Brodrick, so maybe you're one of them, too."

"Don't laugh at me," he hissed, furious. "We're a society of concerned citizens trying to save the world from these demons. We put ourselves at great risk. Some of our people were killed in Europe, you know—martyrs for our great cause. We can't let vampires continue to endanger mankind."

Her eyes widened. She was looking at an honest-to-God fanatic, doubtless somehow behind the effort to kill Desari. "Mr. Brodrick." She tried to be reasonable. "You can't actually believe what you're saying. I know these people. They're hardly vampires; they're just a little eccentric. They travel around singing like most bands do. Darius cooked me vegetable soup the other day. Desari has a reflection in the mirror—I've seen it myself. And I was only kidding about the coffins. The bus has every luxury, including a sleeping area. Please believe me, these are just talented people trying to make a living."

"I saw the mark on you. They use humans. No one has seen them out in the sun. I know I'm right. We almost had them the last time. And what happened to our best marksmen—the ones we sent out to destroy them? They disappeared without a trace. How did Desari escape? How did she live with several bullets put into her? Tell me that. They claim she went to the hospital, and a private doctor took care of her. Ha!"

"That's easy enough to check on."

"The doctor says she was there. So do three nurses and a few techs, but no one else. A famous singer in their hospital and most of the staff can't remember it? And I didn't find one surgical nurse who knew a thing about it. They claimed everyone on the operating team was a specialist brought in from the outside."

"The Dark Troubadours are wealthy, Brodrick. Wealthy people do things like that. But are you openly saying you were part of an attempt on Desari's life?" The admission frightened her; she had the feeling he wouldn't bother to confess unless he planned to get rid of her, too. For the first time she was afraid for her life. Did he have a gun? It was entirely possible. Worse, she believed Brodrick was insane. No one in his right mind would believe in vampires taking over humankind. She'd always believed vampires to be myth—at least until she saw Darius in action. This man was basing his notions on mere foolishness and hoary old legends.

It seemed Darius was far more trustworthy than any human she had met as yet. Not that that did her much good right now, wherever he was. Oh, Lord, she didn't even want to know where he was. What if he really slept in a coffin? The idea gave her the willies. He had mentioned going to ground. What did he mean by that?

Don't think about it, Tempest. That will make you as crazy as this nutcase. Keep focused here. Stay with what's important.

Matt Brodrick was watching her, his eyes narrowed and mean. "I know they need human servants to watch over them during the day. That's what you are. Where are they?"

"You need help, Brodrick. Seriously, you need intense therapy." She wondered if Darius knew the reporter had been involved in the attempt on Desari's life.

"You're one of them," Brodrick accused her agian. "You help me find them while they're sleeping, or I'll have to destroy you."

Tempest was wading faster downstream while Brodrick kept pace along the bank. Her heart seemed to be racing as fast as the water itself. "The truth is, you've told me too much already, Brodrick. You have no other choice but to kill me. I'm not about to tell you where Darius and Desari or the other members of the band are, but they aren't in coffins, and I'm not about to help you put them there."

His lip drew back in an ugly snarl. "Did you know one of the band members disappeared some months ago? I think they killed him. He probably wasn't one of them, and they were just using him for blood until he ran dry."

"You have a sick mind, Brodrick." Tempest was looking around frantically for a way to get free of him. They were so secluded, and she was certain she had left the perimeter of safety Darius was always on her about. If she ever got out of this mess, he'd likely give her a lecture she'd never forget.

She sent her mind seeking into the forest, the sky, calling on the aid of the animals in the general vicinity, needing information, an impression of a hiding place nearby. Brodrick was mumbling to himself, angry with her for not doing as he wished. Very slowly, he withdrew a small revolver. "I think you'd better reconsider."

Tempest could feel the pull of the current on her legs. It was much stronger now, the water louder, more aggressive. She didn't want to run into any unexpected waterfalls, and she was afraid that, or rapids, was where she was heading. She waded to the opposite bank from Brodrick, although still within easy range of his gun. She was still barefoot, her shoes strung around her neck by the laces. What an attractive way to die, she decided. And who else would get caught shoeless when she had to make a break for it across the rocky, uneven ground? What was it about her that attracted trouble?

Far above the bird screamed again, a high-pitched, unusual cry. She instantly received the impression of a steep cliff. She was out of the water, back pedaling quickly, keeping her eyes warily on the gun. It never wavered from her heart, though Brodrick didn't follow her across the fast-moving stream. Evidently he didn't want to get his shiny shoes wet.

His first shot reverberated loudly. A bullet whined close to her ear and kicked up dirt and pine needles several feet behind her. Tempest stumbled backward but refused to run. The rocks underfoot were sharp, tearing at her soles. The lacerations barely registered, though as a second shot had her backpedaling again, moving as fast as she could, her gaze riveted on the ugly little gun.

Time seemed to slow down. She could see individual leaves rustling in the faint wind, hear the bird overhead scream its warning. She even noticed the way Brodrick's eyes became flat and cold. She kept moving backward.

"Why are you doing this? What if you're wrong? Then you have killed an innocent person because you *think* her traveling companions are vampires. I'm out here in the hot sun, in broad daylight. Doesn't that tell you anything?" She tried to buy herself time.

"That mark on you is all the proof I need," Brodrick explained. "You're their human servant."

"Then half the teenagers in America are slaves to vampires. Don't be stupid, Brodrick. I'm a mechanic, nothing else." The rocks were slicing her feet, and Tempest was beginning to feel desperate. There had to be a way out of this mess.

Behind her, she felt empty space under the heel of one foot. The rocky expanse ended abruptly on the edge of a cliff. She stood on that edge, over open air. She could feel the unstable dirt beneath her feet crumbling. The bird screamed again, this time much closer, but she didn't dare take her eyes from Brodrick to look up at the sky or behind her.

"Jump," he ordered, grinning at her, waving the gun. "If you don't jump, I'm going to take great pleasure in shooting you."

"It might be preferable," Tempest said grimly. Falling to her death didn't seem highly desirable.

Tempest, I can feel your fear. The voice was calm and steady, with no hint of haste or emotion. *Your heart beats far too fast. Look at what it is you fear, that I may also see what you have gotten yourself into.* Darius sounded far away, miles away, a disembodied voice.

She kept her eyes trained on Brodrick. *I'm certain he was partially responsible for the attempt on Desari's life a few months ago. He said as much.* She stared intently at the gun.

Brodrick pulled the trigger, the bullet striking inches from her foot, the ricochet zinging off a rock and flying into space. Tempest cried out, losing her precarious balance, her arms flailing to aid in regaining her footing.

She never saw the gun turning slowly but surely toward Matt Brodrick's temple, never saw his finger tightening on the trigger. She wasn't a witness to the beads of perspiration dotting his forehead or the horror in his eyes. Tempest never saw the weird battle with Brodrick's unseen opponent, the struggle for control of the weapon. In Darius's present state, with his great strength low in the daylight hours, he had to use tremendous mental powers to overcome the human's own strength. She heard the loud report of the gun as she fell over the cliff's edge.

Darius swore, deep within the ground. Tempest *would* get into trouble now, of all times. It was still too early to rise; he was weak and vulnerable, unable to go personally to her side. Few but the strongest, the most ancient of his kind, could give aid at such a time. Only his iron will, honed by centuries of enduring, and his terrible need of her allowed him to do battle with the human who threatened her. With the sun high, with the earth covering him, still his will prevailed.

Tempest's fingernails scraped frantically at the cliff's side, trying to secure a purchase that she might prevent herself from falling to her death. She slid, the crumbling dirt and rocks scoring her hands and breaking her fingernails as she fought the soil for anything she might hold onto. It was a tree root jutting out of the craggy rocks that broke her fall. It hit her squarely in the stomach, knocking the wind out of her. Still, she grabbed it with both hands, hanging on with all her strength while she wheezed and fought for air.

Even her slight weight made the root teeter precariously so that she cried out and wrapped her arms around it, her legs dangling helplessly in the air. Above her, she heard the rush of wind, wings beating strongly as the huge bird plummeted toward her, diving straight for her face. Tempest buried her eyes in the crook of her arm and remained as still as she was able, terrified she was near the large bird's nest.

She had never seen an eagle, but the bird was too large to be anything else. The eyes were beady and clear, the beak hooked and wicked looking. The wing span had to be close to six feet. Tempest was certain she must have fallen near its nest. "I'm sorry, I'm sorry," she repeated like a litany.

The bird had pulled up sharply and was once again circling, dropping lower as it did so. Tempest took a cautious look around. The fall was steep and long, several hundred feet. She would never survive. She glanced up, trying to determine whether she had a chance of climbing. At any moment she expected Brodrick to lean over the edge and take another shot at her.

Above her, the cliff was too steep, and she couldn't see a single indentation to try for with her fingertips. How long could she hold on? Darius would come for her, but not until nightfall. How many hours could she hang suspended there? And would the flimsy root hold? She could see the dirt falling away at the base of it, and the wood itself was rotten and dry. Her arms held the slender length in a death grip.

Tempest. The bird will make another pass for you. As it approaches, release the root. As always, Darius sounded tranquil; they could have been discussing the weather.

If I let go, I'll fall, Darius. She did her best not to sound hysterical, but if there was ever a moment when it was warranted, she figured this was it.

Trust me, honey, I will not allow you to die. The bird will carry you to safety.

It isn't strong enough. I weigh a hundred pounds.

I will aid it. Do as I say, Tempest. It is making its dive now.

She felt more than the mesmerizing, hypnotic persuasion of his voice; he was mentally pushing at her. She felt the need, the compulsion to obey him. He was implacable in his resolve. No one defied Darius.

Tempest heard the long, keening cry as the raptor plummeted toward her. She could feel her heart slamming with alarming force against her chest. Dangerous as it sounded, she was going to do what Darius had ordered. She couldn't stop herself. Already the need to obey was upon her, loosening her death grip on the root she never could have released if Darius hadn't commanded her to do so.

The bird raced at her, talons extended. With an inarticulate cry, Tempest let go. Instantly she was falling through space. The raptor was a terrifying sight as it came at her, its feathers blowing in the rush of air as it descended, its speed incredible. At the last moment Tempest closed her eyes. The sharp talons snagged her in midair, digging through clothing into soft skin, puncturing painfully. Then they dropped together, the bird's enormous wings flapping hard to keep them aloft, to compensate for the extra weight of its burden. Her shoes swung and nearly choked her, and she had to clutch at them to keep from being strangled by the laces.

Pain burned through her, her neck, her ribs on fire. Drops of blood traced down her sides to her hips. The eagle gripped her harder with its claws as it fought to bring her to safety. It was unable, even with Darius's help, to lift her above the cliff, so it made its way to the nearest outcropping, dropping her onto the ground. But its talons were caught in her ribs, its wings flapping strongly in an effort to break free. Tempest tried to help, extracting the piercing claws digging into her muscles. Then she collapsed into a heap on a pile of pine needles and dirt and rocks as the large bird rose high and soared away.

Tempest pressed her hand to her side, and her palm came away stained with blood. She coughed several times to relieve the pressure on her throat. Still, there was no doubt in her mind that this was a better fate than being shot or falling to her death on the rocks below. She struggled to a sitting position and tried to assess the damage done to her body and where she might be. Despite what she told Darius, she had a terrible sense of direction.

I know. Stay where you are.

Tempest blinked, unsure whether she had really heard his voice or whether she merely wanted to hear it. He was so far away from her. She tried to rise, focusing on the sound of water. Where was Matt Brodrick? As weak as she was, she couldn't afford to run into him, but she needed to get to the water.

Wait for me, Tempest. The voice was stronger this time, an order if she'd ever heard one.

She supposed he had the right to sound imperious when he was always having to save her, but it grated just the same. Tempest staggered toward the stream, ignoring her screaming muscles, the sound of the bird calling to Darius, and the fear that Brodrick might come dashing at her at any moment. The only thing that mattered to her was reaching the water.

The stream was icy cold, and she lay down in it, full length, wanting the water to soothe the burning slashes in her skin, to numb her enough that she could think again. She stared up at the blue sky and saw only the agitated bird. She sat up slowly and pulled herself to the streambank. The wind combined with the icy water began to seep inside her, and she started to shake.

You should have stayed within the perimeters I set for you, Darius said quietly, with only the slightest edge to his voice.

Shut up about your stupid perimeters, she snapped. Even though she'd expected it, she couldn't bear to be lectured over some idiot reporter who thought he was on to a nest of vampires. The hell with that. "What are you saying?" she asked herself aloud. "There *is* a nest of vampires. Or maybe it's called a coven of Carpathians. No, covens are for witches. But whatever it is, it isn't my fault that some nut wants to shoot everyone."

Her neck and side were throbbing. So were the soles of her feet. She examined one, winced, and put them back in the water. *It isn't safe around you, Darius. Things just happen. Bizarre things.*

It is very safe around me, but you do not know your limits, and you seem to have a problem listening to reason. If you had stayed where you were supposed to stay, none of this would have happened.

"Oh, go to hell," she muttered aloud, certain he couldn't possibly hear her. Did he have to be so blasted superior all the time? She hurt everywhere; the last thing she wanted to do was listen to an infuriating male. Not that she wasn't grateful for his help. She could tell by his voice, by the fact that he was so far away, that his intervention had been difficult. Still, that didn't give him the right to chastise her, did it?

I have the right because you belong to me and I can do no other than to see to your safety and happiness. The voice was calm and very masculine, holding a dark promise she didn't want to think about.

"You can do no other than shut up," she muttered resentfully. Clenching her teeth against the pain, she eased her shoes from around her neck. She didn't want Matt Brodrick sneaking up on the campsite and shooting Desari or Darius from some bush.

He cannot, Darius said soothingly. This time there was a hint of laughter in his voice at her rebellion.

Go to sleep or whatever it is you do, she snapped. *I'll make sure no one can hurt you.* She added the last just to set his teeth on edge.

She immediately received the impression of gleaming teeth, that predator's smile, his black eyes burning with the promise of retaliation. Tempest pulled her mind abruptly from his, mostly because he could intimidate her even from a distance, which was hardly fair. Wincing, she eased her sneakers on over her wet, damaged soles and gingerly stood.

She swayed, her every wrenched and punctured muscle protesting, from holding up her own weight. With a sigh, she followed the stream, hoping to find her way back to the campground. It wasn't easy going, the terrain rough in places as she moved steadily upward away from the stream bed. Twice she sat down to rest, but finally she reached the stand of trees where she had first spotted Brodrick.

Tempest looked around carefully, certain she was in the correct spot, but the man was nowhere in sight. A black feather floated from the sky, a slow swirling in the breeze that dragged her attention skyward. Several large birds circled above the trees, more gathering even as she watched. Her heart nearly stopped. Buzzards.

She sat down abruptly on a rock, her heart pounding loudly. *Darius?* Even in her own mind, her voice trembled, wavered, sounding forlorn and lost.

I am here, honey. He sounded strong and reassuring.

Is he dead? I don't want to find his body. You didn't kill him, did you? She was pleading with him, hoping he hadn't, but it suddenly occurred to her just why he had assured her Brodrick couldn't hurt them and why, earlier, she didn't need to go to the police and report Harry's attack on her. Why he had suggested neither assailant would bother anyone again. Had she always known? Had she simply pretended to herself that Darius was always sweet and gentle, if a bit too imperious? She had known all along he was a dangerous predator; he had said as much himself. And when he said she was under his protection, it meant something to him. Darius was not human. He had his own code he lived by. *Did you kill him, Darius?*

There was a short silence. *He died by his own hand, Tempest,* he finally replied.

She covered her face with her hands. Could Darius have somehow forced him to do such a thing? She didn't know. Just how powerful was he? He could shape-shift. Convince a raptor to rescue her from a cliff. What else could he do? And did she want to know? *You're very dangerous, aren't you?*

Not to you, honey. Never to you. Now go back to camp, and allow me to get my rest.

But his body. Someone has to call the police. We have to take his body to the authorities.

We cannot, Tempest. He is a member of a society of assassins. These so-called vampire hunters would come at the first word of his untimely death, and all of us will be in danger. Leave him for some hiker to find later, once we're gone. He has been unstable for some time, and they will rule it a suicide, as they should.

He did it himself? She sought reassurance.

Anyone who would come after me or mine is clearly suicidal, he answered enigmatically.

She wasn't going to touch that one. *And the other man who attacked me? Is he alive?*

Why would you think such a man should live, Tempest? He preys on women. He has done so for years. What does the world need with such a person?

Oh, God, she could not think about this. Why hadn't she considered the consequences of staying with a creature like Darius? *It is wrong to kill.*

It is the law of nature. I have never killed wantonly or indiscriminately. This is tiring, Tempest. I cannot sustain this communication for long. Return to camp, and we will continue this discussion when I rise.

She recognized an order when she heard it.

Chapter Eight

Tempest was gone. Beneath the earth, black eyes snapped open, burning with fury. The ground rolled slightly, an ominous rippling across the park's surface. Then Darius rose, bursting into the air, soil spewing like a geyser all around him. He felt the curious, disorienting wrench, then the overwhelming sense of loss, the black stain spreading across his soul.

His breath was coming in painful, hard gusts. Red flames flickered and danced in his eyes. There was a pounding at his temples, and deep within him, the beast roared and raged, demanding to be unleashed.

Darius tried to regain a semblance of self-control. Tempest didn't understand his world, the necessity of death. In her world, she clung to the belief that one who killed was bad. He battled with his own hard arrogance that she dared defy him, dared to leave him. Most of all he battled the beast within, strong now and demanding that he claim what was rightfully his.

Rise. All of you, rise and come to me now. He issued the order to his family, knowing they would obey.

They gathered around him, their faces serious. Only a few times over the centuries had Darius called them this way. Dark fury was etched into the harsh lines of his face. There was a cruel edge to the beauty of his mouth. "We will get her back. Before all else, she will return."

Desari glanced uneasily at her lifemate. "Perhaps we should not, Darius. If Rusti has run a second time, it is her wish not to stay with us. We cannot force her to our bidding. It is against our laws."

"I feel her desolation beating at me," Darius declared, his fury mounting. He was more dangerous at that moment than he had ever been. "She fears me, fears our life together. She is aware of what we are."

A collective gasp went up. The members of his family stared at one another. Barack broke the shocked silence. "True, she has seen some things unfamiliar to her, but it cannot be that she knows all, Darius."

Darius regarded them impatiently. "She has known since the first day. She is no threat to us."

"Any human who cannot be controlled is a threat to us," Barack said warily. He moved subtly to place his body in front of Syndil.

"Rusti is no threat," Syndil chastised softly. "You were eager enough to use her to feed, despite the fact that she traveled under our protection."

"Aw, Syndil, do not start again," Barack pleaded. "You've just begun speaking to me again. Do not get all worked up once more."

Darius waved a hand impatiently, dismissing the argument. "I cannot survive without her. She must be found. Without her I am lost to the undead. She is all that matters in my world, and we must retrieve her."

"No," Desari gasped, unable to believe that her brother could be so close to turning.

It was Julian who shrugged casually. "Then we can do no other than return her to our family. She is young, Darius, and human. It is natural for her to fear what we are, to fear your strength and power. You are no easy man to deal with. You need patience."

The burning black eyes settled on Julian's face for a moment; then some of the tension eased from Darius's shoulders. "She is hurt and alone. She does not understand the need to merge her mind with mine. She fights herself continually. I am worried for her health." Darius sighed softly. "And she seems to have a penchant for getting herself into trouble whenever I leave her on her own."

"That, I fear, is a woman thing," Julian declared with a wry grin.

Desari thumped Julian's chest. "Where is she, Darius?"

Tempest sat huddled on the seat near the window, peering out with sightless eyes at the countryside flashing by. She had been lucky to flag down a bus once she made her way to main highway, even luckier that the driver had allowed her on board. But the farther the bus carried her from Darius, the heavier her heart had become. It was now like a leaden weight in her chest. Sorrow was pressing in on her. Grief. As if by her leaving him, Darius had died. Intellectually she knew it wasn't so, but in her resolve to get away, she firmly forced herself to stay away from the path to his mind. And that left her feeling unutterably alone and lonely.

She could hear small snatches of conversation flowing

around her. A man, two rows back, was snoring loudly. Several young people were laughing together, exchanging travel stories. At least four military men were on the bus, returning to their homes on leave. Everything seemed to flow around her as if she wasn't there, as if *she* were no longer alive.

Tempest knew blood was seeping from the puncture wounds on her rib cage and most likely from the scrapes down her back. Someone was bound to notice if it didn't stop soon. She tried to concoct a plausible story, but she couldn't keep her mind on anything but Darius. It took every effort, every bit of concentration and control not to call out to him, not to reach for him when she needed him so desperately. Her shoes were squishing with her own blood. If anyone really looked at her, they'd probably turn her over to the authorities. She huddled down farther in the seat. She just wanted to disappear, become invisible. Even her clothes were damp from her plunge into the stream. She hadn't returned to the campsite, so she had no money, no tools, no plan. More than anything she wanted to feel Darius beside her.

The miles accumulating between her and Darius were putting more and more of a strain on her. She could feel tears burning behind her eyes. It was becoming difficult to breathe. Even her skin was sensitive, needing the feel of his. Tempest closed her eyes tightly against the pounding in her head, the constant strain of keeping her wayward mind from reaching out to his.

"Looks like we're running into a freak storm," the bus driver announced, peering through his windshield at the sky.

The weather was indeed changing rapidly. Rising directly in front of them was a huge cloud shaped like a dark, old-fashioned blacksmith's anvil. Almost instantly the bus hit a sheet of driving rain, so thick and hard, it was nearly impossible to see. Swearing, the driver slowed the vehicle significantly. The rain turned an ominous white. The driver ducked instinctively as hail pounded the roof and windshield. The sound was alarming, like the chatter of a machine gun.

The hail soon took the driver's visibility to zero, and he slowed even more, trying to reach the side of the road. The only warning the passengers had was the hair on their necks standing on end before the flash of lightning struck directly in front of the bus. Thunder crashed, shaking the mammoth bus, rattling the windows. There was silence for perhaps ten seconds, then several girls screamed and a child began to cry. Just as abruptly as the hail had started, it stopped.

The driver peered out, trying to see as he parked the bus, hoping he was safely off the road. Lightning arced from cloud to cloud, and thunder crashed again. Staring out the windshield, he found himself ducking as a huge owl flew straight out of the driving sheets of rain.

"What the hell?" he demanded, even as the creature veered away at the last possible moment. Thinking he was safe, the driver leaned forward to check visibility. Instantly a second bird, than a third, flew directly at the windshield. The birds were huge and vicious-looking. He yelled and covered his face with his arms.

There was another eerie silence, broken only by the rain. Then the driver found himself reaching to open the door. He swore he saw a huge jungle cat flash by in the rain, striking terror into his already pounding heart, but even so, his hand continued to open the door. He couldn't stop himself, no matter how hard he tried. His hand was shaking as he gripped the release. Outside he could hear the beating of wings, strong and ominous. He could hear whispers, insidious whispers, urging him to open the door. Yet he sensed that when he did, he would be letting in the devil himself.

A man's solid frame filled the entrance. He was tall, muscular, his face in the shadows. As hard as he tried, the driver could not see his features. He had only the impression of enormous strength and great power. The dark stranger wore a long, swirling black trench coat that added to his mystery. Only his eyes, burning with fire and suppressed rage, gleamed like a predator's stare from the shadowed face. The man ignored the driver and turned his black, merciless gaze on the passengers.

This time the silence was complete. The wind and rain ceased, as if nature itself was holding its breath. Tempest peeked out at the imposing figure through her fingers. Despite his Old-World elegance, he gave every impression of being a modern-day mobster. No one on the bus would dare defy that impressive figure of sheer power. She huddled down, making herself into a small ball, even though her traitorous heart was rejoicing and her treacherous body instantly went up in flames at the sight of him. He was so incredibly sexy. Tempest wished she didn't think so, but there it was.

The burning black eyes settled unerringly on her face. "We can do this either of two ways, honey. You can come out, quietly, on your own two feet, or I can throw you, kicking and screaming, over my shoulder and carry you out." His voice was low, a purr of menace, a blend of iron and black velvet. Sorcery. Dark persuasion.

Every head in the bus swung toward her. All eyes were on her, all ears waiting for her answer. Tempest sat for a moment in silence before moving. She wanted to pretend she might resist him, but the truth was, she wanted to be with him. She was only gathering her strength.

Heaving an exaggerated sigh, just to show him he was annoying her, she made her way down the narrow aisle to the front of the bus, trying not to wince with every step as the cuts on the soles of her feet burned.

As Tempest neared the bus driver, the man stirred. She looked very small and fragile to him, her clothes torn and smeared with blood. "Are you sure you'll be all right, miss?" He carefully avoided looking at the man towering over her.

The black eyes suddenly left Tempest's face and bored into the driver. Ice cold, graveyard eyes. Tempest pushed at Darius's broad chest, backing him up, away from the driver. "I'll be fine," she assured the man. "Thanks for asking."

Darius dragged her beneath the protection of his shoulder, his arm circling her slender waist. She looked as if she would fall down if he allowed her to stand on her own for too long.

The driver watched them descend the two steps. Behind them the doors snapped closed. Sheets of rain slammed down from the sky, obscuring his vision. Blinking hard, he peered out the windshield, but he couldn't see anyone. The mysterious gangster and the woman were gone as if they had never been. There wasn't so much as a car around.

Without a word, Darius scooped Tempest into his arms and covered the distance to his waiting family using his preternatural speed, blurring their images as he did so. Tempest lay against the solid wall of his chest, cradled in his arms, peeking out at the group suddenly crowding close around her.

"Are you all right?" Desari asked gently.

"She is fine," Darius answered before Tempest could

speak. "We will join you on the next rising."

"We haven't many more days before our next concert," Dayan reminded. "We will need you there."

The black eyes flamed. "Have I ever failed to be where I was needed?" It was a clear reprimand.

Tempest curled her fingers in the lapels of Darius's overcoat. "You're angry with me, Darius, not with them." She whispered the words, forgetting they all had his incredible hearing.

Do not say anything more, Tempest. I am more than angry with you. I am furious.

"That's a big surprise," Tempest muttered resentfully under her breath.

You are not nearly as afraid as you should be right now, Darius rebuked her, his voice soft yet intimidating.

Tempest wasn't impressed by his posturing. Intuitively she knew he would never harm her. She probably really was the safest person on earth. She simply settled closer against him, her arms circling his neck trustingly. He might hold her captive, but she couldn't find it in herself to be afraid. Not of him. Maybe of his possession of her. Of his intentions, perhaps. But not of Darius as a man. He would never hurt her.

Do not be so sure I might not spank you for your childish defiance, he said severely, sounding tough. He swung around and carried her into the dark night.

"I hurt," she announced quietly against his throat.

"You think I do not feel your pain beating at me?" he demanded. "Worsened because I could not help you as I should have?"

"I'm not dead," she pointed out.

He swore eloquently, switching from English to an ancient tongue. "You came close, honey. Brodrick had every intention of killing you. Why do you insist on leaving the areas of safety I provide for you?"

"I told you," she said honestly, "I have trouble with authority figures."

"Get over it," Darius ordered firmly, meaning it this time. She was driving him to the brink of insanity. "Do you have any idea what it is like to wake when I am bound to the earth, feeling your fear, knowing my strength is at its lowest ebb and I am unable to aid you?"

He was striding across a field filled with flowers crushed by the barrage of hail. Rain poured over them. Above their heads, lightning flashed from cloud to cloud, and thunder roared ominously.

"You came to my aid," she reminded him staunchly.

"I had to use an animal that unintentionally hurt you in the process, though I thank God it was there to use. Why do you do these things?"

"It isn't as if I go out and look for things to happen, Darius," she objected. "I had no idea Brodrick was anywhere around." She glanced up at his set features, then touched a fingertip to the hard edge of his perfect mouth in an attempt to soothe him. She was catching a glimpse into his mind, into the red haze of fear and rage.

"This cannot continue, Tempest. It is dangerous, not only for the two of us but for all mortals and immortals alike. You cannot leave me. What made you do such a foolish thing?"

Was there a note of hurt mixed in with the beautiful if severe tone of his voice? She hadn't wanted to hurt him. "We're too different, Darius. I don't understand your world. I don't even know what you mean by being bound to the earth, and you never explain these matters to me. I don't know all you are capable of doing, whether, say, you can actually kill someone from a distance. All of it is . . . unnerving, to put it mildly."

Christine Feehan

Tempest shivered in his arms, drawing his attention to the driving rain. Darius inhaled deeply to center himself and to calm the fury of the storm he had used to regain her. At once the rain slackened to a light drizzle. Overhead the towering cloud began to break apart. The wind rose to help push the mist away.

"You are hurt, Tempest. Instead of waiting for me—and you knew I would come to you the instant I rose—you ran from me." He took a running leap in the air effortlessly, shape-shifting as he did so.

Tempest gasped and clutched at the leathery scales rippling over his body. She closed her eyes against the earth falling away from her, against the wind rushing around her. She felt safe and protected in his arms, as strange as those two appendages now appeared. It was amazing to her that he could do that—shape-shift, fly through the air, and expect her to accept it as an everyday occurrence.

Darius whisked them across the glittering sky, needing the feel of her close to him. He took her over a mountain and back toward high ground near a waterfall. It seemed as if they hovered there alone on top of the world. Below, the mist rose to meet them, vapors from the waterfall rising to encompass them, to surround them in a cloud.

As the huge dragon's clawed feet touched down, Darius was shape-shifting again. One moment Tempest was staring up at a wedge-shaped head bending toward her, recognizing only the familiar hunger burning in its black eyes. Then, as the head moved closer, the dragon became Darius, his perfect mouth hovering inches above hers. Her breath caught in her throat, and her heart slammed alarmingly.

"You can't," she breathed against his lips.

172

"I have to," he countered, meaning it. There was no other choice for him. He had to taste her, hold her, possess her totally. His fear had been so great that, on his rising, his mind and body could accept no other than completing the ritual, making her irrevocably his. It no longer mattered to him that it was against his law, against everything he believed in. He had to have her, have the right to keep her safe at all times.

His lips moved over hers, gently at first, a sweet coaxing that rapidly changed as he fastened his mouth to hers hungrily. Tempest felt flames rushing throughout her body. He had started a fire there was no way to quench. A fire that would consume them both. Yet Tempest didn't care. Her heart might pound with a mixture of fear and excitement, but nothing would change what would be. And she knew it would be. She would belong to Darius for all time. Once he possessed her, he would never let her go.

"I would never have let you go anyway, honey," he murmured against her throat. "Never." He was carrying her with his usual casual strength up the faint trail leading to the top of the falls.

"Are you planning to throw me over?" she asked, bemused by the intensity in the depths of his eyes, by the fire racing through their bodies.

"If I had any sense, I would," he replied gruffly.

There was a cavern behind the falls, and he carried her right through the mist and moisture to it. The cave was narrow, sloping downward into the mountain itself.

"Have I mentioned to you that I have a problem with small spaces?" she asked, trying not to put a stranglehold on his neck.

"Have I mentioned to you that I have a problem with anyone who disobeys me?" he countered, stopping in the narrow tunnel to find her mouth once again.

Perhaps he intended the hard kiss as a punishment, or a distraction, but the earth was already moving under their feet, the world tilting and spinning crazily the moment he touched his lips to hers. Hunger was a craving they fed one another. When he lifted his head, his dark eyes were blazing at her. "If I do not have you soon, baby, the world itself will go up in flames."

"It isn't my fault," Tempest absolved herself, touching a finger to her mouth in awe. "It's you. You're lethal, Darius."

He found he could smile then. In spite of the urgent, painful demands of his body and the fear she had put him through, even his anger that she had tried to leave him, she could make him smile. She could melt his heart. Here he was, the leader of his people, an ancient, one with enormous strength and tremendous knowledge, his word law, his commands obeyed without question. She was a small, fragile, human female, and he was putty in her hands.

The tunnel led deep within the bowels of the earth itself. It was warm and moist, the sound of water ever present. It seeped from the sides of the tunnel and trickled from the curved ceiling above their heads. Tempest inspected her surroundings warily, not liking the fact that they were in a volcanic range of mountains and it was decidedly warm. "Have you ever been here before?"

He heard the note of nervousness in her voice. "Of course I have, many times. We spend a great deal of our time below ground. The earth speaks to us of its secret places and shares its healing strength and great beauty with us."

"Did it happen to mention this was a volcano while it was whispering to you?" she asked, her green eyes searching the tunnel frantically for signs of running lava. She could smell sulfur.

"You have a mean mouth on you, woman," Darius observed, taking a fork to the right that led deeper into the mountain.

At once the faint light creeping in from the cave's entrance disappeared, plunging them into complete darkness. "I thought you liked my mouth," Tempest retorted, doing her best not to scream hysterically at being in this dark, sulfurous, underground hole. "In case you haven't noticed, Darius, it feels as if we're entering hell. Since I already have this faint notion that you could be the devil tempting me, this isn't the best choice of hotels." The humidity was thick, nearly choking her, and she felt as if she couldn't breathe. The inky black interior pressed down on her, suffocating her.

"It is your fear choking you," he said softly. "The air is perfectly breathable down here. The mountain is not crushing you. You fear what I will do once we are together." His thumb was feathering lightly over the pulse in her wrist, back and forth, a gentle stroke but eloquent.

Her green eyes were enormous in her pale face. "What *will* you do, Darius?" Her heart was pounding in the confined space, the rhythm frantic.

He bent his head to hers, his black eyes burning with possession, with intense hunger, with stark desire. "I will put your life and your happiness above my own. You have no need to fear for your life with me." His voice was black velvet, turning her heart over with tenderness.

Tempest tightened her hold around his neck, leaning more closely into him, uncertain whether from need or from fear. She was tying herself to a creature whose powers she had no real knowledge of. What precise code did he live by?

Darius's response was to swing down an even narrower tunnel and emerge at what appeared to be a solid dead end. She knew it was solid because she reached out and touched it with her palm. But Darius waved his hand, and the barrier simply parted. A single strangled sound escaped Tempest's throat. What couldn't he do? How could she tie herself to a creature who wielded so much power?

"It is easy, Tempest," he said softly, reading her mind, her doubts. "Like this, just like this." His mouth took hers again, hard and commanding, tempting and enticing, whirling her out of the dark cavern and into a world of colors and light. He took away her every sane thought until there was only him. Only Darius, with his blazing eyes and his perfect mouth and mesmerizing voice. His hard body and strong arms.

He lifted his head and once more waved a hand. At once hundreds of flames leapt, lighting candles around the huge underground chamber. "In these last centuries, we have all found our own retreats. This is one of mine. The candles are made from nature's most healing elements. The earth here is particularly welcoming to our kind."

Tempest stared around her at the beauty of the chamber. And it was beautiful, a room where the very walls were crafted of nature's art. Pools of water shimmered in the light from the candles. Crystals hung from the ceiling, and diamonds embedded in the walls glittered, reflecting the dancing flames.

Tempest began to struggle for air. Darius was too powerful, able to create and command forces she had no knowledge of. Terror took the place of dark sensuality.

Darius merely tightened his hold and gave her a small, gentle shake. "You still do not see, do you? Try to imagine what life is like with no feeling, Tempest. Nothing but raw, ugly hunger gnawing constantly. Hunger that can never be sated. Only the life in your prey's blood whispering to you of power. No color to brighten your life, everything in black or white or shades of gray. No textures or richness." His long fingers stroked her skin, lingering on the satin softness. "I have taken nothing in this life for myself. You are the light in my world of darkness. Richness when I had nothing. Joy where there was emptiness. I will not give you up because you cannot overcome your fear. Would you have us come together for the first time in a struggle, in violence? Trust me as your heart tells you you must."

In his arms her slight body was trembling uncontrollably. She buried her face in the hollow of his shoulder. "I'm sorry I'm such a coward, Darius. I don't want to be. Everything is so overwhelming. You are overwhelming. The intensity of your feelings is overwhelming. When I live alone, I know the rules, and I like it that way."

He was carrying her farther into the heart of the chamber toward the shimmering pools. "No, you do not, Tempest. I know your mind; I have traveled in it often. You want me."

"Sex isn't everything, Darius."

He set her gently on a flat, smooth rock near a steaming pool. "You want me, Tempest, and it has little to do with sex."

"You think," she muttered, while fire raced up her leg as he removed her shoes to inspect the soles of her feet. His fingers shackled her ankles, firm, strong, yet inevitably gentle. She felt that curious wrenching in the vicinity of her heart.

Darius was frowning as he examined the lacerations. "You should have taken better care, Tempest." His voice was dark and moody, his black eyes suddenly rising to meet her green ones.

Her tongue found her dry lower lip, and her pulse raced faster. With his hands so gentle on her, his gaze hungry and burning with stark desire, how did she know he was furious? Once the knowledge seeped into her, more pieces of the puzzle began to assemble themselves. The terrible fury of the storm had been his rage, volcanic rage seething just below the surface of what appeared to be perfect tranquility. She glimpsed it when her mind sought his, inadvertently touching without her intention or his consent.

Tempest drew in her breath. *She* had done this. Where nothing in his centuries of existence had managed to shake his utter calm, she had. "Darius." She whispered his name in the beauty of the cave, her voice aching with sorrow. "I never meant to hurt you."

At once his hands framed her face. "I know that. I am here now. I can heal these wounds. But do not neglect your health again, baby. I am not altogether certain my heart could take it." His hands dropped to the hem of her cotton top.

At the first brush of his fingers against the bare skin of her stomach, her breath caught in her throat, and her body went still. Darius pulled the shirt over her head with a single fluid motion, leaving her vulnerable and exposed. He barely gave her lacy bra a thought, using a razor-sharp fingernail to dispense with it. His attention was on the puncture wounds on her side, the scrapes on her back.

He swore. She knew that was what he was muttering although she didn't understand the language. And then he bent his head low, his thick mane of midnight-black hair brushing her ribs, sending darts of fire dancing over her skin. At the first touch of his tongue, she closed her eyes, unable to believe the exquisite beauty of the moment. She felt his lapping, velvet soft yet slightly rasping across her damaged skin, a mixture of soothing sensuality.

Even as he took time and great care to see to the wounds on her body, the clothes covering his skin became unbearable, confining his bursting muscles, drenching him in heat and sweat. He shed them easily, as he did everything else, with a single thought to ridding himself of the discomfort. His body moved against hers, hot and aggressive as he bent to his task. His hands caught at her hips, bending her back to get better access to the puncture on her rib.

His hair brushed the underside of her breast, and she jumped as if he had scorched her. At once he lifted his burning gaze to hers. She was swamped with his hunger, his need. It was there in his eyes.

He watched her throat move convulsively as she swallowed a tight knot of fear. Very gently, with infinite tenderness, his hand spanned her throat so that her pulse beat into the warmth of his palm. "Give yourself to me, Tempest," he whispered softly, his voice so beautiful that it entwined itself around her heart. "Tonight, come to me as my true mate. Be with me the way I hunger for it to be. Give me this gift I have lived lifetimes without."

His mouth was only inches from hers, and every cell in her body cried out for her to close that tiny gap. How could she deny him anything when his need was so great? She moved until her lips were against his. "I want whatever you want, Darius." Even as the consent entered her mind, formed the words, breathed them into his being, her heart jumped, wondering what she had committed herself to doing. Did she really trust him so much? Or was his need feeding her own, the urgent hunger beating at him in waves, swamping her as he touched his mind to hers?

His kiss was gentle, tender, a reverent exploration that only added to her great need of him. "I want the water to heal you, honey," he said softly. "I want nothing but pleasure for you this night." His hands found the buttons to her jeans. His gaze held hers as he slowly dragged the material over her hips, taking her white lace panties with them.

Then he lifted her into his arms. "The water is hot, baby, but it will aid in the healing I do." He was holding her over the steaming water. "I think it is time you realized I will not be defied any longer. You are under my protection, Tempest. Every time I sleep, you get into trouble. I will not allow it to continue."

His arrogance set her teeth on edge, but at the moment she was more concerned with just how hot the water really was. He was lowering her feet close to the surface. It smelled like sulfur. Tempest clutched at his bare shoulder, her nails digging into his flesh. "You know, Darius, I have a major aversion to mineral water." His body was powerful and masculine, the heated thickness of him pressed aggressively against her bare skin as he lowered her toward the waiting pool.

"I think you need to trust me more, Tempest." Darius dipped her feet into the water. She gasped at the stingings, her fingers curling around his biceps, holding on to him for safety. The problem was, she had to lift her legs around him to keep from touching the water. Instantly it brought her hot core of femininity, liquid with need, to press fully against his thick, fierce arousal.

Darius groaned aloud, every sane thought, every good intention, flying out of his head. In its place was a need so strong and urgent that he fastened his mouth fiercely to hers. In primitive, stormy, almost violent possession. His mouth fed on hers. He swept her away from the crushing mountain, from the pain of her wounds, and from the steaming water. She could feel his hands sliding possessively over her skin, slow and deliberate, as if he were committing every curve and hollow to memory. She could feel the soft earth pressing into her as he trapped her beneath him, his body, so large and strong, blanketing hers. His mouth never stopped its series of long, drugging kisses that seemed to steal her will and arouse him beyond all human boundaries of need.

Tempest found her hands clutching his wild mane of hair, hanging on for dear life as the firestorm raged around them, through them. His hands cupped her full breasts, slid along her ribs to her belly, found the triangle of curls below, and caressed her thighs. Everywhere he touched he left flames behind, on her skin, inside her body, until she wanted to scream for relief.

She thought to be afraid of his enormous strength, but that thought, too, was swept away on a tidal wave of passion as his palm pressed into her heat. She made a single sound, a low moan in her throat that ignited the fuse smoldering in him. Darius's mouth left hers for the first time, trailing fire down her neck to the thrusting tip of her breast.

She cried out, arching into him, nearly exploding as his fingers found her tight, hot sheath and his mouth pulled strongly, his teeth scraping and teasing the swell of her breast. His knee nudged hers apart even as his tongue lapped at the valley between her breasts. He was above her, his face harsh yet sensual, his eyes black, burning coals.

It was happening too fast. Way out of control. Tempest felt him, thick and aggressive, pressing into her. He

181

seemed far too large for her to accommodate. Trapped beneath his body, she couldn't move, almost couldn't breathe. His teeth scraped the swell of her left breast, an erotic enticement that set her arching toward his mouth. Yet fear beat at her as he surged forward, his body pinning hers, invading hers, taking possession as if he had every right to her. She felt as if he was invading her soul, thrusting so deeply within her that she would never get him out. Instantly she stiffened, whimpering into his shoulder. She felt his teeth piercing her breast, spreading white-hot heat, sinking possessively into her skin as his body buried itself in hers.

His mind pushed into hers, breaking through every barrier until they were completely one. She felt the heat of her own skin, the exquisite ecstasy of her tight, hot, velvet sheath gripping him, releasing, sliding over him, her blood, hot with life and light, flowing into him, the joy and searing flames, his insatiable hunger and terrible need. She saw the erotic images in his head, the things he would do to her, the things he wanted her to do to him. She saw his iron will, his implacable resolve, his ruthlessness, his merciless, predatory nature. He saw her fears, her modesty, her blind faith in him, her need to run away. He felt the slight discomfort of her body at his thickness and instantly changed his position to accommodate her. He fed her own passion with his, building the fire between them until it raged out of control.

Darius was everywhere she was. In her body, in her mind, in her heart and soul. They shared the same blood. And, God help her, she could deny him nothing. Not when he was rising above her, surging hotly into her, his body slick with sweat, his mouth in a frenzy of hunger and need. It was the most erotic thing she had ever encountered. Tempest didn't care if she ever returned to herself. She was flying, soaring, sating his terrible hunger for the first time in all his centuries of living.

The sense of power that gave her was incredible. She was in his mind, knew she was giving him sweet agony, molten fire. Knew it raged in him as it did in her. She surrendered to him completely, holding nothing back, her fingernails in his back, her soft cries, pleas for more, in his ear. She wanted this with him, wanted to give him this exquisite torment.

Her eyelashes fluttered, and she cradled his head, her body moving with his, faster and harder until she was rippling with pleasure, exploding, fragmenting until he caught her safely in his arms. He lapped his tongue over the pinpricks in her skin, closing the tiny wound his fangs had left. His body clenched and raged for release, burning with a terrible need only she could fill. He was in her mind, and he took control, commanding her to do as he bid, not allowing her to think or know what he was asking.

At the first touch of her mouth on his chest, his body shuddered with the effort for self-control. It had to be. She had to complete the ritual, deliver herself into his keeping for all time. Her tongue tasted his skin, the touch so erotic, his hands pinned her hips that he might bury himself ever deeper, even harder than before. Her teeth teased, scraped, and he heard his own hoarse cry. A thousand years of need. This one time had to be his.

Darius lengthened a fingernail to slash his chest, then caught the back of her head and pressed her to him. Her mouth moved as he had commanded; her hot sheath, slick and velvet soft, tightened in demand, squeezing and kneading until his body clenched and thrust helplessly, mindlessly, aggressively into hers, spilling his seed deep within her, claiming her for all time.

He spoke the ritual words. He needed to say them aloud. Needed to seal her to him, make them one. His need to chant the words was as urgent as the taking of her body had been. It was every bit as primitive and instinctive as the hunger to take her life force into his body and give her his in exchange. "I claim you as my lifemate. I belong to you. I offer my life for you. I give to you my protection, my allegiance, my heart, my soul, and my body. I take into my keeping the same that is yours. Your life, happiness, and welfare will be cherished and placed above my own for all time. You are my lifemate, bound to me for all eternity and always in my care." He murmured the words above her head as he cradled her to him, as his powerful, ancient blood flowed into her body, as his seed exploded into her. The power of the ancient words surrounded her, seeped into her to seal her soul, her mind, and her heart to his, to bind her to him irrevocably.

Chapter Nine

Tempest opened her eyes slowly, drowsily, sexily. Darius smiled down at her, touched his finger gently to her swollen lips, caught a ruby drop of his blood on the pad of his finger, and brought it to his own mouth. She blinked to bring him into focus. Her body was locked with his; she could feel him, thick and heavy, buried deep within the tightness of her core. His smile was lazy and sated, his black eyes holding masculine satisfaction that he had done so much more than simply please her. He looked as if he might start purring over his own prowess.

Tempest found her smile hovering too close to the surface. He was moving with slow, languid strokes that kept heat scorching her body, kept her nipples pressing into the muscles of his chest. The flickering lights from hundreds of candles illuminated the fine sheen of sweat on his skin. His long hair was damp, falling around his face, lending him the look of a pirate. She reached up and gently traced the hard line of his jaw.

Darius captured her hand, brought it to his mouth to kiss, then laced his fingers through hers. He stretched her arms above her head and held them there, leaving her body open and vulnerable to his continuing invasion. She was no longer afraid of him. He had been wild and insatiable, even rough at times, but he had ensured her pleasure before his own. She could read the satisfaction in his eyes, the light in his soul, and she was thankful to be able to bring him relief from his endless, barren existence.

Darius savored the hot, slick wetness of her, the perfection of her satin skin, the silken mane of her hair. The wildness inherent in his nature ran as deep in her. Her passion matched his. She was made for him, and in his deepest heart, his very soul, he knew it absolutely. He bent his head to place a kiss in the tempting hollow of her shoulder. It was unbelievable to him that he was here with her like this, that it was not some dream his mind had created to appease his dying soul.

Where he had been wild and aggressive before, he was slow and gentle now, moving with long, sultry strokes, his gaze locked with hers so he could see the pleasure he brought to her on her expressive face. Her eyes clouded with passion; her lips parted as her breath came in little gasps of wonder. She was so beautiful, she destroyed his tranquillity, that absolute calm he had long ago acquired, and she made him as helpless and out of control as a youth. He wanted her for all time. Not the short span of years they would have, but for an eternity. He wanted it all.

Darius closed his mind to that possibility, that temptation, and bent to take her mouth with his, his tongue dueling with hers, sweeping over her teeth, exploring the moist interior, demanding that she do the same to him. He thrilled to the tiniest details. The brightness of her hair, the length of her eyelashes, the curve of her cheek—all an abundance of riches along with the feel of her body surrounding his. Hot velvet gripping him, teasing him.

He felt her tighten around him, her muscles rippling with the intensity of her pleasure, and he allowed the sensations in her mind and body to become his own. He felt the deep ripples begin like an earthquake, building and building until her shattering release. She was making little sounds in her throat, her arms taut as she writhed beneath him, trying to break free from his grip, but he held her and watched and experienced the strength and power of his body joined with hers, the tidal wave ripping through her, fragmenting her mind as the rush came. Only then, still holding her mind firmly with his, did he allow himself to rebuild his own conflagration, so that she could feel the pleasure she gave him.

His body surged more strongly into hers, each stroke harder and longer, going deeper until they were fully one being. He wanted her to know what she did for him, the beauty of her priceless gift. The rush took over, consumed his mind, consumed his body, until every muscle was bursting with need. Still he held her gaze so that she could see the tension on his face, the wildness in his eyes, the hunger and rapture, the sweet agony and ecstasy her body brought to his. He erupted into her, over and over, a volcano of molten seed, of burning fire, and the terrible darkness that haunted his soul. She was dragging him back to the light, and he felt the purity of it as his cries of joy echoed hoarsely throughout the cavern.

Christine Feehan

Tempest's legs held him tightly, nearly as possessive as he. Their hearts were beating in the same wild rhythm, their labored breaths matching. He finally released her wrists and lay his head on her breast, even as his elbows held his weight from crushing her. She could feel his tongue lapping at the small beads of sweat on her breasts, and each feathery stroke sent an aftershock rippling through her. She brought her hands down to tangle in the disheveled mane of his hair, to just hold him. They lay like that, their silence speaking more than any words could have.

Darius took their combined scents into his body, the feel of her hot skin, her breast beneath his cheek, the silken strands of her hair against his sensitized skin. Every sensation seemed heightened, seemed to echo through his body and linger there. The taste of her, rich and filled with life, was in his mouth and heart, and for the first time he could ever remember, his terrible craving for hot blood was momentarily sated. He would never again be tempted to make a kill to feel a rush of power, as one so close to turning often was, when he held the ultimate satisfaction in his arms.

He stirred then, a slight frown touching his mouth. "I did not heal you properly."

Instantly he was off her, leaving her feeling somewhat bereft. She also felt lazy and drowsy, the stifling heat of the cavern and his uninhibited lovemaking wearing her out. "I don't care. I want to sleep. You can heal me later." Her wounds no longer hurt, when earlier they had been burning and throbbing. He had successfully introduced her body to other, much more enjoyable sensations.

Darius ignored her sleepy command and lifted her easily into his arms. "I was more than selfish. I should have attended to your discomfort first, before my own."

Tempest laughed softly at his serious expression. Her fingertip smoothed the hard edge of his mouth in a gentle caress. "Is that what you felt? Discomfort? Hmm. Perhaps I should make you feel that way more often."

He growled—a warning or assent, she wasn't certain which—but she laughed at him anyway. "If I felt any more for you, baby, I would go up in flames," he admitted and padded on bare feet to the steaming pool.

She caught at his neck, scowling at him. "I really don't like being immersed in boiling water, Darius."

"It is not boiling. It is the same temperature as a hot tub," he chided.

She had a death grip on his neck. "It looks boiling to me. I don't want to go in. And anyway, I never go near hot tubs. Everyone always wants to get naked, and I don't know anybody that well."

"We are not wearing clothes now," he pointed out, wading into the steaming pool. He was trying not to laugh as she scrambled higher into his arms.

"It's too hot. How can you breathe in here? You know, Darius," she added seriously, "this is an honest-to-God volcano. Lava could fill up this chamber at any time." She peered into the depths of the pool. "It's probably bubbling up through the ground right now. See those bubbles? Lava."

"What a baby. Put your feet in the water," he instructed, amusement climbing from his voice to his eyes.

Her eyes began to throw off sparks, her temper showing. "I don't want to go in, Darius."

"Too bad, baby. It is good for you." Ruthlessly he lowered her feet into the steaming water.

Tempest tried to jerk her toes away from the hot mineral water, but he lowered her even farther, so that her

Christine Feehan

calves, then her thighs, were immersed. She gasped. "It's hot, you ape! Let me out!" But the water was already doing its job, soothing the lacerations on her feet, loosening cramped muscles, though she wasn't going to give him the satisfaction of telling him so.

His gaze was on the beads of perspiration running between her breasts to her stomach and disappearing beneath the surface of the water. He lowered her until her feet touched bottom and the water reached her waist, so that his hands could find her hips and hold her still for his inspection. He bent his head to the underside of one satiny breast and caught a droplet in his mouth. "Do you have to be so damned beautiful?" he murmured softly.

Her fingers tangled in his hair and dragged his head to her breast so that she could arch into the moist heat of his mouth. The water lapped at her skin. Bubbles burst all around her. Steam rose. "Do you have to be so damned sexy?" she countered, wanting the feel of his mouth feeding erotically on her.

Darius's hands skimmed over her hips in a light, possessive caress. He wanted to know he could touch her this way, that she was his. He wanted her to touch him. For the first time in all his centuries of existence, he was truly alive. Her soft skin, so like satin, brushed against his body. Her hair, so like silk, feathered over his shoulder, sending heat waves coursing through him.

His mouth wandered lower to find the places where the bird's talons had pierced her skin. He winced, remembering the feeling of lying beneath the earth, helpless, while she struggled for her life. "You scared the hell out of me," he told her softly, his tongue bathing the puncture wounds.

Tempest pressed herself closer to his soothing ministrations. "You have a curative agent in your saliva, don't

190

you?" she asked, suddenly comprehending. He had to. That was how he closed the pinpricks his fangs made in her neck, never leaving evidence behind unless he wanted to brand her. It was how her bruises had healed so fast. Darius. So tender and gentle, carefully healing each laceration, every bruise. "And you must have an anticoagulant in your teeth." It was a guess, but a fairly safe one.

He lifted his head, his dark eyes moody and unreadable. "I can heal you completely, but you must stay very still and accept what I do."

She nodded solemnly. He was so beautiful, in a purely masculine way. She loved the hard bones of his face, the deepness and purity of his voice, the rippling of power beneath his skin. His beautiful face now showed intense concentration. He had withdrawn into himself. Tempest found the way his hips indented fascinating. He was so physically perfect. Her hands, of their own volition, reached out to touch those smooth indentations.

The feel of his skin beneath her fingers sent flames dancing in her stomach. She explored farther, the palms of her hands sliding over his muscular buttocks. A sound escaped his throat, a soft warning growl, and his hands shackled her wrists, holding her palms against him. "Just what are you doing?"

Her large green eyes stared innocently up into his fathomless black ones. "Touching you." Her palms pressed closer. "I like touching you."

"I cannot possibly concentrate if you continue, Tempest." He meant to reprimand her, but one of her hands had slipped free to explore the hard columns of his thighs. His breath caught in his throat. Her fingers felt so good on his skin, an erotic fantasy began to take over his mind. His sexual needs were far greater than hers.

Christine Feehan

He was a Carpathian male with a need as elemental as time to take his mate. He had promised himself he would remember that she was human and give her as much space as his nature would permit, but she wasn't helping him at the moment.

His body hardened with a savage, aching rush of fire that added to the heat of the cavern and the pool. Her hand brushed against him beneath the water, slid the length of him, settled around him like a glove. He pushed against her, craving the feel of her surrounding him. "This will not help my concentration," he managed to point out.

"Really? And I thought you were so good at blocking out all sorts of things, Darius," she teased, exploring him more fully, more boldly.

He bent his head to the hollow of her shoulder, his teeth scraping roughly. Beneath the steaming water, his hand slid to the junction between her thighs. Tempest accommodated him, pushing against his palm. His fingers slid into her, urging her to climb with him. "I want you to need me the way I need you," he whispered against her throat.

"How is that?" she asked through clenched teeth. In her hand he was growing even harder and thicker, velvet over iron. His fingers were driving her insane, taking her closer and closer to the edge of a cliff. The water swirled around them, fizzed and bubbled against their skin.

Darius lifted her into his arms, the hot water sluicing off her and onto him nearly unbearable in his sensitive state. "Put your legs around my waist, Tempest," he ordered huskily, barely managing to get the words out. His body screamed for hers. She complied, and slowly he lowered her over his waiting shaft. At her hot, moist entrance, he paused, watching the expression on her face. He seemed large and intimidating to her, but her sheath was tight and velvet soft, gripping and enfolding him. The ecstasy of it tightening around him, slowly accepting his invasion, was almost more than he could bear.

The heat in the cavern made it nearly impossible for Tempest to breathe. Or maybe it was the way Darius lowered her with such excruciating slowness over him. She laid her forehead against his chest, gasping as his body invaded hers, ever deeper, the steam surrounding them like smoke from the fire their bodies were creating.

His fingers dug into her waist as she settled around him, taking him fully into her. She moved then. It was she, not he, who moved. She could feel the pleasure in his mind, in hers, so intense that it was close to pain. She rode him slowly, the beauty of the moment forever etched in her mind. The beauty of his face as she engulfed him, retreated, returned. It was erotic just to watch the pleasure she brought him. She knew precisely what to do to enhance that pleasure from his mind merged with hers. She snagged the images in his mind and made some slight adjustments, arching her back so that her breasts slid over his damp skin, letting her hair tumble over his shoulders, sensations he found unbearably sensual. Deliberately she prolonged the moment of release, moving slowly, then faster, slowly, then fast, her muscles clenching around him, reluctantly releasing him, then capturing him once more.

Even as she felt him swell within her, heard him fighting for breath, his heart pounding against hers, she felt her own body begin the climb toward the stars. She couldn't concentrate on his release when she felt herself start to fragment. At once Darius took control, his hands digging into her hips, thrusting into her with sure, hard strokes, pushing her higher and higher so that he was taking her with him. They soared together, breaking free, their cries filling the cavern. Steam wrapped them together as one body, one mind, one skin.

At the end Tempest was totally exhausted. She closed her eyes and rested her head on his shoulder. "I can't move, Darius. Don't ask me to move ever again."

"I will not, baby," he murmured tenderly, lifting the wet hair from her shoulder to place a kiss on her bare skin. He carried her from the hot water to the next pool, which was several degrees cooler, its source outside the mountain rather than within. He sank into the water, taking her with him.

She felt instant relief and released her grip on Darius's neck, lazily floating away from him. If she kept her eyes closed, she could pretend she was out in the open, with the sky above her and trees nearby. The oppressive layers of soil and rock simply disappeared from her mind. But she couldn't keep her eyes closed forever. She tried to concentrate on how Darius made her feel, on the beauty of the cavern, on the glittering diamonds the volcano had produced over the long centuries.

"What is it?" he asked softly.

"Being in this cave is making me feel like a bat. It's beautiful, Darius—don't get me wrong," she added hastily, not wanting to hurt his feelings, "but we're so far underground, and it's very humid."

Darius swam to her, his body rippling with power, his long hair wet and midnight black. "You will get used to it, honey."

She felt her heart jump. What did that mean? She didn't want to stay underground long enough to get used to it. Biting her lip she forced her mind away from the issue and swam a few strokes, taking pleasure in simply watching Darius swim, the fluid way his body moved. She yawned, her movements slow, exhaustion settling into her body. It was impossible to have any real sense of time underground.

"You have had a difficult day," Darius said as he surfaced quite close to her. His hands caught her waist and drew her against him. "I want you to rest while I perform the healing ritual on you."

"What is it?" She was wary, but her fatigue was making her more compliant to his demands.

Darius studied her face, the shadows beneath her eyes. She was drooping with weariness. He didn't ask for her consent; he merely lifted her into his arms and took her to a small alcove where the rich soil was soft and beckoning. He waved a hand so that a cotton sheet floated to cover the grounds, then laid her down with great care.

"You just made that sheet, didn't you?" she murmured, staring up at him.

He brushed back the wet hair from her forehead. "You would be surprised at the things I can do," he said softly.

"I don't think I would anymore," she countered.

"Do not distract me from my task this time, Tempest. I will free myself from this body, and my energy will go into yours. I can heal your wounds from the inside out. The healing process is much faster, and if any infection is present, I can rid your body of it. But I cannot be aware of my own body during this time. My focus must remain on what I am doing. Do you understand? I cannot reenter my body abruptly when I am really in yours. So do not distract me in any way."

She lay very still, watching his face. He was withdrawing from her—she could see that. Withdrawing from the world they were in, he turned his entire attention inward. She wanted to touch his mind with hers.

It was becoming easier for her to do, but she didn't want to take any chances on distracting him, the very thing he had said not to do.

Tempest felt him then. She felt his entry into her body, pure energy moving through her, like an inner light, examining her, warm and soothing. In her mind she heard a voice. Soft, comforting, it whispered like butterfly wings in her mind. The words were none that she knew. Still, she knew she had heard them before. A chant. She tried to distinguish individual sounds, but it was impossible. She received only impressions, like silvery bells, like water skipping over rocks in a brook, like a gentle breeze floating through the leaves of a tree.

Her skin was warm. Her insides were warm. The soles of her feet ceased to sting and actually felt good. Whatever Darius was doing was obviously working, and she wondered at how he was able to heal as he did. At that moment he seemed a perfect miracle to her.

Darius returned to his own body and gazed down at Tempest's beautiful face. She looked very young, and he felt like a criminal, knowing she had no way to fight him, no way to fight his claim on her. He had made certain of that. She had no idea what the ritual entailed, and perhaps the truth was, neither did he. But Darius felt the difference in himself, the difference the words he had uttered, binding them together, had caused.

He no longer had any choice in the matter. He had to be with her, near her. He knew they could not be comfortably apart for any length of time. Whatever those words had wrought, it was out of their hands now. They had to abide by the results.

Darius touched her face with a gentle fingertip. "Do you feel better, Tempest?" He knew she did. His mind was becoming accustomed to slipping in and out of hers, and he could feel the relief in her body. He had even soothed her feminine core, so that his wild, rather primitive taking of her would not make her sore.

She nodded solemnly. "It's incredible that you can do such a thing. Can you imagine what it would mean to the world if humans could learn to heal like that? Perhaps we really could cure cancer. Think of the good that could come of it. We wouldn't need drugs, Darius."

"It is not a human way of healing, Tempest."

"But you healed me, so it can be done on humans. Maybe you should become a doctor instead of a bodyguard. You could help so many suffering people."

She meant it. The compassion in her was overriding her good sense. Darius leaned over her, and his hand spanned her throat possessively. "I am not human, little love. If those people you want me to heal knew me as I am, they would drive a stake through my heart. You know it is so. I cannot have intimate dealings with humans. No close encounters. Desari entertains humans because she has the voice of an angel and can do no other. Ceasing to do so would make her unhappy, so I must protect her. But I do not deal closely with these people."

Her hand slid over his, and a small smile curved her soft mouth, melting a dimple into her right cheek. "I am human, Darius, and you deal quite well with me."

"You are different."

"No, I'm not," she protested. "I'm just like everyone else."

"You saw the beast in me first, Tempest. You relate to animals. You instinctively accepted my primitive nature. You know I am a predator, more animal than man. We Carpathian men are a combination of the two. You alone among humans understand and accept that."

"You think and reason like a human," she said, sitting up and pushing back her hair, which hung heavy in the humidity of the cavern. She was sweating again, little beads dotting her skin. She looked around for her clothes, so tired she couldn't remember what she'd done with them. "You're more like a human than you think, Darius."

Darius gathered her against him and cuddled her close. "You want me to be human because it is easier for you to deal with that thought." A note of censure tinged his voice.

Tempest pushed at the wall of his chest, then thumped him for good measure with her fist. "Don't give me that attitude. You know at this point I could care less if you're some weird creature from this underground chamber from hell. I know you know that. You've been in my mind the same way I've been in yours. You know what I think of you. I find you intriguing. And, actually, you're not half bad."

"You find me sexy," he corrected and kissed her nose.

She pushed him away and got to her feet, swaying a little with weariness. "Don't let it go to your head. I also find you a pain in the butt." She was wandering around the cave, seemingly inspecting the floor.

Darius got up with a sigh and followed her. "What are you doing?"

"Looking for my clothes."

"You do not need your clothes." He said it very decisively.

"Darius, if you make love to me one more time, I think I might just die. Since we can't have that, it's much safer to find my clothes."

He caught her hand and led her back to the little alcove. "You do not even know what you are saying or doing anymore." Another wave of his hand produced two pillows.

Tempest yawned. "I'm really tired, Darius. I love talking to you, but both of us need to face the facts. Even if you're not human, I am. I have no idea what time it is, but I need to sleep."

He smiled at her, a teasing flash of his teeth. "What do you think I've made up this bed for? This is one of my retreats. I sleep here."

"I gathered that. But you need to take me back."

"Back where?"

Something in his voice warned her. Her green eyes fixed on his face. There was a stillness in him she didn't like. She could hear her heart pounding. "I want to get out of here. You can sleep here, and I'll sleep in the campground, in whatever vehicle they left for us. I don't care. I can sleep under a tree."

"There is no chance, honey, that I will allow you to sleep apart from me." He said it casually, as if it wasn't a big deal to sleep with an entire mountain—a volcano, at that—crushing down on her. He reached out and shackled her wrist. Not hard. Lightly. A loose bracelet of fingers, no more, but it was a warning all the same.

"You can't mean for me to sleep here," Tempest protested, jerking away from him. "Stay under the earth all day while you sleep? I can't do it, Darius. Not even for you."

"You will sleep beside me where I know you are safe, Tempest," he said in his soft, implacable way.

She backed away from him, visibly pale. "I can't, Darius. When you're distracting me, I don't feel as if I'm suffocating, but I could never lie here in utter darkness and try to sleep. I can't see the way you can. If the candles melted down or a draft made them go out, I would go insane. I'd feel buried alive. I'm not like you. I'm human."

"I will not take you to the surface and leave you on your own. Each time I allow you freedom, something happens to you." Her fear was beating at him. He touched her mind, found desperation, panic. "You will not awaken, Tempest. You think I cannot ensure this? I can command the earth itself should I choose to do so. I can create storms, tidal waves, set lava boiling. Why would I be unable to see that you rest beside me undisturbed?"

The tip of her tongue touched her lower lip. Her eyes were wild with fear. "We need to meet up with the others, Darius. I can drive all day. You can sleep and meet me wherever the designated campsite is. I'll be there, I promise."

He rose slowly, his body relentlessly masculine. He moved with fluid grace, a predator's rippling power, toward her. She actually backed away from him, her hand going up between them for protection. Darius stopped immediately, his black gaze on that small, fragile hand. It was trembling.

He sighed softly. "I cannot allow this to continue, Tempest. I have attempted to allow you as much freedom as you need, but we have to have a balance between us. I cannot risk your life, yet when I ask your permission, give you explanations, your fear only grows. If I take command of you as I should, you would feel no fear, no risk. Do you see that you are giving me no choice?"

He moved then, his speed so blinding that he was on her before she blinked, before she was aware of the impending danger. She struck at him blindly, struggling against his superior strength, her mind in chaos. "How could you do this after what we shared?" she demanded, her voice so fearful that he felt his heart melting.

He detested frightening her, even though he knew it was for her own protection. Nothing would happen to her here. The mountain wouldn't crush her. She could breathe the air with no problem. Her frantic blows were no more to him than the batting of butterfly wings, yet each struck to his heart.

"You said you wouldn't hurt me," she continued even as he wrapped her in his strong arms and held her to comfort her. "You said you would always see to my happiness. You lied to me, Darius. The one thing I believed was that I could always trust you, trust your word to me."

Her words were like small blows to his soul. Did she believe that of him, that he would lie to get his way with her? He hated that she was afraid, but what other choice did he have? "I have not lied to you. It is my duty to see to your health, to see to your protection. I can do no other than ensure your safety."

"Darius, I don't care what you are, what kind of power you wield. I will fight you with my last breath for my freedom. You have no right to dictate to me, even in matters of safety. You don't. You can't 'allow' me to do anything. It's my free choice. I won't have it."

Darius regarded her passionate face calmly. He simply held her wrists pinned together, seemingly undisturbed by her outburst. "Be calm, honey, and breathe deeply. Your fear of being beneath the mountain is overcoming your reason."

"I won't stay here with you, Darius. I mean it. I'll go away, so far away you'll never find me," she threatened, her emerald eyes swimming with tears, sparkling like gems.

His face hardened perceptibly, his perfect mouth all

at once edged with cruelty. "That will never happen, Tempest. There is nowhere you can go that I cannot find you. I would come for you, and I would never stop until I retrieved you. You are the very air I breathe. You are my light. The colors in my world. There is no life without you. I will never go back to emptiness, to darkness. You and I are tied together, so we have no choice but to find a way to make this work. Am I making myself clear?"

"Perfectly clear. You intend to be a dictator, and you expect me to be a puppet. It isn't going to happen, Darius. I've been in your head; you're not the type of man to beat a woman because she defies him."

His free hand slid to the nape of her neck, a light, caressing touch that sent a responsive shiver down her spine and started a fire in her abdomen. It angered her that he could do that—with one touch send her body into flames even as he was denying her rights. She could not let him do this to her. She wasn't weak; she wasn't the type to give in simply because he made her knees weak.

"I do not have to beat a woman to make her do what is necessary for her own protection." He said it softly, his voice velvet soft, mesmerizing. "You are not my puppet, honey. I would never want you to be. Do you not realize that it is your courage I admire? But I cannot allow you to place yourself in danger." His arms slipped around her from behind, circled her slender body, and drew her tight against him. "The hour grows late, Tempest. I need to sleep. I want you to lie down beside me and sleep, too. Nothing will wake you. Nothing will harm you."

"I can't breathe down here," Tempest said desperately, wiping at the tears spilling onto her lashes and running down her face. "Darius, let me go. Please let me go."

He lifted her struggling body as if she were no more than a child and buried his face in her neck for a moment, savoring her scent, the feel of her skin. "There is no need to fear this place, honey. It is a place of healing." His voice dropped an octave, taking on a compelling, hypnotic rhythm. "You will sleep in my arms, sleep until I call your name and awaken you."

Darius lifted his head so that his black eyes could stare directly into her green ones, so that he could trap her gaze in his black ice. Mesmerizing. Relentless. She could not pull her gaze away no matter how strong her will. He felt her resistance and admired her for it, but he was unyielding. This he could not give her. He would have to face her on the next rising, but this day she would be safe.

Chapter Ten

"This is all we have." The photograph was tossed on the table. It was of a slender young redhead standing in a stream with her arms outstretched. She was laughing, her face turned up toward the sun, while hundreds of butterflies fluttered around her.

"Matthew Brodrick is dead. The police say there's no question but that it was a suicide. But I say differently. Matt was one of us. He knew what he was up against. He wouldn't have taken pictures of just anybody." Brady Grand drummed his fingers alongside the photograph, then tapped it twice. "This woman knows something. This stream is the same stream where Matt's body was found."

"Come on, Brady," Cullen Tucker protested. "Look at that picture. It's full sun. Broad daylight. No way is that woman a vampire."

Grand's cold eyes traveled around the circle of men.

"I didn't say she was, only that she knew something. For all I know, she was helping Matt. Find her, and we can get at the truth."

"The 'truth' is, we haven't gotten anywhere," Cullen snarled. "You say this band is a group of vampires. The only 'proof' you've offered so far is some obscure quotation based on the Persian word *Dara*, referring to the troupe's singer, Desari."

A low murmur of approval went around the room. Then the others shifted nervously. No one wanted to cross Brady Grand outright; he was just too mean. But they had lost six men in the first attempt against the band, excellent marksmen, and now they'd lost Matt Brodrick.

Brady looked around at the others. "Is that what you think? That I'm wrong about these creatures? What of the fact that we sent six military-trained assassins to kill supposedly defenseless civilians, and all our soldiers ended up dead, the creatures still alive and well? Tell me how that happened, Cullen. You tell me how some simple security guard singlehandedly destroyed all six of our men and their remains. They had a foolproof escape plan but disappeared. They sprayed the stage with bullets, yet the band members were relatively unhurt. Explain that, Cullen, because I don't see how it's possible."

"The band got lucky. Maybe their bodyguard is better than you think, paramilitary himself. What do you know about the big guy? Not too much gets by him. Is it possible the team went in with poor information? That maybe it was you who screwed up?"

Brady's fist clenched tightly until his knuckles turned white. A muscle twitched in his jaw. "I know for certain that the singer is a vampire. I know it, Cullen. The team knew, too, or they never would have gone in to make the hit. We wanted to bleed her as much as possible, weaken her, and take her alive. Our people have wanted a live specimen to study for years. But if the only thing we can get is a dead one, than so be it."

"All we've accomplished so far is to make the world think we're a bunch of crazy fanatics," Cullen objected. "I say we target someone else, someone not so damned popular. The cops love Desari. The merchants in every city she goes to love her. The audiences love her. If we kill her, they'll hunt us down like dogs."

"That's your trouble, Cullen—no sense of commitment. This is war. It's us against them. Do you believe they exist? With all the proof I've given you, do you really not believe?" Brady demanded. "After what you saw with your own eyes? Or was that just a tale to get you inside our group?"

"Hell, yes, I believe vampires exist," Cullen said. "But not this singer. She's just some woman with a beautiful voice and a bodyguard as lethal as anything I've ever seen. So she sleeps during the day. What do you expect? She works all night. So we can't find their campsites even when we track them all the time. They're very careful, very private. But no one ever dies. No kids are killed. They never leave a trail of drained carcasses behind. If they're vampires feeding off people, where are the bodies? Every vampire I've heard about kills. The reason we can't find these people when they camp is because their bodyguard is good. *That's* why there are no pictures, not because we can't get anybody on film. This guy does his job and does it well. Thus, no unauthorized pictures."

"And the leopards?" Brady demanded.

"Part of the show, the mystique. They're in show business, Brady. Everyone has some kind of gimmick. They like leopards. Big deal. Vampires like wolves and bats. Isn't that what we've been told?" Cullen drove his point home.

The man nearest Cullen cleared his throat. He was a little older than the others and generally very quiet. "It is possible Cullen is right in this case, Brady," he said softly. "There is no evidence that any in this group were ever in the Carpathian Mountains or even originate from that area."

"Wallace," Brady protested, "I know I'm right about this singer. I know I am."

The older man shook his head. "It doesn't add up. Vampires seem to have some sort of thing about their women. Possessing them completely. Yet this singer recently paired up with someone from the outside world."

"You prove my point," Brady said triumphantly. "She hooked up with Julian Savage. He is from the region long suspected of producing vampires. And he's been under suspicion for a long time. Suddenly he shows up, and he and the singer fall in love? It seems too big of a coincidence to me." Brady let that sink in, knowing he had made his point. Julian Savage was definitely high on the list of the society's suspects and had been for a very long time, though he had eluded their hunters at every turn.

There was a short silence. Everyone was looking to the older, soft-spoken man, William Wallace. He had been a member of the vampire-hunting society for more years than any of the others. He had lost family members to vampires. He had hunted them in Europe, and when he spoke, everyone, including Brady, did what he said.

"It is true," Wallace mused softly, "that wherever Julian Savage goes, death follows, yet he is never under suspicion by the police. He had a home in the French

Quarter in New Orleans, and several members of our society vanished there, never to be found. We could not prove he was in residence at the time—it appeared he had sold his family home—but even vampires can falsely generate the proper paperwork and credentials. He travels often from country to country, a very wealthy man," Wallace continued. "Now he travels around this country with a group of singers. It is indeed suspicious." He leaned over to look at the photograph. "You're certain this was taken at the same place where Brodrick died?"

Brady nodded. "I personally inspected the site. It's the same, all right. Matt took a series of photos of this woman."

"Have you ever seen her before?" Wallace asked.

Everyone shook his head. "Matt didn't have a girlfriend, either," a pimply-faced youngster volunteered. He was the most recent inductee to the society and wanted to be noticed, to prove himself. "So if he did recently meet a woman and take all these pictures in the area where the Troubudous were rumored to be camping, she would have to have some connection to the group."

"Do any of the other photos show her face up close?" Wallace asked.

"This is the best. She was staring straight toward the camera. I say we find this girl and get a few answers," Brady replied.

"Perhaps," Wallace said, "we should investigate a little further. If this girl knows something, it shouldn't be all that hard to get it out of her. Find her and bring her back here to our headquarters for interrogation."

Cullen Tucker looked uneasy. "Suppose she knows nothing at all? Maybe she's just some girl Matt found photogenic. If you bring her here and she sees all of us, finds out what we seek, we'll be exposed to the world."

Wallace shrugged casually. "Sometimes small sacrifices are necessary. Regretfully the young lady will be disposed of in order to protect our identities."

Cullen glanced around the room, studying the faces, looking for someone who would protest along with him. But the faces were blank, the faces of followers. Prudence dictated that he keep his mouth shut.

"Do you have a problem with that?" Brady growled, his cold eyes suddenly alive with a fever for blood.

Cullen shrugged. "No more than anyone else," he temporized. "I don't have to like it, Brady, just because it's necessary. I'll start looking for her at the band's next concert. It's in northern California. I'm sure they're heading that way now. She shouldn't be hard to spot, but just in case I'm wrong, send someone back to the park. Maybe she was a local or a camper. The park rangers might have seen her."

Brady Grand was silent a moment, quieting the urge to fight. He nodded. "Take Murray with you. It's safer if there's two of you." He indicated the youngster, knowing the kid was eager to do something violent, prove himself to the group.

"I always work alone—you know that," Cullen protested. "Two of us will only draw that bodyguard's attention. We can't count him out, you know. I'm willing to bet he's the one who took down our team."

"Maybe," Wallace mused, "but more likely it was Savage. He showed up right around that time. I hardly think Desari's bodyguard is a threat to us—unless, of course, he's one of them himself."

Cullen bit back his retort. What was the use? Brady Grand had become as fanatical as William Wallace in the last few years. They carried weapons constantly and trained a small army. They both seemed to think they were fighting a war. Cullen simply believed that if something as evil as a vampire existed, it should be exterminated. He believed it because he had been in San Francisco a few years back when a serial killer was on the loose. Except it was no serial killer. The creature had murdered Cullen's fiancée right in front of him, draining her blood and laughing while he did so. The police didn't believe him—no one did. Until Brady Grand found him. Now Cullen wasn't certain anymore whether the bloodthirsty Grand and Wallace were much different than the vampire.

Cullen glanced once more at the picture of the laughing redhead. She was beautiful, with joy and warmth in her smile, compassion in her face, a sweet innocence in her stance. Beyond her slender body and wealth of red hair, he saw someone worth something. He saw a woman with the same natural goodness his fiancée had possessed. He sighed and pocketed the photograph. It was amazing to him the others couldn't see the innocence in her face. She had nothing to do with vampires.

"I'll leave now," he said gruffly. "I'll be calling in to see if anyone picked up any leads, so have someone on the phones."

Brady regarded him strangely. His nod was slow, and his cold snake eyes followed Cullen as he went out the door. Cullen inhaled the fresh, crisp night air deeply, wanting to rid himself of the stench of fanaticism. He had followed the society members out of a need to avenge his fiancée's hideous death. Now that need didn't seem so great. He wanted to be free of anger and hatred and start his life over again.

The photograph seemed to be burning a hole in his pocket. The smart thing to do would be to disappear. Get out. Hide. But he knew Brady Grand. The man liked killing and thought that in the society he had found a legitimate outlet for his psychotic tendencies. Even the U.S. armed forces had kicked him out, discharging him for his repeated vicious attacks on new recruits and civilians. There had been two incidents noted on his record, two suspicious deaths no one could quite prove were murders. Cullen knew all about those; he'd had a friend access the military reports. Brady Grand was not the kind of enemy he wanted hounding him for the rest of his life.

Cullen's Jeep started easily, but the photograph continued to burn through his clothing to his skin. Suddenly he swore. He couldn't just leave the redhead hanging out there. He would have to find her and warn her. The singer, too. She might have the best bodyguard in the world, but if Brady Grand was persistent enough, sooner or later the society would get to her.

Pounding the steering wheel in sheer frustration, Cullen turned the vehicle north.

Far away, deep within the bowels of the earth, Darius held Tempest to him. Something was moving through his mind, a warning signal, one that had stood him in good stead these many centuries. It was strong enough to bring the beast roaring to life. In his mouth he felt the ominous lengthening of his fangs. He lifted his head, his ice-black gaze sweeping the interior of the chamber. Slowly he turned his head toward the south, toward danger. Something threatened Tempest, something coming from that direction. Nothing would harm this woman he held in his arms. Nothing, he vowed.

He glanced down at her face, so young-looking and vulnerable in her sleep. The light from the candles caressed her skin lovingly, throwing tempting shadows across her, inviting his touch. Darius felt the surge of need rushing through his body and allowed it to happen. It would take centuries to sate his appetite for her. Centuries. But he had chosen otherwise. Had chosen to keep her human and die with her when her time came. So he would have to be more careful in his possession of her; he could not afford to keep taking her blood during mating.

He was out of control when his body demanded hers, dangerous for both of them. But he wanted her. He would never stop wanting her. It felt savage and primitive, yet tender and gentle. But he was not a gentle man. The long centuries had seen to that, honing his ruthless side, his predatory nature. Yet he found that when he looked at her, he was different. Something inside him melted, went soft.

He knew from centuries of existing the exact moment when the sun above ground sank low, the night enfolding the earth above them. His time. His world. Darius stretched lazily and turned to run a hand possessively over Tempest's satin skin. He had not slept in the welcoming soil, nor had he slept the rejuvenating sleep of his people, because had something gone wrong, he had not wanted Tempest to awaken alone beneath the mountain with what would appear to be his dead body beside her. In the Carpathians' sleep they shut down their heart and lungs—a useful thing, a rejuvenating process, something their bodies required to keep them at full strength, but it was frightening to humans.

Without fulfilling his customary process, Darius's sleep had been fitful and uneasy. But Tempest was young and used to going her own way, so he had sacrificed his restorative rest to ensure her cooperation and security. Now he rubbed strands of her red-gold hair through his fingertips. Red hair. Green eyes. Hot temper. Strong will. Her skin was warm and alluring. In her trance-induced sleep her heart beat strong, and her breath caused the rise and fall of her full, creamy breasts.

Darius bent his head to taste her skin even as he issued the command for her to awaken. His mind caught hers as she drowsily complied, feeding his own urgent hunger to her, building erotic images of his desires in her head. His mouth moved over her slowly, languidly, his teeth occasionally nipping, claiming every part of her. He could feel the rhythm of her heart change to match his. His body hardened, demanded; his blood rushed in heated need. He felt her body answer as hot blood surged through her veins, carrying flames, carrying need.

Before she was fully awake, fully aware of her surroundings, he turned her world into an erotic fantasy. Darius tasted the warmth of her throat, his hand moving to cup her breast possessively. Though she was small of stature, her bones delicate, her breasts were full, fitting into his palms as if made for him. He took an almost savage joy in the way his body hardened in aggressive male response.

His mouth moved over her shoulder, stopping to dwell in the small hollow there. His tongue lapped gently, insistently, tracing the valley between her breasts, paying close attention to each nipple, a task that sent fire racing through his blood. He closed his eyes for a brief moment, savoring the texture of her skin, the fire spreading through his own body. But it soon became necessary to trace each indentation along her ribs, to inspect her stomach with his tongue.

His hands moved lower still, to the slender curve of her hips, caressing the satin skin there. Beneath his palms, she moved restlessly, still drowsy, only partially aware of what he was doing. But her body was alive with need for him. He shared that, connected in her mind as he was. Darius smiled to himself, enjoying the knowledge that at his every rising she would be with him, her body soft and welcoming.

Her legs were shifting, and his hands began a slow caressing of her thighs. A soft little sound escaped her throat as she tried to decide if this was some erotic fantasy or if it was real. She had no sense of where she was, only of the mouth moving lazily but thoroughly over every inch of her body.

Darius pushed his hand into the nest of tight curls, felt her pulsing heat. As she moved to press closer, he simply lowered his head to taste her. Tempest cried out, somewhere between alarm and pleasure, her fists tangling in his hair, drawing him closer. White heat, blue lightning rushed through her and into him. The sensation was astounding, Darius feeling the way her body rippled with pleasure.

His own body was brutally relentless, so full and heavy that he was afraid he might break her if he moved too fiercely. As they shared her shattering release, Tempest's hands moved over the carved muscles of his back to rest on his hips. Darius lifted his head, his eyes burning down into her.

Normally modest, Tempest should have felt shy. Instead she caught the images in his mind, his hungry need, and she felt like a wanton temptress—and liked it. She pushed him backward so that he lay down. Her hands inspected his chest. Smiling a little, she bent her head to lap gently at his hot skin. He even tasted masculine. With his mind firmly entrenched in hers, she could feel the fire sweeping through his blood, feel the relentless, aching need of his body. Deliberately she allowed her silken hair to fall over his sensitive skin, heightening the sensation even more.

Darius whispered her name, his white teeth coming together helplessly. She was taking her sweet time, driving him crazy with anticipation, her mouth traveling leisurely over his flat belly to find the indentations at his hips. Her hand brushed him, and his body tightened even more. He bit out her name again, a command this time, but Tempest refused to listen. Her tongue tasted him in a long slow caress that brought his hands up to clench her hair, forcing her head to him.

She had the audacity to laugh at him, her warm breath adding to the conflagration building in his body. Her hand moved up and over him, testing his weight, the thickness of him. Then he was shouting hoarsely. The silken feel of her mouth on him was incredible. Hot, tight, moist. She knew what he liked by the images in his mind, and Darius was lost to the world. Lost in the beauty of what they shared.

She teased him. Tortured him. Reveled in her power over him. He stood it as long as he was physically able to; then he dragged her head up by a fistful of red-gold hair. No matter if he was brutal, it was the only thing he was capable of doing at that moment. His hands found her waist and pulled her over him.

With their gazes locked together, Tempest slowly lowered herself over him so that he speared her, inch by inch. Her waiting sheath was so hot and moist, so tight and velvet soft, that Darius's fingers bit deep into her hips to keep him from exploding. Where was his centuries-old self-control?

Tempest found it amazing to know exactly what he wanted. She started to ride him slowly, but it fast turned into a frenzied motion, her muscles clenching around him, taking him deep within her. His hands moved over her body, inspecting her small waist, narrow rib cage, and full breasts. Then he was leaning up toward her, a slow, inexorable movement that nearly stopped her heart. She could feel the hunger in him, his need to take her blood—more a sexual urge than a physical hunger. He had done so many times, but she had never seen his teeth other than perfect. Now he made no attempt to hide his lengthening incisors from her as he bent his head to her throat.

He thrust upward, burying himself deep within her as his teeth sank into her soft throat. He shared the ultimate sensation with her, their bodies and minds joined, sharing the very essence of life together. His body was on fire, the conflagration building and building until there was no controlling it. He swept her along with him until they were both exploding wildly, the very earth shaking beneath them.

He forced himself to stop taking more of her blood simply to satisfy his insatiable craving for her. Already he had noted the differences in her, her ability to hear and see much more acutely. He was inadvertently enhancing her senses. Altering the humanness he had vowed to preserve. Darius swept his arms protectively around her. Nothing was going to hurt her. Not ever. Not even he.

Tempest was content to lie upon the hard strength of his body, feeling sheltered and thoroughly loved. He was a perfect lover, careful of her even at his roughest moments. She could hear their hearts beat in perfect rhythm, and she lay there for some time getting her breath back. As she inhaled to slow her breathing, she felt oppressive heat. Her teeth sank into her lower lip as she looked around her.

They were still in the cave. Humiliation washed over her. She had been so distracted by his lovemaking, she hadn't even considered where they were. She doubted she would have noticed if they were in the middle of a street. Where was her pride? This man had practically kidnapped her, held her in the center of the earth without the slightest remorse, and then taken shameless advantage of her.

Tempest lifted her head, her long lashes veiling her eyes before he could read her expression. But Darius became a shadow in her mind, feeling her guilt and anger at herself, her sense of humiliation that she had allowed this when she was so angry with him.

Immediately he rolled her under him, trapping her slender body with his much larger frame. He tangled a fist in her bright, silky hair and drew it to his mouth. "I must apologize for taking advantage of you while you slept. It was wrong of me when we had unresolved issues between us. But you are so beautiful, Tempest, that I lost control."

Her long lashes swept up, revealing green eyes blazing fury at him. She actually shoved him, the palm of her hand hard against his chest. He was so startled by her reaction that he forgot to move, to pretend he felt the push. Heat curled in him, a wave of desire so strong that he nearly kissed her angry mouth.

"You are so full of it, Darius. Don't even think you can snow me with a line like that. You didn't lose control. You knew exactly what you were doing. You wanted to have sex, so you did. And I'm such a ninny, I went along with it, like one of those idiot heroines in a steamy novel." She realized she hadn't budged him with her push, and that raised her temper another notch.

"I wanted to make love to you," he corrected, his voice black velvet.

Just the sound of his voice sent a rush of heat coursing through her bloodstream. It required tremendous effort to pull her gaze away from the burning intensity of his eyes. And God would have to save her himself if she looked at his perfect mouth. It all added fuel to the fire. "You think you can get your way by seducing me, Darius, but it won't work. I don't much like myself right now, and I know it wasn't all you, but let me tell you before you get too puffed up with your own ego, I don't respect you nearly as much right now as I did yesterday." She paused. "If it was yesterday."

"You can bathe in the pool." He tried not to make it an order. His body seemed to respond to the merest touch of hers. He didn't dare start anything with her green eyes blazing fire and her red hair sparking flames.

"Are you giving me your permission?" she asked sarcastically.

He bent his head to hers because she had made that little moue with her lips he could never pass up. His mouth found hers and tasted the warm honey of her even in her anger, capturing it forever in his heart. "No wonder you are always in trouble," he murmured, his kiss sliding over the corner of her mouth to her dimple, lower still to find her chin, then her throat. Her pulse beat beneath his mouth, igniting his hunger. It came out of nowhere, rushing at him with the same speed and intensity as his body hardened, urging him to take her again and again.

Tempest pulled away, her emerald eyes all at once wary. He was so strong, his power overwhelming, when she had no control at all in the situation. She was his captive, hidden beneath the earth, his to keep for all time if he desired. The idea had not occurred to her until that moment, and it leeched the color from her face instantly. "Darius?" His name came out strangled, a plea for reassurance.

He touched her mind, found her fear easily. His arms encircled her, drew her close to his protection. "As soon as you bathe, we will go to the surface. I need to hunt. You need food."

The relief was tremendous, and she believed the purity of his voice. Despite her anger at him, she clung to him for just a moment, waiting for her heart to stop pounding so violently. "Darius," she confided, "I really am afraid down here."

Darius tightened his hold on her, crushing her slender body against his. He had not known the real meaning of fear until she had come into his barren existence. She brought that definition to life for him. He feared he would lose her, feared someone or something would harm her. Fear made him edgy and dangerous, like one of the cats in their most unpredictable, moody states.

"All of these things are minor differences we can work out, Tempest," he assured her. "No obstacle between us is insurmountable."

She took a deep, steadying breath. "Okay, Darius, I'm all for that. Just don't be so in control of me. I like my freedom. It's who I am."

"Who you are is my other half, as I am yours," he said.

She pulled out of his arms and rose, turning away from him so that she didn't give in to the urge to kick his shins. He was so arrogant, spouting his Old-World non-sense, that she wanted to push him into the pool and watch him lose his magnificent and oh, so irritating cool.

Darius hid his smile. He couldn't help saying things

just to get under her skin. He liked to watch her eyes glitter like gems, the flash of fire that inadvertently exposed her deeply passionate nature as well as her anger.

Tempest stepped into the pool and found the clear water on her skin more erotic than she would have liked. She knew his black eyes were burning over her as she swam, and something feminine and wild in her seemed to take over. She rinsed her hair out slowly, turning so that her profile was to him, so that the water lapped at her waist and ran down her exposed breasts. Beckoned to him. Taunted him.

With her increased hearing, she caught his muffled swearing. A smile curved her soft mouth, all anger disappearing as she caught sight of his body making demand on him, his arousal impossible to hide from either of them. Deliberately she bent over, rinsing her hair a second time, giving him a good view of the curve of her hips and buttocks. He deserved a little suffering. And she was enjoying herself.

Little red-haired witch. She was deliberately driving him crazy. He knew it. He also knew she was having fun, getting back her feeling of control and power. Darius let out a low, husky groan of frustration. Her answer was a stifled laugh, hastily drowned out by the splashing water. Little minx. A man could take only so much. In any case, hunger was clouding good judgment, and nothing tasted like the rush he got from their erotic encounters. Still, he could not afford to take too much of her blood. Replacing hers with his was a dangerous pastime, altering her in ways he was not completely certain of. The few times over the centuries when he had encountered human women converted, they had become vampire and deranged, feeding on children. He had been forced to destroy them.

The thought terrified him. What if he was somehow bringing Tempest to that very edge? Their minds were already continually reaching for each other. Could he be placing her in danger? Would Julian have the answer to that? Distasteful as it was, he would have to ask Desari's lifemate for his knowledge in this matter. Pride meant nothing if Tempest was in harm's way.

He turned to look at her again. She was exquisite. Everything about her touched him, brought out intense feelings, whether protective, sexual, or emotional. He found himself fascinated by the line of her throat, the span of her waist, the curves of her breasts and rib cage and bottom.

Tempest wrung out her hair carefully and waded out of the pool. She was within a couple of feet of Darius before she scented the husky call of his body, felt the heat rising from his skin. She grinned at him, teasing, challenging, a faint, derisive quirk of her lips at his obvious discomfort. "Having a problem?" she taunted aloud.

He was magnificent. There was no other word for his body. And it amazed her that she could produce such a reaction in him, in a creature so powerful and controlled as Darius almost always was. That she could send him so out of control mystified yet excited her. It was exhilarating, like leaping onto the back of a tiger and hanging on for dear life.

Darius waited until she sashayed past him before reaching out to claim what was his. He merely caught her arms from behind, then moved them forward to place her hands on the flat surface of an accommodating rock. At once his body trapped hers, pushing aggressively against her bottom while his seeking fingers assured him that she was creamy with her own need of him. He caught her hips firmly and surged into her tight, moist sheath. It was slick and hot, waiting for him. Darius allowed himself the natural instinctive domination of the males of his race. His teeth found her shoulder and pinned her in place while he buried himself again and again with hard, long strokes.

Tempest felt the sweet rush of fire consuming her, the strength in his hands gripping her hips, the hard thickness of him plunging deep within her, only to withdraw and return. She felt his mouth on her skin, the white heat as his teeth pierced deep and he held her in a submissive position. A part of her felt intensely vulnerable, but he was adjusting his position to accommodate the tightness of her feminine sheath, and all the time he was building the fire higher, ever higher. She could feel her body tightening, gripping his, beginning to spiral outward. She didn't want it over so soon, so fast. She wanted this time with him, afraid it might never happen again once they were back in her world, the world she knew she belonged in. This was too much. Too much of everything. Too much fire and too much feeling.

"Darius." She breathed his name in a whisper, somewhere between agony and ecstasy.

"Only Darius," he growled against her skin. "You are mine." Somewhere deep in his heart he knew she still thought of them separately. That he wouldn't stay with her, that she could walk away, *would* walk away at some point. She wanted him yet was terrified to need him, to be part of him, no Darius without Tempest, no Tempest without Darius. He, on the other hand, had accepted that almost from the first moment he laid eyes on her. His body swelled, hot and slick, velvet steel, and still he moved, wanting to prolong the moment, wanting to bring her to a fever pitch.

He wanted to hear those soft little sounds she made in her throat, the ones that melted his heart and sent arrows piercing his soul. Those sounds drove him crazy. In his mouth was the delicious taste of her, and against his skin was the feel of hers, bare and soft and so vulnerable, all for him. He savored the moment, prolonged it, reaching higher and higher until her body was gripping and clenching around his, wringing his very essence from him, milking an explosion of heat and flame, a firestorm of ecstatic pleasure that consumed them both.

Her breath was coming in little gasps, and he had to hold her up to prevent her shaky legs from giving way. She turned her head to look at him, her green eyes glittering jewels. "I had no idea it could be like this, Darius. You're incredible." She meant it sincerely. She had read books—who hadn't? She'd lived on the streets, grown up around hookers. Naturally she'd asked a few questions. No one had described anything like the feelings Darius produced in her. The graphic mechanics, perhaps, but not the beauty and passion of what they did together.

"It is us together," he explained patiently, wanting her to understand. Tempest was so programmed to be alone, to live her a solitary existence, that her mind refused to comprehend the true meaning of their joining.

"You don't feel this way when you make love to other women?" she asked, struggling to believe that a man as virile, a man who made love as often and as vigorously as Darius did, had not needed hundreds of partners in the past. How could any one woman possibly keep up with his demands, possibly satisfy him? She had no real experience. How could she keep him happy?

He found himself frowning as he read her thoughts. Darius swept her into his arms and waded back into the pool to rinse her off one more time. "You keep up with my every demand," he pointed out. "And you satisfy me perfectly. There can be no other woman, Tempest. You can touch my mind with yours. I cannot lie to you. Read my thoughts. I speak the truth. There is only you in my heart. It is only you my body will accept. There will never be another. It is for all time."

"I will grow old and die, Darius," she pointed out. "In another hundred years you will find someone else." She laughed softly at her own ego. "Notice I gave you plenty of time to grieve for me."

"Put your arms around my neck. Look at me." He commanded it, wanting her complete attention. "I love you, Tempest, not any other woman. It is not the love of humans; it is more encompassing and violent than that, yet more pure and cherishing."

She shook her head. "You haven't known me long enough to feel real love. You're attracted to me sexually, that's all." She sounded desperate even to her own ears.

"I have been inside your mind countless times, Tempest. I know everything about you. Every childhood memory, good and bad. I know your secret thoughts, thoughts humans never share with anyone else. I know the things you do not like about yourself. I know your strengths and the things you consider weaknesses. I know more about you in the time we have had together than any human male could know in a lifetime. I love you. The entire you."

His hand moved to wash the evidence of their lovemaking from between her legs, his fingers soothing, gentle. "I know you think I am the sexiest man you have ever met. You think I am handsome. You love the sound of my voice. You particularly like my mouth and my eyes and the way I look at you." His black gaze moved over her face, the faint humor fleeting as he continued. "You fear my powers, yet you accept them and the differences in me with surprising ease. I make you feel safe and protected, and you fear that feeling because you do not trust such a concept. You do not want to tie yourself to me fully because you do not trust that you could ever hold a man as powerful as myself, and you cannot allow yourself the pain of losing me."

She was attempting to pull out of his arms, but he held her tightly to him, so she glared at him instead. "While you were inspecting the inside of my head, did you find out just what I want to do to you half the time?"

His mouth softened with mocking male amusement. "You mean when you are not wanting my body in yours?"

Furious, she nodded. "Like now, for instance."

His palm stroked back wet strands of hair from her forehead. His eyes burned into hers. "You have an astonishing penchant for feminine-style violence," he commented drolly.

"I'm beginning to think violence might be the only way to handle you." Tempest inserted a hand between herself and the wall of his chest and steadily increased the pressure until she lost her own strength. If he didn't notice subtle hints to let her go soon, she *would* resort to violence, and then he'd be sorry. A serious dunking just might do his inflated male ego some good. She glared at him again, hoping to wither him on the spot. "I don't believe in love. It's a myth. People use it to get their way. There isn't any such thing. It's mere physical attraction."

Darius practically tossed her out of the pool. "You actually believe the nonsense you spout? I am the darkness. You are the light. I am a predator. You hold compassion and goodness within you. Yet *I* must teach *you* about love?"

"Your ego is showing again," she declared, a faint haughtiness in her voice. "You know, Darius, it isn't necessary that we think or believe alike all the time. I don't have to see everything your way."

Something deep and dark and terrifying flickered in the depths of his eyes, and she held her breath. He blinked, and the illusion was gone, leaving her wondering if she had seen only the flames of the candles reflected in his eyes.

"You have clothes on the sheet. Get dressed, Tempest. I must feed."

The moment he uttered the words, she became aware of her heart beating strongly. It sounded overly loud to her, like the beat of a drum. Worse, she could hear his heartbeat. The water pouring from the walls, too, was nearly deafening, whereas the night before she had hardly noticed it. And she heard something else—a high-pitched, far-off sound ominously like what she imagined a great number of bats might make.

Tempest took a deep breath, her teeth biting nervously at her lower lip. She didn't like Darius's using the word *feed*. She didn't like the fact that her hearing had suddenly become so strangely acute. What did it all mean? He had bitten her several times. Could he infect her with whatever made him the creature that he was? Slowly she pulled on the clothes he had supplied—something else she didn't want to examine too closely. They weren't her clothes. Just where had they come from? "You're in way too deep this time, Rusti," she murmured aloud.

Darius was beside her, immaculate, elegant, powerful.

He ruffled her hair affectionately. "Stop talking to yourself."

"I always talk to myself."

"You are not alone anymore. You have me, so there is no further need to continue this habit. Are you ready?" His black eyes flicked over her pale face, settling for a moment on her trembling mouth. It amused him somewhat that periodically she scared herself with her own rousings and anxieties. It amazed him that she wasn't always terrified of him, that she accepted his differences the same way she accepted differences of skin color or religion. The same way she accepted animals.

Tempest unexpectedly reached out and took his hand. "Even if you are the most arrogant being I've ever encountered, thank you for last night. It was beautiful, Darius."

It was the last thing he'd anticipated, and it moved him as nothing else could. He turned his head away from her so that she would not catch the shimmer of tears that suddenly touched his eyes. That in itself was a small miracle. He had not believed himself capable of tears, yet he wanted to weep because she had thanked him. Despite her anger at him, her fears of his powers and this place, their night had meant enough to her that she had thought to thank him.

As he took her toward the surface of the mountain, he realized it was the first time anyone had thanked him for anything. His role as his family's provider and protector had been established long ago and was thus now taken for granted. This small woman, so delicate yet so courageous, made him remember the reason he had chosen the role of provider and protector.

Chapter Eleven

The night was the most incredibly beautiful thing Tempest had ever seen. It was clear and slightly cold, and overhead thousands of tiny stars were trying to outsparkle each other. She inhaled the scent of pine. A slight breeze carried the hint of wildflowers to her. Mist off the falls cleaned the air around them. She wanted to run barefoot through the forest and revel in the beauty of nature. For a moment she even forgot Darius as she raised her arms toward the moon, a silent offering of joy.

Darius watched her face, felt the happiness consuming her. Tempest focused on whatever she was doing at the moment, taking it into her mind and body and enjoying it to the fullest. She seemed to know how to really live. Was it because she had had so little joy in her lifetime? Was it because she had fought so hard simply to survive? He touched her mind, a silent, watchful shadow hovering in the background, that he might share the intensity of the moment with her.

And he did. He saw it all. Each separate, vivid detail of wonder. The exquisite beauty of the leaves bathed in silver light. The individual drops of mist sparkling like diamonds in the air around the waterfall. The prisms of color flowing from the frothy cascade. Bats wheeling and dipping at myriad insects. Darius could even see himself, tall and powerful, intimidating, masculine. His long hair flowed to his broad shoulders, and his mouth was . . . He brought himself up short, a smile hovering close. She definitely liked his mouth.

Tempest thumped him hard in the chest. "Get that smug smirk off your face. I know exactly what you're thinking."

His hand came up beneath hers and trapped her small clenched fist against his chest. "I notice you do not attempt to deny it."

Her green eyes sparkled a teasing challenge. "Why should I? I have good taste. Most of the time," she added pointedly.

He growled low in his throat, a sound meant to intimidate her, but instead she laughed. "Down, boy. Anyone with your arrogance can take a little bit of ribbing." As he brought her hand to his mouth and nipped her knuckles menacingly, her laughter changed to an abrupt squeal of alarm.

"Do not count on it," he cautioned, his white teeth gleaming like a predator's. "I am like any man. I expect the woman I love to adore me and think me perfect."

She gave an inelegant snort. "You'll have a long wait for that one."

His black eyes, so compelling, burned over her face. "I do not think it will be so long, honey."

"Go find yourself food. We have to meet the others," Tempest said a little desperately. He could not look at her that way. He just couldn't.

"And if I go, what will you do for me?" he prompted, rubbing her knuckles along his shadowed jaw. The sensation sent dark fire racing through her blood.

"I'll be a good little girl and wait right here for you." She made a face at him. "Don't worry so much, Darius. I'm not really the adventurous type."

He groaned at the blatant lie. "My heart could not take it if you were any more adventurous." His black eyes pinned her. "Obey me in this, Tempest. I do not want to come back and find you hang-gliding off another cliff."

She rolled her eyes. "What trouble can I possibly get into up here? No one's around for miles. Really, Darius, you're becoming totally paranoid." She strode to a boulder with a flat top. "I'll just sit here and contemplate nature until you return."

"The other alternative is for me to tie you to a tree," he mused, straight-faced.

"Try it," she dared him, green eyes flashing fire.

"Do not tempt me," he shot back, meaning it. He examined the boulder for himself. With Tempest, anything was bound to happen. A snake under the rock, a stick of dynamite blowing it up.

Tempest laughed at him. "Go away. Do you have any idea how pale you are? I'm afraid in a minute you'll decide that I'm your midnight snack." Swinging one crossed leg back and forth, feigning indifference, she blinked up at him, wishing she could take back the words. She didn't want to give him any ideas. "Do have any idea how truly bizarre all this is?"

He loomed over her, tall and enormously strong. "I only know you'd better be sitting right here when I get back." He made it an order. No velvet over iron this time. Just pure iron. He said it between his teeth to show her he meant business.

Tempest smiled up at him, all innocence. "I can't think what else I would possibly do."

He kissed her then because she was so damned tempting that he thought he might incinerate if he didn't. Her mouth was incredibly soft and pliant, such a mixture of sweet fire and hot honey that he had trouble pulling away. Hunger was beating at him to the extent that he was finding it difficult not to nuzzle her throat and seek the taste of her, rich and hot, flowing into his body. He felt his fangs lengthening at the thought and quickly jerked away. His restless sleep and long night of sexual activities had drained his control. He needed to feed.

One moment Darius was kissing her as if he would never let her go, the next he was gone, just disappeared. In his place was a trailing vapor of mist, streaking away from her toward deeper woods. She watched the cometlike phenomenon almost idly, not certain if it was really Darius or some strange effect created by the lofty atmosphere and the waterfall. It was beautiful, a prism of colors and lights flickering like countless fireflies through the trees. She wondered if he had scented prey, and she shivered at the choice of words that had come to her mind.

She inhaled then, taking the scents of the night into her lungs. It was amazing what tales the various smells could provide. Darius was right; it was only a matter of holding oneself very still and listening with one's entire being. Focusing. It was almost overwhelming. The trees, the water, the bats, the animals. She patted the boulder, liking that it felt so solid. She felt as if Darius had awakened her and brought her up from the very bowels of the earth to rediscover the beauty of nature.

Something slightly off-key inserted itself into her magical world, but it was so slow, so insidious, she barely noticed it. Everything around her was so exciting, seen through new eyes, a true awakening. The color of the water particularly captured her fascination, the way the wind played with the surface, tugging and teasing it into a frothy foam. But the nagging intrusion was persistent, a mournful note, a jangle, as if something was out of step with the rightness of all she was seeing.

Tempest frowned and rubbed her forehead. It began aching, throbbing, getting worse as she sat still. She stood, shifting her weight from foot to foot, and very carefully took stock of her surroundings, trying to see without the vivid colors and details, to perceive the reality around her.

Her foot began aching, and she slipped off her shoe and knelt to rub the sole. But the pain wasn't where she had hurt herself. It was deep within the tissues, and she knew it wasn't her pain; she was feeling the echo of something or someone hurting. A sudden stillness seemed to sink into the forest, quieting all wildlife. She heard the rush of wings and thought she understood the sudden silence. An owl hunting would keep mice and small animals cowering in their snug homes. Yet the bats remained busy with the insects above her head. Thoughtfully she replaced her shoe and straightened.

A thin ribbon of a deer trail led into the straggly timberline. She wandered over to it, something pulling her in that direction. She wouldn't go far; she just wanted to find the jarring note intruding on the beauty of nature. The feeling persisted even as she followed the minimal trail. At times it led into thickets of bushes and brambles. She sensed the presence of rabbits crouched below the thorns. They remained unmoving, only their whiskers twitching.

The new intensity of nature's colors and details began to overlap her need to hunt down the mournful sound seeping into her brain. She found herself sneaking glances at the starlit sky and occasionally turning in full circles to admire the forest. Ferns were becoming taller as she walked deeper into the interior. Moss covered the tree trunks rising skyward. She touched the bark of one and was in awe at the complex blend of textures.

It occurred to her that her senses were so heightened that no mind-altering drug could ever compare. She wandered away from the trail for a moment so she could study an unusual rock formation. The boulders were covered on one side with lichen and tiny life forms, minute insects creating their own world. Tempest glanced up at the sky again, amazed that she could see so clearly even within the deep shadows of the trees.

She was moving into thicker woods, where it was much darker, yet she could see quite well, her eyesight as acute as her hearing. She turned the focus of her new-found senses inward. Her stomach was slightly upset. She felt full; the thought of food made her slightly sick, yet she was thirsty. She became aware of the sound of the stream bubbling happily toward the waterfall. She angled toward the water, pushing her way through the brush.

As she knelt at the edge of the stream, she became aware of the discordant note again. It was louder this time, jarring her, making her head hurt. Somewhere close by something wasn't right. Something was in pain.

She dipped her hand in the running water and brought it to her parched mouth. Her mind was tuning itself to Darius's, automatically seeking him. She needed the contact. Tempest didn't know why, but if she didn't reach for him, find him, just for a moment, she knew she would be terrified. She needed him.

The idea of needing him alarmed her, but, unerringly, her mind had already found his. Giving it the lightest of touches, she was no more than a faint shadow sliding in, seeking the comfort of knowing he was alive and well, that he was sating his voracious hunger. Her heart pounded wildly for a moment. She withdrew immediately, annoyed with herself for needing him, annoyed that her first thought had been to wonder if he was seeking sustenance from a woman. She should have been concerned for his prey, not jealous of it, however momentarily.

Tempest blinked and refocused. Where was she? How had she gotten here? Nothing looked familiar. Where was the deer trail? She would follow it back to the boulder where she had promised to wait. "You did it again, Rusti," she chided herself under her breath, worried that Darius might touch her mind and feel her confusion. Slowly she straightened and took a good look around.

There was no deer trail in sight. "Why have you no sense of direction?" she muttered to herself, not wanting Darius to pick up her unspoken thoughts. She wasn't going to live this one down unless she could find her way back before he returned. She decided to follow the stream. She knew it ended at the falls several feet above the little clearing overlooking the cliffs. If she came out above the falls, she could climb down to the clearing. It all made perfect sense.

Breathing a sigh of relief, she began to walk briskly

along the edge of the rapidly moving stream. The problem became apparent at once. The stream doubled back in several places, seeming to meander through the thickest parts of the forest. Brambles tore at her jeans, and the vegetation around her seemed to loom to jungle proportions.

As she moved steadily forward, the mournful note that had set her off in the first place seemed to increase. She knew she was close to whatever it was.

An animal in pain. She knew it with sudden clarity. A large animal, and it was suffering terribly. It was wounded, the laceration infected, and the paw hurt when pressed onto the ground as it attempted to walk. It was broadcasting loudly, the vibrations in the night air finding her a ready recipient.

It wasn't as if the animal was making actual noise; it was more that Tempest had always been able to communicate with animals, and she could hear, in her head, a silent scream of pain. She tried to ignore it, even took several more steps along the bank of the stream, but the animal's distress level was overwhelming. "I can't just leave the darn thing," she argued. "It could be caught in a trap. One of those awful steel things that crush an animal's leg and make it die a hideous death. I'd be as guilty as whoever put the stupid trap out in the first place." She was already turning back, resolutely following the vibrations in her head.

She had no actual warning that she was practically on top of the animal until she parted some bushes and saw a large mountain lion crouched above her on a rocky ledge. Its yellow eyes stared down at her with malevolence. The cat was heavily muscled, a bit on the thin side, and broadcasting as much hunger as pain. Why hadn't she caught that before?

Tempest sank her teeth into her lower lip in agitation. Okay. This was it. The last straw. She was going to be in so much trouble when Darius found out about this one. The cougar was staring at her, frozen in place, only the tip of its tail flicking back and forth. Tempest thought about running, but she knew the animal would definitely attack her if she was that stupid. She reached for the cat's mind.

Hunger. Anger. The cougar was moody and in pain. There was something in its paw, something sticking in and hurting each time it tried to hunt. The cat had tried to bite and gnaw it out but had been unsuccessful. The cat had not eaten in several days, and hunger was riding it hard. And now it was staring at easy prey with obvious satisfaction.

Tempest tried to soothe the cougar, tried to send the impression that she would help. She could remove the painful thorn; she could provide fresh meat. The yellow eyes continued to stare at her, an eerie portent of death. Tempest forced her mind away from the possibility of an attack and continued to send impressions of aid to the cat. She kept the fear from her mind so the animal would not leap at her.

The cougar shook its head, puzzled. Tempest sensed confusion, a need to feed, yet the animal found her strange, unfamiliar, perplexing. The mountain lion needed the thorn out, and Tempest concentrated on that. Images of the thorn removed, the paw healed. If she didn't help the creature, it would remain unable to hunt, and it would perish. The cougar was young, a female; she could reproduce. Tempest knew the cat was extremely dangerous; hunger and pain could force any animal to strike out. But it just wasn't in her to walk away without trying to help. She had managed to control large dogs. Once a tiger at a zoo had bonded with her.

She stood quietly, watching the animal closely for signs of acceptance. She had infinite patience. Hers was a God-given gift, and she believed in it implicitly. Others might call her a freak, but she knew she could help animals, really help them at times like this. She spoke quietly, soothingly in her mind, sending images of the thorn out, the paw feeling so much better. She swamped the cat with the images, kept the animal off balance.

Most cats were curious by nature, and this big one was no different. It snarled silently, but the resolve in its head to kill and feed instantly was fading. It wanted the terrible thorn out, the pain to be gone. Tempest pressed her advantage, sought to expand her mental images and vibrations of goodwill. The cat became more relaxed, the yellow eyes squinting, not so fixed and merciless.

Tempest allowed herself to breathe more deeply and moved cautiously closer, her gaze flicking to the sore paw. It was quite swollen and pustulent. "Poor baby," she crooned softly. "We need to take that thing out of there for you." All the while she built the images of the cat accepting her extracting the thorn. "It might hurt, so I'm thinking we should decide up front that you won't lose your mind and eat me. In the long run, it would be far better for you if you just let me take the thing out." She was quite close now, close enough to touch the animal.

The wound was worse than she first thought; infection had really taken hold. It was possible she couldn't help the poor thing. Tempest sighed. She didn't want to give up. There was always a chance that if she could remove the foreign object embedded so deeply in the paw, the cat might survive. It was more accepting of her, curious that she could communicate, that she understood its pain and hunger, overcoming, for the moment, its desire and need to eat.

Deliberately Tempest shifted her focus, instinctively knowing that when the cougar felt the intense pain as she removed the object, it would want to lash out at whatever was closest. She amplified its feelings of curiosity. "Unfortunately, baby, that's me. Don't you think I'm rather interesting? You haven't seen too many like me around, have you?" Tempest crooned softly. Taking a deep breath, she bent her head to examine the vicious wound, for the first time trusting to luck as she took her eyes off the face of the cat.

Terror. Sheer, unadulterated terror. There was no other word to describe his emotion. Darius could feel his heart pounding so hard that it was in danger of exploding out of his chest. He had left Tempest sitting peacefully on a boulder by the waterfall. Why had he expected her to be sitting there still? Into the terror crept the realization that he hadn't really expected it. He knew her too well. Trouble followed her around. No, it was more than that. She sought it out.

Anger. Black and terrible. A ferocious wave of rage that threatened to consume him. He fought it down and remained very still, becoming a part of the night itself, as only he could do. His hot inner gaze never left the mountain lion, watching for the first sign of aggression. He knew how fast a cougar could move. Injured, this one was even more dangerous. He could kill it from where he stood. He could seize control of the animal, hold it helpless while she worked. He had options. He was even fast enough that he could remove Tempest from danger long before she or the lion knew he was even close. He did none of those things. Darius listened to her voice. Soft. Soothing. Its style reminiscent of the healer's chant. She was actually talking the cougar into allowing her to aid it.

Pride. It welled up in him out of nowhere. Sheer pride. She was frightened by the situation, just as she was frightened by his power, by his wild, untamed nature. Yet she was determined to save the beast. Darius was in her mind, a dark shadow staying still and quiet so he didn't distract her, yet he was there, and her focus was absolute. She was determined to give the cat a chance at survival.

Something in him he hadn't known existed, something long buried or forgotten, welled up, strong and overwhelming. The emotion was so intense that he shook with the revelation. *Love*. If he had not loved her for herself before, he knew he did now. He had walked through his barren existence feeling no real meaning other than to protect and preserve his little family. She had given him deeper purpose and life, a joyful reason to move through the world, to exist. He admired her courage even as he silently swore she would never defy him again, never again place herself in danger this way.

He admired her. The revelation was amazing to him. He admired the way she went through life accepting people as they were without judgment, without expectations. He admired her tremendous courage, her sense of humor. What was the best way to help her? Darius studied the situation carefully. The cougar was definitely unpredictable, afraid, in pain, and hungry. Immediately Darius begin to add his mental strength to Tempest's. It gave her additional control over the beast.

When I remove the thorn, Darius, can you rid the poor thing of the infection? Despite the fact that she was holding rigid control of the animal, her voice was soft but firm in his mind.

He should have known she would sense his presence immediately. The lightest of his touches brought her attention. She was tuned to him now, her mind and body, her heart and soul. He had bound them together. She could find him much more easily than before. And she was sensitive, far more so than most humans he had come into contact with. Still, she held her focus on the injured animal. She was amazing.

Heal an animal? He would do it because she asked it of him, because he knew that if he did not, she would attempt to find another way to heal the cougar. *You do not need me for this,* he whispered softly, realizing it was true. She was capable of holding the pain-wracked creature in check while she worked on it. He could feel the strength in her, the determination, and it was her own.

Tempest didn't look around to see Darius; she knew instinctively he was there. A small smile touched her mouth, revealing the intriguing little dimple that always drove him wild. She could feel his strength of will pouring into hers, doubling her control. It should have made her feel less confident in herself, but Tempest always knew when she had an animal in the palm of her hand. This cougar was receptive, and she laid a hand on its leg to allow it to get used to the feel of her.

She poured her reassurance into the mountain lion as she examined the vicious wound. The cat trembled beneath her ministrations, its fur darkening to a muddy brown. She breathed for it, for both of them, as she dug for the offending thorn. It was buried deep, the entire area swollen and angry-looking. It was more difficult to assert her domination over the cougar as she caught the end of the thick silver and began to extract it.

Darius watched the cat closely, its facial expression and the images in its mind. It wanted to strike out, end the terrible pain, but Tempest was in command. She pulled the thick thorn, a good inch in length and tapering to a nasty point, out of the paw. The cougar shook, howled, but remained still. Darius couldn't help himself. Even though he knew Tempest was in complete control, he stilled the beast, capturing its mind and holding it helpless with his merciless control.

Tempest glanced at him once, but she didn't protest. She could feel Darius's driving need to protect her. It would have been the same as asking him to put a gun to her head to ask him to back off and leave her to her task alone. She was grateful when he focused on the cougar's paw and used his energy to draw out the poison until it boiled up and exploded out of the ugly wound. Tempest watched it run down the cat's fur into the earth.

Back off now, Tempest, Darius commanded firmly. This was as much as his heart could take.

She's very hungry. Can you find her some game?

Back off, Tempest. He bit the words out, a crisp, imperious order.

Tempest rolled her eyes in exasperation. The man was going to drive her crazy. She reluctantly backed away from the animal, very slowly, careful not to trigger the instinct to pounce in the cat. *Try not to sound so much like the king of the castle. It's very annoying.*

She slipped into the brush and began to amble along the trail toward the top of the falls. Darius was summoning an old doe for the cougar. The animal was injured, its mouth filled with sores, rendering it unable to eat. She was glad he had managed to find something that was suffering rather than a young, healthy animal.

"Where are you going?" Darius materialized beside her, his stride slowing to match her shorter one. His body barely brushed hers, yet she was immediately, acutely aware of him.

"Back to the falls. Where do you think?"

Darius shook his head. "I think I am going to get you a compass."

Tempest stopped abruptly, her smile mischievous. "I never quite got the hang of reading one. I mean, I know the needle points north and all, but where does that get you? I never know what's to the north."

His eyebrows shot up. "A map?" She was already shaking her head, her smile widening to a heart-stopping grin. "You cannot read a map?" He groaned. "Of course you cannot read a map. What was I thinking?" His hand found her elbow. "You are heading away from the falls, Tempest."

"I can't be. I'm following the stream," she pointed out with her faintly haughty air.

Again one eyebrow shot up. He glanced around them. "The stream?"

She shrugged. "It's around here somewhere."

Darius burst out laughing, his arm circling her shoulders. "It is a very good thing you have me as your keeper."

Her green eyes glinted at him. The night stars seemed to get caught there, sparkled and glowed. "So you say."

His mouth found hers, a little roughly, a little tenderly, somewhere between laughter and a blatant brand. She melted into him, accepting his warring emotions. Her arms crept around his neck, her body, soft and pliant, pressed against his.

Darius simply lifted her, his mouth fastened to hers. "I must get you to the others this night. You need food."

The words were whispered into her mouth, the sensation warm and sensual, though Tempest wasn't the least hungry.

But already she could feel the change overcoming him. It started first in his mind. She saw the vivid image. It was breathtaking, real, each individual feather perfect. Darius lifted his head, breaking the kiss reluctantly as his body began to shape-shift. She watched in awe, still amazed that he could actually do such a thing. Through it all her mind stayed merged with his so that she could examine his emotions.

The sense of freedom was overwhelming. The powerful wings stretched a good six feet. *Climb onto my back.*

Tempest shook her head, suddenly afraid of hurting him. "Darius, you're a bird. I'm too heavy for you to carry."

I refuse to argue with you. She caught the unspoken threat. It was in his mind. He would force her compliance. Despite the fact that he was a bird, Darius was as powerful as ever.

"You remind me of a spoiled little boy, always having to have your own way," she sniped indignantly. But she was obeying him, not daring to take the chance that he might impose his will on her. Certain things she could not accept. Forced compliance was definitely one of them.

The owl was tremendously strong. She could feel its strength beneath her legs. The flap of the wings was graceful yet powerful, the rush of wind nearly somersaulting her off backward. The ground fell away fast as the owl accelerated. Tempest gasped, her breath catching in her lungs, her heart nearly stopping. The feathers were soft, the silence complete. She was in a whole other world.

Tempest glanced down, saw the tops of trees, and

quickly squeezed her eyes shut tight as the owl climbed higher and higher. It took her a few minutes to remember she needed to breathe. Several deep breaths calmed her enough that she was able to look around. "It's really okay, Rusti," she murmured aloud to herself. "It isn't real. You know it isn't. This is some weird fantasy thing the king of the castle stuck in your head. Just go with it. No big deal. Everyone always wants to fly. Enjoy the hallucination."

She couldn't hear her own words. The wind whipped them away so that they fell into the silence behind them. *You still find it necessary to talk to yourself. I am right here. You can talk to me.*

You aren't real. I made you up.

His mocking laughter brushed at the walls of her mind, sent heat curling like molten lava through her abdomen.

Why do you think that? he asked.

Because no real man would have your eyes. Or your mouth. And no one can possibly be as arrogant and confident as you.

I have every reason to be confident, baby, he taunted, his male mockery setting her teeth on edge.

Have you ever been plucked? It was the best threat she could come up with on short notice. *I bet it's extraordinarily painful.*

His laughter made her smile. She knew he didn't often laugh. He was the most serious man she had ever encountered, yet he seemed to be discovering a sense of fun. At least with her.

She found, as time passed, that she was enjoying the sensation of soaring. The night enfolded her, the stars crowding the sky overhead. The moon threw the landscape below into sharp relief. The sense of freedom was incredible. She relaxed even more, finding herself becoming light, part of the owl, part of Darius.

They covered hundreds of miles, the strength of the owl enormous. The air was cool against her skin, the night jewel-studded, a perfect foil for the ride of her life. She felt as if she had been given a great gift. *Darius*. She breathed his name into the night, took it into her heart. He was magic. For just a moment she allowed herself to want their union to be forever. The real thing. The fairy tale. He made her believe it might be possible.

Darius never quite left her mind. It seemed so much safer that way. Tempest, out of his sight, was at her most dangerous. He knew she could talk herself out of their relationship at any moment. Inside the owl's body, he smiled, a small, secret, male smile. She had no idea of his power. That was his Tempest. She was accepting of his nature, of his special talents, but it wasn't in her to question closely things she didn't understand. That he really meant he wouldn't let her go never crossed her mind. She just couldn't conceive of him wanting her the way he said. Needing her.

Below them, the vineyards in the Napa Valley began to take shape. Tempest could make out the mountains rising majestically above the rich green valley. A lake shimmered in the distance, reflecting the silvery sheen of the moon. The owl seemed to be making its way toward that body of water, circling lower, dropping into the shelter of a thick stand of pine trees. It seemed much darker beneath the trees, yet Tempest was able to see more clearly than she ever had at night before.

She spotted the troupe's campsite tucked neatly into the trees. Parked there were the huge motor home, the truck, and the red sports car. Her heart took an unexpected plunge. She thought it rather silly to be dismayed when she'd just soared through the sky on the back of an owl; a few people shouldn't daunt her in the least.

No, honey, they should not bother you. I have told you repeatedly that you are under my protection. Do you not understand that I would protect you with my life? Darius's voice was soft and soothing in her mind.

The owl glided to the ground, wings spread wide, gave a short hop, and waited for her to slide off. Tempest touched the feathers lightly, regretfully, one last time as they began to disappear. At once muscle and sinew rippled beneath skin. She felt the familiar wave of heat as Darius's arm curved around her shoulders and his thick mane of black hair caressed her face.

"These people are my family, Tempest." His voice was soft, mesmerizing, compelling. "That makes them your family."

She turned her face away from him, closing her mind to that possibility. Her large eyes searched for trails almost automatically, as if seeking escape. Darius tightened his arm, guiding her toward the camp. Desari's soft laughter floated toward them. It did nothing to calm Tempest's wildly pounding heart.

As they walked into the circle, Desari smiled at her in welcome. Tempest noted that Julian was close by, his posture protective of his mate. "Rusti, I'm so glad you're here. You won't believe what happened. Somebody sabotaged the truck. I think the idea was to slow us down. It was most likely one of those obnoxious reporters always snooping around or making up wild stories about us."

Tempest's relief was overwhelming. "Rusti" could meet the group much more easily as their mechanic than as Darius's girlfriend.

Girlfriend? His eyebrows shot up. *Is that what you think you are?* That taunting male laughter mocked her.

She glared at him. *No, that's what you think I am. I know better.* Her voice was deliberately haughty.

Darius burst out laughing. His family turned toward him, startled by the rare sound. He ignored them to lean down, his warm breath against Tempest's ear, speaking softly though he was well aware the others, with their enhanced senses, could hear him perfectly. "I want you to eat before you do anything else. You can look at the truck later."

Tempest's eyes flashed fire at him. "You can stick your little owl's head in the nearest tree, too," she hissed, furious at him. "Why do think you can get away with always ordering me around?"

He grinned at her, totally unrepentant. "Because I am so good at it." His eyes flickered over Syndil. *Help me out here. She must eat.*

Dayan seemed to be having a coughing fit. Desari and Julian were openly laughing. Syndil pushed Barack out of her way, glaring at him so that he groaned out loud. She stalked over to Tempest and took her hand. "Come on, Rusti. Do not pay any further attention to these men. They think they can rule us, but in truth, it is the other way around." As she spoke, she looked down her nose pointedly at Barack.

"Come on, Syndil," he pleaded. "You cannot hold one mistake against me for all time. You are supposed to be compassionate."

"Yes, I can," she said sweetly as she guided Tempest to the bus.

Barack swore, leaned down, picked up rock, and hurled it in sheer frustration. It embedded itself halfway into the trunk of a pine tree. "That woman is the most stubborn creature in the world," he said to no one in particular.

Darius walked over to Julian. "I ask for your help," he said formally, pushing down his dislike of such a thing. All that mattered to him was that he safeguard Tempest.

Julian nodded and fell into step beside his brother-in-law. "Of course, Darius," he replied, equally formal. "We are family."

"I have encountered human women turned by vampires. They were deranged, preying on the children of humans. I was forced to destroy these abominations. Now I fear I am placing Tempest in such peril. How are these women changed? I know that she is already different. Her hearing and vision are far more acute, and she is having trouble eating human food."

"It takes three blood exchanges to convert a human woman. Obviously you have not completed the ritual; it is a very painful process. If such a thing were to occur, you would have to send her to sleep once it was safe to do so in order for her body to convert without enduring too much pain to manage."

"Would she become deranged?" Darius was worried. He had already put her in danger, exchanging blood twice with her. "Has there ever been an instance when a human woman survived the ordeal intact?" Not that he intended to take the chance, but he needed the information in case of an unfortunate accident.

"Prince Mikhail, the leader of our people, successfully converted his lifemate. Their child is the lifemate of your elder brother, Gregori. My own brother, my twin, accidentally completed a conversion started by a vampire. Alexandria is his lifemate. If a human woman has psychic ability, it appears she can handle conversion by her

Carpathian lifemate. And Tempest is undeniably your lifemate."

"When you use a phrase like 'it appears,'" Darius said, "it worries me. I would never want to take the chance of harming Tempest."

"What is the alternative, Darius?" Julian asked gently. "She has brought you into the light. If you lost her, you would be destroyed. You know you would never survive. You would turn vampire, the undead. You would lose your soul."

"I have chosen to grow old and die when she does," Darius announced.

Julian caught the echo of his own lifemate's gasp. Desari was stunned and saddened at the notion. It took a moment for Julian to fight back his own protest of such a decision. "You know the danger our race is in. There are far too few of us to ensure the continuation of our people. We cannot afford to lose even one pair. And certainly not one involving a young, healthy woman capable of bearing children."

Darius shook his head. "I know so little of our race, Julian."

"It is necessary for every Carpathian male to find his lifemate. If he fails to do so, he must choose to face the dawn and end his life before it becomes too late and he loses his soul, becomes the undead. We are predators, Darius. Without a lifemate to bring meaning and light into our darkness, to make us complete, we will become vampire. But so few Carpathian females survive childhood that most of our males are turning and must be destroyed. Before I found Desari, I had made up my mind to end my life. Prince Mikhail, through Gregori, sent me to warn her that she was in danger from the human society of vampire-hunters. Of course, we had no idea any of you were still alive after the massacres in our homeland. We thought Desari human and mistakenly in the society's sights. But when I saw colors in her presence, I knew she was my lifemate, that she was meant to be with me."

"So Dayan and Barack must find their lifemates soon, or they are in danger of turning, as was I," Darius noted thoughtfully, worried.

Julian nodded soberly. "There is no doubt, Darius. That is why those of us who can must try to have female children. It is the only way our race has a chance of surviving. Even so, we may be too late. Most Carpathian women give birth to males. If a female is born, she must struggle to survive that first difficult, dangerous year."

Darius remembered just how hard it had been to keep the two fragile little girls who were Desari and Syndil alive so many centuries ago.

"It is necessary to try to provide lifemates for our kind, our brothers and friends," Julian went on quietly, persuasively. "However, you must also consider that if you bind Tempest to you without converting her, like all lifemates, neither of you will be able to bear any physical or mental separation. You, a Carpathian, must sleep in deep ground. She will need air. When you sleep the true sleep of our people, she will be unable to reach you. No lifemate can take that for a prolonged length of time. It will not work."

"Tempest is already bound to me, and I cannot bear any separation from her. This she does not understand, though. She thinks in human terms," Darius admitted with a sigh.

"It cannot continue for long," Julian said. "We are hunted. Through the centuries we have been hunted.

We are not invulnerable, despite our many gifts. She must be protected as one of ours."

Darius shook his head. "I have asked much of her these last days. I would not ask this—conversion—of her also."

"Before you close the door on the notion, Darius, give it thought. The other women I spoke of are happy in their lives. It took some adjustment, and I will not say they did not suffer, but in the end they accepted the inevitable."

"Because they had no choice," Darius pointed out softly. "The last thing I want is to cause Tempest any more suffering. She has had enough in her young life."

Chapter Twelve

Tempest sighed and put down the wrench she had been using while double-checking her findings. She didn't want to make any mistakes and miss buying a part she might need later on. It seemed unusually hot. She wiped the sweat from her face, and she thought about the night before. Syndil had been so sweet. While they talked, she had fixed a vegetable broth for Tempest. Tempest's stomach seemed to rebel against the broth, but she didn't want to hurt Syndil's feelings, so she tried to eat it. Even so, without Darius's aid she probably wouldn't have kept it down.

Darius had been so quiet when he joined her. He watched her work on the truck, clearly unhappy when she made a list of things she would need that they didn't already have. That meant she would have to make a trip to the nearest town during daylight hours. He hadn't argued, but he told her he would sleep the sleep of humans, not Carpathians, so that he would be available should she need him.

Tempest cleaned up carefully as she contemplated what Darius might have meant. What was the difference? Would it somehow harm him? She knew none of his family members agreed with his decision, none of them liked it, yet no one argued with him or even went so far as to register a simple protest. Their uneasiness caught at her. She could tell none of them blamed her for Darius's resolution, yet she knew they were concerned about Darius and what he was doing.

The money they had handed her so casually was quite substantial. She folded it, shoved it into her pocket, and resolutely climbed into the little sports car. She had a bad feeling about Darius coming to harm, so she wasn't going to take any chances on getting lost. Twice last night she had driven the route to town with Darius beside her, just to reassure him she would be able to make her way there and back without a problem. Still, her sense of dread persisted. She just seemed to attract trouble everywhere she went.

Tempest enjoyed the solitude of the drive, the highway winding down a mountain, the tight turns, the speed and smoothness of the vehicle, but there was a heaviness in her heart, growing much more difficult to ignore. She found herself needing the touch of Darius's mind. She actually felt grief seeping in, troubling thoughts. That something had happened to Darius. That he was lying hurt somewhere. That he was in danger. It was nonsense, her brain told her, but nevertheless she found herself wanting to weep uncontrollably.

Calistoga was pretty town, rather famous for its mud and mineral baths. She found the auto parts store without incident, purchased the supplies she needed, and made her exit. Thinking about Darius instead of watching where she was going, she nearly tripped over the man lounging against the little red car at the curb. The man steadied her easily even as he smoothly removed the packages from her arms and stowed them in her car. Tempest blinked up at him. He was looking at her as if he knew her. He wasn't particularly tall, but he was handsome in a blond, surfer kind of way. "Do I know you?" she asked, unable to place him.

"My name is Cullen Tucker, ma'am," he drawled with the slightest of Southern accents. He held out a photograph.

Biting her lip, realizing this was the trouble she had been expecting. Tempest glanced at the picture of herself. "Where in the world did you get that?" It was a great likeness of her, with butterflies thick in the air, alighting on her head and shoulders. Her arms were stretched out, and she was laughing. The sun was behind her, and her feet were in the stream.

Cullen examined her expression. "Did you know the man who took this photograph?"

"No. I certainly didn't pose for it." Tempest edged around him, preparing to bolt into the driver's seat. She was an excellent driver, and more than once in her rather misspent youth she had even outrun the police. She had confidence in the car, too. If she could get behind the wheel, she would be gone.

"Don't be frightened," he said softly. "I'm actually trying to help you. Can we go somewhere to talk?"

"I'm in the middle of a big job," she hedged.

"Please, it's important. A few minutes. We'll go somewhere public, so you won't be afraid of me. I don't want to sound dramatic, or like a nutcase, but it's a matter of life and death," he insisted.

Tempest closed her eyes for a moment, sighing in resignation. Of course it was a matter of life and death. What else would it be, when she was involved? She finally introduced herself, offering her hand. "I'm Tempest Trine." There was something about Cullen Tucker that she couldn't define, but she believed him to be inherently sincere. Simultaneously she wanted to groan aloud at her own introduction; Darius had her thinking of herself as Tempest instead of Rusti. It was pitiful that she couldn't get out from under his spell for even a moment.

Cullen shook her hand gently. "Do you mind if we get something to eat? I've been traveling for a couple of days and didn't take much time out."

Tempest walked beside him, relieved that so many people were on the street. Cullen didn't give her a bad feeling the way Matt Brodrick had, but she still preferred not to be alone with him.

Cullen waited until he had ordered his meal in a café they found before he started his explanation. "I'm going to tell you some pretty bizarre things. I want you to hear me out before you decide I'm crazy." He tapped the photograph of her with one fingertip. "Some time ago I joined a secret society that believes that vampires really exist."

Tempest felt the color drain from her face, and she sat back in her chair, needing the support. Before she could reply, Cullen held up a hand to stop her. "Just listen. Whether or not you believe there are vampires among us doesn't really matter. What matters is that the people I was affiliated with believe it, and they are out to capture, dissect, and destroy any they might find. Some of them have gone completely off their rockers, I'm afraid. The singer that you're traveling with—and don't deny that you're with her; I've done my homework—is being targeted by the society. They've already made attempts on her life, and believe me, they'll do it again."

Tempest drummed her fingers nervously on the table-top. "Why aren't you going to the police? Why tell me?"

"The police won't believe me—you know that. But I can try to help you and maybe even your friend the singer. This picture was taken at the same place where they found Matt Brodrick's body. He was part of the society, and, unfortunately for you, this picture condemns you in its eyes. They sent me to track you down and bring you back to them to see what they can learn about your group before . . . disposing of you. And I'm sure I'm not the only one they'll be sending. I want to get you out of here, get you somewhere safe, where you can lay low until they lose interest in you."

Tempest shook her head. "Just like that? I'm supposed to believe you and take off with you? If all this was true, the only thing I could do would be to warn Desari and the band, go to the police, and hope they catch these nuts."

"Don't be so damned stubborn," Cullen hissed, leaning across the table, his face inches from hers. "I'm trying to save your life. These people are dangerous. They believe Desari is a vampire, and likely her new boyfriend, too. They are going to capture her or destroy her. Killing her would be doing her a favor, given what they have in mind as the alternative. But you're first on their list, because they see you as a way to get information about her and her troupe. You have to go into hiding, get the hell away from the band. It's your only choice, Tempest."

"Do they think I'm a vampire? For God's sake, they have a photo of me outdoors in broad daylight. I'm having lunch with you in a diner in the middle of the day," she replied, exasperated but a little afraid. Darius was going to kill her when he realized she was having lunch alone with a man involved with human vampire-hunters and Matt Brodrick. Maybe she didn't dare go back to the band. Maybe she would be leading the enemy straight to them.

"You're no vampire," Cullen said grimly. "I've seen a vampire, a real, honest-to-God vampire. Those idiots in the society have no idea what one of the undead is truly capable of doing. Desari is no vampire either. But they're already suspicious of me, so I'm going to have to go into hiding, too. Likely they'll send their 'military' after me because I know them all, their identities. I've seen their faces and been to their secret meetings. You have to come with me, Tempest."

Tempest tilted her head to one side. She wasn't a vampire, but there was something definitely different about her. She could hear Cullen Tucker's heartbeat. A loud, strong, healthy pounding that echoed through her own bloodstream. She could hear the swish of water from the kitchen, the clink of individual dishes, the low murmur of conversation between the cook and a waitress. A couple across the room were have a whispered quarrel. She smelled food cooking, various perfumes and colognes, all mingling, overpowering each other until her stomach lurched from the onslaught.

Colors were vivid and bright, almost like when she was with Darius. She noticed the thin veins in the leaves of the daisy in the glass vase on the table, the extraordinary petals and each round pollen center. Her gaze hung there, entranced by the flower's unusual beauty, the precise creation of nature.

"Tempest!" Cullen hissed across the table at her. "Are you even listening to me? For God's sake, you have to believe what I'm telling you. I'm no crackpot. These people won't stop. They're hunting you. Let me at least get you to a safe place. I'll try to protect you, although you'll probably be safer without me. They might give up hunting you, but once they know I've betrayed them, they'll never stop hunting me. You just have to hide out for a few months. And it's imperative that you distance yourself from this group."

"What about Desari? She's done nothing wrong. If I go with you, these crazy, dangerous people will still be after her. Maybe this time they'll kill her." Tempest shook her head. "I can't run away and leave her to them."

Cullen wanted to reach across the table and shake her, grab her, and haul her little butt out of there. He had seen another woman die, one he loved, one with that same innocence in her eyes. "Damn it, you're so stubborn, so unreasonable. They'll get you, Tempest. If I was still with them, you'd already be on your way to their hideout." Frustrated, he stared out the window, trying to think of anything that might convince her to leave with him. If she didn't go, he would have to stay and try to protect her. And that meant he was going to die. He would have no chance at all.

Tempest remained silent while the waiter placed their plates in front of them. Immediately her stomach lurched at the overwhelming odor of food. She was no longer able to eat anything without Darius's aid. Her insides had changed somehow. She didn't know how she knew it, but she knew. It was the same as her enhanced hearing and eyesight.

"I can't help but notice that you aren't shocked and horrified at the idea that vampire-hunters are after you. Why is that?" Cullen's blue eyes were serious, almost accusing. "Why is that you aren't scoffing at the very idea of vampires?" he demanded.

Tempest indicated the picture. "Brodrick was always intimating that he thought Desari was a vampire. I thought he was an isolated nutcase, but now I can see he was part of a bigger organization. Why in the world did they settle on Desari? She's so sweet to everyone. Why would they believe such a weird thing about her?"

"Her nocturnal habits. Her mesmerizing voice. And when they sent an organized paramilitary hit squad after her, she somehow managed to escape, while the 'soldiers' died or disappeared. These people were professional killers. They sprayed the stage with automatic gunfire, yet she escaped death."

"That's it? That's why she's a vampire?" She wanted to believe he was making up the entire thing, but she knew, deep in her heart, that he wasn't.

"She stays up all night; no one has ever seen her during the day."

"I've seen her during the day," Tempest lied valiantly. She was becoming agitated. She couldn't afford to get upset. Darius was so attuned to her, she knew it would disturb his sleep, and she was worried about his health since she had observed his family's concern.

Cullen shifted position in the straight-backed chair and regarded her steadily. He shook his head and sighed as he picked up his fork. "You're going to die, Tempest. And it won't be an easy death. Damn it, why won't you listen to me? I swear to you, I'm telling the truth."

"I believe you. I don't know why I believe you, it's so absurd, but I do. I'm even fairly certain you aren't trying to lure me into going with you to put me in their hands." Tempest fiddled with her glass of water. She was beginning to sweat. Her head pounded. She needed to touch

Darius. Just for a moment, just to assure herself he was really alive and well.

"Why don't you let me hide you, then? We can warn Desari if you think it will help, but don't go back there. Stay away from them," Cullen begged her.

"Why are you doing this?" Tempest asked. "If you're telling me the truth, your people will never forgive you for this. Why would you risk your life for me?"

Cullen stared sightlessly at the food on his place. "A long time ago I was engaged to the most wonderful woman on this earth. She was loving and gentle—there was no one quite like her. We were in San Francisco, doing the tourist thing together. She was murdered."

Tempest felt his sorrow like a knife. "I'm so sorry, Mr. Tucker." Tears swam in her eyes, tangling in her long lashes. "How horrible for you."

"The police thought the murderer was a serial killer who had been terrorizing the city, but I saw it happen. The creature sank his teeth into her neck and drained her of blood. Then he threw her body down like it was so much garbage. Her blood stained his teeth and chin. He looked right at me and laughed. I knew he was going to kill me next."

"But he didn't." She touched his hand, wanting to comfort him.

Cullen shook his head. When he looked at her, his eyes reflected a deep, piercing pain. "For so long I wished he had. But something or someone scared him off before he could. A light, like a comet, came streaking through the sky toward us. The vampire hissed and turned his head toward it. It was like watching a repulsive reptile move, that slow, undulating way snakes have. Then he literally dissolved in front of my eyes and streamed away from the light coming at us. I watched it chase him

260

across the sky toward the ocean. He was the coldest, cruelest thing I'd ever seen. I wanted revenge. I wanted to hunt him down, hunt down anything that even resembled him."

"I can understand that," Tempest murmured gently.

Cullen shook his head. "No, you can't, and that's the point. You remind me of her. She had great compassion, the way you seem to have. She'd never seek revenge; she'd try to find a way to forgive him. I think that's what you would do." He sighed and moved the food around on his plate. "They're going to torture you for information. Even when you give it to them, they'll kill you. God, Tempest, don't you see? I can't live with that."

Tempest shook her head. "Darius won't let them take me."

Cullen's eyebrows shot up. "Darius? He must be the bodyguard. I'll admit the man is good, but it won't matter how good he is. They'll get you. They'll find you and kidnap you. You don't understand—these people are dead serious."

She leaned forward to stare directly into his eyes so that he would know she spoke the absolute truth. "No, Cullen, you're the one who doesn't understand. They don't understand. Darius would come for me. No one could stop him. Nothing on this earth could stop him. He is utterly relentless. He's merciless. He's as silent as the leopard and moves like the wind. They wouldn't see him, wouldn't smell him, as he sped through time or space. And he would never stop, not until he had me back and had removed any threat to me for all time. That is who they'd be dealing with."

Cullen sat back as if she had struck him. His face paled visibly. "He's not human? You're saying this bodyguard is a vampire?"

"Mr. Tucker, you have vampires on the brain. Of course Darius isn't a vampire. Do I look like the kind of woman who'd go out with a vampire?"

"The bodyguard is your boyfriend?" Cullen asked, incredulous. "He—" He forced himself to stop abruptly. "Are you sure you know what you're doing? He sounds dangerous, Tempest. Very dangerous. I thought maybe he was involved with the singer."

"He is. Darius is Desari's older brother." Tempest pushed at her hair, suddenly wondering what she must look like. She had been working all morning and hadn't thought to clean up before coming into town. She was tired, too. She had stayed up all night with the band and Darius, and now the sun was getting to her. She even felt as if it were burning her eyes and skin. Sunburn wasn't unusual for a fair-skinned redhead, but this burning was different. Deeper. She tried not to be alarmed.

"The bodyguard is not invincible, Tempest," Cullen said, "even if he does seem pretty amazing to both you and the vampire-hunting society."

"I want to thank you for risking so much to warn us," Tempest said softly, and she laid her hand gently on Cullen's. "I'm terribly sorry for your loss, but please don't worry about me. Darius will take care of all of us."

Take your hand off that man now, Tempest! Raw fury, black rage made the velvet voice menacing. *If you value his life, do as I say.*

Tempest snatched her hand away from Cullen and ducked her head to hide the fire in her eyes. *You have no right to order me around. You have no idea what's going on here, Darius.*

I know you are with a male.

Well, gee, what a crime. Sarcasm dripped from her voice.

"Tempest?" Cullen brought her attention back to him. "What's wrong?" He couldn't help but notice she had stiffened, her mouth tightening as if she were annoyed.

She shrugged. "Not much. I just have some weird organization of vampire-hunters wanting to kidnap, torture, and murder me. Not too big of a deal. I can handle it. Mostly I'm worried about Desari. She doesn't deserve any more trauma."

"I wish you'd listen to me. What if I come with you and talk to the bodyguard myself? If he's as good as you say he is, he might be able to use the information I can give him," Cullen ventured, not certain why he offered. He knew he would follow Tempest, try to protect her as best he could. Even if he didn't actually go to the camp, he would try to guard her against others coming after her.

Tempest was already shaking her head.

Bring him back with you, came Darius's order.

I won't do it, Darius. I have no idea what you'll do to him. This man has suffered enough.

You should trust your lifemate.

I would if I had one, she sniped back. *All I have is some bossy male who thinks he can order me around. Go back to sleep.*

You are very brave when you think I cannot touch you, honey. All anger was gone from his voice, replaced by amusement. She felt the brush of his fingers around her throat. His touch sent the familiar wave of heat curling through her bloodstream and butterflies fluttering in her stomach. No one else could do that, touch her physically without being present. She knew Darius was far away; she felt the distance between them.

"Tempest?" Cullen was afraid he was losing her. She

263

kept turning inward, focusing on something other than the danger she was in.

Tempest tilted her chin. "Why would you want to put yourself in more danger, Mr. Tucker? Aren't you taking an even greater risk by joining us? Your people might not find out that you warned me today, but if you actually came to the camp, they'll think you've changed sides."

"I know," Cullen admitted, suddenly weary. "I feel I owe the singer something. I didn't know they'd ordered a hit on her until it was too late, but I was a part of that wacko group for a time, and I feel guilty." His eyes jumped to the window, the door, continually checking in case Brady Grand had sent someone after him.

"Guilt isn't a very good reason to put your life on the line," Tempest pointed out.

Quit arguing with the man and bring him back.

I don't want him hurt.

If he is telling the truth, no one will harm him, Darius assured her.

"I can't let these people kill you, Tempest," Cullen argued. "Matt Brodrick had your picture in his camera when he died tracking your band. They know what you look like, and they'll come for you." Cullen Tucker paused. "How did he die, anyway? It appeared he shot himself, but weren't you there?" Cullen tapped the picture one more time. "This is the exact same spot where his body was found."

"I have no idea. I had no idea he was even taking my picture. He must have been hiding in the bushes close by. It's a heavily wooded area." Tempest tried to throw Cullen off track with the improvised explanation.

"It doesn't stand to reason, Tempest," Cullen said quietly, "that Matt would take your picture and then blow himself away. The police bought it because there was absolutely no evidence of anyone else being around, but I knew Matt. He was a sadistic son-of-a-bitch. He never would have killed himself."

For a moment she couldn't breathe, remembering the way the reporter had looked at her with his cold, calculating eyes.

I am here, baby, Darius reassured her. *This man asks many questions, but I do not sense a trap.*

She took a deep breath and began telling Cullen Tucker the truth. "I didn't see him kill himself. He was going to shoot me, but I fell backward off a cliff and down a ravine. I heard a gunshot, but I have no idea what actually happened."

"No one else was there?" Cullen prompted.

"I didn't see anyone," Tempest reiterated truthfully.

Cullen sighed softly. "Let's get out of here. The longer we stick around, the more likely it is we'll be spotted. Why did you have to drive such a distinctive car?"

"You're right," she agreed. "No one would have noticed the touring bus with the huge block lettering on the sides."

He grinned at her, and Tempest realized it was the first time she had seen the man smile. "I bet you give the bodyguard more trouble than the entire band put together, don't you?" he teased.

She tilted her chin, ignoring Darius's silent laughter. "Why in the world would you say that?"

"Because I know the bodyguard type. And this one is clearly powerful, maybe even deadly. I'd say he'd be dominant, aggressive, and the extremely jealous, possessive type if he ever fell for a woman."

"What an interesting assessment." *Take that, Darius,* she added happily. *He hasn't even met you yet, and he knows exactly what you're like. Rather interesting description, don't you think?*

What I think is, you had better bring your lovely little butt home fast, honey, or I might be tempted to spank it.

You're welcome to try, she said haughtily, knowing she was perfectly safe.

Cullen Tucker stood up, tossed some money onto the table, then held her chair. She sighed. Her nice, solitary existence used to be so simple, so quiet. She heard Darius's low growl of aggression when Cullen guided her toward the door with his palm at her back, and she sighed again. The words echoing in her mind were in another language, one she was unfamiliar with, but the blistering tone told her Darius was swearing.

Step away from him. He has no business putting his hands on you.

He's simply being polite.

Cullen yelped, removing his hand from her to bring it to his mouth. "Something stung me."

"Really? I didn't see a bee." Tempest looked as sympathetic as she could under the circumstances, but she felt an unexpected urge to laugh. *Spoiled little king of the castle.*

Learn some respect, honey, Darius ordered.

Cullen opened the car door for her, then yelped a second time when he held her elbow to help her in. He frowned at her. "What the hell's going on?"

Tempest was fumbling for dark glasses. The sun seemed to be sending shards of glass into her eyes. Almost at once they were swollen and red, streaming in response to the burning light. "I can't think what you mean," she told Cullen.

She drove back to the campsite at a much more sedate pace than she had used heading for the town. Aware that Cullen was following her, she took care to keep to the speed limit, annoying though it was. The road was made for the sports car—winding, narrow, climbing upward, sheer drop-offs on one side, the mountain rising on the other. She had to fight the inclination to let loose and enjoy what the car could really do.

Once in the forest itself, she moved through the network of dirt roads like a professional. Cullen needn't know she had practiced driving the route so she wouldn't get lost. She maneuvered through the maze of narrow tracks, selecting one bearing to the right. At once she felt a curious, mood-wrenching sensation, the dark oppression of entering a time warp of evil—the perimeters Darius had set around the camp to keep others out. She was more sensitive to them than she had been before. It wasn't so bad that she couldn't drive through the barricade, but she feared Cullen might have a problem.

He pulled up behind her, not quite to the barricade. "What's the hold-up?" he called.

She pulled her car forward, waiting for him to see what would happen. Cullen drove toward her a few feet, then stopped abruptly, slamming on the breaks. Tempest glanced in her rearview mirror and noted that he was trembling, beads of perspiration dotting his forehead. *Can he make it through the safeguards? Does it get worse?*

For a mile or so. He can take it.

Can you get rid of it?

Lead him through it. Darius was implacable. He would not lower the barrier when he knew they were hunted, when he was aware Tempest could be in imminent danger.

Muttering about stubborn men, Tempest got out of the sports car and walked back to Cullen. His breathing was labored, his hand clutching at his chest.

"I think I'm having a heart attack," he managed to get out.

"Move over," she said. "I'll drive. It's just a kind of security measure Darius dreamed up. He's a genius, you know," she said briskly. "It drives people away from the area."

"It feels evil, like something is waiting to drag us into hell," Cullen said, but he obediently moved over.

"Yeah, well, after you meet Darius, you might think that's just what happened," she replied grimly. "God help you, Cullen, if you're not on the up and up. Darius is no one you want to try to lie to."

"If he designed this particular security system," Cullen said with a certain degree of admiration and awe, "I believe you."

"Is it letting up?" she asked hopefully. She didn't want to leave the sports car where someone might find it and give away their location, and it was too hot to drive him to camp and walk back to retrieve the car.

"Enough that I know I'm not having a heart attack. I can follow you. Just get us out of this as fast as you can," he pleaded.

Tempest patted his shoulder and slid out of his vehicle and back into hers. They made good time weaving in and out of the trails, Cullen practically tailgating her.

The camp appeared deserted when they arrived. Tempest knew the band and Darius were sleeping somewhere in safety. The cats, scenting a stranger, immediately started roaring their opposition to such an invasion. Cullen refused to get out of his car, hearing what sounded like a den of leopards, hungry and determined to have him for lunch. Tempest spent a few minutes silencing the cats, exasperated that Darius had chosen that moment to bow out and leave her on her own.

"Where is everyone?" Cullen demanded, finally emerging from his car and gingerly looking around the deserted camp. He followed Tempest to the truck.

"Darius is somewhere in the woods. He likes to string a hammock between two trees far away from all of us and have what he affectionately refers to as his quiet time."

Very funny, honey. You are the worst liar I have ever met. And stop touching that man. If I get any more jealous, I will be the one to have the heart attack.

Go back to sleep. You're annoying me, Tempest said severely. She smiled sweetly at Cullen. "He's so moody, you know."

"And Desari? Where is she?" He glanced uneasily at the motor home.

Tempest caught his look and burst out laughing. "She's in a coffin in the bus. Would you like to see? I can let the cats out while you take a look around."

Cullen looked sheepish. "I guess I am being pretty silly. But those cats are another reason Desari was marked by the society." He absently handed Tempest a tool she pointed at. "Vampires supposedly have some animal from hell looking after them in the daytime. Those cats fit the description."

Tempest laughed with him. "Actually, the bus is empty except for the cats. I use it more than the others. They're up a great deal at night, either rehearsing or performing or driving to their next destination. I take care of the vehicles, so I go to town and do the shopping and take care of business. Desari and Julian are probably up already," she improvised. "They like to hike. Personally, I think that's their excuse to make eyes at each other with no one around."

"Julian Savage? He's high on the society's hit list. He

269

has quite a reputation. Some of them think he's the reason Desari escaped the hit," Cullen confessed.

Tempest banged her knuckles, muttered a few choice words, and bent back to her task. "The way I heard it, he did save her life."

"Did he kill the entire squad?" Cullen asked, curious.

"I don't know. I never even knew they were dead. I rarely read the newspapers." She said it almost absently, as if she were barely listening.

"I don't think it was Julian," Cullen said carefully, watching her closely. "I think the bodyguard killed them."

She not only banged her knuckles this time but her forehead as well. She turned to glare at him. "I have work to do. Get out of my hair for a while, will you? Go check the woods for the band. Dayan has one of those little tent things. Don't wake him up if he's sleeping, though; he's a grouch if you disturb him before he gets his eight hours. Syndil could be in the bus with the cats if you want to look," she offered, knowing full well he wouldn't take her up on it.

Cullen shook his head. "That won't be necessary. I don't want to get anyone riled up. I'll just look things over to see if I can figure a way to tighten security around here."

"Oh, yeah, that's all we need, one more bossy male telling us what to do," Tempest muttered under her breath.

I am impressed with your ability to give the illusion we are all out roaming in the sun.

See? I'm an accomplished liar when I need to be, she said. *Guess it comes with living the kind of life I had when I was a kid. It might come in handy if these maniacs get their hands on me.*

Darius could hear the faint echo of fear in her voice. She was trying valiantly to pretend the things Cullen had revealed to her didn't frighten her, but he was dwelling in her mind, and he knew she was afraid. *Torture and kill.* Those were the words Cullen Tucker had used, and Tempest had a vivid imagination. *You are under my protection,* he reassured her gently.

Tempest smiled at his arrogance. She knew that his comment was supposed to make her feel instantly better, but she was used to relying on herself, not on the protection of some man.

Some man? Darius echoed.

She could hear his soft laughter, the gentle teasing that always managed to melt her heart. *I'm trying to work here, Darius. Go away.*

You really do have trouble with authority figures.

And you have trouble with anyone saying no to you, don't you? she countered and promptly banged her knuckles again. *Damn it, Darius, you're distracting me. See what you made me do?*

Pay attention to your work, and stop looking at that male.

I'm not looking at him, she denied hotly, glancing up to see just where Cullen was. She didn't want him snooping around the bus and being eaten by the two leopards, may be even at Darius's command.

Soft, mocking laughter echoed in her head. *There you go, looking again. Pay attention to what you are doing or we might have to fire you.*

Desari wouldn't let you. Go back to sleep while the sun is still up.

Chapter Thirteen

Syndil emerged from the trailer, confirming Rusti's belief that Darius was able to communicate privately with each member of his family as he did with her. He must have filled them in on what had transpired while they slept and the cover stories Tempest had provided for each of them.

Cullen nearly fell over backward watching Syndil approach. His mouth actually fell open, his gaze on her swaying hips and her wealth of raven hair. Syndil smiled in her sweet, shy way at Cullen as Rusti introduced them. She looked unusually beautiful, an exotic beauty who could steal a man's breath. Indeed, Cullen looked as though someone had struck him in the head with a two-by-four, as he stammered out a greeting to the black-haired musician.

"How nice of you to join us, Mr. Tucker," Syndil said softly, her voice as soft and gentle as the breeze surrounding them. "I hope Rusti is seeing to all your needs. We have plenty of refreshments in the bus."

Cullen shoved a hand through his blond hair, messing it up even more than the long ride had done. "Oh, yeah, sure. She's been great."

"And the truck is fixed, Rusti?" Syndil asked politely, trying not to smile at Cullen's reaction to her. It had been a while since anyone had made her feel beautiful and desirable. She knew that was her own fault, hiding from the world, but now, with Cullen Tucker making her feel alive again, she was suddenly happy.

"No problem," Tempest replied.

Syndil reached out and caught Tempest's right hand, turning it over to examine the scraped knuckles. "You are bleeding. You have hurt yourself." There was tremendous concern in her voice, on her expressive face. She glanced up at Cullen, a mischievous and sexy smile on her mouth even while her palm settled over Tempest's, soothing the scrapes. "Does Darius know you have a friend visiting?"

Tempest felt color sweeping into her face. Syndil knew very well why Cullen Tucker was there. She was just subtly teasing her. Syndil smiled at Cullen. "Darius is crazy about Rusti, and he is a very jealous man. Perhaps you should stick close to me so I might offer my protection."

Cullen looked happy with that idea. "Do you think I need protection?"

"Oh, absolutely," Syndil assured him, flirting outrageously. "Darius never allows anyone near Rusti."

"That isn't true, Cullen." At least Tempest hoped she was telling the truth. Darius allowed the women around her. It seemed to be only men he objected to.

"Is this a party?" Dayan came striding out of the

woods, a backpack on his shoulders and a small tent folded neatly into a cube in his hands. "Why wasn't I invited?"

"Because you're such a grouch when we try to wake you up," Syndil greeted him, winking at Tempest. She went up on her toes and brushed a kiss on Dayan's chin. "It's okay. We forgive you. You can join us now if you like. Rusti has invited a friend to visit."

Dayan instantly offered his free hand to Cullen, a welcoming grin on his face. "My name is Dayan. Any friend of Rusti's is a friend of ours." He rubbed his chin thoughtfully, his eyes shifting from Cullen to Tempest and back again. "Does Darius know you're here? Have you met him?"

Cullen glanced uneasily at Tempest. "I'm beginning to think coming here wasn't such a great idea. Just how jealous is this bodyguard?"

Dayan laughed softly. "Darius has this thing about his little darling."

"I am not his 'little darling'!" Tempest denied hotly. "I'm not his anything." *I know you can hear every word being said. You're deliberately making Cullen squirm. Come out here right now!* she groused to Darius.

It is not only Cullen Tucker who appears to be nervous. Darius responded complacently. *And you are mine, my everything.*

You really need to get out of fantasy land, Darius.

Dayan had the audacity to ruffle Tempest's hair as if they were old family friends. "You are definitely Darius's only love, and he does not share well."

Syndil nodded solemnly. "He really does not. I don't think he learned how to as a child." Her dark eyes were lit with mischief, something those around her were grateful to see. "Really, Mr. Tucker—or may I call you Cullen—I will protect you."

Cullen again ran a hand through his hair. "No man is willing to share the woman he loves, Syndil. But Tempest and I met only a few hours ago in town. I brought some news she thought all of you should hear. But the bodyguard doesn't have anything to worry about. I wasn't hitting on her."

Dayan's eyes were suddenly hard and cold. "I hope we did not give you a false impression of Darius. He would never *worry*. That is not his way." The voice, even more than the words, supplied the threat.

Tempest groaned out loud, wishing she knew Dayan well enough to hit him over the head. She reached out to reassure Cullen, who was looking as if he'd stumbled into a nest of vipers. Dayan moved subtly, deliberately inserting his solid frame between Tempest and the human. Syndil took Cullen's arm and walked him toward some lounge chairs set up beneath a shade tree.

Darkness was falling fast. Bats began their nightly ritual, assaulting the insects, performing their acrobatics in the sky. A cool breeze had come up, gently rustling the leaves in the trees. Desari and Julian, complete with hiking boots and backpacks, walked hand in hand into the circle. Both looked surprised to see a visitor, but Tempest knew by their appearance that the surprise was feigned.

Julian moved his body protectively in front of Desari even as he offered his hand to Cullen as they were introduced. Cullen looked uneasy as he murmured a greeting. This was the man the society absolutely believed was a vampire. Cullen studied him closely, receiving an immediate impression of sheer power. Julian Savage was enormously strong, although careful not to crush Cullen's bones when they shook hands. It was impossible to tell his age; his face looked timeless. Physically he was almost beautiful, in a purely masculine way, like the Greek statues of their gods.

"You are a fan of my wife's singing?" Julian ventured.

"He came here with Rusti," Dayan offered with a grin.

Julian's eyebrows shot up. "With Rusti? Then you have not met Darius as of yet, Mr. Tucker."

"Don't start," Tempest said. "I mean it, Julian. We've gone through this already. Darius is hardly the ogre you're all making him out to be. He could care less if I had a dozen men here to visit."

Do not ever risk that one, my love, Darius said softly in her mind, the snap of his white teeth audible.

"Do you want a mass murder taking place?" Dayan teased.

Tempest tilted her chin in a challenge. "Darius isn't like that at all."

Darius came striding out of the woods, tall, elegant, power personified. Cullen actually came to his feet. The bodyguard was the most impressive man he had ever seen. His body rippled with leashed strength. Power oozed from his every pore. His midnight-black hair was pulled back and held with a tie at the nape of his neck. The harsh planes and angles of his face seemed carved of granite. His mouth held latent sensuality and a hint of cruelty. His black eyes took in everything, the smallest detail, yet never left Tempest's face.

Darius moved silently, like a stalking panther, straight to Tempest's side, his arm curving around her possessively, drawing her beneath his shoulder. He bent his head to find her soft, trembling mouth with his hard one. "You look tired, baby. Perhaps you should lie down and rest before we move out tonight. You have been working all day."

The moment his perfect mouth touched hers, Tempest forgot his teasing and gave herself up to the sizzling chemistry between them. Her arm slipped halfway around his waist, her fingers bunching in his shirt. "I'm fine, Darius. The truck is running, so we can leave as soon as we need to go. I brought this man here to speak with you."

The black eyes at once rested on Cullen Tucker's face. Involuntarily Cullen shivered beneath the icy gaze. It was like looking into a graveyard, the eyes of death itself. Cullen felt as if the bodyguard could read his every thought and was judging him worthy or unworthy—and that his very life might be hanging in the balance. He watched as the bodyguard carefully, deliberately raised Tempest's right hand to his mouth, his tongue moving slowly, almost erotically over her scraped knuckles, those black, burning eyes never leaving Cullen's face. Cullen could feel Syndil at his right side, close yet not touching him. He was aware that she was holding her breath.

"I'm Cullen Tucker," he introduced himself, grateful that he still had his voice. Tempest had been telling the truth about this man. He would go after anyone who attempted to take her from him, and he would never stop. The bodyguard, as he'd guessed earlier, was the type of man who was utterly relentless, who had no mercy in him.

"Darius," the bodyguard replied briefly. His hands went to Tempest's shoulders, and he pushed her toward his brother-in-law. "Julian, perhaps you would take the three women to shelter while I speak with this gentleman. Desari, please see to the needs of the cats, and make certain Tempest eats before she goes to bed."

Syndil moved closer to Cullen, for the first time in her life defying Darius. *I will stay here and listen.* Her chin was up belligerently.

Without warning Barack was there, his handsome face a twisted mask of fury. He literally shoved past the other men and caught Syndil's arm, yanking her away from the human. His eyes were burning with rage. "What are you thinking, Darius, that you allow this man to come into our camp while our women are unprotected?" he demanded, forcing Syndil backward despite her struggles. His body was a solid wall of muscle, pressing her softer one away from the group.

"How dare you treat me this way!" Syndil hissed, outraged.

Barack turned his head, his black eyes blazing at her. "You will do as I say in this matter. You know better than to put yourself in a vulnerable position."

"Barack, have you lost your mind?" Syndil demanded.

He growled, a low warning that rumbled in the air, his white teeth snapping like a predator's. *I refuse to argue with you. If you do not wish to suffer embarrassment, Syndil, you will do as I say right now. Do you think that I did not know you actively sought this man's company?*

Syndil moved backward into the shelter of the trees, partly because Barack was giving her no choice and partly because she was so astonished. Barack was the most easygoing of all the males. He tended to be amused by everything, and he flirted outrageously with human women, enjoying his image of the playboy of the band.

You have no right to tell me what to do, Barack. If I wish to seek out a thousand men, it is my right.

Like hell it is. Barack literally lifted her by the waist and carried her deeper into the woods. "Who is this man, that you suddenly wish to be with him? You have never displayed interest in human men before."

Syndil's chin went up. "Well, perhaps that has changed."

"What has changed? What did this man do, bewitch you? I warn you, Syndil, I am in no mood for this foolishness. You touched him. You put your hand on his arm, flirted with him." His eyes were blazing at her.

"And this is considered a crime? Should I remind you of all the times I have known you were with human women? Do not dare to judge my behavior. This man makes me feel beautiful, desirable, like a woman, not some shadow to be ignored. He looks at me, and I feel alive again," Syndil defended herself.

"That is the reason? He makes you feel alive? Any man can do that, Syndil," Barack snapped.

"Well, he is the one I want," she said defiantly.

His hand closed around her neck, his dark eyes furious. "I have waited patiently for you to recover, been as gentle as I know how to be. But this I will not give you. If you dare to go near that man, I will tear him apart with my bare hands. Now get in the trailer, where I know you will be safe, and stay away from him."

Syndil blinked up at him, shocked and wide-eyed at his uncharacteristic outburst. "I am going, but not because you order me. I do not want a scene in front of an outsider."

Barack pushed her toward the bus. "I do not care what foolish reason you come up with to do as I *order* you. Just do it. Go now. I mean it."

"Where did you get the idea that you were my lord and master?" she indignantly threw back at him over her shoulder as she went toward the motor home.

"You just remember that I am, Syndil," he snapped and watched to assure himself that she did as he commanded before he returned to join the men, who were questioning Cullen.

Rusti and Desari met Syndil at the door to the bus. Desari wrapped an arm around Syndil's shoulder. "Was Barack very angry?"

"I do not know about him," Syndil said, "but I am. What is he thinking, treating me that way? As if I am his daughter, his baby sister. Do you have any idea how many women he has been with? It's disgusting, that's what it is. It makes me sick, the way the men have such a double standard—one for their own behavior and another for ours. The only reason I even listened to him was because this is a matter of your security, Desari. Otherwise I would have told him to go straight to hell. I may yet. In fact, I may just leave altogether after this next concert of yours. I need a vacation from that idiot."

"Maybe I should go with you," Tempest ventured. "Darius is even worse than Barack. What is it with these men?"

Desari laughed softly. "They are overbearing and domineering and often royal pains. Julian is forever trying to lay down the law with me. The thing is, you have to stand up to them."

Syndil pushed a hand through her hair in agitation. "You and Rusti, maybe, but I do not belong to anyone. I should be able to do as I wish."

Tempest sank into a deep, cushioned chair. Both leopards immediately wrapped themselves around her legs. "I don't belong to Darius. Where does everyone get the idea I'm his girlfriend? And even if I were, I wouldn't have to do a darn thing he says."

"Rusti," Desari said gently, "you cannot defy Darius. No one can, not even one of us, and we are very powerful. Finding a lifemate is not like a human marriage.

More powerful instincts are at work. Each of us has only one true lifemate, you as well as Darius. You must be the other half of his soul. The light to his darkness. You cannot change what is simply because you fear it."

Syndil nodded in agreement. Taking up a brush, she removed the clip from Tempest's hair so she could tame the thick red-gold mass. "Darius is always so gentle with you, but there is great darkness in him. You must understand what he is. You cannot think of him as human; he is not human. He is quite capable of forcing your compliance in matters of your health or your safety. The men always protect the women."

"Why? Why are they so dominating? It sets my teeth on edge."

Desari sighed softly. "Darius has saved our lives over and over again. The first time he was only six years old. He has done miraculous things, but to do them, he had to believe implicitly in his own judgment, and with that comes a certain arrogance."

Tempest gave an inelegant snort, but a part of her was awed at what Desari was telling her. She had seen glimpses of Darius's life in his memories, had heard some of his stories, and they astonished her, his implacable resolve to keep his family alive.

"Julian told me that the Carpathian race is dying out," Desari continued. "There are few women—fewer than twenty, counting Syndil and myself. We are the future of our race. Without us, the men have no chance of survival. It used to be that a woman waited a century before she settled with her mate and even longer to bear children. But now the males have no choice but to claim their lifemates when they are mere fledglings. You must see why it is of vital importance to all of them that we are protected," Desari said.

Tempest felt her heart skip a beat. It was easier not to think too much about what she had gotten herself into. When Desari said the words aloud, she knew terror was waiting a heartbeat away to claim her. She bit down hard on her lower lip. Both women heard her suddenly pounding heart. She was human, not Carpathian, and she didn't feel safe in their world.

Desari sank to her knees in front of Tempest. "Please do not fear us," she said softly, persuasively. "You are our sister, one of us. No one in our family would harm you. Indeed, Darius would give his life for you. He *is* giving his life for you." Her dark eyes filled with tears.

Tempest's green eyes widened at Desari's obvious distress, her choice of words. "What do you mean, he's giving his life for me?"

"We Carpathians have great longevity, Rusti; that is both our blessing and our curse. Because you are his lifemate, yet mortal, Darius will choose the human way of things. He will grow old and die with you rather than remain an immortal," Desari explained gently.

"Already he shows signs of stress," Syndil added. "He is refusing to go to ground to sleep properly."

"What does that mean?" Tempest asked, curious. Darius often used that phrase, but she still wasn't certain exactly what it meant.

"The soil is healing to our people," Desari said. "Our bodies require sleep in a different way than yours. We must shut down our heart and lungs to rejuvenate ourselves. Without doing that, we cannot sustain our full strength. Darius is our protector. He is the one who must face the human assassins and hunt the undead who threaten us. Unless he goes to ground as he must, he will lose his great power."

Tempest felt her breath catch in her lungs. The

thought of Darius in trouble was frightening. "Why doesn't he just go to sleep the way he's supposed to? He spends the entire time driving me crazy, always talking to me, giving me orders, and mixing in a threat or two just to keep things interesting."

"Darius would never leave you unprotected. He could not. You are his lifemate. He cannot be apart from you."

Tempest sighed, enjoying the way the two women made her feel, as if she belonged in their family circle. "Well, he'll just have to get over it already. I'll insist he go to sleep the way he's supposed to. If he won't, I'll have no choice but to leave."

Desari shook her head. "You still do not understand. Darius can never be apart from you. It would destroy him. Do not think that anything will change if you attempt to leave him. He will only put a tighter leash on you, Rusti. He has never once, in all the centuries of his existence, wanted anything for himself. But he wants you. Needs you."

"Perhaps I don't want him," Tempest said. "Don't I have rights?"

Syndil and Desari both laughed, the notes like silvery bells, like water tripping over rocks. "Darius can do no other than make you happy. He dwells in your mind. If you did not want him, he would know. Can you not understand, Rusti?" Desari asked her. "You cannot be without him any more than he can be away from you. Do you not feel it when you are apart? When he is sleeping the sleep of mortals?"

Tempest ducked her head, the memory of that precise discomfort firmly in her mind. For a moment she felt close to tears. At once he was there in her mind. *Tempest? I am here.* He flooded her with warmth, with reassurance.

I'm okay, just being silly.

I will come to you if you have need.

Your touch is enough. And it was. The two women were right. She needed him whether or not she was willing to admit it to anyone other than herself. She felt the brush of fingers, a tender caress that trailed over her cheekbone, down to her mouth. She could feel the instant response of her body, the warmth, the heat, the distress when the contact slipped reluctantly away.

"Rusti?" Desari asked softly. "Are you okay?" She turned Tempest's hand over to examine the scraped knuckles. "How did you do this? Has Darius seen this?" She closed her palm over the scrape in the same way Syndil had. At once Tempest could feel a soothing warmth.

"Of course," Tempest admitted, blushing slightly as she remembered the feel of his mouth on her skin. "He doesn't miss anything. What exactly are the undead? You said Darius hunted the undead. Are you talking about vampires?"

"If our males do not find a lifemate, in time they eventually lose their souls to the darkness within them. They become vampire, preying on our people as well as humans. They must be destroyed," Desari answered.

Syndil touched Tempest's shoulder to draw her attention. "The one who attacked me, the one who was raised as my brother, my family, my protector—he had turned vampire. He nearly killed Darius. Had Darius not been so powerful, he might have succeeded. As it was, Darius was severely wounded. I, too, would be dead, and perhaps Desari as well. Who knows?"

"Cullen told me he had seen a vampire in San Francisco. That the woman he had intended to marry was murdered by one," Tempest said. She reached up to take

Syndil's hand with her free one, so that they were all connected. "Could Darius still turn?" There was a note of fear in her voice.

"Not unless something happened to you." Desari was examining Tempest's knuckles again. "We need to clean this scrape."

"Is there a possibility of a child? Could we have children together?" Now there was a distinct quaver in Tempest's voice.

Desari exchanged a long look with Syndil. "I do not know for certain, Rusti," Desari answered honestly. "Julian told me of one woman who was born to a human mother and a Carpathian father. She was not raised in our ways and had a difficult time surviving. There was no one to teach her, to love her, to help her grow properly because the mother committed suicide and the father turned vampire. The child did survive, however, and eventually was discovered by her true lifemate."

Tempest closed her eyes tiredly, rubbing her suddenly pounding forehead. "So I guess if I stay with Darius—and I don't seem to have too many other choices—I might or might never have children. I never really considered I'd have the whole fairy tale."

"Darius is giving up his life for you," Syndil pointed out gently. "When the sun is high, members of our race are vulnerable. Even Darius. In the ground, few could harm us, but while he sleeps the sleep of mortals, he cannot go to ground. Anyone who found his resting place could easily kill him. As time goes on, and he loses more and more rejuvenating sleep, his great strength will weaken substantially."

"What can I do to remedy the situation? I don't want this. I never asked him for this. I couldn't bear it if something happened to him because he was trying to take care of me. It's insane for him to neglect his own needs because he's watching over me." Tempest couldn't think beyond that. Everything else was far too overwhelming. "Has an ordinary human woman ever before become a lifemate to one of your kind? Surely I can't be the only one. There must be someone who knows what to do. I can't have Darius endangering himself." The idea of some assassin or vampire stumbling upon Darius while he was vulnerable was frightening.

Desari tightened her hold on Tempest's hand. "Julian told me his brother's lifemate was human."

Tempest jerked her hand away, unwilling for Desari to feel her elevated pulse. Desari had used the past tense. "She's dead?"

"No! Oh, no, she is one of us now. She is like we are." Desari glanced at Syndil, well aware Darius would not thank them for imparting this information and worrying Tempest.

Syndil hugged Tempest gently. "I am going to fix you more vegetable broth. You are quite pale."

Tempest shook her head, answering almost absently, her mind clearly somewhere else. "I'm not hungry. Thanks, though, Syndil. What do you mean, she is like you now? How is that possible?"

"Darius can convert you," Desari admitted carefully. "He has said he will not, that he would never take the chance of something going wrong. He has made up his mind to live as a human until your death. Then he will go with you."

Tempest stood up, scattering the leopards, pacing restlessly. "How is it done? How would he convert me?"

"He must make three complete blood exchanges with you. It is obvious he has made at least one, perhaps even two." Desari watched her pacing, nervous that she had told her things Darius had purposely kept to himself. "But Darius will not even consider the idea. He feels it is far too risky, as only a couple of women have survived such conversions . . . intact."

Tempest stiffened. "Exchanged blood. He has taken my blood. What is an exchange?"

There was a small, telling silence. And suddenly she didn't want anyone to say anything; the knowledge was already seeping slowly into her pores, her brain. Tempest pressed her hand to her mouth. The idea was so frightening, she pushed it out of her head in an attempt to understand what the women were telling her. "That's why I see things and hear things so differently," she mused aloud, looking to them for confirmation.

"And why you are having trouble eating human food."

There was another silence while Tempest digested what they were saying. Her mind worked at it from all angels. "So if he converted me, I would have to have blood."

Syndil stroked a light, soothing hand down the length of her hair. "Yes, Rusti, you would be like us in every way. You would have to sleep our sleep, stay out of the sun. You would be as vulnerable and as powerful as we are. But Darius refuses to take the chance. He has made up his mind to keep the risk all his own." She said this softly, gently, her voice a beautiful blend of soothing, comforting notes, yet it didn't help.

The sides of the trailer were suddenly closing in on Tempest, suffocating her, crushing her as the mountain had done. Tempest pushed herself away from the two women and stumbled toward the door. She had to breathe; she needed air. She flung herself out of the bus, wanting to run into the night, run to freedom.

Darius caught her small, flying figure as she leapt down

the steps, and he pulled her into the safety of his arms. "What is it, baby?" he whispered softly against her neck. "What has frightened you?" He didn't invade her mind, because he wanted her to trust him enough to tell him herself. If she refused to tell him, he could always merge with her.

Tempest buried her face in his neck. "Take me away from here, Darius, please. Just get me out into the open."

He raised his eyes, black and furious, to meet his sister's guilty gaze before he turned and moved away from the camp. Once out of sight of prying eyes, he poured on the speed, so fast that the trees around them blurred. When he stopped, they were in a secluded clearing tucked into the rolling hillside by a grove of trees.

"Now tell me, honey." He was still permitting her to speak the words rather than reading her mind. He wanted her trust. He wanted her to volunteer what was causing her fear. "We are under the open sky. Only the stars are looking down upon us." His hand caressed her cheek, her throat, slid down the length of her arm to find her palm. Very gently he brought her knuckles to the warmth of his mouth, to the soothing, healing moisture his velvet tongue provided.

She closed her eyes tightly, savoring the feel of him. She had missed him these last few hours. Missed him so much that she didn't even feel alive unless he was bugging her. "I don't know how to be a part of something, Darius, a part of you." She pressed her forehead against his shoulder, afraid to look at him. "I've been alone all my life. I don't know any other way."

Darius held her closer, warming her. "We have all the time in the world, honey. You will learn to be comfortable with a family, and if it is too much all at once, I will take you away from the others until you learn to be a part of me. You do not have to contend with the entire group of us all at once if you find it overwhelming."

"What if I can't do it, Darius? What if I just can't?"

His hand found the nape of her neck, his fingers moving in a slow massage, easing the tension out of her. "Baby," he said softly in his black-velvet voice, the one that could command the wind and the very forces of nature. The one that sent her pulse racing and set every nerve ending in her body on fire. "There is nothing to fear. I can do no other than ensure your happiness. Trust me to do that."

"I could lose you, Darius. You know I could. It's so much easier to be alone than to lose someone." Her voice was low and trembling, turning his heart over. "Already you are neglecting to take care of yourself. You're taking advantage of my ignorance of your needs, your ways. Something could happen to you because of me. Don't you see that? I couldn't bear it."

Silently Darius cursed his sister. He felt Tempest's fears and fatigue beating at her, at him. Her body needed nourishment, yet she couldn't eat. His fault. He had done that to her. "What nonsense has my sister been spouting? You cannot be responsible for choices I make. I want to be with you. Live with you, love you, be a family with you."

Tempest shook her head, then pulled back to look into his eyes. "You know that can never be. I won't let you do this, Darius—throw away your life, make yourself vulnerable, perhaps sick. I know sleeping above ground the same way I sleep will eventually weaken you. I won't have it. Why are you doing that? I don't need constant protection. I've taken care of myself for a long time."

He answered her the only way he knew how, by fastening his mouth to hers. The rush was there, instantly arcing between them, sizzling and snapping as hunger rose sharply and flames began to lick at their skin. Darius poured everything he felt for her into that kiss—the fire, the hunger and need, his absolute commitment to her. Then he caught her face between his palms to hold her still beneath his searching gaze. "Look at me, honey. I want you to believe me. Merge your mind with mine so that you will know that what I say is true. I want this. I have no reservations, none at all. I want to spend my life with you, grow old and die with you. It would be a wonderful miracle to have centuries together, but I accept that it cannot be, and I do not wish it otherwise." He leaned down to kiss the corners of her mouth. "Do not fear our union. It is what I want with every cell of my body. It is the only thing I want. I will be happy with our life together."

Tempest reached up to circle his neck with her arms, pulling his head down desperately to kiss him, moving against his body restlessly, needing him with almost Carpathian hunger. He could feel the tears on her face and knew she was crying for him, knew she was afraid of bringing him harm, knew that any moment she could be so overwhelmed by this sharing of her life that she might bolt.

"Why didn't you tell me what you were doing to yourself, Darius?" she whispered against his throat. His fingers were moving beneath her shirt, pushing the edges up until he found her silken skin, his palm hot and inviting, caressing her breast. She could hardly think with the fire racing through her and the hunger for him raging in her soul. "You have to promise me you'll never do it again. I can look after myself while you're in the ground. I'll stay wherever you ask me to stay. I promise I will, Darius."

His mouth was now at her breast and she cradled his head to her, her fingers spearing through his thick hair while waves of heat raced through her body.

She was silk and satin, warm honey, and the clean, fresh scent of the night he loved so much. She was everything good and beautiful in the world, everything he could ever want. His hands slipped reverently over her body, sliding over every inch of skin he could reach. He pushed at her jeans to get at more of her.

Darius was consumed with hunger for her, with a fierce need to bury himself in the perfection of her body. He needed her hot, tight sheath gripping him to take away the terrible fear for her safety he couldn't quite shake. He pushed her jeans away from her slender hips, caressing her, shaping her body with his hands, cupping her bottom in his palms so that he could crush her against him, press her into his hard, thick arousal. He groaned at the feel of her, moist and hot, beckoning him, her body's wild scent calling to his.

She seemed so fragile that he had a fear of crushing her, of becoming so out of control that he would forget his own enormous strength and hurt her. He tried to be gentle with her, to see to her fulfillment before her own, but the scent and feel of her was so exciting to him that his animal instincts threatened to take over.

"What am I going to do with you, Darius?" she whispered softly against his bared chest. Her mouth was moving over him, tasting his skin as hungrily as he was tasting hers. There was an ache in her voice.

His mouth immediately fastened on hers again in long, drugging kisses that fanned the flames more. "Love me back, Tempest. Need me the way I have need of you."

He was everywhere, his broad shoulders blocking out

the night sky, his breath taking hers, his body molding around hers, sweeping her into their own world where nothing else intruded. "You do not know what you put me through with your blatant disobedience." His mouth was on her throat, her breasts, a frenzied hunger that seemed to know no boundaries. "You must learn to obey me." His hand moved between her thighs, found her hot, moist acceptance. He heard his own groan as his body hardened even more, a sweet agony only she could relieve. "God, baby, I am going to explode if I do not take you right now." His fingers found her feminine sheath, explored, teased, made her crazy for him.

Tempest was kissing his shoulder, soft little nips she couldn't stop, her body moving restlessly in enticement, demand. "Darius, please, stop giving orders for once and just make love to me."

He pressed her back against a fallen tree, turning her in his arms so that she could brace her hands on the huge trunk. He caressed her bottom, traced the indentations, the cleft, the two small dimples at her lower back. Impatient, Tempest pushed against him, and he grew instantly heavier with need. His hands went to her hips to hold her still, and as he pressed his velvet tip into her hot entrance, the breath was stolen from his lungs.

"Darius!" she wailed, trying to push backward, to take the length of him deep inside her.

"Promise me," he growled softly, his hands caressing her hips, sliding over her buttocks to deliberately enflame her more. The sight of her, so petite and perfect, sent streaks of lightning whipping through him.

"I promise," she bit out rashly, unable to think clearly.

Darius reached around her to cup her breasts in his palms possessively. He thrust into her mind even as his hips surged forward to bury himself deep within her. She was even hotter, softer, tighter than he remembered. He nuzzled her neck, his teeth scraping erotically. He felt her body grip him harder in anticipation, and, despite his every good intention, the wildness in him took over; his fangs lengthened and sank into her neck.

He took her hard and fast, thrusting deeply, his body surrounding hers as hers did his. He was in her mind, feeding her erotic images, his savage, primitive, bestial nature rising, a wolf claiming its mate, a leopard holding its female in a submissive position. At the same time he was Darius, taking her higher and higher, pushing their shared pleasure beyond human to ecstasy. Her body rippled with her release, driving him over the edge so that his hot seed erupted again and again into her depths.

He held her still, locked to her, not wanting to give up their physical connection, the taste of her. Reluctantly he forced himself to close the pinpricks in her neck. He had fed well before he had approached the camp, knowing he would take her before the night was over, knowing he might still, regretfully, have to kill Cullen Tucker. He did not want to risk inadvertently converting Tempest, to chance that something might go wrong.

He stroked her body, explored her every curve. His mouth followed the line of her spine, kissing the length of her back. "Do you have any idea how I feel about you, baby, any idea at all?" he growled.

Tempest's legs felt rubbery. She wanted to lie down somewhere. They had been up all night the night before, and she had not so much as grabbed a nap. Suddenly, with all the intrigue, the work, and their shared, wild lovemaking, she was exhausted.

Darius knew it instantly. He slowly withdrew from her

body, feeling slightly bereft. It shamed him that he could need her so much, hunger for her blood, the taste of her body, the feel of her surrounding him. He had to find a way to strike a balance between treating her gently enough to keep from scaring her off and forcing his will on her so that he could keep her always safe at his side.

Darius tenderly pulled her up against his hard frame, where Tempest slumped, blushing wildly at how wanton she had been, begging him to take her. She shoved her hands through her hair, and at once his palms covered her upthrust breasts, sending fire sizzling to her sensitive nipples and back to him again. She buried her face against his chest, too tired to stand on her own, and Darius instantly swept her up into his arms. She closed her eyes as they moved in a blur through time and space.

Whatever he said to the others, however he had made it happen, she was grateful that the campsite was empty, except for the bus when they returned, both of them stark naked. When she was making love to Darius, she felt totally free, totally uninhibited. But once they were back in the real world, her private nature reasserted itself, and she was painfully modest.

Darius carried her into the trailer to the sofa bed, placing her among all its pillows. "You will rest now, Tempest." It was decree, an order delivered in a voice meant to be obeyed.

She caught at him as he went to move away from her, drawing him back to the bed, down beside her. Her hand stroked the hard angles and planes of his face, a gentle caress that totally disarmed him. Darius was instantly lost in the contentment, the sheer pleasure of having her with him. He lay down beside her, just for a few minutes, and pulled her into his arms.

Chapter Fourteen

"What are we going to do about these people stalking Desari?" Tempest asked as she snuggled into the curve of Darius's arm.

He looked down at her, his mouth brushing her forehead tenderly. "We? What is this 'we'? As I understand it, the society's first objective is to acquire you. You are going to do exactly what you promised and obey me to the letter."

"Actually," Tempest said calmly, ignoring his ruthless tone, "I thought Cullen Tucker said that the society considered Julian a vampire for certain. I would say he was their first target."

"Security is a matter for the men, Tempest, not for you. From now on, you will do as I say and stay out of trouble."

Tempest was drowsy, content to lie in his arms and smile up at the black fury gathering in his eyes. Idly she touched his mouth, a feather-light caress tracing the perfection of his lips. "I do love your mouth," she admitted before she could censor the words.

Darius found he was instantly distracted from his anger. One touch from her and he couldn't remember his own name, let alone his lecture. He kissed her hard, possessively, taking his time to explore her sweetness, to show her exactly where she belonged. When he lifted his head, her emerald eyes were bemused, beautiful, and so sexy that he found himself groaning aloud.

"Rest while I fix you something to eat," he ordered.

Her long lashes swept down, her velvet soft lips just asking to kissed again. Darius had to look away from her or he wouldn't have the strength to leave her.

She caught at his hand. "I'm really not hungry, Darius. Don't bother fixing anything. It will only be a waste of time. In fact, I feel slightly sick."

Guilt swept him. It was his fault she was having trouble eating. He touched her face, his heart melting. "You will eat what I fix, honey. I will ensure it stays down." But he was talking to himself; she was already asleep.

Darius spent a few minutes staring down at her, absorbing the rhythm of her breathing into his body. His life. It came down to that. This delicate, fragile creature was his entire life, his entire world. He needed to take better care of her, pay greater attention to her health and safety. Tempest seemed to go from one crisis to the next. He would have to put his foot down, get her under some semblance of control. She would start by taking naps in the evening hours to build up her strength.

Absently Darius fashioned a pair of jeans and pulled them on, carelessly buttoning them as he padded on bare feet to the door of the bus. The leopards were off in the forest, and he prompted the animals to return to the safety of their camp. As he opened the door, the night breezes washed over him, carrying scents and sounds from miles around.

At once his black eyes became flat and merciless. A low hiss escaped as he exhaled sharply. The enemy had found them. Not one or two but, if his acute sense of smell had not failed him, a virtual army surrounded them. The men were moving slowly through the forest, ringing the campsite. He smelled their fear, their adrenaline, their sweat. He smelled their excitement. He read their intentions, their eagerness for the kill.

A low growl rumbled in his throat in response to the threat. He was anchored to the trailer and Tempest, unable to act as he would had he been alone. A snarl lifted his lip, revealing lengthened canines. The truth was simple. He welcomed the fight. He had had enough of the threats to his family, and his way had always been one of action. He sent out the eerie call of the leopard, warned the others of the danger, and turned to wake Tempest.

She surprised him, listening to his explanation and donning the clothes he provided almost without question. "Do you have any weapons in here?" she finally asked.

His eyebrows shot up. "As in guns?" he prompted.

She laughed. "I'm from the streets, Darius. Don't let the fact that I was attacked a couple of times fool you. I was blindsided. If you don't see it coming, it's a little hard to defend yourself."

"Our guns are in the case just inside the closet. But use them only if it is absolutely necessary to protect yourself. Let me handle these idiots," he cautioned warily. Tempest with a gun in her hand was a scary proposition.

"Where are the others?"

"They have gone ahead to our next stop, taking Cullen Tucker with them. He had nothing to do with this that I can detect," Darius said calmly.

He sent himself seeking out into the night while she hastily prepared the bus for a quick getaway. He found one man approaching from the north, a long rifle in his capable hands. A sniper in camouflage. Darius directed the male leopard to hunt. The female cat was sent after the man closest to the sniper, a few feet to his left. They were in thick brush, easy targets for the cats, and Darius knew their deaths would be swift and silent. He was torn between staying in his present form and protecting Tempest and going out into the forest, where he could do more good.

"Go," she said softly, feeding shells into the guns she had laid out. "I know you won't be far if I need you."

Darius leaned down to kiss her soft mouth. There were shadows in her eyes, and she was trembling slightly, but she looked him in the eye, and he could feel the resolve in her mind. "Do not allow anything to happen to you, Tempest. For the sake of all mortals, see to your safety first." He glanced at the arsenal she was preparing. "And do not shoot me when I return."

"I'll resist the temptation." Her hand stroked his neck. "See to it you come back to me." The ache in her heart was real and strong. *Fear*. She tasted it in her mouth.

He disappeared. One moment he was real and solid, standing in front of her, the next he was gone. Tempest had no idea if he had dissolved into vapor or moved so quickly that she hadn't seen him. Outside in the darkness, the wind began to build, emitting a low, eerie moan. It spoke of death. Tempest shivered, wondering how she knew but knowing it anyway. The wind was death. Darius was the wind.

She saw herself in the mirror. Pale, her hair wild, her eyes wide with fear. She looked absurd, a small woman in blue jeans and T-shirt loading a big gun, but there was grim determination to the set of her mouth. Her feet were bare, and she remedied that quickly, certain she would have to leave the illusion of safety the trailer provided. She sat on the step, a gun in her lap, two others behind her within easy reach, and she waited.

Darius streaked through the sky, noting the position of each attacker. There were seventeen men, all armed. The campsite was surrounded, heavy trucks positioned across each trail leading to the main highway to prevent the bus from leaving. Forest was dragging the body of the eighteenth man through heavy brush. The male leopard was moving silently, his powerful body sleek and deadly, undetected by the hunters creeping forward within a few feet of him.

Darius dropped behind a large man armed with everything from hand grenades to a machete. He simply snapped the man's neck as if it were a matchstick. There was no time for a sound to escape, only the rush of wind that carried Darius to the next assailant in line. This one was crouched low, peeking into the trees, trying to catch a glimpse of the silver bus. The wind caught him in a death grip, like a huge hand at his throat, and slowly strangled the life out of him while his body dangled helplessly a foot from the ground, then fell unceremoniously to the forest floor.

"Murphy?" A voice hissed off to Darius's right. "I can't see anything. Where's Craig? He was supposed to stay close."

Darius loomed up, larger than life, his features harsh and relentless, his black eyes burning coals of fury. Long white canines revealed themselves as he smiled. "Both of them lost." His words were soft and mesmerizing. The man froze in horror, unable to do so much as lift his gun as the apparition moved toward him with blinding speed. The hunter felt the impact in the vicinity of his chest and stared down in horror at the gaping hole there. He wanted to scream, but no sound emerged. He died standing up, facing Darius, his face a twisted mask of shock.

As merciless as the wind itself, Darius moved on to the next attacker. This one was young, with pitted cheeks, scrubby mustache, and paint smeared on his face. He was breathing heavily, adrenaline pumping through his body. His finger continually stroked the trigger of his automatic weapon. Darius moved past him, a blur of muscle and sinew, razor-sharp talons ripping out his throat as he passed.

Some distance away a gun erupted, spouting red flame into the darkness. A man's high-pitched scream mingled with the unearthly cry of the female leopard. Darius turned toward the sound. Several guns spewed bullets wildly, raking the area where the sounds had come from, until an authoritative voice several yards off to his left barked an order.

Tempest came to her feet, her first thought for Darius. Automatically she reached for him, wincing when she felt the red haze of killing fury in his mind. Breaking contact, she sought out the cause of the cry. Instantly she knew the female leopard was in jeopardy. Swearing beneath her breath, she tried to calm herself enough to decide what to do. Sasha was hurt; she could feel the pain and anger in the cat as she dragged herself through the foliage back toward the bus and her human companions.

Tempest hesitated only one second before she stuck a pistol into the waistband of her jeans, gripped the automatic, and ran toward the trees. She sent Sasha quick reassurance that she was on the way, she would help get the cat to safety and stop the pain.

There was another shout, much closer than she would have liked, followed by a volley of shots. Again Tempest reached out to touch Darius's mind, terrified that he was hurt. He was in the middle of shape-shifting, his body accommodating the muscular form of a panther even as he was leaping for a low tree branch. He crouched above a sniper who was slithering on his belly through the vegetation. The Sniper's gun was trained on Forest as the leopard made its approach toward another intruder, who was firing at Sasha as the female cat retreated.

Tempest gasped aloud as she shared Darius's mind. He was utterly without mercy, emotionless, calm and cool, relentless in his pursuit of those who threatened his family. He leapt upon the sniper, silent, merciless, deadly. As his wicked canines sank deep into the gunman's throat, she broke away, unwilling to witness Darius killing his adversary.

Tempest ducked low beneath the canopy of low, sweeping branches, trying hard to be quiet and not rustle any bushes. Petite, she was able to move easily on the narrow trails established by small animals, but she nearly stumbled over the silent, wounded panther. Sasha was crouched motionless in the large ferns growing beneath the trees. Tempest laid a calming hand on the cat's back and sent it waves of reassurance as she knelt to inspect the injury.

The leopard's back right leg was coated with blood. Tempest muttered unladylike swear words beneath her breath. The cat was too large for her to lift by herself. She wrapped an arm around its belly and lifted just enough to allow Sasha to crawl forward. The ground was uneven, and the panther was in tremendous pain, leaning more and more of her weight onto Tempest as she limped toward the bus.

Sasha suddenly turned her head to the left, curling her lips in a snarl of warning, then freezing into stillness. Tempest dropped flat, eyes searching the area to her left. A man loomed up, his head turned away from her, a gun cradled in his arms, another strapped to his shoulder. He was dressed in dark clothing, his face smeared with black stripes. He looked like a gorilla coming out of the gathering mist.

While the night had been clear, fog was now rolling in fast, gathering into a white, eerie vapor on the forest floor. Tempest lay against the injured panther, shaking with fear, weak from lack of food, and already exhausted. Even the gun felt heavy in her hands. It seemed an impossible task to get the leopard back to the comparative safety of the bus.

The man disappeared into the trees, the fog surrounding him. Tempest got to her feet, her knees rubbery, her mouth dry. Sasha crept forward with Tempest's help. They inched their way over the ground—a slow, painstaking process that seemed never-ending. The heavy fog was their only protection once they emerged from the forested area to the campsite itself. Tempest sent up a silent prayer that the thick vapor would prevent their presence from being detected.

Darius felt the disturbance ahead. He had made his way through the line of intruders, the male leopard coming from the opposite side to meet him at the campsite. Twice Darius had used the heavy fog to wrap a sniper in its deadly grip, choking the life out of the intruder. He had left behind no living enemy and knew Forest had done the same. The numbers against them had been significantly reduced, Sasha accounting for two before she was shot.

Darius was very much aware of where Tempest was at every moment and what she was doing. He had made no attempt to stop her from reaching the cat because he would have had to force her compliance. All the same, he was terrified for her, and the fear was nearly paralyzing him. He sensed the man rushing out of the fog at her, his gun pointed at her head. Sasha tried to throw herself over Tempest, protecting her at Darius's command, even as he took control of the weapon, using his mind and the eyes of the female leopard to force the barrel back around toward the killer.

The man screamed horribly as the gun he was holding, seemingly of its own volition, turned slowly, inexorably, toward his own heart. Even as he tried to tell his brain to stop, he felt his own finger tighten on the trigger. Darius had been moving with preternatural speed and arrived on scene just as the man fell. He leapt toward Tempest, slamming her into the earth. A bullet caught him high in the back of his shoulder, burning and tearing through his body, stealing his breath.

Darius wanted to lie there a moment and rest, but the man who had succeeded in shooting him was moving in for the kill. Putting aside pain, he focused his will on the enemy. Already, however, he was directing the male leopard, stirring up the wind, and creating the dense fog, and he was weary now, his great strength draining, along with his life's blood, onto the ground.

Still, he rose up like an apparition, his body contorting, his face lengthening into a long muzzle, fangs exploding into his mouth as the wolf surged forward and tore into the oncoming wall of a man's chest. The enemy was so frozen with terror at the sight of something half man and half wolf, he could only gape in horror.

Tempest had hit the ground so hard, it knocked the wind out of her. For a moment she could only lie there, trying to collect her scattered wits. She wasn't even certain who had tackled her. It was Sasha who prodded her into action, with her mewling, painful cries, the harsh images of torn flesh. Tempest rolled over to see Darius drop a body onto the ground. She cried out a warning, and he instantly turned and met a huge attacker rushing him with a machete.

He caught the man's raised arm with his casual strength and stared at him a moment, his eyes holding the other captive. Slowly he bent his head and drank, needing to replace his own loss, needing the nourishment and power of adrenaline-laced blood. The rush hit him hard in his weakened state, and he drank voraciously.

Darius! Tempest whispered to him urgently. Something in her knew she had to stop him. She didn't understand why; she knew he had killed, but not this way, never this way. *Darius, I need you now.*

The soft, beautiful voice penetrated his mind, subduing the raging, beast, appeasing the wild hunger for death and blood. He forced his teeth away from his prey and dropped the man into the dirt while he still lived. Without looking into the woods, he sent his message to the male leopard. The man must be destroyed, leaving no witnesses to what had happened here. It was necessary to the survival of his race.

"I will carry Sasha," Darius said gruffly, the beast still strong in him, red flames flickering ferociously in his eyes.

Tempest gasped when she saw the blood, inky black

in the darkness, running down Darius's back. "Go. I'll cover you."

"They are coming in from the left," he said, pushing her ahead of him, bending to lift the huge cat.

She stepped behind him and laid down a covering spray of automatic fire, the bullets zinging viciously, giving him time to get Sasha into the bus. Tempest was backing toward him when he caught her in his arms, taking the weapon out of her hands.

Darius was well aware that she wasn't shooting at anyone, only keeping them away. Tempest did not have one killer instinct in her body. Courage, loyalty, yes—she would never leave him or the cats, and she would do her best to protect them, but she would have a difficult time actually killing another human being.

Ruthlessly he took the decision out of her hands. "See to Sasha. Use the herbs in the closet. She will allow it." He literally tossed her into the bus, turning away before she had time to protest.

At once it began to rain. Not lightly, but sheets and sheets pouring from the sky, drenching the forest and campsite, as if the heavens had opened up and dumped an entire ocean on them. Tempest concentrated on her task. Sasha was flicking her tail back and forth in agitation, a low, menacing rumble coming from her throat.

Darius protected the bus, shielding it from the hidden hunters who had now become *his* prey. His form, real and solid, shimmered in the driving rain briefly, then simply evaporated. In the silver sheen of the downpour, blood-red drops occasionally splashed to the ground.

The wind rose to a frantic pitch, screaming through the trees, as sharp as any knife. The male leopard was a whirling blur of savage fangs and claws, an instrument of revenge. For a brief moment the forest was alive with moans and cries and the horror and stench of death. When at last it was over, only the sound of the wind and rain remained.

Darius knelt for a moment in the rain, weary, wounded, revulsion for the necessity of this deed welling up in him. He bowed his head while the water began to flow in small streams around him. The bodies looked as though they had been attacked by wild animals, yet if they were studied, there would be a roar of interest heard halfway around the world. He could not allow that.

He spent considerable time arranging the area in a way humans would accept without too many questions. A battle had broken out between fanatical factions of weekend warriors, and they had killed each other, their bodies then disturbed by a multitude of scavenging animals. He took great care to remove any traces of his family's presence from the area. They couldn't afford to leave even tire marks in the campsite. The accumulating water would take care of that for him. He could hide the bus, blurring it from prying eyes until they were on a main highway.

Exhausted, he finally called in Forest, and man and cat made their way back to the bus together. Sasha was lying quietly, and the big male leopard went to her side and touched her several times, examining the wound, stitches, and wrapping. Tempest turned to look at Darius, her heart in her eyes. He felt he had come home, the weariness dropping away, the stench of death replaced by her welcoming light.

"You're bleeding," she said softly.

"I will live," he answered. Ordinarily his kind shut down heart and lungs to preserve their blood, but Tempest and he were not safe yet. They still had to run the gauntlet of trucks blocking every road to the highway, and Darius knew others would be in those trucks waiting for them.

"Tell me what you need," she said, aware that his body healed differently than hers.

"The herbs and soil I need are in the cupboard above the couch."

He sounded tired, and that frightened her. She looked away, careful to avoid allowing tears into her eyes. The sight of Darius, soaking wet, weary, streaked in blood and mud, his black hair plastered to his head, nearly broke her heart.

She worked on him quickly. It was easier than she had envisioned, as the bullet had exited his body and he had started sealing off the wounds from the inside out. But it required tremendous energy on his part to heal his insides without benefit of the earth and rejuvenating sleep. Tempest packed his wound with the mixture of his healing saliva, soil, and herbs. It was strange to follow his directions to mix dirt with his saliva, but she accepted his explanation that Carpathians were of the earth and took advantage of its healing properties. Her hand caressed his neck, her fingertips conveying her growing love when she still could not voice it to him.

Darius caught her hand and brought it to his mouth. "I am sorry, Tempest. I never would have willingly exposed you to this side of our life. We are often hunted by mortals. Down through the centuries many of us have been massacred. I wish I could have spared you this."

"I don't wilt in the sun, Darius, or melt in the rain. I'm tough, you know. Now let me drive us out of here. You go to sleep. Real sleep. I know you can't go into the ground, but you can sleep the way you're supposed to and trust me to take care of you." Her green eyes captured his black gaze and held it every bit as easily as he could do. "You do trust me, don't you, Darius?"

He found himself smiling. In the midst of blood and death, pain and weariness, she made him smile. "With my very life, baby," he responded, his voice velvet soft, brushing at her insides like the touch of his fingers. He cupped her chin in his palm. "I promise you, I will rest when I know we are safe."

Resignation crept into her eyes. There was no point in arguing with Darius when he had made up his mind. "Tell me what to do."

"You will have to drive the bus. The storm is coming to its peak. We must take advantage of it. The water will pour into the streams because the ground cannot hold it, so there will be flooding. We want to time getting across the bridge before the wall of water hits it. We cannot use the roads, as they are blocked," he explained.

She bit down hard on her lower lip, but that was her only sign of apprehension. She squared her shoulders and turned resolutely to walk to the driver's seat.

Darius caught her around her small waist and fastened his mouth to hers. He tasted her fear, her sweetness, her compassion. He tasted her love for him, growing inevitably with every moment they shared. He took his time, his kiss fiercely possessive, savoring the closeness with her. Reluctantly he lifted his head. "We should get going, honey." His eyes darkened even more as he studied her slightly bemused expression. She was so beautiful to him. Color had swept into her face, and her lips were slightly parted, an invitation he couldn't find it in himself to resist. He kissed her again, this time hard but brief.

Tempest seated herself behind the wheel of the bus. The rain was beating at the windshield, visibility at an all-time low. She glanced back at Darius, unsure of herself for a moment, but he was peering out the window, directing the violence of the storm. She read the certainty in him that she could do what he had asked of her. He believed in her absolutely.

"There's a faint trail, Darius," she called back to him. "It's disappearing under water, but I think I can stay on it." The bus moved sluggishly in the muddy track, rotted tree branches floating along in the water, bumping against the sides.

"Do not use the lights," Darius warned softly.

"I need them. I can't see that well in the dark," she objected. "If the water's too high, we'll get stuck."

"You can see. I see through your eyes. It is the human mind in you that refuses to rely on your own senses," he corrected absently, as if his thoughts were elsewhere.

Tempest exhaled slowly. The moment she felt calm and in control, she moved the large vehicle carefully through the swirling water. Her mind played tricks on her; she thought she saw eddies of deep red blood in the dark stream. But the rain was beating down so hard, she could barely see. The windshield wipers had no hope of keeping up with the deluge pouring from the sky.

Tempest felt Darius standing behind her, the warmth of his body seeping into the cold of hers. He reached around her to frame her face with his palms, his fingertips brushing away her tears. "You weep for the death of those killers." He made it a statement, neither good nor bad. He could feel the intensity of her sorrow beating at him.

"I'm sorry, Darius." Her voice was low, strangled, as if she was choking on her anguish. "They had families, mothers, wives. Brother and sisters. Children."

"They would have killed you, honey. I could read the

intent in their minds. Some of them thought they would enjoy you before giving you your death. They would kill my sister and destroy her chosen lifemate. I could not allow such an atrocity," he said quietly.

"I know," she agreed softly, "and I'm not blaming you for what had to be. I realize the position they put you in, but I still feel sadness for their families and the waste of their lives. Perhaps some of them felt they were doing the right thing. It doesn't make it right, but they were living beings."

Darius swept the thick mane of hair from the nape of her neck and bent to kiss her exposed skin. "You do not have to explain what I already know, my love. I dwell in you as you may do in me at any time you choose." His hands rested briefly on her shoulders, the intensity of his love for her shaking him. It rose up, a flood of emotion that threatened to swamp him when there was still so much for him to do. He had to turn away from her before the need to crush her to him, to feel her skin against his, overcame him. He took a deep breath to steady himself and deliberately put distance between their bodies.

Tempest drove through the murky water as it continued to rise. Twice she crossed a paved road and found another dirt track. Once she came very close to a huge truck parked across the road, one of its occupants smoking a cigarette. She nibbled at her lower lip worriedly but got past the truck without incident. She glanced back at Darius, noting his coloring. He was gray and drawn, lines etched deeply in his face. The strain of masking with illusion an object as large as the bus was enormous. In his weakened state, he was actually trembling.

Tempest hastily averted her eyes, her heart pounding

as if it might explode in her chest at any moment. The idea of anything happening to Darius was terrifying. She drove as fast as she dared over the unfamiliar terrain, feeling her way carefully, focusing her mind on the dangers the volume of water presented. At times she chose a path so narrow that the tree branches scraped the sides of the trailer with a screeching metallic sound she thought might haunt her for all time.

As the bridge loomed up in front of them, Tempest wiped at her face, hoping to wipe away the veil that was making it so difficult to see. Between the rain and the fog, she felt as if she were driving blind. She felt the bridge sway beneath the bus, and instinctively she let up on the gas pedal, nearly panicking.

At once Darius was there, his bare foot covering hers, pressing the accelerator so that the bus fishtailed before the tires found traction. "Keep going, baby," he said softly.

He didn't give her a choice, his foot firmly over hers. Tempest held on grimly to the steering wheel, her heart in her throat. Water was pouring over the structure, pushing at the bus hard enough that she had to fight to keep them on the bridge. The water wanted to lift the trailer and carry it into the swollen stream. She allowed herself to breathe only when the vehicle cleared the bridge. Then she pushed at Darius's leg, making him let up on the gas. She was shaking so violently, her teeth were chattering.

"You are doing great, honey," Darius whispered, his hand stroking a caress down her bright hair. "We are almost out of this."

"Almost?" She turned her head to stare up at him. "There's more? I'm getting so tired, Darius." She felt silly telling him that when he was wounded and in more need of rest than she. "I think I've had enough adventure for one night."

He ruffled her hair, affection in his touch. For a man part beast and all predator, he found he had a side he had never expected. Tempest made him go soft inside. "Hang in there, honey. We face one more barrier, and then we will reach the open road."

She heard a muffled roar and realized a wall of water was building upstream, pushing everything in its path in front of it. Immediately she started the vehicle moving forward, inching their way through the the heavy vapor and rain. Without warning a truck loomed up only scant feet from them, directly in her path. A man was leaning against the hood, night goggles pressed to his eyes.

Lightning flashed, strike after strike, lighting the night as if it were day. The man dropped the goggles into the muck, his hands over his eyes as she swerved off the road, barely missing a huge tree. Clenching her teeth, she fought the heavy bus for control, bringing it back onto the road beyond the parked truck.

Darius slumped into the seat beside her, his face so gray and drawn that she nearly slammed on the brakes. "Go lie down, Darius," she ordered, frightened by his lack of color. "I'll get us to the resort where Desari is supposed to be. Konocti Harbor Inn and Spa. It's somewhere near Clearlake. I can find it." The route was well marked, an easy thing to follow, she hoped. She was bad at directions, but surely she could follow road signs.

Darius staggered to the back of the bus without argument and lay down on the couch, the injured leopard on the floor close by. "You know you will get us lost without guidance, little love."

Her heart turned over at the note of tenderness in his voice. She wanted him to sleep the rejuvenating sleep of his people, to heal himself in the earth so that he would be at full strength again. The pain from his wound was on him, hunger from blood loss beating at him, yet when she touched his mind, she found only thoughts for her, for her safety.

"You just think you're indispensable," she scolded him, deliberately sarcastic. "I'm perfectly capable of finding my way to the resort and the campsite where they plan to settle tonight. Now go to sleep, and I'll wake you if I need a wounded warrior."

"Do not ever attempt to leave me again, Tempest," he murmured so softly that she barely caught the words. There was an unguarded ache in his voice that brought a fresh flood of tears to her eyes.

In her life, no one had ever wanted her. No one had ever needed her. Certainly no one had ever been so loving and caring toward her. For all his overbearing, dominating ways, she couldn't ever say he didn't put her first. She couldn't say her heart wasn't totally captivated. He had woven a spell around her so strong, she didn't think the tie could ever be broken.

As she drove down the highway, the rain began to lessen to a drizzle. She made every attempt to keep her mind from what had happened. The idea of all those men throwing their lives away, attacking people they really knew nothing about, was devastating to her. She had no idea just how many adversaries there had been, but she knew the cats had managed to kill two humans apiece. She had caught the images in their minds. Darius had killed the others, but she had no idea how many, and she didn't want to know. It was better not to know, not to allow herself to think too much about insanity of what was happening in her life.

Carpathians. Vampires. Vampire-hunters. It was all too bizarre.

Chapter Fifteen

Tempest drove the bus onto the shoulder of the road, parked, and rested her head against the steering wheel. She felt as if she had been driving forever, but it was the road conditions and driving rain that finally defeated her waning strength, not the hour of night. Exhausted, she struggled to keep her eyes open. In any case, she had stayed on the main highway until there was a confusing fork in the road. She had gone right around the bend, hoping she wasn't supposed to take the road branching to the left. She rubbed her eyes, feeling faint.

Her heart nearly stopped when a cloud of vapor streamed in through the window she had cracked open, hoping the cold air would revive her. Julian Savage shimmered into a solid state beside her, then went at once to Darius, concern etched on his handsome face. Tempest laid her head back against the seat, too tired to question him.

"How long has he been like this?" Julian demanded.

"He was shot," Tempest said without opening her eyes. "I told him to sleep, that I would find the rest of you."

Julian bent close to Darius, tore at his own wrist with his teeth, and pressed the wound firmly over Darius's mouth. "Take what is freely offered that you might live both for your lifemate and yourself." He was unexpectedly gentle, his voice a blend of concern and hypnotic compulsion.

Darius moved then, for the first time in hours, his hand rising weakly to grip Julian's wrist and hold it to his mouth. Julian began the ritual healing chant, and from several miles away, the rest of the Carpathians, linked as they were with their unique telepathy, joined in. All of them felt Darius's weakness and pain. All of them knew he would not go to ground as he needed.

Tempest pushed herself from the driver's seat and staggered down the trailer until she could drop to her knees beside Darius. "Is he going to be okay, Julian?"

"He is weak. He went into battle already drained of his strength. He used mental energy to focus the storm and hide the bus." Julian looked worried, his eyes filled with concern. "He must go to ground and heal. He needs to sleep the sleep of our people."

Darius roused himself, the blood of the ancients flowing strong in his veins. "She was lost again, was she not?"

"I wasn't lost," Tempest protested, her voice drowsy. "I was simply looking for a good place to rest."

Julian shrugged. "She took a wrong turn a few miles ago. I will drive both of you to the others. You must sleep, Darius."

"I must protect Tempest." It was an implacable statement, an order given by a being used to being obeyed.

Tempest leaned her head against his leg. "You're about as much protection as a wet noodle right now, Darius. I'm protecting *you*." She would have glared at him, but she didn't have the energy to lift her head. "Get it? I'm taking the responsibility for a change."

Julian shook his head at them. "You are both a sorry sight. I have no choice but to offer my protection. I will drive. You two rest."

"Good idea," Darius and Tempest said simultaneously.

Darius reached down until he found Tempest's hand and laced his fingers through hers, connecting them together. They were content to be silent for a long while, the swaying of the bus curiously comforting. Then Darius's thumb began to move, a feather-light touch brushing gently back and forth across her knuckles. "I need to feel your body beside mine," he murmured beneath his breath.

Tempest heard the urgency of his need in his voice. He never tried to hide it from her, never worried that he sounded vulnerable. She was exhausted, so much so that it was an effort to lift herself to the other side of the low couch. Sliding beside him, she fit her body to his. Darius instantly turned to wrap his arms around her. She felt as though she was home, safe and protected, where she belonged. She closed her eyes and slept, not realizing Darius had given her a slight mental push to help her drift off peacefully.

Tempest jerked awake just under an hour later as Julian parked the trailer at the chosen site and opened the door for the others. Desari rushed in, a soft cry of alarm escaping as she saw her brother and Tempest. Her hand went to her throat. "Julian?" Her ethereal voice wavered for a moment as she sought reassurance from her lifemate.

"He needs more blood and the earth to heal him," Julian supplied.

Darius pushed himself into a sitting position, his black eyes moving over his family crowding around him. "Do not look so worried. It is not as if I have never been injured before. It is nothing." He turned to look down at Tempest.

She simply didn't have the energy to move. She lay, her body like lead, just staring lovingly up at his face. His hand stroked her cheek, then settled around her neck. Darius was looking at her as if she were his entire world.

Desari stroked back Tempest's hair. "You were wonderful, Rusti, so brave. I can feel your body's terrible weariness."

Tempest managed a wan smile. "Don't tell me Darius was broadcasting a blow-by-blow report while it was all happening."

"Of course. We needed to know in case something went wrong and we had to return to give aid," Desari explained. "To help with the illusion, we created in the minds of those who saw us traveling on the highway the memory of the trailer traveling with us. If the authorities question anyone, they will state that all vehicles were traveling together last night, long before the horrible battle where we had camped."

"A regular sports commentator, aren't you, Darius?" Tempest asked, annoyed that he had expended even more energy than she had first thought. No wonder he was looking gray and gaunt. "Take him wherever he's supposed to go and put him to sleep and leave me to rest."

Darius's hand tightened around the nape of her neck. "We will not be separated. You must eat something before you sleep, Tempest. You have not taken any sustenance for twenty-four hours."

Her eyebrows shot up. "Oh, I get it. You don't have to take proper care of yourself, but I do. It isn't going to happen that way, Darius. You can growl at me all you want, but if you're insisting on forcing this relationship on me, you can darn well see to it that you take care of yourself so there's no possibility of your leaving me alone."

Darius felt the curious melting in the region of his heart that she always caused. Tempest was trying hard to lecture him, to be tough, but her voice wavered, her fear for his well-being clearly evident to him. He leaned over to brush a soft kiss across her mouth. "You will do as I say, honey, as you are meant to do."

Tempest's eyes flashed fire. "That's it. One of you go get me a club. A big one. He clearly needs to be hit over the head to bring him back to his senses. He must have lost them somewhere in the forest. You idiot, I'm not your child to be dictated to. I'm a grown woman perfectly capable of making my own decisions. Now just this one time in your life, do what you're supposed to do and go to ground or whatever you call it."

Julian made the mistake of allowing a laugh to escape, then hastily tried to cover it with a cough. Darius glared up at him, noticed the others grinning openly at him. "I am certain you all have things to do," he instructed pointedly.

"Not really," Barack answered.

Dayan shook his head. "Much more entertaining here, Darius. You know, I'm still trying to get this relationship thing down, so is necessary to observe one up close."

Syndil took the more innocent approach. "Naturally

our concern is for you and Rusti, Darius. Nothing is more important than aiding you."

Julian smirked at him. "This is enlightening. I am new to your particular ways, Darius, and do not mind learning how to handle the women properly when they refuse to be obedient."

Desari's eyebrows rose. "I'll show you obedient," she threatened.

Darius groaned. "All of you, go away."

"You go away, too," Tempest directed, fitting her body more closely into the pillows. "I need to sleep."

He could hear the utter weariness in her voice. "It is unsafe, baby. We cannot stay here. We are hunted, and none of us can remain above ground in our weakest hours. There are caves close by. You will be comfortable there, I promise."

Her lashes fluttered for a moment, her heartbeat audible to them all. "It's the bat thing again, isn't it?" She forced humor into her voice. "I think I'm going to have to go into therapy if we keep doing the bat thing. Closed-in places don't agree with me."

"I will make you sleep," Darius said gently.

"Let's do it then." She lifted her lashes long enough to catch Desari's worried expression. When she glanced at the others, she could read the concern on their faces. "What is it? What's wrong?"

Darius's black eyes suddenly came alive, burning with a kind of fierce protectiveness. His gaze swept over his family.

Tempest sighed heavily and sat up, pushing at her wild mass of hair, which was tumbling everywhere. "Darius, I'm too tired to figure this out. What is it everyone is worried about? It's unfair to keep me in the dark just because I'm unfamiliar with your needs."

"He must sleep our sleep in the ground," Syndil blurted out, not daring to look at Darius.

"Isn't that what we're doing? I'm going to the blasted cave. I'll sleep while he's in the ground," Tempest said. "That's the plan."

Syndil shook her head, ignoring Darius's warning growl.

Tempest clamped her hand over Darius's mouth to shut him up. "Tell me."

"He will not go to ground. He will sleep as a mortal with you above earth because he fears to leave you vulnerable to attack."

There was a silence while Tempest digested the information. It was clear to Tempest that Darius was displeased with Syndil for interfering. Very gently Tempest stroked his neck with loving fingers, soothing him while she thought it all out. Eventually she shrugged. "So put me to sleep, and then both of us can be in the ground." The idea of it turned her stomach; it sounded like a burial. But if she was completely unaware, it was a small thing to attempt if it helped Darius.

Her calm statement brought a collective gasp of admiration. "You would be willing to do such a thing for Darius?" Desari asked, gripping Tempest's wrists. "You suffer greatly from confined spaces. Darius has told us this."

Tempest shrugged. "I wouldn't suffer if I was asleep," she pointed out. "Let's get to it, Darius. I'm tired." And she was. Her body felt heavy and cumbersome. She didn't look at him, not wanting him to see the revulsion and horror at the idea of being buried alive reflected in her eyes.

Darius's arm swept around her and brought her small body into the shelter of his, his heart swelling with pride in her. He didn't need to see her expression to read her true thoughts. A part of him was dwelling in her mind like a shadow. The terror burial and caves held for her was clear to him, yet she was willing to make the sacrifice if it meant his health. "This is a great gift you offer me, Tempest, but it is impossible. My body is made to shut down my heart and lungs. Your body is not. You would suffocate in the ground. It may take a little longer, but my body will eventually heal," he assured her.

Over her head, Darius's black eyes blazed at his family. No one dared defy that look, except Julian, who grinned at him. Desari kept a death grip on Julian's hand to deter her lifemate from riling her brother further.

"Please fix Tempest a vegetable broth," Darius instructed his sister.

Tempest shook her head decisively. "I really couldn't eat a thing, Desari, but thank you. I just want to go sleep for a week or so."

Darius glanced at his sister, a quick, steady look she could read all too easily.

She nodded almost imperceptibly. "Come on, we must allow them to clean up a bit."

Barack growled low in his throat. "Syndil, Sasha has need of our healing powers. I will carry her, and you bring the herbs."

Syndil's eyebrows shot up. "Have you forgotten we are entertaining a guest? I was going to fix him dinner and then take a walk with him."

Barack caught her arm just above the elbow. "Don't keep baiting me, Syndil. I have only so much patience."

She gave him a haughty look. "I do not have to answer to you, barbarian. Not now, not ever."

"Dayan can walk with your precious guest into the

woods. I will send Forest hunting him," Barack snapped. "You will stay with me."

"I think you have forgotten yourself." Syndil glared at him. "I am leaving for a while, taking a small vacation."

There was a moment's silence. Darius's head snapped up, his black eyes burning, but he refrained from the violent protest welling up within him. Dayan paused in the act of heading out of the bus, his face all at once harsh. Even Julian stilled as if Syndil had dropped a bombshell.

"With that human?" Barack hissed softly, menacingly, between clenched teeth.

Syndil stuck her chin in the air belligerently. "It is not your business."

Barack's hand slid up her arm to the nape of her neck. He caught her chin in his palm, holding her still while he bent his head to hers. His mouth fastened on hers right in front of them all. Hot. Burning. Sweeping away everything that had gone before and replacing it with heat, with a smoldering fire. Barack lifted his head reluctantly. "You are mine, Syndil. No one else will have you."

"You cannot just decide that," she whispered, her hand pressed to her mouth, her eyes wide with shock.

"No?" He placed both hands on her shoulders. "In the presence of our family, I claim you for my own. I claim you as my lifemate. I belong to you. I offer my life for you. I give to you my protection, my allegiance, my heart, my soul, and my body. I take into my keeping the same that is yours. Your life, happiness, and welfare will be cherished and placed above my own for all time. You are my lifemate, bound to me for all eternity and always in my care." He spoke the words aloud, decisively, furious with her that she couldn't see it, that she refused to acknowledge his right to her.

"What have you done?" Syndil wailed. She looked at Darius. "He cannot do that. He has bound us together without my consent. He cannot do it. Tell him, Darius. He must obey you." She sounded on the verge of hysteria.

"Have you never wondered why Barack did not lose his feelings as Dayan and I did?" Darius asked her gently. "He laughed where we could not. He felt desire where we could not."

"With every human groupie who gave him the eye. I do not want such a lifemate," Syndil said firmly. "Take it back, Barack, right now. Take it back."

"Well, that is too damned bad," Barack snapped. "I am your lifemate, and I have known it for some time. You merely refused to see it."

"I do not want a lifemate," Syndil protested. "I will not have some pompous male directing my life."

Barack's harsh features softened to sensual male beauty. "Fortunately for you, Syndil, I am not pompous. I have a need to discuss this with you while we are alone. Come with me."

She was shaking her head even as he was drawing her out of the bus.

When they were gone, Desari turned to her brother. "Did you know? All this time, did you know?"

"I suspected," Darius answered. "Barack saw colors. He retained so much of what Dayan and I lost. When Savon attacked Syndil, Barack was a monster unlike anything I had ever tried to control. He raged for weeks, so much so that Dayan had to lend me his strength to keep him under control."

"I did not realize," Desari said softly.

"We kept it from you because he was so violent and angry, we worried for his sanity. After losing Savon, we didn't want to worry you with the possibility of losing Barack also. I realized he was experiencing not only the male need to protect but also the grief and rage, the violation and betrayal, Syndil was feeling."

"He went to ground for some time," Desari remembered.

"I sent him to sleep to keep mortals and immortals alike safe. He was so distraught, in so much pain, I could do no other. Syndil needed the time to let the horrifying experience fade enough that Barack could cope with her pain."

"That's why he was so quiet, so unlike himself these last weeks." Desari nudged Julian. "Why would he wait so long to claim her?"

Julian shrugged with his casual, elegant grace. "It is long since we have had women born close to their lifemates. I know of no such case, so I cannot answer. Perhaps the proximity allows the male many more years of freedom."

"Freedom?" Desari glared at him. "Do not talk to me of male freedom, lifemate. You stole my freedom from me just as Barack has stolen Syndil's."

Tempest stirred, caught by the conversation. "She can refuse him, can't she? I mean, these are modern times. Men can't just carry women off against their will can they?"

"Once a male Carpathian recites the ritual words to his true lifemate, they are bound, soul to soul. She cannot escape him," Julian said softly.

"Why?" Tempest asked, turning her head to give Darius the full benefit of her censuring green eyes.

Darius didn't so much as wince or even look repentant. Nor did he deign to answer her. He had the audacity to look amused.

"A true lifemate is the missing other half of our soul. The ritual words bind the soul back together again. One cannot exist without the other. It is very"—Julian searched a moment for the right word—"*uncomfortable* to be apart from one's lifemate."

"And the man can choose to bind the woman to him whether she wants it or not?" Tempest was outraged. She wasn't entirely certain she believed him, but if it was so, it was barbaric. Totally barbaric.

Darius circled her shoulders with his good arm. "Practical only, honey. Women seldom know their own minds. But a woman cannot escape the need of her own lifemate, either. He is *her* other half, as well, you see."

Heedless of his injury, Tempest shoved him away from her. He didn't budge even an inch. She knew he was teasing her, laughing at her, although his face remained perfectly expressionless. "Well, I don't believe it anyway. I'm not Carpathian, so it can't work on me. And I'm going to talk to Syndil about this nonsense."

Darius kissed the side of her neck. Not a brief, elusive kiss but one that lingered, that sent tiny shivers down her spine, sent fire dancing in her bloodstream. She glared at him. "I thought we agreed, none of that. Didn't we have a lengthy discussion about this?"

His teeth scraped her collarbone, his chin nudging aside the neckline of her shirt to find bare skin. "Did we? I cannot seem to recall."

"You recall everything else." Tempest did her best to sound severe, but it was difficult when electricity was arcing back and forth between them. "Darius, you're hurt. Act like it, will you? We need paramedics and stretchers and maybe a dozen knock-out pills."

He moved then, with his easy, familiar grace, fluid and supple with the strength of an ancient's blood flowing in his veins. His arm was rock hard around her waist, taking her with him toward the bathroom. "I need to clean the stench of the kill from me, Tempest, before I can touch you properly."

It came out unexpectedly, a confession. Tempest touched his mind, astonished at the ease with which she could accomplish the feat. He felt sorrow. Not for those he had dispatched in battle. He was pragmatic about that; he did what was necessary for his people and would do so again. He would protect Tempest without feeling remorse or sadness for those who were evil enough to threaten her. But he felt sorrow for his inability to come to her as an innocent man. He did not want her to look upon him as a beast, an undisciplined killer. He wanted her to understand that he was a dispenser of justice, very necessary to his people.

He lifted her into the tub with him, and the water felt cool on her hot skin, breathing some life back into her depleted body. Very carefully she washed the blood from his shoulder and back, wincing at the sight of the angry wounds. She reached up to shampoo his thick mane of hair, massaging his scalp with gentle fingers. Darius bent his head forward to make it easier for her.

Despite her exhaustion, finding herself pressed naked against him sent her pulse skyrocketing. His body stirred to life, pushing hard and thick against her. "We can't possibly," she whispered. But her tongue flicked out and caught the water droplets running down his stomach. She traced the path lower still, feeling his body clench. Her hands, of their own volition, slid over his hips, massaging, kneading, tracing the firm muscles of his buttocks.

She loved the feel of his hair-roughened skin against her softness. He made her feel beautiful and feminine. Hot and restless. Hungry and sexy. He made her feel safe, as if she would never be alone again. She clung to him, pressing herself close to the shelter of his body.

Darius forced his mind away from her teasing mouth. She was drooping with exhaustion. He could have her—she would never refuse him, and he knew he could ensure her pleasure—but her body cried out for rest and nourishment. Before all else he needed to see to her health and protection.

He pulled her head up so he could kiss her gently, tenderly. "You are right, baby," he said softly. "We cannot possibly until you have rested. I want you to sleep."

He held her against him with his one good arm while the water cascaded over them, washing away the stench of blood and death.

"Make me be like you." Her words were so low, barely discernible even to his acute hearing, that he wasn't certain he had heard her correctly. Perhaps his mind was simply playing tricks on him.

"Tempest?" He said her name against her neck, his heart pounding with temptation. He closed his eyes, praying for strength to resist the velvet seduction of her words.

She raised her head so that her emerald eyes could search his face. "You could do it. Make me like you. Then you could rest without worry. Sleep the way you're supposed to sleep. Just do it, Darius. Take my blood, and give me yours. I want you to live."

There was resolve in her voice, in her mind, yet her slender body was trembling at the enormity of what she was going to do. Her thoughts were centered only on him, on his well-being. Darius groaned, fighting the selfish beast, the one that wanted it all—his lifemate, the fires of ecstasy burning between them for all eternity. She didn't realize what it would cost her. The sun. The blood. The hunters. Humans abhorring what she would become. Even the danger of such an experiment.

His fingers crushed her hair in his hands. "We cannot, Tempest. We cannot even consider such an action. Do not bring this up again, as I do not know if I have the strength to refuse such a temptation."

Her hand stroked his face, sending living flames piercing his body until he could think of nothing but possessing her. "I've thought a lot about it, Darius, and it's the only way. If I was like you, there would be no need for you to worry about my safety. I could be with you in the ground."

He felt the hard slam of her heart when she said it, saw the mental image of the earth closing over her head, of being buried alive. She pushed the thought away, but her pulse was racing.

He caught her hand to still her caressing fingers before he lost all good sense. Her scent was beckoning him; his body was hard and full with need. His mouth could actually taste her, the hot, tempting spice of her blood. He had never wanted anything more. "I will not even consider such a thing, Tempest. The danger to you is too great. I have made the decision to live as humanly as possible. I am willing to age as you age, to die when you die. Converting you is a risk I am not willing to take."

"Watching your health and strength slowly dwindle is not something I'm willing to do, Darius," she protested, wrapping her arms around his waist. Her fingers settled over his buttocks and began a slow, erotic motion that threatened to turn him inside out. "I'm not making an impulsive decision without thought. I've really given this a good amount of consideration. It's the only answer for us. The only thing that makes sense." Her mouth skimmed over his chest, her tongue lapping at his nipples, lazily tracing a bead of water to his flat stomach, swirling around his belly button so that every muscle in his body cried out for her.

"You have not thought it through." His voice was a husky ache of need. Unable to stop himself, his hand skimmed over her satin skin, moved up to cup the soft weight of her breast, his thumb stroking her erect nipple so that she shivered and pressed into him. "You cannot abide closed-in places. The thought of being buried in the earth is repulsive to you. Your mind cannot deal with the idea of drinking blood."

Darius had thought to make her wince with that deliberately graphic image, but she seemed preoccupied with catching a drop of water that was sliding over the tip of his throbbing erection. Her tongue sent a storm of fire surging through him, like a wild wind out of control. Her mouth was tight and hot and so exquisite, he bunched fistfuls of her hair in his hands, holding her there for a long moment, somewhere between agony and ecstasy.

He felt his hunger rise, the need to dominate, to take what was his, to feed on her voraciously, to feel her mouth taking him into her body as a true lifemate should. His fangs lengthened dangerously, and the beast fought for freedom. She had committed herself to him. It had been her idea. He could take her without guilt, bring her into his world and have her for all time. The temptation was so great, he forced her head up, his hands wrapped in her hair, her soft throat vulnerable and open for his assault.

She went to him willingly, without the slightest fear

of him, lifting her chin to give him better access. At once Darius spun her around so that her back was to him. Locking her to him with one strong arm, he buried his face in her shoulder, breathing hard, breathing away the temptation beating at him so fiercely. For the second time that he could remember, tears slid down his face and mingled with the water running down her shoulders. He ached to have her, to taste her, to teach her his ways. But more than that, he was humbled that she would make such an offering. That she could love him enough to come willingly into his life.

It wasn't as if she accepted or acknowledged to herself that she loved him. She hadn't even shared his mind enough to know him as he knew her. That was what made her gift so incredible to him. Her complete acceptance, her willingness to put his life, his health, before her own. He knew every one of her fears. He dwelt in her mind. Yet she was willing to give up everything she knew so that he would live safely the way he was meant to. No one had ever thought to protect him or put his needs first, not in all the long centuries of his existence. He doubted if anyone had given a thought to his desires. It was his duty to provide for the others, to hunt, to protect, to guide, to control. It simply was.

Tempest was offering him unconditional love. She didn't recognize it for what it was; she didn't think about it. He needed something, and she was willing to move heaven and earth to provide it for him. He read her determination easily. And she was quite capable of seducing him into it. He wanted it. He needed it. He hungered for it.

"Baby," he whispered softly, his teeth scraping back and forth on the soft temptation of her pulse. "I will not put you in danger. I cannot risk your life. If I did this thing and something went wrong, we would both be lost. Thank you for your willingness to give me such a great gift, but I cannot accept. I cannot." He was humbled by her, humbled by his own overwhelming love for her.

"It has been done before, Darius. If you fear my reaction, I have thought up solutions to some of the problems. You could put me to sleep before we go into the ground, at least until such time as my brain is accepting of your way of life."

He resolutely turned off the water, needing a reprieve from the seduction of her offer. "That is true, Tempest, but—"

"Wait before you protest. Twice now you have given me your blood. I didn't even know you did it. You can provide for me while I learn your ways. It shouldn't be that difficult." As he wrapped her in a towel, she caught his hand, held his palm against her breast. "I am already half in your world and half in mine, at home nowhere. You can't live without your strength, and I can't bear to see it drained away from you. It isn't what you were meant for. There is greatness in you, Darius."

He smiled, his black eyes softening, the hard edges of his mouth tender. "And what of you? Do you think yourself less than me that you must sacrifice so for me?"

She shook her head hastily to disabuse him of that notion. "Of course not. In fact, I think you need me around to keep you from being an arrogant, overbearing dictator, to keep you on the straight and narrow."

"Overbearing dictator?" he echoed, male amusement sliding into the velvet timbre of his voice. He nuzzled the nape of her neck.

"Exactly." The smile faded from her face, leaving her solemn. "I'm not like other people, Darius. I've never fit in anywhere. I don't know if this will work out between us, but if you can manage not to try to rule every aspect of my life, I'm willing to try. I know I want to be with you. I know I'm not afraid of you or your people."

His eyebrows shot up at her blatant lie.

"Oh, shut up." She threw a towel at him. "Don't look at me like that. I know you would never hurt me. Never, Darius. I don't believe in too many things, but I believe in you." She looked around for clean clothes and was disappointed when she realized she hadn't thought to bring any with her. Fatigue was crowding in, pushing out her need to convince him. She wanted to lie down and sleep for a week.

"Just promise me you'll think about this, Darius. It's really the only sensible solution. And if it doesn't work out between us, by the time we know, I should be able to take care of myself." She sank down onto the edge of the tub, too weary to stand any longer.

Darius tamped down his hunger, his raging desire, and the emotions that were clouding his good judgment. He caught up the robe he had made a day or two earlier for her. It was hanging on the door, thick and warm. He enfolded her in its softness. "We will eat, honey, and then we will sleep. All of this can be sorted out on the next rising."

"Isn't that the first day of Desari's performance? Whoever sent those men after her will try again. She'll be so vulnerable, Darius. We have to resolve this before she goes on stage."

He could hear her weariness. It clung to her like a second skin. The Carpathian male could do no other than protect his lifemate, see to every aspect of her care, so he simply took possession of her arm and, without further conversation, led her into the kitchen and sat her at the table.

Desari had prepared a bowl of steaming vegetable broth. The aroma filled the bus, but Tempest merely pressed a hand to her stomach and tried not to gag. *See, Darius? I can't eat anyway. I can't have one foot in my world and one foot in yours. I'm willing to risk the conversion to have a chance at a future with you.*

He ignored her soft, persuasive voice and thrust his mind deliberately into hers. Not gently, but firmly taking control, giving her no time to fight him. *You will eat this broth, and it will stay down and nourish you.* It was a command. He forced her obedience, even when her stomach rebelled, attempting to rid itself of the food.

Tempest blinked up at him, finding her soup bowl empty. She shoved her damp hair away from her face, her long lashes drooping tiredly. "I just want to sleep, Darius. Let's go to sleep."

He wrapped her in his good arm, lifted her easily, and carried her out of the trailer and into the night. They were back to their warrior and captive roles, but Tempest didn't care. She closed her eyes and settled closer against his chest.

The tunnel he chose leading into the earth was warm with geothermal activity. At once it robbed her of breath, inducing a feeling of suffocation in her. She tried to hide it from Darius, not wanting him to know she was uncomfortable. She burrowed closer to him, giving herself up to his protection. She knew he would not go into the soil because she could not go. He would make them a sleeping area in the safety of the earth where she could sleep the sleep of humans and he could try his best to follow suit. But he needed the rejuvenating soil, especially now that he was wounded. He needed to shut down his heart and lungs and sleep the Carpathian way. Tempest smiled against his heavy muscles, suddenly confident of her ability to persuade him to her way of thinking. She just needed to rest first before she renewed her attack. Darius could not resist her forever. She had been in his mind, felt his vulnerability. He would give in if she persisted. He wanted her conversion with every cell in his body.

She knew Darius felt he had to protect her, that she was fragile and delicate. But Tempest knew she wasn't. Perhaps physically she was weak in comparison to his race, but she had a tremendous strength of will. It was every bit a match for his. She would find a way to keep him safe, protect him in the same fierce way, with the same fierce love as Darius did her.

Chapter Sixteen

The Konocti Harbor Inn, famous for its food and concerts, was built on the edge of a large lake nestled in the mountains, cool and shaded by majestic pine trees. The resort drew large crowds to its outdoor concerts, its large amphitheater, and the more cozy indoor venue where guests could dine and watch their favorite performers. The Summerfest was legendary, bringing visitors from all over the country to the festivities. It was one of Desari's favorite places to perform, and she scheduled concerts there each time she was in California. To Darius and Julian, the security was a logistical nightmare.

The head of security appeared to be in his forties and had the air of a man who knew his job and could handle any situation that should arise. He listened attentively to the group's special problems. Already aware of the attempt on Desari's life a few months earlier, he had made additional preparations himself. Still, he was open to their ideas and more than cooperative. Darius found himself liking the man, going so far as to give him the grudging respect he generally reserved for his own kind. Darius expected cooperation and got it either through consent or compulsion, but it was easier when he had the full cooperation of the security team.

Desari was to perform indoors. All three men agreed on that. It was safer and the environment much easier to control. The head of security showed them around, going over the recent renovations with them, showing them floor plans and every possible entrance and exit. He was easy to work with and had a fairly competent staff for the small resort. Still, for the kind of problems they expected, all of them knew it wouldn't be enough.

Locals, mostly young, were employed as event staff, and they were far too inexperienced to handle the kind of threat Desari's enemies posed. Darius and Julian knew they would have to check the entrances themselves, testing each individual's thoughts as he or she moved through the doors. Dayan and Barack would be able to help at least up until the actual performance. With the ability to mask their appearance at will, they could blend in with the security staff and not look like band members.

While the men were occupied with pre-show security arrangements, Tempest enjoyed the shower in the suite of rooms provided by the resort. Darius had come up with a wardrobe of clothes for her, and she had never had such clothes in her life. The jeans didn't have holes in them, the dresses clung and swirled, and everything fit perfectly. For a moment she almost didn't wear them, feeling like a kept woman, but then she couldn't resist. She was part of the troupe, like it or not. Desari and Syndil were both elegant, striking women. She couldn't very well run around in her oily bib overalls.

She stepped out into the night air, remembering at the last moment to pin the little tag in place identifying her as a member of the band's crew. She wandered around outdoors, inhaling the scent of pine trees and flowers. The lake was a stone's throw away, boats docked in rows, waves lapping at the shore. The lake called to her, the breeze blowing gently in her face.

Tempest felt free walking by herself, even though Darius would have a fit. He was becoming more and more protective of her, so much so that she was thinking of breaking out of prison for a few hours, maybe during the concert. Darius would be busy and unaware of what she was up to.

Do not count on it, my love. You are not to wander around unescorted. Go back to the room while I am working. Later you may come and listen to the concert.

His very voice held magic. A velvet caress that sent heat pooling low within her. How could he do that from such a distance? How could he brush the nape of her neck with his perfect mouth and span her throat with his palm, make her pulse race and her blood turn to molten lava?

How kind of you to give your permission, she retorted. *Concentrate on your work, Darius. I'm just looking at the lake. What possible trouble could I get into?*

His laughter, low with mocking male amusement, brushed in her mind like butterfly wings. *I would not be surprised if you managed to sink the entire pier. If someone told me you were singlehandedly trying to rescue seven drowning victims, I would not raise an eyebrow. There will be no heroics, no hang-gliding, no speedboat racing, and no flirting. I absolutely forbid your helping the security team deal*

Christine Feehan

with drunks, brawls, or any other situation. Go back to the room.

I'm not that bad, she reprimanded indignantly. *Pay attention to what you're doing, and leave me in peace.*

I do not wish to force my will on you, honey. It was a clear threat.

But you will if I don't obey. Her hot temper surged forth. If he was standing on the edge of the pier in his elegant suit, she would have shoved him right off the edge into the water. *You have no right to dictate to me, Darius. In case you've forgotten, this is the modern era. Women have rights. You're irritating me.*

I do not have time for this silly argument. Now go. There was the slightest hint of resignation in his voice, in his mind, and it made her smile. Darius was slowly but surely getting the message that dictating to her did not necessarily get him his way. And she was beginning to understand his driving need to protect her. More and more she was sharing his mind, including memories of his childhood and his life.

"Tempest!" Cullen Tucker's voice nearly made her jump out of her skin. "I have to admit it's a bit surprising to see you out without Darius."

She rolled her eyes in exasperation. "Is it catching or something? Come on, Cullen. Why would I need an escort at every moment?" She knew she sounded belligerent, but after Darius's little lecture, she was annoyed with the entire male population of the earth.

He instantly and prudently held up a hand in surrender. "Hey, Tempest, you can pack that redheaded temper away. I don't think you need a bodyguard at every moment, but Darius seems to keep a close watch on his property."

Her eyebrows shot up, fury gathering in her green

eyes. "For your information, Mr. Tucker, I am not *any-body's* property. Least of all Darius's. Don't encourage him."

You are definitely my property, Darius said, laughter in his voice.

Oh, shut up, she whispered sweetly.

"Okay," Cullen said to appease her, discretion being the better part of valor. He waved a hand toward the glistening lake. "It's beautiful, isn't it?"

Tempest nodded, her eyes on the waves. "There's always something soothing about water."

Cullen gestured toward a riverboat that looked like something that should be on the Mississippi River. "That's pretty cool. I hear you can rent it for private parties or take a three-hour tour on it around the lake. There's a big bachelor party tonight. Darius had me go over the guest list to see if I recognized any of the names."

Tempest raised an eyebrow and quirked a little grin at him. "A bachelor party? Complete with a stripper jumping out of a cake?"

Cullen laughed. "Who knows?" He sighed softly. "You know, you were right about this driving at night business. I'm usually a morning person, but after traveling all night, I swear, I couldn't wake up today. When I finally managed to drag myself out of bed, it was seven o'clock, and everyone was already up. Even Julian." He glanced around to assure himself no one was in hearing distance. "To tell you the truth, I did kind of suspect him of being a you-know-what, but I saw him eating dinner with Desari. They were almost finished when I went into the dining room. I watched him eating myself."

How can that be? Tempest demanded, fully aware that

Darius was monitoring every word of the conversation. *Eavesdropper.*

We can eat. We simply remove the offending substance from our systems as soon as possible.

Yuck! Tempest pushed down the mental image and turned her attention back to Cullen. "The whole idea was a little farfetched."

"I saw a vampire," Cullen snapped defensively. "I saw him kill my fiancée in San Francisco. It wasn't some delusion."

She rubbed her hand up and down his arm soothingly. "I know, Cullen. I believe you. I was speaking of Desari. She's so sweet and good to everyone. Why anyone would think she was a monster, I can't imagine."

Out of nowhere Dayan and Barack suddenly appeared, casually positioning themselves on either side of Tempest, inserting their larger frames between Cullen and her. The move was subtle, but they definitely removed her hand from Cullen's arm. Tempest heaved an exaggerated sigh, fully aware the two Carpathians had been sent by Darius to retrieve her.

You're a skunk, you know that? But it was hard to keep the laughter out of her voice; of course she should have anticipated his move.

I know you do not need to be touching other men. I told you to go back to the room, where I know you are safe.

I was going.

Not fast enough to suit me.

Barack took possession of Tempest's arm. Not tightly, but she knew she couldn't break his grip. It was all she could do not to burst out laughing. *I take it Barack isn't a man?* A soft growl was Darius's only answer to her teasing. Deliberately she smiled at Cullen. "I would think it might dangerous for *you* to be out in the open like this. What if the society sends someone here and you're spotted?"

Cullen shrugged. "I'm hoping I can spot them first. It's the least I can do under the circumstances."

Barack was applying pressure, slowly drawing her away from the human, back toward their rooms. "Darius wants you with Desari and Syndil, little sister. He is very insistent." He had heard the growling, too.

Dayan stepped smoothly to Cullen's side, grinning good-naturedly at him. "Darius is the very devil with that woman. He keeps a close watch on her and has a protective streak a mile wide."

"It seems all of you do," Cullen responded.

"It is our way. So you are stuck with me, the bachelor." Dayan walked him toward the concert hall. Darius had made it a point that they watch over Tucker. He might not be Carpathian, but he had warned them of danger at great risk to himself, and Darius was not about to let him die. Dayan understood some of Cullen's feelings. The man grieved for his lost love, felt totally alone, and Dayan knew that feeling well. More and more as the others could feel emotion, the darkness was spreading in him, a stain he couldn't seem to remove. He could touch the others and momentarily feel emotion through them, but it only increased his own barren existence when he slipped from their minds.

Tempest paced alongside Barack, fuming that Darius was forcing his will on her. Barack didn't seem to notice her deliberately lagging steps, simply taking her with him to the room allotted to Desari. He reached around her and opened the door, all but pushing her inside. She glared at him. "You know, Barack, you could use some lessons in manners."

"Probably true," he agreed softly, "but then, you could use a few lessons in obedience."

Syndil slammed the door in his face. "That man is a total brute. I do not know where he got the idea that he can suddenly boss us all around, but I swear, he has been hanging around Darius too long."

From the other side of the door, they heard Barack's mocking laughter. Syndil threw her shoe at the door. "Jerk!" She flung herself into a chair and glared up at Desari. "How do you put up with Julian?"

"Not easily," Desari admitted. "When he gets out of hand, I just go around him. It is much easier than butting heads with him."

"I would very much like to butt Barack in the head," Syndil said. "You should hear him. He thinks he can just start ordering me around because he was an idiot and tied us together."

Desari laughed softly. "He could not tie you together if you were not true lifemates, Syndil. You know that very well."

"I know he has spent centuries bedding women. Who would want him?" Moodily she flung her other shoe at the door, wishing the wooden panel was his head. "And you should hear him go on about my flirting and about men wanting me. I tell you, Desari, he can fling himself into the lake."

"He has not made his ultimate claim," Desari observed. If Barack had made love to Syndil, all of them would have known immediately, as they had with Darius staking his claim on Tempest.

"I refused him." Syndil looked down at her hands, sudden tears welling up. "He has been with so many. I have only had Savon, and that was rape. It was horrible, and it hurt. I could not take the chance. I almost wanted to, but I didn't dare. If I couldn't make myself accept him in that way . . ."

Desari circled her shoulders, pulling her close. "Oh, Syndil, it would not be like that. You should have shared your fears with Barack."

Syndil shook her head in agitation. "I cannot. I closed my mind to him."

Tempest laced her fingers with Syndil's. "Savon committed a violent crime against you, Syndil. When you're with someone who loves you, he takes great care to ensure your pleasure above all else. If Barack does love you and wants to be with you always, he would treat you gently."

"What if I did not please him? What if I cannot do as he wishes? I think about it, wanting him, but then the memories come, and I don't think I could take his hands or his body on me," Syndil explained miserably. She sounded as if her heart was breaking.

Desari stroked her hair. "A lifemate dwells in the mind as well as the heart and soul. He would see to your needs, help you overcome your fears. You must give yourself a chance at happiness, Syndil. What Savon did should not be allowed to destroy your life as well as Barack's. Remember, what happens to you, happens to him."

"Why do they have to make it so damned hard on us?" Tempest asked. "They act as if we should be in a convent when we're not with them."

"They have the old values, Rusti," Desari said. "After all, they were born centuries ago. And there are so few Carpathian women. You cannot really blame them for wanting to protect us."

"I'll never fit in," Tempest said sadly. "Even if I convince Darius to convert me, I know I'll never be able to take the way he tells me what to do." Her feelings for Darius were growing at an alarming rate, winding deep into her heart and soul so that she had to see him with all his dark memories, had to see him for the man he truly was. She needed to love him and protect him in the same way he needed to love and protect her.

Syndil and Desari exchanged a long look. "You asked Darius to convert you?" Desari asked, shocked.

Tempest shrugged. "He won't do it. He says it's too dangerous. Is it? Does anyone know?"

"I asked Julian," Desari said eagerly. "He said that you must have some psychic ability. Otherwise, as a human, you could not be Darius's lifemate. And believe me, Rusti, it is rather obvious you are his true lifemate. I have never seen my brother like this."

"I don't have any psychic ability," Tempest protested, looking confused. "I really don't."

"Of course you do," Syndil said. "You communicate with animals."

"Oh, that." Tempest shrugged. "That's not anything special."

"It is what enables you to understand Darius's predatory nature," Desari explained, excited. "The conversion would work. I just know it would."

"And if it didn't?" Tempest prompted.

Desari chewed her lower lip nervously, her gaze sliding away from Tempest's. "You could become a deranged vampiress and would have to be destroyed."

There was a small silence. "A deranged vampiress," Tempest said sarcastically. "No wonder Darius doesn't want to chance it." She leaned over to meet Desari's eyes. "What else are you keeping from me?"

Desari glanced at Syndil, who nodded. "Julian says the conversion process is very painful."

Tempest shoved at the hair spilling around her face. "Oh, yeah, I'm into pain. Did you know all this when you first brought up the subject? You did mean for me to think about it, didn't you?"

Desari looked guilty. "I am sorry, Rusti. It is just that I love my brother, and I can see the strain in him already. He would never shirk his duties. Even though his strength is lessening, he will continue to fight those who threaten us. I was thinking of him, not of you. I ask your forgiveness."

"Darius was furious with both of us," Syndil admitted. "He did not raise his voice—he does not have to—but he fairly shook with rage."

Tempest paced the length of the room. "What kind of pain?"

A flood of remorse slid over Desari. As much as she wanted her brother to live, he would be furious at this conversation, at Syndil and Desari for using Tempest's feelings for Darius to persuade her.

"You cannot be serious." Desari jumped up and caught her shoulders. "It was wrong of me to suggest such a thing. It is against Darius's wishes. He has told me he has made the decision to age and die with you, that he has no regrets. I must accept his will, although it is difficult."

Syndil nodded. "Darius says the woman should not have to risk her very life for a man." She looked down at her fingers, remembering Darius's chastisement. "He said it was bad enough that he taken away your choices, your old lifestyle, and he would never willingly risk your life." There was pain in her eyes when she raised them to Tempest's. "We should not have continued to discuss this."

"But then, it really isn't his risk or his decision, is it?"

Tempest asked softly. "I have as much right to worry over his health and well-being."

"It is the male's duty to see to his lifemate's health and happiness," Desari pointed out. "He can do no other."

"My happiness," Tempest repeated softly, almost to herself.

The sound of a knock on the door made her heart pound. Inside she was turning over their revelations. Could she do it? Chance it? Did she have that kind of courage? The words *deranged vampiress* did not conjure up a pretty picture. She didn't like the sound of that at all. But the thought of Darius losing his great strength, growing old when he did not have to, was a heavy weight on her heart.

Did she believe in the fairy tale? Darius might believe he would grow old with her, but perhaps he would soon tire of her as men often did of their women. No man could really devote himself to one woman for all time. Certainly not for an eternity. She was a loner. Solitary by nature. Yet the thought of an eternity of solitude wasn't all that appealing. Tempest didn't mind going around once in life, but over and over didn't sound all that great. And then there was the blood thing.

Tempest made a face. Sucking the blood out of somebody's neck was a sickening thought.

Baby, you think the most depressing thoughts. Just put the whole thing out of your head. I will be fine, I will not tire of you, and you will never be allowed to suck anyone's blood. I, however, will have the pleasure of sucking on your neck and other parts of your anatomy as often as possible. After I strangle my two little sisters, everything will be fine.

You don't have to strangle them. I was the one who asked.

I will not leave you, my love. His voice was a soft caress, but it carried total conviction. As their minds were merged, she could clearly see his thoughts, his beliefs, even his memories of the time before he met her. His had been a bleak, barren existence. She was his world. She would always be his world. He believed that implicitly.

"I need to find the courage," she whispered aloud to herself.

Desari leaned into her. "You are our sister, beloved for what you have given Darius. You already have shown great courage, just to brave being with him. Do not let us make you fret. Darius has chosen. So be it."

And you think this will relieve you of the responsibility for making my lifemate fear for me, little sister? Darius demanded.

Desari shook her head as if he could see her. The knock came again, signaling that it was time for the band to make an appearance on stage. "Come with us, Rusti," she invited.

Tempest stepped back, suddenly shy. She had never liked crowds, and she definitely preferred to be anonymous. "I'll listen from a distance. Good luck, you two."

Syndil was appearing with the band for the first time since the trauma of her rape. Out in the hall, Barack and Dayan were waiting, along with several security and event staff, to escort them on stage. Julian and Darius were at the entrances. Security would remain tight for the duration of the concert, and there would be little chance for patrons to wander about the auditorium unobserved.

Tempest followed the band from a short distance, looking around for Darius. When she couldn't find him, she stayed just outside the door and listened. A roar went up, signaling that Desari was on stage. The band began a slow, moody ballad, one particularly suited to Desari's beautiful voice. It filled the hall and spilled out, dreamy, sexy, mystical.

Tempest touched the door with reverent fingers. No one had a voice like Desari. Once heard, it was impossible to forget. It conjured up dreams, fantasies, evoked intense emotions in all who heard her. Tempest felt a surge of pride in her. Somehow she had become part of them all. Accepted. Respected. A member of their peculiar family.

Cullen hurried up, obviously out of breath, his heart loud enough for Tempest to hear. "Where is he? Where's Darius?"

"At the entrance to the balcony, I think," she replied.

"The riverboat party. The bachelor thing. I saw Brady Grand among the passengers boarding the boat, but I don't think he got on. If he's the one who booked that boat, then it's a set-up. He's got a crew here."

"Who's Brady Grand?" Tempest was pacing alongside Cullen as he raced toward the stairs to find Darius.

"He's someone you don't want to meet. He heads up the society here on the West Coast. Damn it, where's Darius?" Cullen started up the stairs but was stopped by a uniformed security guard. He pointed impatiently to his tag and pushed past the man.

Tempest turned and ran to the door, rushing outside, running around the building toward the marina. The riverboat was still tied to the dock. Men were laughing and shoving one another as they moved up the pier to board the boat. She had no idea exactly what she was looking for. They all looked like normal partygoers to her. She stood very still, trying to see one thing that jangled, that jarred. The revelers continued to board the boat, their jokes lewd, a lot of playful pushing and shoving going on. Most of the men looked as if they'd already indulged in a great deal of partying before they arrived.

She shook her head and moved away from the bushes toward the marina store. Almost at once she felt a sharp object poking into her back. Thinking it was a branch, she started to turn. She saw a blur coming at her head, nothing she could identify, but she had no chance of getting her arms up to protect herself. Whatever it was smashed against her head, hard, and she was falling.

Inside the building Darius froze in place. Not a muscle moved. It was as if he stopped breathing. Then he was moving, far too fast for the human eye to see. He burst from the building, the beast raging for release. He felt it growing stronger and more lethal within him. He let it consume him, reaching for it, so that the thin veneer of civilization was gone. The savage predator was loose, and there was not one shred of mercy in its soul.

Tempest. Her name was a whisper of sanity in his mind, the only thing keeping him from a berserker's rage. He could not kill everyone who crossed his path. He had to stay focused. She had been taken from him. But because she did not answer his call did not mean she was lost to him forever. He would know if she was dead. His soul would know. No, they had knocked her out in some way, made it impossible for his mind to reach hers. They had baited a trap, and in his arrogance, he had fallen into it. Thinking Desari the ultimate target, he had concentrated his protection there. Cullen had been right all along. They wanted Tempest.

Julian, they have taken Tempest. Stay and protect Desari and Syndil. Alert Dayan and Barack. I will go after her.

It is a trap.

Of course it is. Why else would they grab her when we

*were all here for the taking? They are using her for bait. I
will go.*

Darius moved swiftly away from the crowds, needing
the open spaces. He sent a call to the night, sent a wind
seeking his answers. It brought the scent of his prey,
sharp and pungent, to his nostrils. Darius took to the
sky, shape-shifting as he did so, his body becoming that
of a winged night hunter. Below him he saw the winding
ribbon of highway, the car speeding over the mountain
road. They would be taking her somewhere close. Leading him into the trap.

Darius plunged straight down, streaking through the
sky toward the windshield of the car, his huge expanse
of wings spread wide. The bird completely eclipsed the
glass, and the driver screamed and instinctively ducked.
At the last moment Darius pulled up and disappeared as
if he had never been. The car swerved wildly, fishtailing
dangerously close to the cliff. The rear end swung
around, smashed into dirt and rock, bounced off, then
slid several feet before the driver could regain control of
the vehicle.

Brady Grand swore as he clutched at the seat in front
of him. "What the hell are you doing, Martin? We almost crashed. Slow down if you have to. Wallace says
she has to be alive. We need information, and the only
way to lure one of them to us is through a woman."

"You didn't see it?" Martin wiped the sweat from his
face. "It was an owl. The biggest damned owl I ever saw."

"There wasn't anything there," Brady snarled. "You're
just chicken. All you have to do is drive." Brady swept
back the red-gold hair falling across Tempest's face so
he could examine the ugly cut where Martin had hit her
with the billy club. "You hit her too damned hard. She's
bleeding like a stuck pig back here."

A gust of wind hit the side of the car, blowing it several inches into the other lane. Ahead of them ominous black clouds gathered from out of nowhere. Veins of lightning zigzagged from cloud to cloud. Thunder crashed so loudly, it shook the car. Martin ducked again and swore out loud. "This is getting out of hand, Brady. I say it's a warning of some kind. If something's doing this, I don't want to challenge it. Let them have her."

The car was slowing, pulling to the side of the road. Brady slapped the back of Martin's head hard. "Drive! This is what we want. He'll follow us. We have a poison that will render him helpless. We'll actually bag one of them. Just drive the damned car."

A cloud, black and sinister, poured into the car through a back window that was cracked open an inch. It flowed in, spreading a dark vapor that obscured all vision. Brady grabbed at the woman but felt something tugging her away from him.

"No way! I'll kill her!" He jerked his gun into position and pulled the trigger as fast as he could. It was too late. The vapor had wound itself around his throat and was pulling tighter and tighter. He felt his captive slide to the floor and tried to aim the gun at her head, pulling the trigger again, cursing as he did so. The reverberations from the shots were loud in the close confines of the car.

"You thought you could take my woman from me," Darius said softly.

The venomous black vapor suddenly felt real, felt like a solid noose, a garrote cutting deep into Brady's throat, slicing through flesh so that his blood ran like a river down his neck to soak into his immaculate white shirt. He was still cursing as he died.

Darius snarled silently as the stench of gunpowder drifted out the window and the black cloud slowly solidified. Blood was dripping from his left thigh, and another bullet had caught him near his hip when he had flung his body over Tempest to protect her. She wasn't moving, and it scared him to death. The driver was dead. Grand had shot him with his wild barrage of bullets.

Tenderly, carefully, he drew Tempest's motionless body from the bloodstained car. He clamped down hard on his own pain, taking time to examine every inch of her before launching himself skyward. Droplets of blood splashed to earth as he flew, mingling with the soil. He took her to the cave.

One of you needs to take care of the car. It must be destroyed, and then we must find the head of this organization that continues to hunt Desari and us. We cannot take any further chances with them, Julian. They must have a hideout nearby.

You are injured. I will come to you and give you aid.

Do not leave the women until it is safe to do so. Darius's voice held hard authority. He knew Julian was unlike the others. They were used to following his orders, while Julian had long been a loner, answering to no one except on the rare occasion when he had contact with his Prince or the Dark One, the healer of their people. Julian chose his own way always. He would likely ignore Darius and accede to Desari's wishes that he aid her brother. Darius let his breath out slowly, acknowledging that Julian would make his own decisions. *I cannot protect them at this time, and I am relying on you. As soon as the concert is over, put them somewhere safe, and all of you meet with me to ferret out this predator.*

There was a small silence. *You are safe?*

I am. Darius was uncertain if he spoke the truth. He was not at full strength, and he had lost a great deal of blood. Ordinarily he would have instantly shut down his heart and lungs to preserve the precious fluid until his kindred came to provide for him. But he didn't have the time or luxury to do so now. Tempest was hurt.

Tempest stirred and moaned softly, raising a trembling hand to the gash on her head. "Ow." Her long lashes fluttered, rose, and she smiled at him. "I knew you would come, Darius, but I've got a hell of a headache."

He leaned over her and pressed a wet cloth to her head. "Close your eyes, honey and lie still so I can see what I can do about this."

"They wanted one of you to follow, didn't they?" she murmured, her lashes drooping. She felt sick.

"You have a slight concussion, Tempest." Darius knew his voice reflected his weariness. It was impossible for him to keep the pain at bay with his strength waning by the moment. Fortunately, she had not recovered enough to notice his wounds. He scooped up handfuls of rich soil, mixed it with his healing saliva, and packed the gaping holes in his body.

Darius sent himself seeking outside his own body and into hers. It was difficult to focus as completely as he must while his great strength and energy were draining away. He had tried to slow his heartbeat, to slow the loss of blood, hoping to give himself more time. He could feel her fear, the pounding and throbbing of the pain in her head. She had lost blood, but not the copious amounts head injuries often led to. She would not need a replacement.

He tested the bruising, meticulously worked at healing it inside her skull and then outside until the wound was closed. He took her headache away and retreated, slumping wearily onto the floor of the cave.

For a long while there was only the sound of their heartbeats. Tempest lay floating in a kind of a dream state. After some time she became aware of the differences in the rhythms of their hearts. They always beat the same when they were close to each other, yet now his heart seemed slow, almost stuttering. Tempest forcibly roused herself. She turned her head slowly toward Darius and, to her horror, found him slumped in an awkward position against a boulder, his skin drawn tight over his skull, his face gray and dotted with crimson beads of blood.

Gasping in alarm, she came to her knees, reaching for him. His shirt and trousers were soaked in blood. "My God, Darius!" she whispered, horrified.

There was no response. She reached for his wrist to check his pulse, found it thready and weak. Tempest knew immediately that he had seen to her needs before his own. He was unconscious. He had lost too much blood. She was afraid he was going to die. They were stuck deep within the earth. There was no way she could drag his body out of the cave and to help in time.

Tempest forced herself not to panic. He wasn't human. What could she do to revive him with what she had at hand? She had no way of contacting the others. The private mental path the family used only worked among them. She noticed the soil packed in his wounds. He had tried to stop the bleeding using the richness of the earth. Quickly she looked around, searching for the soil he'd said was filled with minerals and healing agents. She mixed a fresh pack and spread it over the wounds.

"Darius, tell me what to do," she whispered, feeling more lonely than she ever had before. Smoothing the hair from his forehead with gentle fingers, she felt her heart turn over, then begin to pound. She had somehow fallen in love with him. He wasn't human. He was overbearing and dominant. They probably didn't have a chance in hell of making it work, but she wasn't about to fail him.

Somehow in the short time they were together, Darius had become her other half, more important to her than her own life. He shared his life, his memories, with her; he laughed with her, took care of her injuries before his own. He showed her in a thousand ways that he loved her. Despite his arrogant ways, he cared for her, cooked for her, saw to her every need. She *felt* his love. More important, through his memories, when their minds were melded, she saw his greatness. And she knew absolutely that he was willing to grow old and die for her.

Well, she was not about to lose him. Tempest eased him down so he would be more comfortable. No one else was around to give him the one thing he needed most. So she stretched out beside him, turning so that her head was pillowed on his shoulder.

"Here's the deal, my darling," she whispered. "You are going to take my blood, as much as you need to heal you. If it works, you'll wake up and save my life. Hopefully I won't be deranged." She made a face. "I really don't want to be deranged. So let's just do this and not think too much about it. Okay? This is my decision." She leaned into him and brushed her mouth against his neck. *You understand me, Darius? This is my decision, my free will. I want to do this for you. Take my blood. I'm offering my life for yours. I think you're a great man and well worth it.*

She dug the pocket knife out of her jeans and, biting her lip hard, slashed a hideous gash in her wrist, instantly pressing it to his mouth. *Drink, love. Drink for both of us. We live together or we die.* She meant every word. There were no doubts, no regrets, but it hurt like hell.

At first she felt her blood flow into his mouth on its

own, but then he moved weakly, bringing his hand up to capture her wrist, to press it tightly against him. His lips moved, drawing the precious liquid into his faltering body, a mindless, blind instinct for survival.

Tempest closed her eyes, allowed the gathering darkness to float her away.

Chapter Seventeen

Water dripped slowly from the ceiling of the cave and seeped from the walls, collecting into pools along the floor. It mixed with the rich red soil, making it look like blood lying in puddles on the steaming surface. Somewhere far off a rock fell, clattering against other boulders. Then there was silence again.

Darius became aware that he was lying on the ground, his body heavy and cumbersome. Hunger was a raw, gaping wound in his gut. He was aware of pain; he seemed to be floating in a sea of it. Something held him pinned to the ground, but he had no idea what had happened or where he was. He turned his head slowly, shocked at how difficult it was to do so. His mind seemed to be clouded, to be moving slowly. It took a moment for his eyes to focus. As they did so, the hand covering his mouth fell limply onto his chest.

The cry of pain and fear was torn from his very soul.

It echoed in the cave again and again, tormented and deep, reverberating to the heavens. Darius caught Tempest's wrist and hastily sealed the terrible gaping wound that had saved his life. "Baby, baby, what have you done?" He dragged her close, his hand over her stuttering heart. She was laboring for breath, her heart working far too hard. The blood loss was mortal. Tempest was dying.

Without a second thought, he tore a wound in his wrist and forced it over her mouth. A small amount of his blood would keep her alive until he had a chance to feed and supply her with a transfusion. His mind was a blank. There was only the litany of prayer. She could not die. He would never let her go. She could not die. He swore it to himself, to God. He sent her to sleep, commanding her to stay alive, forcing the edict into her brain, his will like iron. He made it clear that she dared not defy him in this.

When he was able, he left her, taking to the sky to hunt. He wasn't particular in his prey; he fed fast and voraciously, ruthlessly dropping his victims one by one onto the ground before he could kill them, his mind filled only with his need to get back to Tempest. It no longer mattered to him whether anyone else lived or died. There was only room for her. His entire will was bent on holding her to the earth with him.

This time, with his renewed strength, he pulled her into his arms, cradled her against his chest, and cut open a line over his heart. He fed her lovingly, ensuring that she took enough to live. When her body began to respond to the sustenance, she tried to move away from him. Darius merely forced her closer, held her tighter. She would obey him. That was all there was to it. He had given her far more freedom than he had ever thought possible, even when he could have compelled her obedience, but now he gave her no choice. This was for her life, for his soul. If she died, he was damned. He would never go quietly into the sun. He would wreak vengeance upon the world such as it had never seen. He would deliberately choose that course to get at those who had taken her from him.

When Darius was certain she was completely renewed, he gently inserted his hand between her mouth and his chest, closed the laceration, and laid her down. He would have to clean the blood from both of them before she awakened. He closed his eyes, reaching inside his body to repair the damage from the inside out. His hip wound was nasty, the bullet shattering the bone and doing more injury than he would have liked. The thigh wound was easier to repair; he was able to align everything and close off all the veins and arteries without much effort. He even bathed in the steaming pool before replacing the packs on his wounds. This time he mixed herbs with the soil and saliva.

Tempest began stirring restlessly. Darius went to her immediately, lying down beside her to encircle her shoulders in his arms, drawing her up so that she could rest her head against his chest. Her long lashes fluttered, but she didn't lift them. Darius traced the curve of her cheek and slipped his palm over her throat to feel her pulse beating into it.

"Wake up, honey. I need you to open your eyes," he coaxed softly.

"I'm thinking about it first," she answered tiredly.

"Thinking?" he echoed. "You took centuries off of my life, and you are thinking before you open your eyes?"

"Tell me what I look like first." Her voice was a mere thread of sound.

"You are not making sense." His voice was a black-velvet caress.

"Have my teeth grown? Do I look like a hag? I don't feel deranged, but you never know." Her lashes lifted, and she glanced up at him, laughter in the depths of her green eyes. "I could be, you know."

"Could be what?" She was so beautiful, she took his breath away.

"Deranged. Aren't you listening? After all, I decided on a lifetime of sucking blood from the necks of men."

"From the necks of men?" He could breathe again, really breathe. It was safe to allow his heart to beat again. "You will never, at any time, be sucking on the necks of men, unless, of course, it happens to be mine. I am a jealous man, baby, a very jealous man."

"Why don't I feel like I want blood? Shouldn't I have cravings?" She turned her head to look up at him. His color was back, his clothes once more immaculate. How did he do that? She didn't really care. She was so tired, she just wanted to sleep. "I still don't like closed-in places. I thought I might wake up wanting to hang upside down like a bat or something," she teased.

He caught the worried note, the one she was desperately trying to hide from him. His fingers tangled in her hair in a soothing massage. "We will get through this, Tempest. I cannot believe you took such a chance with your life. I will have much to say to you when you are feeling better. You were told the decision was made, and yet you deliberately chose to place your life in jeopardy. I will not get over this for many centuries." He would never get over her courage, the act of sheer love she had committed for him. *For him.* His heart was melting even as it was pounding in a kind of terror for what would follow.

"Stop lecturing me, Darius," she said softly, pressing a hand to her stomach. Her insides were beginning to feel hot and uncomfortable, as if they were suddenly twisting and turning. "Oh, God, I'm sick."

Instantly he placed his hand over her stomach and felt the writhing inside her body, the building waves of heat. He swore softly. The breath rushed out of her, tore a cry of pain from her throat. She jerked up, then slammed back against him. He laced his fingers through hers.

"It has started, my love. You are going through the conversion." He merged his mind with hers, focused, shouldered as much of the pain as he was able.

The first wave of pain lasted several minutes. An eternity. Darius was sweating and swearing in every language he knew. When she grew quiet, he wiped the beads of blood from her face with shaking fingers.

Tempest moistened her lips, her green eyes cloudy with shock. "If you leave me in the first century after this, Darius, I swear to you, I'll hunt you down like a dirty dog. They said painful. Remind me to tell them that's an understatement."

"They may not be alive for you to tell," he threatened, brushing back the silken strands of her hair, now damp and clinging to her skin. He wanted to strangle Syndil and Desari for their interference.

She tightened her grip on him, her muscles going rigid. Darius had to hold her down as her body seized and contorted, the fire racing to tissue and bones. It squeezed her heart and lungs, reshaping, changing her organs, the pain so intense that it drove all color from her face even when he shouldered the agony with her.

At last the wave ebbed slowly away, giving her another respite. Her nails were digging into his arm. "Can you make it stop, Darius?" The plea was wrenched from her when she didn't want to ask. She knew him enough to know he would stop any suffering the moment he was able. "I'm sorry. I didn't mean to say that." She whispered the words hoarsely, reaching up to touch his perfect mouth with trembling fingers. "I can do this. I know I can." But it was swelling in her body again, red-hot fire that threatened her very sanity.

Darius could not believe she was trying to reassure him in the midst of such agony. He could only hold her, feeling helpless, tears gathering in his eyes, a prayer for mercy in his soul, his mind merged as strongly with hers as possible.

Tempest wanted to scream and scream, but no sound emerged. She was going to be sick, and some shred of mindless modesty had her blindly crawling away from Darius. But he was merged so tightly with her, he could read the needs of her body. It was desperately trying to rid itself of toxins, of the last remnants of human blood and waste. He held her in his arms, blood-red tears etching paths down his face.

He had never wanted this for her, never wanted her to suffer the fires of conversion. He found he could barely breathe, protesting the pain she was enduring on his behalf. She seemed so small and fragile in his arms, so close to shattering.

Stay with me, my love. In another few minutes it will be safe to send you to sleep, where the pain cannot reach you. Please stay with me.

With the fire ripping through her, with her muscles locking and her body convulsing, she still made the attempt to reassure him. Her fingertips brushed his neck in a light caress before her hand fell away. Darius wept, his chest so tight that he felt his very heart had split in two.

The moment there was no chance of Tempest choking to death on her own vomit or blood, Darius sent her into a deep sleep so that her body could finish its work on its own. He held her tightly in his arms, a part of him still locked with her, insurance that nothing could go wrong. Only when he was certain the conversion was complete and she was safe did he strip the filthy clothes from her body and wash her gently and lovingly.

He sat for a long while, exhausted and wrung out by her ordeal, his mind, so often calm, in chaos. He had never conceived of anyone ever loving him enough to suffer the fires of hell for him. He felt humbled by her sacrifice. He kissed her, his touch tender and reverent, before opening the ground. Then Darius put Tempest into the sleep of Carpathians, closing the earth over her so that the soil could rejuvenate her.

As the earth closed over her body, Darius turned his head slowly toward the tunnel leading from the cave back toward the surface. His black gaze was utterly cold, without mercy. He felt the beast in him rising, and he made no effort to stop it. Red flames flickered in his black eyes. He had not hunted down and destroyed these murderers months ago when they had first attacked his sister. His instincts had been to find and destroy all of them, but his kind had always attempted to fit into the civilized world, to avoid drawing attention to themselves and their activities. At this moment, however, there was no longer hesitation; there was not a shred of civility in his body or soul.

He protected the cave with the strongest safeguards he had ever used, determined that no one, human or Carpathian, would go near Tempest while she slept, would not live if they tried to enter the cave. And then he was streaking through the tunnel, bursting out into the night sky, his mind a red haze of vengeance.

The concert was over, Desari and Syndil safe in a closely guarded room, Cullen with the group. They suddenly all went quiet, exchanging a long, knowing look. Julian glanced skyward. "He has risen. There will be no calming him. He is bent on destroying those who took Tempest." He sounded complacent and unhurriedly bent to kiss Desari. Then, with Dayan and Barack, he went out to the small porch off the suite.

Dayan took a running leap and launched himself skyward. "It is rather ironic that we now leave the human with our women." He was shape-shifting even as he spoke, feathers rippling along his wide-spread arms.

"Our women can handle one human male," Barack growled as he joined Dayan, also choosing the body of the night owl to race across the distance, attempting to catch up with their leader. *Syndil, stay across the room from that blond human flirt. If I catch you making eyes at him, there will be hell to pay.*

Oh, now we can handle one human male! I like that. So if I want to take him to the nearest bedroom, you have no say in it.

Do not force me to kill this human. Darius has a fondness for him, although I cannot imagine why.

Barack? There was a short pause while Syndil considered how to phrase her concerns. *Please be careful. I would not want Desari to have to grieve for you.*

He laughed softly, a velvet caress in her mind. *And you wish me to believe that you would not? I never thought of myself as an angel, but my patience with you certainly qualifies me for sainthood.*

I cannot imagine anyone considering you an angel or a

saint. Again there was a slight hesitation. *Be careful, Barack. I feel the intensity in Darius. The darkness is on him. He will not turn back, whatever the danger.*

His lifemate has chosen our way. Did you not feel his sorrow at her suffering? Barack's voice held a note of censure.

At once he could feel the tears gathering in her. *Do not remind me. He shared with us what we had wrought with our meddling. She suffered much for him.*

It is done, my little love. It wrenched at his heart that he had made her cry. *We will remove the threat to you and Desari, and all will be well once more.* Barack was reassuring.

Darius is truly angry with us. He will not forgive us for a long while.

Barack wanted to turn back and comfort Syndil. Instead, he sent her waves of reassurances, warmth, and love. He knew Darius was furious. Coldly furious. He also knew Darius was capable of things neither woman could conceive of. He was a harsh, unrelenting enemy. His woman, the one he deemed his very soul, had suffered agonies this night. He would not forgive easily. Barack flew faster, streaking through the dark sky to catch up with the hunter.

Once the three Carpathians were united with Darius, Julian signaled them to settle to earth. Mostly he wanted to see for himself just how far gone Darius's condition was. All three males fully intended to protect Darius. They knew he had been wounded.

Impatiently Darius's cold black eyes swept over Julian. "What is it?"

They were in an orchard not far from where Darius had forced the car carrying Tempest off the road. Julian had blown the car sky high. Fire and police vehicles were already leaving the scene.

"Cullen told me a man named Wallace came over from Europe and fired up this Brady Grand against the band and Julian and Desari in particular," Dayan volunteered. He was studying Darius's face as he spoke.

Darius looked drawn and harsh. There was a spot of blood on his hip and another larger stain spreading on his thigh. Dayan glanced uneasily at Julian and Barack but refrained from commenting. There was cold fury in Darius's eyes. A strange scarlet glow that seemed to come from the blood-red moon was trapped and reflected back at them from the very depths of those black, black eyes. It was an eerie flame of savage rage, as primitive and unrelenting as time itself. There would be no stopping Darius this night. He was the ultimate predator. His quarry could never escape him.

"Have you heard of this Wallace?" Darius asked Julian quietly.

"A few years back there was a man who hunted our people, our Prince, his lifemate, and his brother. He tortured and killed both humans and immortals alike. That man was named Wallace, but he was destroyed. I know he belonged to a society of fanatics. I can only imagine that the two Wallaces are related, especially if he came over from Europe. He must be at the head of the society now."

"These lunatics are like Medusa, the snake woman. Cut off one head, and another grows in its place. If we take this one, we can hope they will at least be forced to regroup for a while," Darius said softly. "It will give us time to collect more information on them."

Julian nodded solemnly. "Human vampire-hunters have plagued our people for thousands of years. As long as our males turn, there will be those humans who become suspicious and continue to hunt us all."

"Perhaps the solution is to find out more about these fanatics and actively hunt them," Darius suggested grimly.

"We have some of our people gathering information on them. A toxin was developed by one of their laboratories. Injected into the body of a Carpathian, it can paralyze," Julian informed him almost soothingly. "Our healer—your brother, Darius—has found an antidote. But these are determined men. Even if we take this Wallace, they may come after us again and continue to develop new and more deadly poisons against us."

"Not *if*, Julian," Darius returned with quiet menace. "I *will* destroy this man. If it gives our people respite, so be it. If it does not, we will not back away from our duty."

"Do you have the scent of our prey?" Julian asked.

"It is a stench in my nostrils. He cannot escape his fate this night."

"Your lifemate still lives," Dayan said softly.

Darius's head snapped around, his eyes blazing with smoldering fire. "I am well aware of the state my lifemate is in, Dayan. There is no need for you to remind me."

"Tempest is one of those unusual women who never hold a grudge," Julian said to no one in particular. "It is difficult to imagine her harming a fly."

"Thank you for pointing that out to me, Julian," Darius snapped, and he launched himself straight upward.

Few could accomplish such a feat. He was in the sky, a stream of vapor streaking through time and space. Julian laughed softly and followed suit, not to be outdone by his brother-in-law. Dayan shrugged his powerful shoulders, grinned at Barack, and took a running leap.

Barack shook his head at them all and went after them. Someone who had some sense had to go along.

The dark, ominous cloud grew heavier as the separate streams of vapor gathered together and moved rapidly overhead, blotting out stars as it went. Below them animals scurried for cover or cowered in trees and dens. They sensed the dark predators moving rapidly overhead and chose to remain as small and still as possible.

The cloud abruptly stopped, as if the wind had ceased to blow. Darius allowed the breeze to blow around him, through him. It told him exactly where he wanted to go. He had the scent of Brady Grand's companions. He would know them anywhere.

Far below, tucked into the side of a hill, a ranch house sprawled in an L-shape. At first glance it appeared deserted, but there was no way to stop the wind from carrying the stench of their prey to Carpathians. The cloud moved slowly, spreading a dark stain over the hill. The wind rose sharply and should have carried the cloud away, but it stayed stubbornly overhead, a portent of death and destruction.

The wind tugged at the windows of the ranch house, looking for a way in, searching for weaknesses. It grew stronger, rattling the glass in the panes, banging the shutters insistently. Then there was movement at the south side of the house; someone opened a downstairs window and reached out into the night to try to close the shutter.

The ominous black cloud struck hard and fast. It poured out of the sky and streamed into the house through the open window, filling the room like suffocating smoke. The man staggered backward, his mouth gaping open in a silent scream. The sound failed to emerge, muffled by the thick vapor as it moved through

his body, taking his breath, removing the air like a vac-
uum.

One by one the Carpathians shimmered into solid
forms. Darius was already moving. He could hear every
sound in the house. Four men were playing pool in a
room three doors to their right. Overhead, two others
were moving around. Someone was watching television
in a room upstairs and to their left. Darius glided through
the house, a silent predator stalking his prey.

On the ground floor two men lounged in a room, talking in low voices. The soldiers. They waited for Tempest.
Waited for a helpless woman they could torture, use to
draw one of the Carpathians to them. Each of those
soldiers carried a syringe on him. Darius was certain of
it. He didn't care. Nothing mattered to him except that
these were the men who had attempted to harm his lifemate and his sister. Nothing would stop him.

He stood in the open door to the pool room, his eyes
glowing a fiery red, his white teeth gleaming. The men
turned as one being, a slow-motion pirouette orches-
trated by a relentless conductor, performed with the
grace of a ballet. As one they grabbed their heads, clap-
ping their hands tightly over their ears. Darius gave a
menacing smile of mocking amusement. He applied pressure, a steady, relentless application of pain. As one they
dropped to their knees.

"I believe you gentlemen were looking for me," he said
softly, the harshness in his face implacable, his emotions
as cold as ice. He watched them die dispassionately, giving a fleeting thought to the coroner who would have
to try to explain how four men died of brain aneurysms
all at the exact same time. Instantly the victims were
dismissed from his mind.

Julian, Dayan, and Barack could handle those in this

portion of the house. Darius moved like a cold, killing wind to the other leg of the L, where he knew he would find the head of the monster. He moved so fast that one of the soldiers coming down the hall brushed against him without realizing what he had run into. The man staggered backward, looked around, scratching his head, and continued down the hall toward the pool room. Darius dismissed him as already dead. Julian had witnessed the first attempt on Desari's life so many months ago, when men such as these had raked the stage with automatic weapons, nearly killing her. Despite his offbeat sense of humor and his rather sardonic manner, Julian was every bit as lethal as Darius. He simply hid it better. Julian would not allow any of these assassins to escape.

The huge living room boasted high ceilings and a rock fireplace on one wall with a large conversation area grouped around it. Two men were lounging in deep recliners, sipping coffee as they waited for their victim. Darius's large frame filled the doorway. He simply stood there, waiting.

The older man had to be Wallace. He was of medium build with a shock of graying hair, rather coldly handsome features, and empty eyes. His companion was a good twenty years younger, with dark hair and an obvious eagerness to prove himself. Darius touched their minds. In Wallace he found a sick, perverse nature, a man cruel to animals and women. He enjoyed hurting them, found arousal in watching others suffer. This elder Wallace had obviously passed the legacy on to his son, the man killed in Europe by the Carpathians a few years earlier. His hatred ran deep and strong, and he was anticipating a long, pleasurable session with Tempest. The perverted fantasies in his head roused the demon in Darius to an almost uncontrollable pitch. Darius fought for control and won.

When neither man looked up, a situation he found laughable under the circumstances, Darius cleared his throat softly to direct their attention toward him. "I understand you requested my presence. It was completely unnecessary to issue the kind of invitation you did. Although now that I have seen you and looked into the rot of your minds, I understand why you did so." His voice was beautiful, a black-magic weapon he wielded easily. "Please do not feel it necessary to get up," he added to the younger man. "I have business with your boss."

He lifted a hand and rather carelessly slammed the younger soldier back into his seat with ease holding him in his thrall even from a distance.

William Wallace stared at the tall, elegant man filling the doorway. Midnight-black hair flowed to his broad shoulders. His eyes held a demon's red glow. Power clung to him, and his white teeth gleamed with menace when he smiled. He was inordinately polite, but Wallace sensed the smoldering threat beneath the surface. Physically he was beautiful, a handsome, intensely masculine specimen of a man with a sensuality around his mouth matched only by its edge of cruelty.

Wallace felt his heart began to pound in alarm. His fingers curled into two tight fists. "Who are you?"

"I think, more to the point, is *what* am I? Have you ever met a vampire before, Mr. Wallace?" Darius asked politely. "As you have gone to so much trouble to invite one into your home, I would expect you to have a fairly good idea of what you are dealing with."

Wallace glanced at his companion, frozen in place by the mere whim of the intruder. He decided to be as polite as his guest, hoping to catch him off guard. The house was swarming with his men. Sooner or later one would come. In any case, he had a secret weapon, if he could just get the vampire close enough. "Do come in." He waved an expansive hand, indicating a chair close by.

Darius smiled, a show of teeth, a leap of flame in the depths of his eyes, but he did not move. "By all means, let us be civilized. I'm sure you had that in mind when you sent your assassins after my woman. Do not bother to deny your intentions. I can read your thoughts so easily."

Wallace decided to brazen it out. "Evil calls to evil. I know your kind and what you're capable of. Others like you killed my own son, murdered two of my brothers-in-law. Yes, I intended to take my time enjoying the woman. She is pretty enough. It would have been . . . delicious."

Darius put out his hand and studied his immaculate fingernails. One by one, razor-sharp talons sprang to the tips. He smiled again with the menace of a predator. Once more his black gaze touched the older man, and it was like a physical blow, a punch that seemed to shake Wallace's brain so that he clutched his head in pain. He felt the tremendous power of the visitor, and his insides turned to jelly.

Darius glided into the room, fluid and supple, muscles rippling with power beneath his elegant white shirt. He seemed to take up the entire room, seemed to suck the very oxygen out of the air. "I see you have decorated the windows with garlic. Do you believe vegetation bothers me in some way, perhaps weakens my power?"

"Doesn't it?" Wallace countered, stalling for time.

The gleam of stark white teeth was his answer. Darius

moved to the fireplace, reached out, and touched the large silver cross there. "You seem to have all the supplies for bagging yourself a vampire."

Wallace was horrified. He glanced toward the door, suddenly aware of the deep silence in the house.

Darius glided closer. "What is it precisely you wished to learn about me, Mr. Wallace? Now is your opportunity."

Wallace jerked out the syringe filled with the toxin and plunged it deep within Darius's arm. He jumped back, grinning in triumph.

"Ah, yes, the poison you worked so hard to develop," Darius said softly, his voice as beautiful and unconcerned as always. "It is so difficult to know what really works unless you have the chance to test it. Let us observe the results together." The soulless eyes met Wallace's. "You do fancy yourself a scientist, do you not, Mr. Wallace?"

Wallace nodded slowly, staring at the one he thought was a vampire. Darius slowly rolled up the sleeve of his silk shirt, exposing the roped muscles of his arm. He stared at his skin, causing red flames to flicker and dance, and Wallace nearly screamed when golden dots of liquid poison began to ooze from the Darius's pores and run in a stream down his skin to drip onto the floor.

"Interesting, is it not?" Darius inquired in a menacing purr. "You should have known more about an enemy you wished to challenge, Mr. Wallace. It is a poor business to hunt without sufficient knowledge of your prey."

"Where is the woman now?"

Darius's eyebrows shot up. "Are you really so arrogant that you think I would allow your ridiculous assassins to take from me what is mine? I suspect you are more interested in the whereabouts of your soldiers."

Wallace sighed and ran a hand through his shock of

gray hair, leaving it standing on end. "And where are they?"

"What was left of them can be claimed from the local morgue," Darius answered, unconcerned.

"I suppose my other men are also destroyed," Wallace ventured.

Darius sent his mind seeking throughout the house, then smiled in satisfaction. "I must admit, they seem to have been in very poor health. You should choose your companions more carefully, Mr. Wallace."

Wallace's faded eyes flashed with sudden malice. "I see that you yourself have not gone unscathed. You are bleeding."

The white teeth gleamed again. "It is nothing, a mere scratch. My body will heal without difficulty, but thank you for your concern."

Wallace hissed between his teeth. "You mean to kill me."

The glowing red eyes poured over him like molten lava. "With great pleasure, Mr. Wallace. I protect my own. I allowed you to go free after the last threat you made to my family, but you insist on asking for release from your miserable life. I can do no other than oblige you."

"I will go back to Europe, leave you alone."

Darius shook his head slowly. "You had her touched by your filthy servants. You intended to rape her, torture her. Not because you thought her vampire but because it would bring you pleasure. You wanted me here, Mr. Wallace, and now you have the very thing you wished for."

Wallace glanced at his young companion, the one he had chosen to groom as his protégé because he had found the same deviant nature in the young man as was in himself.

Darius had easily picked thoughts of starring in a snuff film with Tempest out of the younger man's head, knew he didn't believe in vampires but was attracted to the violence and sexual rush the vampire-hunting society promised to provide. His black eyes bored into the young man while he contemplated the evil that existed in both his world and the human world. He released the young man from the thrall. Instantly the youth launched himself at Darius, seemingly too dense to understand that Darius had been controlling him.

Darius stood so still that he seemed to be a part of the room, of the earth itself, silent, watchful, unmovable. At the last second, just as the man was about to lay hands on him, Darius shimmered into vapor, dissolved, and reappeared behind the young man.

"Daniel, behind you!" Wallace warned.

Daniel tried to drag the gun from out of his waistband as he turned. Even as he caught sight of the intruder, the vampire's face rippled, contorted, and lengthened into a long muzzle. Teeth burst forth, razor-sharp, jaws rushing forward to bore straight into Daniel's chest, tearing a hole to reach the pounding heart.

Wallace leapt out of his chair, knocking it over as he tried to get to the door. The elegant figure moved, a gliding blur that cut off his line of retreat. Once more Darius looked like a handsome man, black eyes impassive, mouth set and cruel. There was not a stain on his immaculate shirt, although a puddle of thick, sticky blood pooled around Daniel's body. He looked like a rag doll lying in a heap on the floor.

Wallace froze, not daring to get any closer to the terrible fiend that threatened him. "Don't you see?" he hissed. "I'm like you. I could serve you. Make me like you are—immortal."

Darius lifted an eyebrow. "You flatter yourself to think we are anything alike. There are those of my people who have become evil and twisted, rotten shells as you are. They might grant you a short stay of execution, allowing you to live for a while on the meat of the dead while you serve their dark purposes. But that is not who I am."

"Who are you, then?" Wallace whispered. He could hear something else now. Not the silence that haunted this house of death. Not the sound of his men coming to his aid. But low, insidious whispers assaulting his ears. He tried to repress them, not understanding the language but knowing there were more creatures near than the one he was facing. They waited, calling to this one to finish Wallace, to come to them.

"I am an instrument of justice. I have come to send you from this world to another, where you must answer for your terrible crimes against mortals and immortals alike." Darius said the words softly, almost gently.

Wallace shook his head adamantly. "No, you can't do that. You can't. I'm a leader. I have an army behind me. No one can defeat me." He raised his voice hysterically. "Where are you? All of you, I'm in danger. Protect your leader!"

The terrible soulless eyes never left Wallace's face. Those black eyes were completely empty, devoid of all feeling. Then tiny red flames began to flicker in their depths, feeding Wallace's dread.

"There is no one left," Darius said. "Only you. And I sentence you to death for your crimes against all humanity. Please oblige me, sir." Darius gestured toward the hall.

Wallace found he could not fight the compulsion.

Step by macabre step, he moved, his body jerking like a marionette as he moved down the hall toward the stairs. Wallace tried to scream, but no sound emerged. His body continued to obey the commands of the demon he had summoned to the ranch house. Once upstairs, the creature continued to gesture him forward. Inch by inch, step by step, relentlessly, implacably, Wallace was drawn forward toward the pool room.

He gasped as he saw the four men lying lifeless, without a mark on them, in the middle of the floor. Then the compulsion pushed him to the balcony door. Below was a wrought iron fence, each separate post rising like a sharpened stake. Wallace stared down at the lethal pegs and tried to stop his next step. But he felt space beneath his forward foot, then air beneath his other one. And then he was falling, released from the demon's thrall so that his scream echoed in the night.

Darius stared down dispassionately at the body hanging on the fence, a stake driven directly through his heart. He stayed there quietly, fighting down the beast still raging for release, still calling for retribution and blood.

Tempest. Deliberately he thought of her, took her into his body and soul, allowed her light to calm the terrible beast, to once more restore the balance between intellectual man and instinctive predator. He was no longer a savage ruled by instinct, demanding blood and vengeance, but once more her other half. He could do no other than return to her as quickly as possible. He turned then, back to his family, back to his people.

Julian sighed softly. "You must take my blood, Darius, and then go to ground to heal your wounds."

"I suppose I must concede you are right."

"And it nearly kills you to admit that." Julian smirked at him.

A slow smile touched the hard edge of Darius's mouth. "Oh, shut up," he said tiredly but with a glint of real humor in his eyes.

Chapter Eighteen

Darius rose two days later, his body completely healed. With the proper rejuvenating rest, the blood of a powerful ancient, and the rich soil, his full strength was renewed. At once he sought news of his family. He mentally checked with each of them to ensure they were well and safe. He assured them, in return, that he was whole and healed and would soon awaken Tempest.

Darius rose voraciously hungry, and he knew that if all had gone well with Tempest, she would be, also. He hunted, choosing prey close to the cave, feeding ravenously, taking enough for both of them. When he returned to the cavern, he prepared for her rising, crushing herbs to fill the air with a soothing aroma, spreading candles so that little flames danced on the walls and flickered invitingly. He made up a thick bed with soft sheets to welcome her.

Darius descended to her and cradled her in his arms,

floated out of the earth, and closed the deep hole so no sign would remain of what might appear to her to be a grave. Tempest looked beautiful even in her sleep. Even more beautiful than he remembered. Her skin was flawless, her hair a mass of thick red-gold silk tumbling around her face. He carried her to the steaming mineral pool and woke her as he lowered her into the water.

He bent his head to her soft mouth, capturing her first breath as she drew air into her lungs and exhaled. She tasted like light and goodness. She tasted like hunger and flame. Her long lashes fluttered, then lifted, so that he was staring into her vivid green eyes. A faint trace of humor crept into the emerald depths. It was amazing what it did to his heart, melting it and simultaneously squeezing it hard. His chest felt inordinately tight, his heart pounding with fear about the consequences of her courageous choice.

"So, hopefully, it isn't the deranged thing going on here. I don't have a mad desire to turn upside down and hang from my toes like a bat, but I definitely have a craving." The seductive caress of her voice played over his skin like fingers. Her mind, when he touched it, was a mixture of fear and humor, as if she couldn't quite decide which to go with.

"It is natural to be hungry, honey," he reassured her, his palm sweeping the silken strands of her hair from her neck. The water was lapping at their skin, bubbles bursting over and around them, creating a sensation of intense pleasure.

"A bit on the repulsive side, though." She tried to be analytical about it.

"Do you think?" He bent his head to find the pulse beating in her throat, his tongue stroking a brand, feeling the sudden, impatient expectation. "What does it feel like when I kiss you like this?"

He was stealing her breath, her sanity. He was bringing her body to life again, bringing it to a living flame of need. "You know," she accused.

His teeth scraped lightly back and forth over her neck. Her stomach muscles clenched in anticipation. Heat pooled immediately within her, low and urgent.

"What about this, Tempest?" he persisted, his breath warm on her skin.

She arched her neck to give him better access, her entire body on fire for the erotic ecstasy of his bite. "You know, Darius."

His mouth moved to find hers in a slow, languid kiss he needed more than anything else at that moment.

It robbed her of her ability to think sane thoughts, to think of anything but him.

"That is how it feels to me," Darius said, "when your mouth moves over my skin, when your teeth find me and my blood flows into you. It is beautiful and erotic, and my body craves the sharing just as yours does."

His hands moved over her skin, a slow exploration of her shadows and curves, washing the remnants of soil from her. The feel of his palms gliding over her bare flesh, cupping her breasts possessively, sliding down her belly to the triangle of curls, slipping between her legs to seek her creamy heat brought fire to her body. Brought a hungry demand she had never known. He slowly inched a finger inside her. A second. He thrust into her, explored her velvet interior, knew it pulsed with life and need for only him. She pushed against his hand, seeking relief from the gathering fire. Tempest could feel her own inhibitions slipping away as her body initiated its own demands.

She began to stroke his skin, tracing the heavy muscles of his chest, the definition of his abdomen, then moved lower to cup the weight of him in her palm, to dance enticing fingers along the hard length of him. Darius lifted her into his arms, striding out of the pool to lay her on the bed he had made for her, his body blanketing hers.

Tempest smiled and circled his head with her arms, her hands stroking his thick hair. "At last, a bed. Do you think we'll know what to do in it?"

"Oh, yeah, baby. I do not think you have a thing to worry about. I know exactly what to do," he whispered against her throat. Her body felt like satin, her hair like silk. How could anything be so damned soft? He tasted her skin, the sweet honey of it, and allowed his body to swell into a fiery shaft of desire. Need poured into him, strong and urgent, a relentless hunger only her body could sate.

Tempest was caught up in the feel of his hard body and aggressive male domination, his brute strength, the shivering response her fingertips could induce. She smiled, her tongue tasting his neck, reveling in the rich texture of his skin. Her breasts were sensitive, swollen with need, aching with pleasure, pressed against his powerful chest.

And then she became aware of his heartbeat. The ebb and flow of his blood, like the waves of the sea advancing and retreating. The call, the hunger, the all-consuming hunger. Instantly she stiffened, cried out with fear, and struggled to free herself from the weight of his body.

Darius captured her slender wrists and stretched her arms above her head with easy mastery. "Shh, my love, be calm. Turn down the volume in your head. You know it can be done. Already you were hearing things magnified, and you learned to deal with it easily."

She was shaking her head from side to side, trying to block out the sound and smell of blood, the rising, gnawing hunger that seemed to take over her entire being.

Darius held her firmly, calmly. "Look at me, Tempest. Open your eyes, and look into mine. Breathe with me until you are calm. We can do this together. We can. You trust me to know what is right. Look only at me."

Swallowing the tight knot of fear and revulsion, Tempest pried her eyelids open and was instantly caught and held by his mesmerizing black gaze. It calmed her as nothing else could. She did trust in him, believe in him. She loved him totally, without reservation. More than her own life. The terrible pounding in her heart subsided. She dragged great gulps of air into her lungs. Her gaze clung to his, her savior in the madness of what she had become.

Darius smiled down at her with complete confidence. "We can do this together, honey. You and me. We are one. Our hearts, our souls, our minds, and our bodies." His hand slipped between her thighs, his fingers testing her readiness. He pressed his hot, throbbing velvet tip into her scorching entrance so that she could feel his raging need, how thick and heavy with urgency he was. "This is us, Tempest, you and me. Our bodies crave one another, need one another. You feel me demanding you, hungering for you?" He pushed himself deeper with exquisite care, watching her eyes widen in response, feeling her heat close around him, tightening and clenching in reaction to his invasion. The sweet agony made little beads of perspiration dot his forehead.

Tempest moaned softly, her hips moving with her own need. Darius held her still, his body swelling even more, filling her completely, driven by the tightness of her fiery sheath, the demands her own body was making on her, on him. "Merge your mind with mine. I want us to be together as we should." His whisper was pure seduction, sheer magic. "My body is deep within yours." He withdrew and surged forward again, a powerful stroke that buried him ever deeper. Her arms tried to break free, but he held her pinned beneath him.

Darius bent his head to the temptation of her breasts, smiled when her body clenched around his. His tongue lapped lovingly at one nipple before taking her satin-soft flesh into the heat of his mouth. She cried out then, arching more closely into him, needing the feel of his mouth pulling at her. His hips moved in a slow, lazy rhythm designed to drive her crazy. She couldn't move, pinned as she was, so Darius could take his time, arousing her to a fever pitch, exploring her body leisurely.

She felt his hot breath above her breast, and something wild in her seemed to break free. "Please, Darius," she heard herself moan, and she knew what she wanted. She was coming up off the bed, offering her body to his nuzzling mouth. "Please, don't make me wait." She whispered the words in an agony of anticipation, then felt his body respond to the urgency of her plea, swelling, hardening, moving with longer, deeper strokes into her. She felt his teeth scrape her skin gently, his tongue follow with a rasping caress, and then she was crying out as white heat enveloped her, beat at her, as his teeth pierced deep and his mouth moved erotically against her breast, feeding on her. She felt fire bursting in her. All around her. She wanted it to go on forever. Never stop. She wanted to hold his head to her and force him to take her this way over and over again, for all time.

The heat. The fire. The ecstasy of it. She closed her

eyes and gave herself up to it. Waves of pleasure rippling through her body, consuming her, consuming him. Then his mind was thrusting into hers with the same demands his body was making on hers. *This is what it feels like for me. I need you to do the same for me.* His voice brushed in her mind like fingers between her legs, raw and needy and creating waves of fire.

His tongue stroked across her breast. "Do this for me, my love. Give me what I have given you." It was sheer, blatant seduction, the devil's own temptation.

He thrust his hips deeper still, turning her to molten fire. His chest was over her head, pressed against her seeking mouth. Her tongue found his skin. She felt the jolt go right through his mind. Felt his body within hers throb. Her teeth moved back and forth over his beating heart. Hunger consumed her. The need to give him whatever he desired. One large hand caught her bottom, lifting her hips so that he could bury himself over and over in her; the other went to the nape of her neck, holding her tightly against his chest.

"God, baby, you are killing me here. Do this for me. I need this as I have never needed anything else in my life. Please, baby." The words came out raw with need, between clenched teeth, his body straining to convince hers. Then his hoarse cry filled the cave, his head thrown back in sheer ecstasy as her teeth pierced his flesh. She felt it, felt the intensity of his pleasure as he flowed into her, hot and rich with the essence of life and passion. His body began pumping into hers, hotter and faster, swelling and hardening until she was so tight, the friction threatened to send them both up in flames. He felt her body convulse around his, grip his, squeeze tighter and tighter until he was pouring his hot seed into her, filling her mind and body, her veins, with his life.

Christine Feehan

Darius cried out, afraid he might shatter with the pleasure, afraid she would. "I claim you as my lifemate. I belong to you. I offer my life for you. I give to you my protection, my allegiance, my heart, my soul, and my body. I take into my keeping the same that is yours. Your life, happiness, and welfare will be cherished and placed above my own for all time. You are my lifemate, bound to me for all eternity and always in my care." He forced each word out between his teeth, between each beat of his heart, so that there could be no mistake, ever, no way that the ritual was not complete. He wanted her to feel each word in their united soul, their united bodies, in their mind, their heart, and their skin. She was his, and he belonged to her. He would never give her up, never let her go, never allow anything to harm her.

Darius held her to him, his body still hot and hard in the velvet fire of hers. She was slick with his seed, her tongue closing the pinpricks over his heart, her body so exhausted that she couldn't move. He rolled off her, taking her with him, keeping their bodies locked together. "Thank you, Tempest. I do not deserve you, but thank you."

She lay listening to their combined heartbeats, resting in his mind. She saw his implacable resolve to keep her, the deep ties between them that could never be broken, and she was reassured of their future together. She saw that the ritual heat of Carpathian mating only increased over time. She could not see how that was possible without inducing heart failure, but she accepted it. She could also see beyond that possession and that hot hunger for her body. Darius loved her. Tempest. He loved her so deeply, so completely, that it filled his entire being. He loved her enough to give up his life for her. He loved her without reservation, unconditionally.

She lay in his arms, savoring the feel of him beside her, strong and real. "Are the others all right, Darius?"

He pushed the hair from her face with gentle, caressing fingers. "Of course. Julian has a twin brother, Aidan, who lives in San Francisco with his lifemate, Alexandria, and Julian has taken Desari there to meet his family." Because he had to, Darius found the hollow of her neck and scraped his teeth along her skin lightly, his tongue swirling to ease any ache. Then he smiled against her neck. "They took the leopards with them, which should be something, as Aidan has human caretakers, and Alexandria has a little brother."

"And Syndil?" Her body was reacting to the touch of his teeth with inner ripples of pleasure. Her hands found his hips and began to stroke the defined curves of his muscles. At once his body began thickening, hardening in response to her touch.

"Barack and Syndil are together, working out their relationship. Syndil seems happier and much more confident, despite having discovered her temper. She sent me a very warm greeting for you. They are traveling to Europe before the next performance in hopes of meeting Julian's Prince and others like us."

Tempest bent her head to his chest, her fingers dancing over him in answer to the fantasy she read in his mind. She watched his face, felt his heat, his smoldering passion rising with her caresses. "And Dayan and Cullen?" She could barely think anymore, as Darius's mind was now sizzling with all sorts of erotic possibilities.

"With all of us finding our lifemates, the darkness was spreading in Dayan. He needed time to adjust." She felt more than heard the underlying worry in his voice. "All the intense emotions were disturbing to him. He and Cullen Tucker have gone up to Canada. They will travel together for a while, and Dayan will help to ensure Cullen's safety, which should also ensure his own. When the band comes back together to tour, they will return." There was a huskiness in his velvet voice she couldn't ignore. Anticipation.

Catching the rather graphic image of her in his mind, Tempest slowly pushed herself up so that she was straddling him. The movement filled her with his thick heat and widened her green eyes with shock. But she flung back her hair and began a slow, erotic ride, rocking her hips gently, a small smile of satisfaction curving her mouth.

Darius reached up to span her waist with his hands, his thumbs feathering back and forth over her flesh in a caress he couldn't resist. She was just so beautiful, with her red hair tumbling sexily around her face and her lush mouth and enormous green eyes cloudy with desire for him. Her body was so perfect to him, small but curvy, her narrow rib cage emphasizing the creamy swell of her breasts. His hands tightened, moving her so that he could penetrate her even more deeply, so that he could watch her eyes darken with pleasure, and he found himself smiling, too.

"While I have you where I want you," he said softly, reaching up to trace her lower lip with his finger, "I would like to remind you that you could have died very easily from your sacrifice. Any number of things could have gone wrong."

Tempest felt the sudden fear beating in his chest, the swell of anger that rode in like a tide. Deliberately she drew his finger into the moist cavern of her mouth and clenched her inner muscles tightly around the hard thickness of his shaft while she increased the fiery friction. She found a certain amount of satisfaction in knowing she had distracted him momentarily from his male tirade. His hips thrust upward, seeking the ultimate core of her, as his hands cupped the fullness of her breasts. His eyes went black with hunger.

Tempest smiled at him, her nipples pushing into his palms, her body tempting him with every movement. Darius suddenly sat up, his arms sweeping around her, his mouth feeding hungrily at her breast for just a moment before he took charge of the situation once more.

"You will hear what I have to say, honey, and you will obey me in this. There will never again be a time when you put yourself at risk. Is that understood?" He growled the words of the Carpathian male laying down the law to his wayward mate.

Her arms slid around his neck, her tongue finding the sensitive spot behind his ear, swirling slowly, erotically, creating heat and fire, distracting him further. Her mouth then crept mischievously around his neck and burned its way to his throat, all the while her body a tight sheath bent on sending him soaring with pleasure. Darius tried to bring his disciplined mind under control. She *would* obey him; she had to promise. But her mouth was teasing the corner of his, and her silken legs suddenly shifted to circle his waist so that she could draw him even deeper within her.

At that moment, all he could think of, all he cared about, was going up in flames with her, shattering into a million fragments and settling safely back to earth together, wrapped in each other's arms. Soft whispers filled the cave, low laughter, the sounds of bodies moving together, the scent of their lovemaking. They reveled in their newfound love, insatiable in their appetite for one another.

When Darius finally got around to lecturing her, it

was several risings later and didn't carry quite the impact he had originally intended. But it didn't matter, as he knew his future was sealed. Tempest was his, for all eternity, and she would always *be* his Tempest—wildly exciting, distracting him from his commands, tormenting him with her escapades, and always, always loving him.

NEW YORK TIMES BESTSELLING AUTHOR
CHRISTINE FEEHAN

DARK MAGIC
978-0-06-201951-6

DARK GOLD
978-0-06-201948-6

DARK FIRE
978-0-06-201945-5

DARK LEGEND
978-0-06-201950-9

DARK CHALLENGE
978-0-06-201940-0

DARK MELODY
978-0-06-202134-2

DARK DESTINY
978-0-06-202133-5

DARK GUARDIAN
978-0-06-201949-3

THE SCARLETTI CURSE
978-0-06-202136-6